No Place Strange

No Place

Strange

Diana Fitzgerald Bryden

KEY PORTER BOOKS

Library and Archives Canada Cataloguing in Publication

Bryden, Diana Fitzgerald
    No place strange: a novel / Diana Fitzgerald Bryden.

ISBN 978-1-55470-137-7
    I. Title.

PS8553.R94N6 2009   C813'.6   C2009-901318-5

THE CANADA COUNCIL | LE CONSEIL DES ARTS
FOR THE ARTS | DU CANADA
SINCE 1957 | DEPUIS 1957

ONTARIO ARTS COUNCIL
CONSEIL DES ARTS DE L'ONTARIO

The publisher gratefully acknowledges the support of the Canada Council for the Arts and the Ontario Arts Council for its publishing program. We acknowledge the support of the Government of Ontario through the Ontario Media Development Corporation's Ontario Book Initiative.

We acknowledge the financial support of the Government of Canada through the Book Publishing Industry Development Program (BPIDP) for our publishing activities.

Every reasonable effort has been made to secure permissions. Anyone with information on outstanding copyright holders is invited to contact the publisher.

Key Porter Books Limited
Six Adelaide Street East, Tenth Floor
Toronto, Ontario
Canada M5C 1H6

www.keyporter.com

Text design and electronic formatting: Martin Gould

Printed and bound in Canada

09 10 11 12 5 4 3 2 1

To RB
December 6, 1927 – November 22, 2004

Prologue

Who are you, really? Most of us wonder this at one time or another about the people we love. For a handful of Phil Devlin's closest friends and colleagues, that question was at its most challenging in the days directly following his death in 1972—difficult days for Yves Levy and myself, who were with him when he was killed. If I've learned anything useful from that time, it's to be more patient than efficient when interviewing the survivors of trauma. It is just not possible to think clearly when one's world has been up-ended, not right away.

Typical of survivors, for several days after the rocket attack, Levy and I were in shock. While we tried to sort through what had happened and why, the rumours had begun. No reliable information was available then, and when the dust cleared it was to be a long time, longer than any of us might have imagined, before any of the theories and facts surrounding Devlin's death, and that of his interpreter, could be called "reliable." Not until early this year were some of the government files declassified, and there are still travel bans in place, though soon they may be lifted. Perhaps then we may get answers from the woman whom many say cost Devlin his life, but that possibility is not one we should count on; if it's difficult to know one's friends, it's harder still to know one's adversaries—and Rafa Ahmed was, if not an adversary, then certainly a risk—though to his cost (and that of his family and friends), Phil Devlin believed otherwise. Yes, this is where we should begin: with Rafa Ahmed—already engraved on the public consciousness for her actions in 1970—and whatever there is to know of her.

Part One

one

If a stranger had fallen down Lydia Devlin's rabbit hole one evening in 1970, 15 years before the publication of *In Love with Danger*, she would have found the Devlins at home. A family, if not entirely happy, at least acclimatized to its own specific form of discontent. Phil was always away, Elise had admirers, and Matthew and Lydia held regular, whispered discussions about which parent they would most like to live with in the event of a divorce, but these were the occupational hazards of their ambitious, cling-by-your-fingernails middle-class existence. The Devlins lived beyond their means in the embassy district of London, in Kensington. Elise had fallen in love with the house, but she and Phil and, less directly, Matthew and Lydia, and even Elise's mother Rosalie, now lived under the strain of paying for it. Number 18 was white with a black front door and glittering, quartz-flecked steps, just southeast of Holland Park, a stone's throw away from the dull, mud-brown dioramas at the Commonwealth Museum, and only a little further from the adult cinema whose posters, with their glowing fleshtones, were more appealing to Lydia's eye when she was whisked past them.

On this particular evening she'd had her supper and was half asleep, sitting on the floor with a book while her parents drank their pre-dinner drinks and smoked their cigarettes and Phil watched the news. Elise was reading her paper. It was rare to have both parents at home together in the evening, and with Matthew already in bed sleeping his way through a feverish cold, Lydia was determined to milk every minute of it. She sat as close as she could get to her father's chair, shifting gradually along the floor until her back touched his legs. In that way, drowsy and relaxed, she could make herself the recipient of an unconscious caress.

Phil's domestic sojourns in between assignments followed a predictable arc. "I missed my bunnies," he'd say, squeezing one child in each arm. But from those first semi-euphoric days, they could chart his mood as it slipped from elation to contentment to the beginning of a scratchy restlessness, each phase enhanced by taller and taller glasses of Scotch, longer and longer nights out with friends like Yves Levy, Simon Gardner, or Edward Armitage. It was like air being slowly let out, his buoyancy gradually leaking away. He and Elise would start to snipe at each other, the sniping would accelerate into a series of explosive fights, and soon after that he'd be off again. Although as a staff correspondent he despised most of the freelance reporters who swooped in for bombs and assassinations—*disaster junkies*, he called them, hooked on the thrill of other people's pain—apparently he shared their aversion to the cramped patterns of home life.

That night he seemed happy, if preoccupied. When he registered Lydia, leaning against him, he looked away from the TV and rubbed her head distractedly. Then he put his drink down and, as she had hoped, held out his arms. She had to perch on his knee because her legs had grown. She was so pleased to be the centre of his attention that she resented the intrusion of the newsflash that broke up their rare domestic tableau before she even knew what it was about.

Five planes have been hijacked. A revolutionary Palestinian group has claimed responsibility. The announcer's upper lip was shimmering with sweat, though his voice was BBC-neutral. Elise stopped reading her paper and sat forward, closer to the television. *Four of the planes were flown to an airstrip in the Jordanian desert, but one attempt on an El Al jet on its way to London has failed. There were two hijackers, one shot dead by El Al security and the other overpowered.* Lydia was caught between Phil's knees, his chin pressing hard into her shoulder. She could smell his drink and the tobacco on his breath, thick and marshy. *The surviving hijacker, Rafa Ahmed....* She felt his arms twitch and loosen as he let go of her and sat back in his chair.

"Who's Rafa Ahmed?" she asked. No one answered. She was about to ask again when a small photo appeared high on the screen, a woman's face inside a square. The woman had a scarf round her head and heavy eyelids and she was smiling. She looked beautiful and

11

strange—and dangerous, with a hefty gun slung over her shoulder. But her expression was relaxed, almost languorous. If anyone had asked Lydia to pick one word for the look on Rafa Ahmed's face, she would have said "satisfied." As if she'd just finished her favourite pudding. Elise pressed the switch on the TV and the picture zipped shut, the screen crackling as it went grey.

Phil spoke. "She's one of the hijackers." Elise had raised the paper again, but she was listening, Lydia could tell. The edges of her paper were too still.

"Why did she do it?" Lydia's question could hardly convey all that she meant, or wanted to know. *A woman! How could a woman, any woman, be so fearless? What kind of person was she? Why would she risk her life, threaten the lives of strangers?* Phil answered her literally. "The usual. Freedom. Land." He drew her back onto his knee again.

"Freedom for who?"

"Whom," Elise said crisply, without putting down her paper. "Freedom for whom, Lydia. And the answer is, for terrorists." The ice in her glass cracked loudly. Smoke from her cigarette made a ragged question mark in the air.

Phil ignored her. "It's complicated, Lydie. There have been injustices on both sides. As an old Irish Catholic I understand the obsession with territory. And violence." Elise gave a snort from behind her paper. "Time for bed, Lydie." Phil pushed her gently off his knee.

"Will you come and tuck me in?"

"I'll be up after dinner, honeybun." She fell asleep waiting for him, and woke later in the night to hear voices, coming from their bedroom now, rushed and loud. It wouldn't be long before her father was gone again.

two

A warm September day and Mouna Ammari was late for school. Her neighbour Hanan called out as she raced down the stairs. "Mouna! *Yalla! Shoof!* Come here! Look!"

Someone had dropped a *Daily Star* on the stairs: front page, a picture of Rafa Ahmed standing calmly between two young policewomen in *London, England,* the newspaper said. *In custody.* Hanan didn't read English, but Mouna could, some, thanks to her uncle Basman. In Beirut, how you felt about Rafa Ahmed might depend on who you were, who your parents were. If, not unlike Rafa herself, your mother was Palestinian—and not particularly cherished by her in-laws—you might have memorized an image, the one in which Rafa's slanting cheek caressed a machine gun that was almost but not quite as sleek as her. You might have squirrelled away a smeared piece of newsprint that you looked at before you went to sleep. Might, on occasion, have dreamed you were with Rafa, dreamed you *were* her.

When Mouna got to school, her French teacher was facing the blackboard and she was able to take her seat without being noticed. She had run so fast to get there that her underwear had crawled uncomfortably high; she stuck one hand down the back of her skirt to free it. A giggle. The girl behind her, Sara Halil, had seen. Mouna didn't mind; Sara was very pretty, and although she was from a better family than Mouna's, they had eaten lunch together more than once. She was Mouna's only real friend at school.

The other girls didn't like Mouna, most of them; they had become increasingly less restrained in their teasing since the news had spread that Mr. Ammari had returned to Jordan and wasn't coming back. At home, they heard other rumours: that Walid Ammari could be as far away as America now; that Deena, Mouna's mother, was the reason he'd left. Epic mood swings, crazy behaviour. That Mouna's wildness was the main thing that drove her mother crazy.

Mouna's father had soon been overwhelmed by her mother's ups and downs. After the years away, they weren't close to Mouna's aunt Mariam and her family; instead, they leaned increasingly heavily on her uncle Basman, who, as Walid saw it, owed him for the hospitality he'd extended whenever Basman's assignments had brought him to Jordan. Deena had no one much except May, her one good friend, but May's five children took up most of her time, and Deena was lonely. Mouna had spent many evenings lying in bed next to her little sister Nasima, trying to discern the next day's patterns from the register of her mother's voice in the next room, the heavy, masculine hum of her father's frustration, first quiet, then loud and stuttering, and then, finally, silent. When he first left she'd been afraid. What would happen to them? They weren't completely abandoned: Basman loved them, and came whenever he could make time from his work as an interpreter for the news agencies. And there was her aunt, Mariam; Basman said she was a good woman and some day soon they would visit her. Deena looked doubtful when he said this, but after he left that time she seemed better. She petted and sang to Nasima, cooked supper, and things were almost normal.

"Did you hear about Rafa Ahmed?" Sara whispered, just before the bell. Mouna didn't answer. Rafa was hers to hoard and she didn't want to talk about her with anyone else, not even Sara. Undeterred, Sara linked arms with her on the way to lunch, and held hands, her warm wrist brushing Mouna's as they walked together. "What will happen to her?" she asked Mouna. As if Mouna knew. She had her own questions. Would they torture Rafa in prison? Would they lock her up until she was an old woman? "Aah!" Sara pulled her hand free and shook her crushed fingers, which Mouna had been squeezing without realizing. "*Afwan*. Sorry." When more news came, three days later, only Sara had an idea of what it meant to her; the teachers at school simply wondered what had happened to put that rare smile on Mouna Ammari's face. Not long after that, Deena hit the down side of her mood cycle, and Mouna's smile went underground again.

three

"Air Sickness" by Edward Armitage
from his book *In Love with Danger*

September 4, 1970, and the passengers on El Al flight 071 (Tel Aviv to London) have more than usual cause to applaud their captain and crew on a safe landing. As the plane taxis to a full stop, a young woman near its tail end is crying from the pain in her head. A gun butt broke the skin near her temple, inches away from that most fragile spot where the blow might have killed her. Lying face down, her features distorted by pain and fury, she's still beautiful, which it could be argued is an immaterial fact, but given the circumstances, not at all. For one thing, her distinctive beauty compelled her to suffer plastic surgery in order to board 071 without being recognized. Her altered, if undiminished, looks will play their part in exciting the interest of the press, the sympathy of the public. They'll make her jailers more solicitous. Combined with her considerable charisma they've pleased more lovers than might be expected for a young woman not yet 22 who's had more significant things on her mind.

Rafa Ahmed is sprawled in the aisle, face mashed into the carpet, forehead bleeding. Her arms and legs have been restrained, first by passengers determined not to let her up, now by impromptu handcuffs (neckties and rope). Like some high-stress version of a party game, the grenade she dropped in the scuffle—pin still in place—rolled forward, was snatched up by Melissa, a stewardess, who passed it like a hot potato to Josh, the El Al security man whose gun butt had clocked Rafa on the head. Rafa tried to shout a name— "Pablo!"—but Josh's hand covered her mouth, blocking the sound. She gagged, trying to breathe, to make more noise. It wouldn't have mattered; Pablo was dead. Shot by the gun that had stunned her. She hardly knew him, barely knows his last name, which will be rendered differently in various news reports later. They'd met just twice before the hijacking, but he was her only ally on the plane. There can be little doubt that almost everyone else on the plane—children, businessmen, mothers, teachers on sabbatical—would have been, if not happy, then relieved to have seen her die along with him.

While Rafa lies incapacitated, her more successful comrades are supervising the landing of four planes on a desert airstrip in Jordan. Terrified passengers from several points of origin have been informed that their fates now depend on the resourcefulness of their governments. Over the next few hours they will swelter inside the beached planes, keeping their eyes on the hands of the men watching over them. Soon fluids will be rationed, toilets will overflow, the planes will begin to stink. Hijackers and passengers alike will start mouth-breathing, dream of surviving to inhale fresh air again. Doors to the planes—an armed hijacker at each one—will be opened to allow some of that precious air to circulate. Passengers surreptitiously dry-swallow heart pills and Valium, afraid that those who reveal an infirmity will be selected, Darwin-fashion, as the first to die, should it come to that. A strange bond will develop between even these passengers and their captors, as the hours become a day, then two days, then three.

The travellers inside Rafa's plane were lucky. While cruising at 30,000 feet, their air circulated freely, if a little muddier each time as the machinery worked to process more smoke than usual—a frenzy of cigarette lighting after the aborted attack—and the plane maintained its course to London. When they hit rough air, Rafa rolled awkwardly, bruising her shoulder. Pablo's body is in the hold, kept from spoiling by the subzero temperatures there. Once the plane has rolled to a full stop, four men step on board and order the passengers to stay seated until Rafa has been safely removed. They unleash her and snap on real cuffs, taking her into custody, accompanied for the sake of decorum by a female officer who will supervise the strip search. Pablo is sent to the morgue, sharing an ambulance with a coroner and a police officer. Other ambulances are waiting for the passengers, whose delayed responses to shock and tension will hit now that the pressure is off. Rafa will spend the next few hours in the company of British intelligence, then she'll be transferred to Holloway, where she will later be interviewed under guard by a handful of journalists, among them Phil Devlin, a British journalist of Irish descent, father to Lydia and Matthew, husband to actress and radio personality, Elise Marcus. Phone conversations have already been initiated between various governments and their representatives, including the Jordanian embassy just down the street from the Devlin house.

The day after they heard about the hijacking on the news, Phil got the call to interview Rafa Ahmed. It wasn't an interview by his usual standards, but more what he liked to call a zoo visit, heavily supervised, a handful of pre-approved questions allowed. The negotiations for Rafa's release were well underway. According to Phil, the interviews and the photo ops had been designed to show her potentially impulsive colleagues that Rafa was unharmed. She posed with some of the more photogenic female warders. *She's just a girl, like us,* one of them said, anonymously, to the *Daily Mirror. We shared ciggies and talked about men. She wanted to know if I had a boyfriend.*

When Lydia walked home from school that windy afternoon with her friend Caroline and Caro's nanny Joan, they found the street blocked to traffic by police cars. And police, lots of them. Even stranger, some of them carried guns. Guns! Like the policemen in America! Once before, Lydia had seen police with guns: extras in a James Bond film on location in Holland Park. There were two Bonds: a stuntman jumped nimbly over the park fence and then the police chased the famously handsome but less-than-agile Bond actor. These police were different: serious. They were flat-caps, not Dixon of Dock Green patrolmen with their domed helmets and truncheons—though there were some of those too, arms folded, lining the fence in front of the

Jordanian embassy. A faint, gusty roar came from inside the building, vocal tides rolling closer and then further away. Joan tried to hustle them along but Caro and Lydia refused to be herded. They stood beside the solid legs of one tall copper to see a handful of young men spill out of the embassy doors. The men stayed inside the fence, shouting slogans and chanting. Students, Lydia found out later, who had occupied the embassy and were refusing to leave. Most of them were from Jordan or Lebanon. They were protesting the expulsion of Palestinians from Jordan after Arafat's defeat there and insisting on the release of Rafa Ahmed and seven other political prisoners. Some of them waved placards with blown-up images of the same face Lydia had seen on television the night before. "I know her!" Lydia said to Caro, pointing. She had to yell over the noise, which was getting louder.

"No you don't," Caro scoffed at her.

"She's a famous hijacker. It was on the news."

Caro hated it when Lydia knew something she didn't. "Nanny Joan says the news isn't for children." She elbowed her in the ribs. "Ow!" Joan was asking one of the policemen something, listening carefully to his response. Then she took each of them by the hand, holding tight. "Come on girls, this is no place to stand. Let's get you home." They squeezed past the crowd to the top of the street and round the corner to Lydia's front door. "Go on now, get inside." Lydia ran up the steps while Caro and Joan watched and waited until Rosalie opened the door and let her in. "You're home early, Lydie." Rosalie waved in a preoccupied way to the others. Inside the house it was quiet, except for Matthew's phlegmy cough. The house smelled of Vicks and baked beans; Rosalie was making tea.

"I know, Grandma. There's..." she stopped just in time. "I think Caro has her piano lesson." This was what Rosalie might call a white lie. Lydia didn't know exactly which day Caro's lesson was, it *might* be today. On her way back to Matthew, who was calling querulously from the sitting room, Rosalie didn't see Lydia slip out the side door and into the garden, where she opened the gate and went through, back onto Caro's street. It was unlike Lydia to be so bold, and she was a little nervous, but not enough to stop her from wanting to see what was going on. It was strangely exciting, all those men shouting.

This was not, generally, a neighbourhood where seven-and-a-half (*almost* eight)-year-olds went out without their parents or nannies, and she tried to look as if she were used to walking home alone from school, but it didn't matter: no one took any notice of her. People had come out onto the steps of their homes to see what was going on, and some of them wandered up the street without the police trying to stop them. The young men were yelling and waving their signs. Lydia could see more of them hanging out the windows of the embassy, smiling and singsong chanting like football supporters. Reporters were trying to talk to them through the railings and cameras were trained on the embassy front. More cameras were focused on someone chained by the waist to the railing, someone Lydia knew: Jenny Richardson. Her face was pink and her eyes shining, her long blonde hair slipped out of its knot and blowing over her face in the wind. She held a placard and Lydia stood on tiptoe to see what it said: *Free All Prisoners of Conscience.* Another phrase, *Right of Return*, was scrawled in red across the front of her white T-shirt. A small group of people was standing around her, yelling at the police if they came close. *Right of Return* meant Palestinians. Lydia knew that, because Phil had explained it to her last night. Jenny was famous for supporting Palestinians. Depending on your point of view she was *an apologist for terrorists* (Elise, *The Daily Mirror*) or *a supporter of oppressed refugees* (Jenny, Phil). Phil admired Jenny's bravado and, Elise had observed more than once, her tits, which were almost as famous as she was. Even Lydia had seen them, in a racy production of *A Midsummer Night's Dream*—Jenny as Titania had reclined almost naked on a giant red feather. At the moment Jenny's tits were covered by her T-shirt and heaving in front of a fascinated cameraman as she wrestled with two police officers. One of them was trying to cut her chains without hurting her, the other to keep her long arms away from his face. The doors of the embassy opened suddenly and the noise quietened a little. Two people came out onto the steps. One of them, wearing a suit, had blood on his shirt.

Suddenly, a hand yanked Lydia back by the shoulder.

"Lydia Rosalie Devlin. What do you think you're doing?"

"That man's been hurt!" Lydia hoped to divert her grandmother with this shocking news and her lip trembled, half real emotion, half self-preservation.

"Nonsense. Look." The man was talking to one of the journalists calmly and had waved off an ambulance woman. In spite of the blood, Rosalie was right, he did seem to be fine. "Besides, it's none of your business, missy. The police will take care of it." She pulled Lydia by the arm away from the embassy, along the street and through the back gate. Inside the house, Matthew was sitting at the kitchen table eating biscuits. He looked up, his mouth open and disgustingly crammed with paste. "Ith Lydia in trouble?" He could hardly talk through the slimy mass of food.

The Devlins were between nannies, for financial reasons, and Rosalie came over in the afternoons, but today she'd been there all day with Matthew, whose cold had moved to his chest, she said. She often stayed for the evening, too, when Elise was at the theatre, once or twice overnight. But usually, no matter how late it was when Elise got back, Rosalie went home to her own flat, to the privacy she cherished because when she was little, *not spoiled rotten like you two,* she hadn't ever had her own room. And she hadn't been allowed to stay home when she was ill, either. She'd finished school when she was fifteen. And when she fell and scraped her knees her mother rubbed salt in to teach her a lesson.

"Close your mouth, Matthew. And finish your beans. Biscuits are for after tea."

Then back to Lydia. "What do you have to say for yourself?"

Lydia couldn't think of anything.

"Because of you I left your brother alone."

"Why did you?"

Rosalie looked as if she'd like to slap her. "What if those foreigners had turned violent? What then?" Like Lydia earlier, she was exaggerating for her own purposes.

"I just wanted to see if everything was all right."

"What if your brother had fallen and hit his head while I was out?"

Matthew giggled. Lydia opened her eyes wide to stop herself from laughing too.

"I'm sorry, Grandma."

Rosalie stared at her for a minute. They could hear Matthew's clogged, snotty breathing; he snuffled and chewed and gulped his milk. "You're not too old to be spanked, missy." She had never lifted a hand against either of them. And when Lydia fell on her new roller skates, Rosalie took her home and made her tea with six spoons of sugar and rubbed ointment, not salt, into her raw knees. She clicked her tongue. "Oh, come and get your tea."

Two days later, Rafa Ahmed was released, along with her seven colleagues from different jails in Europe and Jordan. Twenty-four hours after that she was back in Beirut, the city where she was born.

four

When Farid started to whine again, Mouna shoved him. Hard. *Walad*, stupid baby, crying over which seat he got to sit in. He fell and smacked his head on the table and when he got up she could see the mark on his cheek. It looked pretty bad. He put his hand to it and for a moment they were both quiet before he started to scream. Mariam came running into the kitchen. "What's going on? *Habibi*, why are you crying?" But she could see. His cheek was red, already swelling up under his eye. Mouna stood still, as if she couldn't hear the unearthly pitch of her cousin's wails, but her jaw was so tight that Mariam could see the ridge of muscle, knotty and hard under her smooth young skin. She grabbed her by the shoulders. "What happened? What did you do to him?" Her thumbs dug into Mouna's flesh and she dropped her hands, furious and ashamed of herself. Mouna ran out of the room. Mariam knelt down and held Farid away from her to look again—there was no bruise yet, but the skin was tight and shiny, as if he was going to have a black eye—then hugged him close. He sobbed, whimpering and gagging on his own tears. She rubbed his back, gently, trying to calm him. "Sshhh. Tell me what happened."

When her younger brother, Basman, had called to ask if they could take Mouna, indefinitely, Mariam had hesitated. She was sorry for him, unfairly burdened with a sense of obligation to their brother's family now that Walid had run back to Jordan. Sorry that Deena, the girl's mother, was ill again. Sorry too, for Mouna, that both her parents found her so difficult. And guilty that even since their return from Jordan she'd had so little to do with the family until now, when they were in trouble. *But still.* She dreaded summer at the best of times. Blame it on memory, the torments of childhood: first, the sweaty, airless city, then dull weeks in the hills with her mother and brothers, watching their father escape each morning along with the other fathers in the city-bound taxis lined up in the main square. Nothing to do all day but run errands for her mother and help prepare meals. She was an adult now and, in theory, summer should be easier with two kids than one. So her husband said: the kids could occupy each other and she would get some time to read and prepare next year's classes. Reality was something else. Since Mouna's arrival, Farid had become obsessively proprietary—favourite chair, special toy, choicest bit of meat. Mariam was embarrassed by his ungenerous behaviour, not least because it reflected her own ambivalence towards this difficult child. Mouna's hostility held them all back. It surrounded her like a poisonous cloud.

Late night, or early morning. Either way, Mariam was awake. Nadim was stroking her shoulder, sliding his hand over to her breast. God, she was tired. She pushed him away, which he took as part of the game, and soon enough it was and they were fucking. Little hitches of irritability and resistance—the urge to slap his hands off, to bite or scratch—still mounted but then caught and dissolved; after Nadim came he finished her off, the familiar tunnelling sensation of her own orgasm, everything slowing and drawing in on the tiny slick bead of flesh that jumped and shivered under his wet fingers. Afterwards she reached for her cigarettes on the nightstand. As Nadim lit one for her, they heard a noise outside in the street: Hamid the baker was shooting his pellet gun at pigeons again. They could hear his hoarse, high voice—"Vermin! Thieves!"—as he ran at the birds. Mariam closed her eyes and could see the ripped and fraying canopy of wings swishing above him. Bird shit splatting Abstract Expressionism all over the pavement in front of his bakery.

Nadim shook his head. "God forbid, one of these days he'll hit one."

"Either that or blind somebody." She stubbed out her cigarette.

"What's the matter?"

"Nothing."

"Why don't you lie in bed, let Faiza handle the kids today."

"Faiza's got enough to do. I'm fine." As she put feet to floor, the hallway echoed with simultaneous outraged yells.

It was going to be a long summer.

five

Nadim said he'd take Farid to the museum and then drop him at home on his way to work. He didn't have a case booked until the afternoon. After they had gone Mariam went into Mouna's room, where she was sitting on the bed still in her pyjamas, staring at nothing.

"What do you think? Would you like to come to the university with me this morning?"

"OK." Her narrow face wasn't giving anything away.

"We can all go swimming later."

"OK."

"Everything is OK, really?"

"Yes, *Umma.*"

"Hurry up and dress, then."

"Yes, *Umma.*" ("She's not my auntie," Mouna had said to Basman. "She is, *habibti.*" "Why can't I live with you?" "*Mish mneeha.* It's not suitable. Don't be sad, it's just for a little while." But Mouna suspected that wasn't true. Since her father had gone back to Jordan, her mother was taking longer to get better, each time. And Mouna was *too defiant, too difficult,* she'd heard it whispered.)

What was she was thinking about, her face set so fiercely? Mariam wondered. Would this child ever let them get close to her? "Come and get some breakfast, and then we'll go."

Everything was different here. So many books. How could anyone read them all? Maybe they'd spent all their time reading until their son came along. They'd had him later than most people. Her mother said people without children had all the time in the world. *They can afford to be selfish,* she said. Sometimes in the evening, Mariam and Nadim didn't even talk to each other, but sat in the same room, reading their big books. There was no quiet place to read at home. Her mother's sewing was all over the place, at different stages of completion. Mouna was a bad sewer, so Deena made her take measurements and keep track of patterns instead, or entertain Nasima, who was too young to help. Mouna thought about her little sister. She was the one who should have come here. Even at two-and-a-half she liked books. She watched other people turn the pages and pretended that she could read the words. Mouna pressed the heels of her hands into her eyes and answered her mother inside her head. *No, Umma, I'm not going to cry.*

When they walked past the bakery, the crazy man who was always yelling at the pigeons waved at her. Caught off guard, she waved back and was rewarded by his beautiful smile. He looked much younger when he smiled, and not crazy at all. His son Ali was about Mouna's age and she could see him sweeping the floor inside. He didn't go to school and he never looked like he had time to play. When he wasn't in the bakery he was carrying trays of coffee or tea and bread to the garage, to the market, to the building sites—the men had nicknamed him "Taxi" for how often he went back and forth—or throwing stones at the pigeons. That was a kind of game, maybe, but not much of one. It didn't look like fun to her. She was staring at the open doors to the bakery when Ali came out, sweeping dust into the street. He crossed his eyes at her and she looked away, but she could smell him. Even from a distance, sesame and thyme and cigarettes. Already he smoked, she'd seen him, hiding in an alley.

Her aunt was speaking to her.

"Have you ever been to the university, Mouna?"

"Are there many big books there too?"

Mariam laughed. "Thousands. Do you like to read?"

"*La.* No."

A minute or so later she said, "My sister, she does."

"Does…? Oh, likes to read. Already? Little Nasima?"

Suddenly Mouna didn't want to talk about her family, and she kept quiet for the rest of their walk.

She had no idea what a university would be like. She looked around her at the huge banyan trees and stone benches and the red-roofed houses—"This is College Hall," Mariam said, pointing at a building as they passed, then an oval garden and more benches. It didn't look much like a school to Mouna, more like a park or a fancy estate in another country. Many people had already gone out of town for the summer, Mariam said, as they kept walking. "The rest will be at the beach." They could hear the echo of something being smacked against a hard surface. "Or playing tennis." She pointed over her shoulder. "The courts are over there, in the old gym."

They went inside one of the buildings and up the stairs. "This way." Mariam pulled out a key. "This is my office." She unlocked the door and held it open for Mouna.

"Shall I get you a book?" She smiled, teasing. "I forgot—you don't like to read."

"Can I look out the window please, *Umma*?"

"Of course! But in case you change your mind…." She went to the shelf and found what she wanted, a book of French fairytales. Two minutes later the book was on the floor and Mouna was leaning with her elbows on the sill, looking out. A breeze blew into the room and she lifted her face to it, sticking her head further out into the air.

"I see some people."

A few minutes later they both heard voices and feet on the stairs, light shoes scraping stone, followed by heavier ones. There was a knock on the door.

"Professor?" The voice had a laugh inside it, waiting to slip out.

A woman stepped into the room and because of the way the light fell, Mouna, twisting around in her seat, could just see her outline and those of the two men behind her. One stood still and the other paced up and down, swivelling his head, right, left, looking down the hallway. Mariam got up from her desk.

"Is it really you?"

"They did a good job then?" The woman smiled, gesturing to her face. She stepped closer. They kissed each other and over Mariam's shoulder, the woman looked at Mouna, just as she had in her dreams.

"But who's this?"

Mouna had never seen a face so exciting to look at, or heard a woman's voice like this, deep and rasping, almost a man's.

"My niece, Mouna."

"Basman? I didn't know he had kids."

How does she know Basman?

"*La*, Walid, my brother who moved away."

"Hello, Mouna. I'm Rafa."

"One of my favourite students," Mariam said, smiling.

"One of your most disappointing, you mean."

Mouna could tell this was one of those adult conversations where everything important was hidden behind the words. For example: *They did a good job* must mean Rafa's plastic surgery. Now her new face was as famous as the old one, and here she was, tall, smooth-skinned, in a tan jumpsuit and a gold chain around her neck. Everything golden except for her hair and her strange ring: a loop of twisted grey metal. Rafa saw her looking. "Would you like to see my ring?"

Everyone knew about Rafa's ring; it was made out of a grenade pin. Mariam steered between them and put an arm round Mouna. "*Yalla*, wait for me out here." And Mouna was pushed, book in hand, outside the door, where Rafa's two men stared at her incuriously. Her face hot, she sat down, opened the book and angrily pretended to read.

Mariam said something Mouna couldn't hear and the sound of Rafa's laughter carried into the hall, making her flip faster through the pages of the fairytale book. But she was captivated momentarily in spite of herself by the perverse, spooky drawings: soft little animals with long claws and princesses with sharp horns peeping out, barely visible, from their headdresses. She shut the book and moved as quietly as she could close to the door. The bodyguards watched her, but didn't say anything as she listened and squinted through the gap between the door and its frame.

"It's good to see you again."

"You too, professor."

"How's your mother?"

"Still a devoted gambler. She's at the Hippodrome every week."

Rafa seemed restless. Her shadow scattered the light as she crossed the room. "I can't say I've missed this place."

"No more school for you."

"Different application of talents—to something that really matters."

"You know I can't agree."

"Things are going to change now that we're here. You might have to pick sides."

Mouna tapped on the door. "*Umma*?" She held the book out. "I've finished."

Rafa laughed. "You can have your auntie back." She hugged Mariam. "We used to laugh a lot together, didn't we?"

"A shared sense of humour makes for good friends," Mariam said.

"More than shared politics?" Rafa turned to Mouna. "And you, little one? What do you think? Must friends share the same political goals?"

Mouna blushed. "I don't know. But…." She blushed more deeply. "I know that Palestine should be returned to its people."

Rafa ruffled her hair. "*Eeafekeh*. Fantastic. Tell your auntie that, *habibti*."

"I don't disagree. We differ on the means, that's all. *Yalla*, Mouna, I'll work another day. Let's find your cousin and we'll go to the beach."

On the way home Mouna was lit up, jittery with excitement. "That was Rafa Ahmed. You taught Rafa Ahmed!"

Mariam took the little girl's hand, which was warm and damp with sweat, and held it tight. "What Rafa did was wrong, Mouna. She could have killed innocent people."

Mouna pulled her hand away. Her eyes were shining as she quoted one of Rafa's most famous—and in Mariam's opinion most banal and cynically misused—phrases. "None of us are innocent."

Part Two

six

Run away, then. But look where you're going. This was Rosalie's advice to Lydia, that summer of 1986 as she prepared to flee Toronto. Not all that useful, as advice went, not to Lydia, not then—arms pumping, legs churning, eyes resolutely forward, desperate to be gone, half-gone already, Armitage's book a wraith, flapping its pages at her. No: an ugly baby squalling for her attention. Let it scream its sordid heart out. All Lydia wanted was to get away. Where? *Who cares?* So said Lydia, anyway, when her grandmother called her bluff. In Rosalie's opinion, the past must be faced some day, and they'd all wallowed in it long enough. They may not love the method, or its messenger, but *Lydia, Lydia, isn't it time?*

No one could deny that it was more than time, in fact, after 13 years, for Elise to ditch the last of her ancient widow's weeds, the stifling good taste and dignity that tend to shroud wives betrayed and bereaved, as if they and not their husbands were the dead ones. Even Lydia knew the truth of this, and she might have been less resentful if her mother had been as "unflinchingly honest" (*The Times*) about her own peccadilloes as she was Phil's. Or if she'd simply been a little less unflinching in who and what she chose to expose, once the urge took hold.

Whatever Elise's motives, their outcome was galling. The Toronto leg of Armitage's book tour: Elise glowing, friends patting her back in approval of her stiff upper lip, her "fearless honesty and complete lack of self-pity" (*The Times* again) while Edward *call-me-Ted* Armitage, "incisive, uncompromising, clear-eyed" (*Newsweek*), smiled and refuelled at the bar. Wine glasses clinked in the atrium of a huge downtown galleria, laughter and talk floated above and away; small bodies, backlit by the setting sun, insubstantial in the cavernous, glass-roofed space. To survive the occasion, Lydia drank too much and was rude to

Armitage and obnoxious to his poor, blameless publicist. She was trapped in a grim performance as churlish daughter, trying not to squirm too obviously as she doggedly recited her one line to journalists looking for a titillating quote: "No comment." Inside her head a storm raged: *Thanks for nothing, mum; fuck you very much, Armitage. You too, dad. A pox on all yer houses.*

Enough. She decided to disappear; like so many young Canadians, to take a post-university year off and find some adventure of the banal, paste-it-in-your-scrapbook kind. Cash in her savings, pick up her last paycheck, sublet her room, book herself a cheap flight to London, and from there make her way to a nice, hedonistic Greek island where no one would give a toss about the news. *Get me away as fast as you can. Jiggety jig.* That was Lydia's plan.

Just before she left Toronto, a premature heat wave stunned the city. She and her fellow citizens were insects domed under glass, buzzing weakly as heat and humidity brewed virulent smog and the pollution count soared. From her desk at the clinic where she was making some last minute cash as a temp, Lydia watched an empty building site cook in the sun: wheelbarrows, girders, and cranes burnished to a toxic shimmer. Lung cancer patients lugged their oxygen tanks through the clinic's waiting room more listlessly than usual; secretaries refused to run errands outside, so Lydia, being expendable, was sent out to the post office. Her first step outside was a burning slap in the face; then she was in one of those bad dreams where you try to run but can hardly move your sluggish feet. By the time she got to the post office her dress was pasted to her shoulder blades and patches of sweat had bloomed under her arms. She bought the envelopes her boss had asked for and walked back as slowly as possible. The usual crowd shunned the hot dog stands, whose operators sat languishing on dripping coolers. At the end of the day, office towers cleared and hospital staff and visitors rushed into waiting taxis with the same fervent shudders as in winter, sprinting from revolving door to cab at 20 below. They sank back against oily seats and sighed, eyes closed until the end of the trip. Lydia took the streetcar, slow boat home through the swampy heat.

Down the Limpopo the barge crawled. With her own eyes shut, she could summon the memory of Phil singing her favourite bath-time song. "Mud, mud, glorious mud. Nothing quite like it for cooling the blood." That was when she hadn't yet reached that mysterious, inexorable Age of Indecency that separates fathers and daughters, and Phil would imitate the hippo of the song by submerging himself and spouting bath water at her, sending a small tidal wave over the edge of the tub, to Elise's irritation.

Home, stewing in her third-floor apartment, Lydia was much too hot to sleep. Her room had been stripped of everything except bed and TV for the sublet. Her roommate, Tree, was doing a night shift at the group home and Lydia had watched enough serial killer thrillers that she couldn't bring herself to sleep alone on the tiny rooftop balcony. Instead, she walked down the street to the parkette and sat there until midnight with other apartment refugees, including a small pregnant woman who hummed while she brushed her black hair in long, languorous strokes. As the park emptied, she went back home to take a cool bath and lie naked in her bedroom. She stared at the television, flipping channels—click, infomercial; click—*aagh!*—Armitage's face on a syndicated book show (inset: a still of Rafa Ahmed in her kaffiyeh); click, Susan Sarandon in a late-night movie—until she dozed out of sheer exhaustion. When she got to work the next morning, there were police all over the building site. Undeterred by smog, unslowed by heat, thieves had looted it during the night.

Ten days later, and already Lydia was unmoored. A day and a night in London was all she had given herself, nipping any nostalgic urges in the bud. She would tell Rosalie—Elise, too, when she felt like speaking to her mother again—that she hadn't felt the remotest urge to visit the past. No trip down memory lane, no mawkish pilgrimage to Number 18 to stand plaintively outside its closed door.

She arrived in London in the morning and floated on a cloud of jet lag through customs, baggage claim, train to the city, each drifting step made more surreal by its tinny soundtrack: *All passengers with connecting flights to Zurich please go to Gate 12…. Would Mr. Thomas Hobbes please come to the information desk…. Delay on the Circle Line…. Mind The Gap….*

The tiny hotel near Paddington had one room available; a closet-sized cubby that she correctly intuited would turn into a Poe horror chamber after dark. Not a room to invite lounging, no. She spent the day buying a train pass and plotting the most efficient, cheapest route to Brindisi, and from there the ferry to Athens. Stopover in Corfu? Why not? Sounded like fun. Sun, sand, cheap wine. People her age laughing and running on the beach. Exhausted but triumphant at her own efficiency, she had returned to the hotel and fallen dead asleep, only to wake with a thundering heart into a darkness that stuck to her like treacle. Water pipes squealed and rumbled, and one floor up, someone coughed and retched into the toilet. Lydia could tell even in the gluey dark that the walls of her room were doing their Poeish worst, getting closer and closer, the ceiling pressing down. She gripped the sheets and shut her eyes and when she next opened them it was after dawn and there was light in the room and the ceiling was back in its place at a suitable distance above her. She sat on the edge of the bed groggily surveying her feet, translucently pale and bony, creatures on the ocean floor, deprived of light. Then she showered, packed her bags and skipped the hotel's complimentary Nescafé for a lard-soaked breakfast across from the train station. *Goodbye, London.*

In spite of the new fast trains, she took longer than planned to make her way to Athens. Once she'd crossed the Channel she decided to stop in Paris—she was travelling, after all, not running away, and there was no need to move on through like a fugitive, ignoring all possibilities. After Paris, a tiny eccentric village in Switzerland, for no reason other than a casual recommendation from a fellow traveller. Then she had been going to visit Milan for a few days, but after being persistently groped and almost mugged in the station, she took the train straight to Brindisi and booked her ferry passage to Greece for the same night. There were showers close to the docks, below ground, like London's public lavatories. She climbed down a steep set of stairs and washed in the back at the end of a stone passage. She watched her bags the whole time, soap running down and burning her eyes.

And now she was sick, she really was. It wasn't just the disorientation of travel. She was in rooms and out of them, up above herself and flying through time. She could see the other beds, a brown suitcase, a pair of jeans crumpled like Christmas wrapping. Tiles on a floor. Not this floor, another one. Black and white. People danced on the tables below, singing. The same people at the ferry. She had paid the cheapest fare for a spot on the ferry's open deck and sat there overnight, wrapped in a blanket and trying alternately to read and sleep, and also not to feel like the loneliest person on board, squeezed between necking couples and rowdy groups of friends all celebrating the start of a wild Greek holiday. She had caught a cold that had turned into bronchitis—*you and your brother have weak chests*, Rosalie said, *and no wonder*. They'd grown up inside a cloud of smoke. Phil lit each fresh cigarette off the dying stub of the one before. Elise half-smoked hers and as soon as she'd crushed it, tapped the next out of its case. The case was an old one with its own perfume, leather and tobacco mixed into a myrrhish scent, dark and earthy. Lydia had loved the smell, used to snap the case open and sniff it when Elise left it lying around.

That day, the day they heard about Phil, Elise had paced the house smoking straight from a pack of his Benson & Hedges. Black and white tiles on the kitchen floor. Black and white in the hallway, too. A smear of ash where Elise's heel pressed, grey on white, a plush little accordion of ash tilting and falling. She went to phone Phil's mother in Ireland, then Rosalie. They waited for Rosalie to come. Burnt toast smell in the kitchen, the yolky puddle of light from the standing lamp. Matthew crying. Lydia dropping to the floor to wipe up the ash and staying down there, hugging his knees. *Don't cry, Moo*: his baby nickname. There were people in the room with her, more than one. Talking and whispering. No more dancing on tables. *Is she OK?* She turned on her side and slept.

"Are you OK?" A woman sat in the bed opposite hers, a sheet wrapped around her and long tanned feet. Curly hair sleep-frizzed around her head. "They said you were sick."

Lydia yawned and sat up, feeling her own head, tentatively patting the sides. "I was. I don't think I am any more."

"You're Canadian, right? Steve said."

Steve's Hotel. Picked out of *Let's Go.* She had arrived there from the docks in a shared taxi, half-hallucinating already. *One step up from a hostel,* said the book, *but still cheap.* One step up meant four to a room instead of eight. Mail-forwarding privileges for long-term visitors. Half-decent showers. A ratty little lounge downstairs, with a door at the back opening on to the street, propped by a chair. Men watching TV and a group of people drinking and swapping travel tips. *Don't take the two o'clock, it's always crowded*: this from an American woman, older than her companions—solidly built and very suntanned, in a green T-shirt with *Steve's* printed on the front. She was the one handing out vouchers, the one who'd steered Lydia and the others to the taxi. Someone else in the group was telling a sinister anecdote about Italian trains, knockout sprays, and slit money-belts. Lydia was already gently woozy with fever at that point. The carpet smelled of sweaty feet; there were posters for island tours, and notes personal and commercial on a piece of corkboard on the wall. *Karl, where are you? Call Elke; SUB-LET AVALABLE JULY 1; Cheap ticket to Turkey, males only, call this number.*

The man behind the bar—in his late 40s, bandana round his forehead, tank top and scuffed leather vest—sold Lydia a beer and some chips that she couldn't eat. As she sipped the beer, a headache moved in and she began to sway. *Better get to bed, darlin.* He stared at her legs. That night under thin white sheets that looked blue in the dark, she tossed and turned, fever dreams in full bloom, barely conscious of the heat or the street noise and the boarding-school sounds of three other sleepers. She slept all through the next day and night and had woken now to lucidity and the face of the woman across the room.

"Francine," the face said. "I'm from Edmonton."

"Lydia. Hi."

"Want to get some breakfast? You must be starving." And she was. But first, to the showers. Lydia's toes retracted from scum-slick tiles, but the warmish water felt good, washing the last of her fever away. Francine soaked her crazed hair so that she could sleek it down into a ponytail. They dressed and went downstairs in search of coffee, then stepped out into a steam bath of a day.

seven

For reasons of safety more than comfort, Mariam and Grace were sitting on the floor of Grace's apartment. Through the open door to the balcony—the same balcony that had been the scene of so many raucous barbecues—they could hear the usual shelling and gunfire in the streets beyond the university but, mercifully, no closer, though violence always lapped at the gates, encroaching; sometimes came inside. The university's president had been shot and left to die outside his office in 1984, over a year ago; supporters of Amal and Hezbollah paced the halls in their red and green armbands; Christian students were attacked on the dangerous route across the city; foreign professors abducted and murdered or taken hostage; agitators from all sides tried to whip their peers into a frenzy. When Grace had fired an orderly for stealing from staff and patients, he'd accused her of being anti-Palestinian and tried to plant a bomb under her car (thwarted, thank god, by a vigilant security guard). Mariam had been called an Israeli sympathizer and a traitor for giving low marks. Everything, it seemed, was now political.

Even love. Grace had just had to say goodbye to her boyfriend, Jorge, who had joined the mass exodus of foreign nationals from Beirut. "It's not the end of the world. I've got my eye on someone new," she said.

"Who? Tell me!"

Grace shook her head.

"I was such a bitch to Nadim this morning," Mariam told her.

Grace laughed. "*You?*"

They were lucky in their friendship. They rarely judged each other, and when things got tough—when Grace had needed surgery for the lump in her breast, when Basman died, and then Mariam's father, or when yet another friend or loved one was added to the lists of killed or wounded, they turned to each other before anyone else.

"So what was it this time?"

Mariam told her. Yesterday, Nadim had been asked to mediate between a group of students who wanted to ban the veil from campus and the Shi'ite followers of "disappeared" imam Musa al-Sadr, who insisted on wearing it. Mariam couldn't stand the Sh'ia, always moaning and complaining, burning with their historic sense of grievance, as if the rest of the world gave a damn whether they followed the seventh or twelfth imam. *Intoxicated with their own suffering*, she'd said to Nadim. Like Ali, the baker's son, to whom Asma, his mother, had passed on her seething resentment of their Sunni and Christian neighbours. Ali, they'd heard, had taken his mother's prejudices to heart and, inspired by the imam Sadr, had joined Amal. Now Amal was targeting the refugee camps. Mariam didn't understand why; none of these rotations of violence made sense to her, only increased her fear for Mouna, risking her life every day that she went to work with the Palestinian refugees, never mind the barricades and the armed men who patrolled all the camps since the massacres at Sabra and Shatila.

Nadim had been talking to the students until past midnight. Then it had been a matter of getting everyone home safely, avoiding the areas where *musallaheen* were known to be taking hostages, and making arrangements for those who would have to stay overnight. Nadim wasn't home himself until nearly two, and when Mariam took him an espresso in bed that morning he was exhausted and preoccupied; she had held the thick white china cup in her hands, its heat slowly burning her palms, while he tried to tell her about his mediations of the day before.

"They have a point, you know. They're just trying to claim their place within the faith, and in the government. No one's allowed the Shi'ites—" She interrupted him: "Twelvers, Seveners. Party of God. Who cares? What difference does it make when it's all just an excuse for murder?"

"How sophisticated of you! And how convenient. Write them all off. Who's left? Christians? Are they so noble? Tell Karim's mother that. And what about Sabra and Shatila?" Karim was an old friend who'd been shot to death at one of the checkpoints by Christian Phalangists. Mariam missed him terribly, as Nadim knew. They both did.

"Please. If anyone looks down on the Shi'a it's your mother… you've heard her! And let us not get started on what she says about *me* behind my back." One of Mariam's cousins had gone to Cyprus to marry a Christian woman, and Nadim's mother never let them forget it. Since the beginning of the war, visceral prejudices that neither Mariam nor Nadim had acknowledged before, to themselves or each other, had begun a slow, rolling boil to the surface. Sometimes it shocked them both, what spilled over and burned.

Mariam was irritated when young women came to her class in *hijab*. A small thing, given everything else, but it touched a nerve, personal as much as political. In her own home she had been criticized once too often—sometimes audibly, if not to her face, at least in earshot—by one or two of Nadim's more conservative aunts. The stresses of the war brought out the worst in everybody.

Certainly the worst in both of us. When they fought, she knew, Mariam became her most haughty and dismissive, Nadim his most condescending. Centuries ago, it seemed now, her mother had warned her that most marital fights come down to differences in habit: that's the way my mother/father/grandmother/great-aunt always did it. *It's the trivial things that you get stuck on,* she had said. *And listen, habibti, don't think that trivial means easily resolved. People can be ridiculously stubborn about habits, including the ones they never thought much about when they were growing up. Those small differences start out unimportant, or maybe they're even what attract you to each other in the first place. Then all of a sudden you wake up one day and* voilà, *they've turned into matters of life and death.* She couldn't have known how right she'd be.

In the middle of their fight this morning Nadim had suddenly stopped, looked at his wife and sighed. "*Habibti*, please. Let's drop it. Let's not get into the family history." He'd stretched out a hand, tried to touch her arm. Moving slightly out of his reach, she had set the cup, probably cold now (hopefully), on the table beside the bed.

"Here's your coffee," she'd said as ungraciously as possible.

"Very mature." Grace was teasing her.

"I know, I know. I lost my head."

"It doesn't sound serious. Tell him you're sorry and you'll be his nice obedient wife from now on. Starting with…." She made a small, indecent gesture with her tongue to signify Nadim's favourite sex act. (He would, of course, be mortified to know that she was familiar with such intimate details.) Jolted out of her melancholy, as Grace had intended, Mariam let out a screech of laughter.

How could Grace stay so calm, so full of fun, with all that she faced at work? How could Nadim, for that matter, keep his head? Their work was more dangerous every day. Sanitary conditions in the medical centre getting worse and worse, violent, drug-addled *musallaheen* stalking each other in the halls and threatening the same people they expected to save their lives.

She had tried that morning—without actually apologizing, of course—to make up for her irritability by reminding Nadim of what life used to be like, what they used to be like together, before the war. When the hotels were still full of tourists, Myrtom House still a favourite destination for sweet-toothed admirers of Viennese pastries, a place to take the kids for a special treat, Al Ajami still somewhere to splurge on your wedding anniversary—*Remember our fifth? Our tenth?*—not a useless set of walls whose shell-holes had been smashed wider by gunmen for easy access. She had talked on like that, but Nadim had stayed silent—either hoarding resentment, or, like her, thinking back to those days when they liked to stroll through Hamra together, holding hands, window-shopping. Now, when Mariam walked through Hamra and its more humble sisters, it was like looking at her own self in the mirror. *It can't be—that building can't have been destroyed, there can't be a sheared-off wall instead of an apartment block, my face can't really look like that, half-drowned and drawn.*

Of the people who were still left in Beirut, except for Grace (and Nadim too, most of the time), Mariam was almost as tired as she was of herself. She knew exactly what they'd say in response to anything that happened, how each fresh crisis would be met; who would talk once again about leaving, yet not go. They had all spent the first few years of the war over-producing adrenaline. Strange rushes of euphoria followed by hours of exhaustion. In the end, they were like those animals in laboratory experiments, the ones whose immunity to pain increases each time they receive the electric shock, so that it takes greater and greater shocks to produce the fear and horror that a small assault would have triggered in the beginning. But what was the reward? There they were, she and Nadim and Grace, on the downward slope of middle age, and they'd used up their best years in this ridiculous place, this state of pointless stress.

Mariam shook her head and tried to shove away the lingering dread and loneliness that had settled in after walking with her stone-silent husband to work, where they had separated at the gates, kissing each other as coldly and dutifully as a pair of estranged spinsters. She had almost told him then that she was sorry, but couldn't quite summon the generosity.

"*Fi shi?* What's the matter?" Grace asked.

"*Ma fi shi.* Nothing. Everything. Do you have any more coffee?"

eight

The ugly light in her office at the refugee camp's clinic was hurting Mouna's eyes, giving her a headache. That, combined with the clanging noise outside and the loud, monotonous voice of the woman in front of her. *Please, Umma, just tell me what I need to know and then shut up.* Mouna tried not to think this, she tried to listen, but there were other people she needed to talk to at the camp today and this woman whose eyes couldn't settle on any one thing was stuck, words that had been jammed up in her throat for too long now pouring out. *Home.* Which home, even? The one with the lemon trees, lost by her parents in 1948, or the mockery of one here? The woman herself didn't know, couldn't say.

Mouna interrupted her. "And your daughter, *Umma*? Where is she?" The woman—suddenly Mouna couldn't remember her name or her daughter's and didn't want to make it obvious by looking down at her sheet of paper to check—was alone today.

In three weeks Mouna would be at a conference in Geneva. She and her colleagues were supposed to have final interviews with this woman's little girl and at least twenty others like her before they completed the report that would be presented there. Mouna, the only member of the team not a doctor or nurse, would present their findings to a special conference sponsored by the UNHCR while they all tried to hope that something useful would come of it. It was hard sometimes not to feel they were torturing the poor kids they interviewed, and their parents.

The woman had stopped talking. She set her dry-skinned, dirty hands on the table and spread them apart. "Dead." Mouna was momentarily dizzy with anger. *Shit.* Someone must have known this. Why hadn't they told her? "How?" "*Qannas.* A sniper." She coughed and turned her head to the side to spit into a stained handkerchief. Then she folded her hands and went back in time, again, her eyes roaming everywhere but Mouna's face, to the house, the one that was stolen from her family, it doesn't matter when. Mouna found herself incapable of asking any of the questions she should—about the death, any improvements (or lack thereof) in the daughter's mental health before she died—she had notebooks full of similar questions and the answers to them. This one kid, her story so much like the others, would be just another statistic to strangers in Geneva, but the hole she'd left in her mother's life would never be filled. One little girl—why the fuck couldn't she remember her name?—who should be buying school supplies, grabbing sweets from shop-owners, running to catch up with her busy mother. Like Mouna and her little sister used to run after Deena, then Mariam in Souk Tawile, before all this shit started. No more shopping for anything but the basics, not like the old days, as Mariam would call them. Holes in the walls in all the souks now, the ones left standing. Grass and weeds rampaging through the fallen souks, swallowing them. *Green, green, I want you.* That was Lorca, his beautiful poem that Sara, romantic that she was, had sent Mouna, but this green was another thing, the colour of ruin. The Green Line, a gash that split the city into two broken halves.

When had those old days started to disappear? One afternoon a few years ago, before they knew how bad things were going to get, Mariam had come home from shopping with a frown—in a jewellery store in Hamra, someone had tried to sell her a crucifix. She'd shown him the miniature Koran she kept in spite of herself. *Not long before you'll need one of each*, he'd said. *The trick will be in knowing which one.*

The old days. There were so many places missing now that sometimes Mouna walked down a street without knowing where she was. Trees had fallen. Birds dropped to the ground, stunned by rocket blasts or hit by stray bullets. In some cities, people collected the birds that flew into glass buildings, even saved a few from dying, but here they left them in the streets along with everything else broken. Yesterday Mariam had opined that they were all crazy, all of them who were still there. She was sipping wine with Grace, had been for a while, and she had launched into one of her monologues. *Why do we consent to live in this asylum? Nothing makes sense. Nothing! Our museum artefacts are encased in concrete. Safe from bombs, invisible to us. You have to buy back your own car from the thugs who take advantage of this chaos to steal it, only to see it incinerated in the next explosion. A woman loses her entire family and then she's killed later the same day by a car bomb intended for someone else. At least that last one might be interpreted as divine pity. Whichever divinity you claim as the justification for all this shitty mess.* Shaking their heads, she and Grace had raised their glasses in a toast: "Stop and Think!" A worn-out joke from when the Israelis dropped their pamphlets in 1982, not so funny any more.

Mouna had seen a photo of the woman Mariam was talking about. A zombie stepping out of the grave, or a quake survivor, grey with dust, her dress shredded, her mouth open. Her apartment building had been hit while she was out, all her family killed. She ripped at her hair, tore out handfuls. People stood back from her. So it was reported, by the journalist who took the photo. Her image was reproduced with the story about her death and wired to more than one international paper, captioned: *The Terrible Irony of War.*

It was impossible for Mouna to believe that she'd be sitting in front of all those compassionate strangers in Geneva in three weeks. Soraya, that was it: the little girl's name. Finally, Soraya's mother stopped talking. She wanted to sit for a while, alone with Mouna. It wasn't as if Mouna could offer her any real comfort, but the office did at least allow for privacy, which was something in a place like this. She fought her sense of urgency in order to allow Soraya's mother that. Afterwards, there was no time for more interviews, so she said goodbye and stepped outside the building into hard, bright light and walked towards the exit: rusting barrels topped with used tires and packed in between with sandbags. Inside the camp, holes blasted into the walls of former houses, and off to the right a small lake of dirty water. How was that possible? There'd been no rain for weeks. There was a car right beside the water, parked permanently on stripped rims. Two men with AK-47s were watching some kids kick a broken plastic jug, pretending it was a soccer ball, and a boy on crutches was also watching the makeshift game. The metallic echo that Mouna had been hearing all afternoon came from up high, two older boys were swinging construction hammers at what was left of a wall, trying to finish by hand the demolition begun by a rocket. There was another kid off to the side, by himself, not watching them, but scratching at the dirt. The way he squatted, hunched over and hump-backed, reminded her of an afternoon when she was young, before she went to live at Mariam's. Basman had come home for lunch to find her alone, moping around the apartment in a terrible mood—Deena must have been off somewhere with Nasima—and he asked her to join him while he ate. He had a copy of *National Geographic* with him. She refused to sit, but grudgingly stood beside him while he fed himself with one hand and turned the pages with the other, trying to elicit some interest from her in a series of photographs of some place far away—*The Galapagos Islands*, the caption said. Basman pointed to a big photo of a turtle—pea-shaped head, long, wrinkled neck and an open, slightly beakish mouth. The turtle looked to Mouna as if it was yawning or laughing. On its back a plated shell, a patch of cream just above the head, and striations and more creamy patches on the dark plates. There was a picture on the opposite page—a field of bright green dotted with more turtles, knobbly domes like giant walnut shells humped all over. In the first photo the turtle's eyes looked back at Mouna wickedly above its open mouth and the folds and wrinkles in its neck, frilled like the skin on the necks of very old people. "You see this guy?" Basman said. "We should envy him." In spite of herself, she had to ask. "Why?" Basman swallowed his tea before he answered her. "Because wherever he goes, he carries his house with him. There's no place strange to him." He patted her hand and got up from the table to go back to work, leaving the magazine open in front of her. She stood looking at the photograph, thinking about what he had said. *But what happens if you smash a turtle's shell? Then it's permanently homeless, right?*

On her way back to the apartment she lit up a joint. People were rushing past her and she ducked into a doorway, trying to anticipate the trajectory of danger this time. False alarm, just a crowd hurrying home. The streets were relatively quiet. She passed an old grocery store with sheets over the windows and newspapers taped to the glass door. The door was propped open, and looking in she could see people inside: women and children, bedding stacked against the wall, pots and pans on the shelves of their new home. A man came to the door and blocked the view with his body, staring at her until she looked away.

She walked by a travel agent, boarded up. She knew the place. Her last year of school—no, was it the last? When? If schools were still open regularly it might have been earlier. Mouna was walking home with Sara Halil, her best friend and more. They were moving fast, hearing gunfire, not close, streets away, but still, enough to make them speed up. So, she and Sara were hurrying home, talking non-stop as usual. They flinched unconsciously at the sound of that gunfire, but didn't let it interrupt their narrative, which was no doubt about the social games of girls too important in the school hierarchy to associate with them. (Beautiful Sara was in medical school now, in Canada. Her escape chute.) They passed one of the bombed-out buildings; glanced at the travel agency as they hurried by, saw shadows moving through the gutted space, quickly, from the interior to the shattered windows on the main floor. *Musallaheen.* A young man with a gun smiled at them.

"Girls, come here!" He beckoned with his free hand. They stopped, frozen.

"*Yalla.* Don't be afraid. We just want to talk to you." He was wearing bell-bottoms and a tight T-shirt: disco handsome. They edged closer. Inside, a cheap chandelier hung from the ceiling, half-detached, faux-crystal coated with plaster dust. It swayed while they stood there. A cardboard hostess, wearing the Air France tricolour, waved at them. *Bonjour! Comment ça va?* A shredded poster showed scraps of the Eiffel Tower. Another man with a gun was kneeling, fiddling with his weapon, cleaning or reloading. A third man stepped forward. He wasn't wearing a shirt. Smoking a cigarette—no, different smell, familiar to Mouna now, but not then. They were stoned. The shirtless guy smiled, mindlessly rubbing his left nipple while he looked at Sara, his gun slung over one shoulder. "Come and play with us," he said, echoing his friend. He had a surprisingly light voice. Then he snickered.

"We have to go home," Mouna said.

The first guy, Disco Boy, spoke again.

"You can go, little girl. Maybe your friend wants to stay."

He smiled in what was supposed to be a charming way, but came off half-cocked, unbalanced. Too far gone to make nice convincingly. No, he wasn't nice. He wasn't really a man, either, she knew that too, now. Eighteen, maybe. His friend perhaps a bit older. Mouna felt unable to move, transfixed by the chandelier. She was sure she could see it swaying; that it was about to fall, the glass bowl and its imitation crystal loops ready to shatter, adding delicate powder to the crushed mess of rubble on the floor.

She should have stayed alert. Because next thing, Disco Boy had stepped out, grabbed Sara by the wrist and was pulling her into the building. She screamed and he put his hand over her mouth. Mouna snapped to it and lunged after them, holding on to Sara's other arm, yelling.

"Let her go!"

"Shut up, bitch." He took his hand away from Sara's mouth and whipped his gun around, thwacking Mouna in the head. She fell down, her hand pressed to her face. Wet. She was bleeding. The man cleaning his gun ignored them, the other one, still stroking his own chest, laughed like an idiot. Sara had started to cry. Mouna got up and ran for them again. Sara's shirt was torn open and the man was grabbing her small breasts. She was crying, gagging, snot running down her face. Mouna smelled sweat (Disco Boy) and piss (Sara). This time she watched the gun, to avoid being hit again—in the moment, though, it didn't occur to her that he might actually shoot—and ran for his stomach, head lowered. She butted it, hard, and he loosened his grip on Sara, who dropped free. They ran for it. Ran and ran until they were at the end of Sara's street, then stopped to inspect the damage. Mouna wiped

Sara's face on her own shirttail. Sara's shirt was torn—she would blame it on sports at school—and Mouna's cheek was bleeding. She wiped that as well. Now there was blood on her white shirt, as well as Sara's snot and tears. She tucked it in to hide the stains. How would Sara explain her underwear? "Can you wash your things when your mother isn't looking?" Sara shook her head. "Here, give them to me. I'll do it." Sara stepped out of them and Mouna balled them up and stuffed them into her pocket.

Mariam told her off for being late. "Mouna, where were you? It's not safe out there." Somewhat distracted, she accepted the explanation of a soccer ball for the mark on Mouna's cheek. At dinner she and Nadim had a familiar discussion about whether they could risk sending the kids to school the next day. Mouna excused herself and when no one was looking she rinsed out Sara's underwear and her shirt and put them out on the balcony to dry. She retrieved them early in the morning and gave the underwear back to Sara before school. She remembered Sara's kiss, beside her ear: "Thank you," she'd breathed. And later, when they could steal some privacy in an empty apartment, more kisses. No small gift, Sara's gratitude. Mouna had her most recent letter tucked away with the others inside an old album cover.

She was home, finally. As she rounded the corner, she snuffed out the joint and lit a cigarette instead. She waved to Hamid, still keeping the bakery open even with the shortages and thefts and his bad heart. "What do you have today, Hamid?" "For you, *habibti*, anything." There wasn't much, but she bought a small loaf. Not a sign of his son Ali, disappeared weeks ago. Tonight they might visit Deena in hospital. They should take some bread, something to eat. At least now the tunnels weren't blocked with people. She pressed the button before she remembered that the elevator was broken again, although they did have power, at least for now. She climbed the stairs, sweating, stopping to shift the bread from one arm to the other. The loaf slipped and fell onto the floor. She picked it up and dusted it off, blowing microscopic contaminants away.

Later that night, eyes closed, she could see the woman in the photo, blurring into the woman who had sat in front of her today. Mariam was right. Total craziness. Whose god would be cruel enough not to kill a woman along with her children? To make her survive—for an hour, a day, 20 years, what did it matter how long? *The point is,* Mariam had said, *what kind of god could countenance such torture in the first place?*

nine

The boats to the islands were small and less stable than the huge float-ing lounge that Lydia had taken from Italy to Greece. On the crowded deck, a group of German girls, white-blond with varnished tans, smoked and drank, and it was the smell of their coconut oil, beer, and cigarettes that almost undid Lydia. Her only chance to avoid puking was to stay prone on the wooden bench. She couldn't close her eyes for fear of a nausea-provoking increase in dizziness; tried to distract herself by inwardly reciting school poems: "I will arise and go now, and go to Innisfree/A small cabin build there, of earth and… *no*, build there, of clay and wattles made." *Fuck! When are we going to get there?* "Nine bean rows will I have there, a hive for the *fucking* honey bee, and live alone in the *fucking* bee loud glade…." Francine had chosen to stand at the rail, nose to the wind, its freshness keeping her insides more or less steady. Hair scooped into two wide sheaves, she looked like an Irish setter sniffing the air from an open car window, an image that made Lydia feel slightly better. Think of family trips to Wales with cool damp air drifting through the car's interior, not the stagnant heat of this deck. Her relief when they reached Mykonos was almost reli-gious. *Oh, blessed land, holy sand.*

Before they boarded the ferry she had phoned Matthew from the post office. Inside the narrow booth she listened to the unmistakable transatlantic ring, echoey and submerged, as if she could actually hear it making its way through underwater cables. The post office was full of young tourists like her, picking up their mail, arranging wire trans-fers, calling home, umbilical cords stretched but attached. After their first hellos she got to the point.

"Did you read *The Times* piece?"

Matthew's answering voice was clipped, brisk, drained of anima-tion, as always when he was anxious: "I'm busy at work, absolutely no time." *Liar.* They were both good at playing ostrich when it suited them. She listened for aural signals of his state of mind. Instead of telling her about himself, Matthew told her how well Ruth was doing at work. She had been given hints that she might be up for early partnership.

"What a star!"

As soon as he could, younger than anyone they knew, Matthew got married. To Ruth: intelligent, stable, six years older, well on her way to being a coveted family lawyer and children's rights advocate. Matthew finished law barely into his twenties, having whizzed through the gifted program in high school and completing university in two-thirds the time it took his peers. No detours, no travelling, no disorganized quest to find himself. Not like his wayward sister.

He and Ruth had met in law school, attracted by a shared sense of social responsibility and the desire to create a more stable family than either had grown up in. Now he articled at a labour law firm, representing unions whose members had claimed unfair dismissal or other mistreatment. Some of his firm's clients were honourable people who'd been genuinely wronged; others were feckless liars who faked doctors' appointments or smashed up their delivery trucks after one too many lunchtime beers. Whatever his private opinion, Matthew treated each client as if they were as painstakingly honest as he was, and Ruth, who had grown up in a family of labour activists and gone to summer camp with the children of the provincial NDP leader, supported him wholeheartedly. How long would it be until they became parents? Matthew had always wanted to be a father, and Lydia had no doubt that some day there would be at least two little Matthews or Ruths, raised to save the earth and improve life for its citizens. On her less charitable days, that didn't necessarily warm her heart, but she loved and admired her younger brother.

"Ruth sends her love." Doubtful. Lydia was pretty sure Ruth lumped her in with Elise and with Phil, whom she'd never known: self-centred, irresponsible, a potential danger to others. Matthew wanted things between all of them, even Lydia and Armitage, to be more congenial than they were. His albatross: the need to fix, the yearning for "normalcy."

Sometimes it seemed unbelievable to her that Matthew should be an adult, and, unlike her, such a competent one. She could remember what it was like to heft him onto her lap when he was a toddler, the smell of his neck, how still he'd lie at night, listening to her bedtime stories, how much he trusted her. In one of her less proud sisterly moments, she had stood by while Matthew had sworn to Mr. Hall that Lydia had not and never would steal chocolate buttons from his shop. "My sister doesn't steal," he'd said. The buttons melted in Lydia's closed palm while Mr. Hall, slowly and deliberately, gave Matthew a handful for himself. He kept his knowing eyes fixed on Lydia and she blushed and squirmed while Matthew, innocently, smiled and thanked him. She had wiped the chocolate off her sticky hand on the inside of her skirt on the way home when Matthew wasn't looking.

"I'll call again when I get back to Athens. Love to Ruth. Give Rosalie a hug for me."

Safely landed on Mykonos, the air was silky, and the hostel they found, a little way from the beach, amazingly cheap and quiet. Most welcome of all, there were only two beds in their room, with half-decent sheets. Bare walls, long windows and billowing white curtains like the ones in a Tampax ad. Look out the window and there were the blue roofs, whitewashed houses, and fat steps. Kodak signs outside the tourist shops, and men leaning against the walls smoking, eyeing the sun-slapped street for ascending tourists who might be pulled in as they struggled upwards against the heat. The ubiquitous postcard racks stood just outside shop entrances, wire frames stacked with views so routinely, picturesquely white and blue they could all be reproductions of one painting. Lydia and Francine leaned out of the windows: they saw backpackers trudging up the steps looking for accommodation, either shaking their heads at the shop-owners or nodding wearily, shrugging off their packs and stepping inside. As they watched, one couple accepted an invitation to go into a jeweller's shop. The man had his arm around the woman's waist and both were smiling at the proprietor.

They decided to go for a swim before anything else. There was a side entrance to the hotel that led onto a street with no shops except for a mini-grocer and a small café, both of whose shutters were closed. Bathing suits on under their shorts, towels in hand, they walked slowly past the limp awnings and down to the beach, where rows of bodies were rotisserie turning on the sand.

They found some free space to lay out their towels, then took turns swimming so that one of them could keep their spot and guard their things. Lydia watched a Spanish man oiling his girlfriend with Piz Buin. She remembered the smell: Ibiza. After Phil died, Elise, in a mad attempt at distraction, took her and Matthew there on a package holiday. Rosalie was supposed to come too, but at the last minute she developed an arrhythmia and the doctor told her she needed to stay at home and rest. They hardly left the hotel premises except to walk down the sloping drive to the beach. Elise preferred them to swim in the pool, while she sat on a striped chair with her sunglasses on and a book in front of her face to deter conversation with strangers. Lydia and Matthew swam or were parked in the hotel "Fun Room" with other kids to play games and watch films, fed a relentless diet of what the hotel correctly assumed to be the preferred foods of the children of holidaying Britons—"Chicken and Chips! Fish and Chips! Hamburger and Chips!" crowed the laminated kids' menu. The radio played last year's Eurovision winner over and over: "Chirpy Chirpy Cheep Cheep." The refrain—*where's your pa-pa gone, where's your papa gone, where's your pa-pa gone, where's your papa gone? Far, far away, chirpy chirpy cheep cheep*—still ran through Lydia's head from time to time. Elise, understandably, was not herself, and fell down on the supervisory job: Matthew got badly sunburned and had to wear a T-shirt in the water for the rest of the holiday.

Lydia wanted to get up and swim. *Come on Francine, my turn.* Here she was. Lydia struck out into the water farther than she should in the effort to empty her head of anything but her surroundings, white heat and blue water. Stroke, stroke, breathe. Good. Yes, that felt better, slicing through the water, recklessly far given that she was a mediocre swimmer, and when she turned back she had to push herself a little, fight down an irrational fear that she wouldn't make it—stroke, stroke, breathe, stroke, stroke, *come on*—and would drown, stupidly, within sight of the holiday games taking place near the shore. She pushed along, trying not to think about how much water remained between her and the safety of the beach. Almost there. Gasping, she let her body float into the shallow surf. Of course no one had noticed her panic; she rested there until her breathing was steady, walked back to her towel nonchalantly with only a slight tremor in her knees. Francine looked up from her book while she was towelling off and held up the tube of sunscreen.

"Want me to do your back?"

"Thanks."

Lying on the towel with her eyes closed, Lydia suddenly fell back into herself. For days, it seemed, she'd been a stick figure, a barely vivified cartoon, strange to herself, hearing her own voice without recognition. The foreignness outside had just been an extension of that "pinch yourself" feeling. Travel brought it on, but it was an old companion, this sudden loss of familiarity. Hovering just outside her skin. *Who are you? Whose is that face in the mirror?* Now—*hold on to this, it might leave in a moment*—she was no longer watching herself. She was here. Thanks to the warmth and the smell of the sea, Francine's company, and the prospect of days saturated with mindless pleasure, at that moment she was absurdly happy.

ten

Standing on his balcony on Palaio Zografou, coffee in hand, Farid stayed in the shade, back from the sunlit edge. *So hot out already.* If he closed his eyes he could be home, at the height of summer. Home as it was once, not now. Now, refugees in the bathing huts at Karantina, shells dropping in the water, hotels looted and burned and occupied by the different militias. Bodies on the lawn in front of Myrtom House. Scorched sheets dangling from a window of the St. Georges. Now the whole city was a blood-soaked demolition site, the hospital a morgue, his family lab rats trained to distinguish different missile types by sound. To wait for the lull that means a bomb is about to drop. How close? Run for the basement? Dive or stay standing? He should be there with them. No, they should be here. By the time Israel was done there'd be nothing left. He drank his coffee and tasted the first cigarette of the day, the combination supplying a little head-rush that made him almost swoon with pleasure. He was his mother's son: cigarettes and coffee.

Mariam, crawling on her stomach to the stove, for espresso. *Without coffee, I don't care if I get shot,* she had growled to Nadim. And they had all laughed, as she had meant them to. Air cooling the hot apartment, slightly. Blowing through empty window frames. The living-room windows, taped for protection, had all shattered. This was a day they came back from the hills. *I'm not hiding any more,* Mariam had said, and Nadim agreed. The road into Beirut was slow, hundreds of cars going the other way, their roofs strapped with bedding. A man with a sling and a patch over one eye drove all over the road. They swerved to get out of his way, almost hitting a red van. They made it over the Green Line. They stared at an overturned tourist bus—in the old days it might have been on its way to the museum—transformed into a makeshift barricade. *The place will be stuffy,* they said to each other, but no, it was an open-air zone because all the windows were gone. The floors in the front rooms crunched and glittered. Mariam shooed everyone away and began the clean-up, but they all hit the floor when they heard rocket fire and machine guns. Farid remembered the feel of the tiny fragments of glass, little teeth nipping at his bare arms and knees. That was when Mariam got her coffee. Then two men came to replace the glass—the second time they'd had to do that, he remembered now, but he couldn't remember the first.

No school that day, like many others. They waited with Mariam for the glazier. While they played cards and drank warm sodas, time stopped, then stretched out, assuming the strange proportions peculiar to the afterlife, the under-life, of war. Shrinking and expanding, pausing suddenly to hover, humming with tension (*does silence mean that the bomb is above us?*). Then stretching mindlessly ahead. His mother said that Beirut-time, wartime, should be added to the list with Greenwich Mean and Zulu, a phenomenon unique unto itself.

Farid finished his coffee and went in to dress and start his day. In a few weeks his cousin would be here for a visit. He would like to persuade her to stay, here where there were so many expatriates, so much sympathy for the PLO that Arafat was a regular visitor. This was less significant to him than it would be to Mouna, but even so he knew she'd refuse. Like his mother, she was stubborn in her attachment to the dying city.

Here in Athens there was a joke going round that if they held the Olympics today, athletes would drop dead from the heat and pollution before they made it out of the starting blocks. It was true that you could hardly breathe in this air. Tourists fresh off the ferry from Brindisi coughed into their Kleenexes and drank pint after pint of beer, gallons of retsina, to compensate for the dust-choked heat. Or—screw the antiquities—they fled immediately for the islands. They had the right idea, those tourists. Farid and George would do the same this weekend: get out of town, take the ferry to Mykonos. Swim, eat seafood, meet girls. *Ay*, time for some fun.

eleven

After swimming, Lydia and Francine took a nap, then wandered the cooling streets until they found a restaurant that appealed to them: a small sign at street level, its red arrow pointing up to the flat roof of one of the white buildings. A faint glow and a hum of sound—voices, glasses clinking, cutlery knocking plates—floated down. When they reached the top of the steps they were faced with a dauntingly romantic scene: couples at candle-lit tables, leaning towards each other or sprawled, relaxed and laughing. For a moment they stood, doubting and self-conscious, aliens on Planet Honeymoon.

Once they had a table, though, their confidence gradually returned. They were giddy from an afternoon's sunshine and salt water, anxious to establish a sense of celebration as rapidly as possible. They drank retsina, with its clinical taste, ate crisp calamari and taramosalata pink and briny with roe so fresh the salty beads popped against their teeth. Salt and alcohol began their alchemy and they started to feel superior, convinced that their independence allowed them a wider variety of fun than all these couples. But then…. Lydia nudged Francine. "Look. Over there." At a table across from theirs, beside the low white wall that edged the roof, a punkish blond man was masturbating his girlfriend. Short brown hair spiked with gel, cheeks flushed by sun, she was poised on the edge of her seat, skirt drifting, legs apart, while he leaned forward as if in intense conversation. Tableside, it was a stereotypically romantic pose. Below, something raw and intimate. Lydia felt her own body respond, sensation telescope, external sound withdraw, view recede as everything concentrated and narrowed to a pinpoint. The waiter arrived, and turning to answer him she just caught the woman's quick, quiet, full body spasm. Next time Lydia looked she was sitting back calmly in her chair, her face empty, the man now using his hand to dip bread into oil. He bit off a chunk of bread and licked his fingers. Looked up to see them watching and winked at Lydia, who blushed. "Wowza!" Francine said. "I'd never have the nerve."

Voyeurs-in-arms, aroused, they laughed and tucked into their supper. Everything tasted better than it should, and they were basking in a golden haze, enhanced by retsina, when the waiter brought more. "But we didn't…." "The two men over there asked me to give you this. Do you want to accept? I can take it away if not." Raised glasses, inclined heads, implicit question: *May we join you?* Francine and Lydia looked at each other. *Why not?* The men weren't unattractive, and they looked harmless enough. So they nodded at their benefactors, who smiled and came towards them, glasses in hand.

Lydia pegged the donor of retsina, the one who zoomed right in on Francine as if he'd been keeping his eye on her. He looked like a polo player or a Greek movie star, glossy waves of brown hair, neat moustache, wide-open shirt, and gold medallion. A little anachronistic, stuck in an earlier fashion zone. There was good humour in his face— the face of a man used to luck. Making room for the extra chairs, Lydia felt suddenly shy. As she slid her chair sideways, her elbow nudged her wallet and it dropped to the stone floor. She leant down—cool stone, she placed her hand on it, resting—and bumped heads with the other man, who had knelt to help her.

"I'm sorry." She lifted her head, bumped him again. "Sorry."

"So polite." He laughed. "It was my fault." He tapped his forehead. "And my head is harder." He handed her the wallet and spilled change, and smiled at her. He was thin and narrow-faced. Young, but older than Lydia. He had thick, very black hair, less wavy than his friend's. "Are you all right? You look… your face, it's a little bit red."

Her cheeks were hot from the day's sun and the wine and she felt light-headed.

"I'm just tired. We got here today from Athens. And then the wine…."

"You should be more careful. And with your money, too." he said, wagging a finger in mock admonition. He looked around. "All the kids on holiday."

His teasing was gentle, somehow flattering.

"Farid," he said, holding out his hand. It was warm and dry, and his grip felt good: not limp but not knuckle-crunching macho, either.

"Lydia."

"So Lydia, tell me about Athens. How difficult the men are. How cheap everything is. How dirty the statues are." His teasing manner was older than he was, but it suited him. He had deep creases around his mouth, in spite of being, she'd guess, 27 at most. (Almost 24, like her, he told her a few minutes later.) He was wearing a long-sleeved cotton shirt, open at the neck, and dark pants. He didn't seem to suffer the heat. (She felt sweat on her lip, was sure her cheeks and forehead were shiny with it.) His wrists were thin, almost hairless, and his watch hung loosely in spite of the extra holes punched into the strap. Not her type, but it didn't matter—she and Francine were ready for some company and he seemed nice enough.

It was an innocent night: no under-the-table manoeuvres for them. They talked and laughed with Farid and George, walked on the beach, then said goodnight at their hotel. Farid invited them to drive round the island tomorrow. He knew a nicer beach for swimming, he said. "And some very excellent ruins." He smiled at Lydia. Did they divide them up by taste, or did he get stuck with her, she wondered? Lying in their beds they talked about the two men. There was something boyish and giddy about George; Francine joked about his medallion, his Omar Sharif looks. As they gossiped, drowsy Lydia drifted between this room and others. The bedroom in the London house where she grew up: sleepovers with her friend Caroline. They drew letters on each other's backs; semi-erotic shivers from the soft scratching through cloth. When they jumped on the bed, static from their nightgowns made blue sparks, their hair crackled. Then the room she and Matthew had shared in the rented Toronto house, dark wood molding and a deficit of natural light. Matthew had nightmares then and he woke her often; she told him stories to get him back to sleep, reprisals of fairytales or books she'd read. Then she'd lie awake, over-stimulated and unable to lull herself to dreamland. Lydia fell asleep while Francine was telling her that George was too short.

She woke with a disoriented jolt in the middle of the night, confused by the room's bare walls, by the presence of Francine in the other bed, the salt-laced breeze coming through the open window. In her half-awake state the scene from the restaurant returned, flooding her receptors. Like a grain of sugar sucked off her lips and held in her throat for its last drop of sweetness, she rewound and replayed it, repeatedly—the man's stretched hand, one finger extended, the woman's lax thighs, the drained expression on her face after—while she touched herself, almost motionless apart from her own finger. Not wanting Francine to wake and guess what she was doing, Lydia reverted to childish habits. Suppressing each shudder, each contraction, she made the whole thing so small that it was no more than a breath held slightly longer than the ones before and after. She fell back asleep, hands tucked between her legs.

Farid's car was an old green convertible, and Lydia was tempted to swan her arms around like a character in an old movie about holiday romance—something with Grace Kelly or Audrey Hepburn—but the parameters of cool forbade it. She was self-conscious about how young, how gawky she might seem to the men, who were joking and laughing already with Francine. Lydia felt a spasm of envy. Then the speed of the car chased away thought—Farid drove fast, and her short hair lifted like the fur on a nervous kitten; Francine's hair flew in the breeze, whipping across her face until she held it back with one hand. When they got to the beach, George and Farid chivalrously spread towels on the sand and Farid went in search of a sun umbrella.

It was less crowded than the main beach, a deep cove with tiered levels of blue sea: pale aquamarine, deeper turquoise, and then, suddenly, dark, impenetrable blue. Most people were sunbathing, already dead to the world, but there were a few swimmers, and as they watched, a man dove under a woman and burst up between her legs, hoisting her on his shoulders. She shrieked and then toppled backwards, falling into the sea with a loud splash. George applauded. He was wearing a bright red Speedo and there was dense black hair on his chest, a runnel of hair from his chest to his navel. He struck a muscle-man pose and his medallion glinted in the sun; throwing off blinding sparks of light. Farid came back with the umbrella, still wearing trousers. Lydia wondered if he was shy about his thinness the way she was about being pale and looking young for her age.

George ran into the water, eager, splashing wildly. Francine went in after him and Lydia admired how womanly she looked in her bikini. She herself was wearing a dark blue one-piece, and glancing down she could see how white her skin was, especially compared to the prone bodies slumped on the sand. Farid took off his shirt. His chest was thin, almost hairless, with a slight indentation just below his breastbone. Then he took off his pants, baggy swimming trunks underneath. The way he held himself had something of the small boy, exposed, self-protective, as if he was shivering beside an underheated pool rather than sitting under the hot sun.

They watched Francine and George goofing around in the water.

"So tell me something about yourself, Lydia."

"Like what?"

"Your parents. Do they not worry that you travel like this, by yourself?" She was mildly offended by the question. "Of course not." Did he think she was a teenager? And that he was her babysitter? She was annoyed with herself for caring. She barely knew him, after all. "God, it's so hot. I'm going to cool off." She ran to the water and waded in until she could plunge into a wave. Shining heads dotted the water beside her and farther out. She dove under into the cool, then resurfaced, fizzing out of the sea. Farid watched for a moment, put out his cigarette and lay back, closing his eyes against the sun. When Lydia came back, relaxed from the water's buoyant cradle, he beckoned her under the umbrella. "You will burn if you stay in the sun for too long." She tried and failed to imagine any of her Canadian boyfriends showing such quasi-parental solicitude. It wasn't bossy or oppressive—he had the knack, like his handshake, of striking the right balance, and now she hoped that he hadn't noticed her mini-sulk earlier, while knowing somehow that he was too observant to have missed it. Afterwards, they all lay on the towels, but George couldn't sit still. He went back in the water, then shook himself off and walked up to the pathway. He came back with drinks and leaned forward to offer one to Francine (touching the cold bottle to her stomach so that she jerked up, gasping). An old scar glistened on his back, pocked with other smaller ones. And on his thigh, another. He smiled and apologized showily to Francine, who pouted, both of them play-acting.

"When do you return to Athens?"

"We're going to Santorini first."

"After, you must stay with us in Athens. We have extra rooms." No answer from either woman.

"No hanky-panky," George said, Groucho-wiggling his eyebrows. They all laughed, but the offer hung in the air between them, suspended. More swimming (and in spite of his unathletic build, Farid impressed her with a fine, powerful front crawl), more lying in the sun—in Lydia's case, out of it: the curse of those descended from the black Irish with their blue-white skin. Her dark hair, first flattened and sleek from the water, dried salt-stiff. Farid smoothed it with the palm of one hand; his touch brought on a little shiver, the same prickle of passive languor that some low, slow-speaking voices induce. He wasn't handsome, with his big, bony nose and his thin arms and legs, though he did have beautiful eyes. George was the physical prototype of a Mediterranean lover, in spite of his goofy persona, but he wasn't her type, either. Nor she his: he was watching Francine (now lying on her stomach, eyes closed) with barely covert admiration. Her tanned legs, her hair soft and curly from the salt water.

That night they had dinner together in one of the many seafood restaurants with plastic chairs and round white tables with candles; Francine and Lydia insisted on paying their share. George and Farid talked a little about themselves this time, snippets of background: George had three sisters, no father; he was the youngest, the favoured baby of the family. Farid was an only child but he'd grown up with cousins, two girls, Mouna and Nasima. His parents were both at the American University of Beirut, his mother a professor in American literature, his father head of surgery at the medical centre. He and George had both been born in Beirut, but George's family came from Palestine, like Farid's aunt, Deena. As kids they lived together on the same street, half a block from each other: friends, co-conspirators, aficionados of movies and travel. No better in school than they should be. "Farid always was with the girls," said George. "*Ay!* True!" as Farid waved him off. "Fast talker," George winked at Lydia. "But now he's all alone. His girlfriend has left him." He played a tiny invisible violin. "The beaches at home are much more beautiful than these," George continued, sounding nostalgic. He and Farid reiterated the offer of a place to stay, and Farid gave Lydia the phone number before they said goodbye.

Lydia and Francine had a couple of days to decide what to do. They checked out of the hotel and carried their small bags with them—for a fee, Gary, the bartender at Steve's, was babysitting their heavier luggage back in Athens—downhill to the docks.

The boat to Santorini was even smaller but less crowded than the other ferry. Prepared this time—they had taken Gravol before but the sea was calm today, anyway—Lydia and Francine could talk and even doze.

"So, do you like him?"

"Not that way. What about George?"

"He's fun…." Francine had known her share of good-time boys— eventually, always, the fun wore off. But she was on hiatus; nothing had to last. She closed her eyes.

Santorini was a purge after the feast. Gorgeous, but ravaged. Thriftier with their money this time, they stayed in the cheapest hostel, a low cement building with a phalanx of open-air showers alongside. Tin heads the size and shape of trimmed sunflowers rained onto a rough cement floor and while they washed in the thin spray of fresh water they could look out at the sea, breathe in its fishy tang. The room they slept in with five others was dirty, drifts of dust and sand in the corners, paint peeling off the wall in scabrous patches. They spent as little time there as possible. Francine didn't trust one of the other women, an Australian with the dislocated stare of either a chronic drug addict or someone who'd been travelling too long (both, in her case); she looked fixedly at their bags, asked too many personal questions. Using the communal bathroom late at night, Lydia found her nodding off on one of the toilets. She helped her to bed and afterwards, lying in her own bed, gave a mental thank you to Francine for insisting that they sleep with passports and money belts under their pillows; like the pea under the princess's mattress, they disturbed her sleep, but were safe.

twelve

The university was—in spite of everything, even the murder of its president and the shelling of the Basic Sciences building—still a fragile haven. It had closed or suspended classes more than once, and no doubt would again, but for now it was amazingly intact. Once through the Bliss Gates and past the soldiers—ignore the bullet holes in the gym's tin roof, the rubble in the hospital parking lot, the little heap of flowers and cards that commemorated a dead student—you might almost not be in a war zone, Mouna thought. Almost. Even during the invasion it had been quieter here, although then the hospital tunnels had been choked with refugees from the camps who used them as bunkers, too afraid to leave. "They'll have to go," Nadim had said after a week or so. "We can't function. People will die." Mouna had asked him: "Where are they supposed to go?"

The day the Israelis invaded, "Khalil Hawi is dead," Mariam had told her. He had shot himself on his balcony, not far from theirs. *Impossible,* was how Mariam had described him, after more than one department meeting. Impossible, difficult, stubborn were all words Mouna had heard her use about him. Even so, Mariam loved his poems. That day, the day of his death, she'd had tears in her eyes for him, but not just for him: "Poor little poet," she'd said. "Poor little Lebanon." They drank a toast to Hawi that night. Mariam read one of his poems at his memorial. *In the snowy nights while the horizon is ashes/ Of fire and the bread is dust;/ You will remain with frozen tears in a sleepless night....*

Every night was sleepless now. Nadim practically lived at the hospital, and if the entrance was not quite as protected as the main gates or the compound where some faculty lived, many days it was safer for him to stay there overnight than to make the short trip back and forth to home. Last week he wasn't home at all. A convoy of nurses coming to work from East Beirut was hijacked and held hostage, and Nadim spent his one day off negotiating for their release. In the end he had been able to convince their abductors that it made little sense to harm the very same people who might be called on to tend them, their comrades, and families, when they got hurt.

In the halls of the hospital, which Mouna reached by the safest, sideways route, the illusion of calm was ripped away, shredded by sounds and smells—and by the sight of *musallaheen* pacing the hallways, jittery, drugged-up, some of them teenagers, playing with their weapons and waiting for their comrades. Patients with blackened phosphorous burns, gunshot wounds, crush injuries. "We're a field hospital now," Grace said. The pediatric unit was shut down. Other hospitals, overloaded, sent staff and patients here, including some of the mental patients from Asfourieh Hospital, which was closed, though every day there was less room for psychiatric patients, with all the casualties coming in. Deena would have to stay at home next time she had a relapse.

Mariam and Mouna had argued over Hawi's death. In Mouna's opinion the Israelis killed him. "I don't believe in political suicides," Mariam had said. "He was a tormented man." Angry as she was at Israel, she insisted, she couldn't blame them for Hawi's choice. "Well, if we're all like you," Mouna had said, "Beirut is finished. We can just roll over and die." Mariam's laughter had been loud and furious.

Mouna heard footsteps behind her accelerating into a run and suddenly Grace was flying by, her rubber-soled shoes squealing, so fast that Mouna almost looked for skid marks like the ones a car would leave when it burned rubber. She flapped a hand in greeting as she ran by. "*Shu fi?*" "Another car-bomb. A small one, *grâce à Dieu*," Grace called back. Mouna sped up to follow her, although she was supposed to be collecting her mother and taking her home. When she turned the corner to the main ER she stumbled into Mariam coming the other way.

"I thought you might want some help," Mariam said.

But instead of turning to go upstairs together, they both followed Grace, as if the pull of disaster was irresistible. Stretchers, blood, someone screaming. Several bodies going straight to the morgue. Then a man lying on a gurney, his face strangely familiar. Mariam stopped. "Taxi!" People stared at her. *Is she nuts?* But Mouna knew him too. From a dream world, so long ago it seemed now. He was older, of course, than the last time she'd seen him, but the face was the same, though how she could distinguish it from the hundreds of others, these thin, bearded, wild faces, she didn't know. But she had seen him before, many times, in another life. Sweeping the dust out of the bakery, hurrying along the street with his deliveries. Ali, Hamid's son, looked at them, his eyes wild and glazed with pain. His hand was clamped to his leg and he had a gun in his hand that he wouldn't give up. The gun wavered. No one wanted to get too close. Grace had come up behind them, and was listening.

"Ali. Do you recognize me? From the bakery?" He nodded at Mariam, but it was Mouna he was staring at. She couldn't tell if he knew her. She had changed too, though maybe not as much as he had. There was not much of the boy in him any more. He was too thin, with the strung-out look of so many militiamen, high all the time on a cocktail of drugs and booze.

"Are you hurt?" Mariam kept her voice low and very level, an old teaching trick effective with overwrought students.

"My leg."

"Can the nurses take a look?" He kept his hand clamped to one pocket.

"They can't give you anything until they see what's wrong." He shook his head but the gun dangled more loosely from his fingers.

"No one will steal your things. *Bou ee dik.* I promise." Now his free hand hovered over the pocket and Mouna felt an eruption of sweat between her shoulder blades and under her arms. The back of her neck felt hot, as if she'd burnt it in the sun.

"What's in the pocket?" The gun snapped up.

"Ali, did you hear about the X-ray room?" Grace was talking

67

quickly and calmly. He shook his head again.

"A grenade killed three people. By mistake." It had gone off in the pocket of a Phalangist whose friends had brought him in. Destroyed the X-ray machine, killed the young man and a friend waiting just outside and maimed the technician, who died later in surgery.

"No grenades," he muttered. He flapped his hand to indicate he wanted her to lean closer so he could tell her. "Hashish. For the boys."

"OK, give it to me. I promise to take care of it for you. We may have to cut your pant leg." He was still uncertain and they were running out of time. "It's safe with me, *bou ee dik*. They don't let me smoke, it makes me paranoid." He didn't smile. "OK? Then the doctors can look at your leg and you can get your medicine." He started to nod, slowly. "OK. First we need the gun." For a minute Mouna thought he'd say no, but he let Grace take it, and the brick of hash, which she put into her pocket; it bulged like an overstuffed wallet. She would reek of hash later, Mouna thought, and almost started to laugh. Then an orderly wheeled him to another examining room, by which time he was almost unconscious from pain. Grace mouthed *merci* to Mariam. Aloud, she said to Ali: "You know, one of these days I might need some of that brown stuff myself. Just to take the edge off...." Mouna couldn't hear if he answered her.

A memory of Ali the boy, tapping on their door. Some manoucher for Mariam, who was recovering from flu. And soup. Hamid had made lentil soup for her. Ali stood at the door with the bread and a jar of soup. "For your mother." "She's not my mother," Mouna had said, and she could tell he didn't understand. He pushed the food at her. Mariam called out. "Who is it, Mouna?" "Ali, from the bakery." Mariam came slowly to the door. She was wearing a robe and Ali stared when it fell open. He looked as if he wanted to bury his head there, in her breasts. He looked, for a second, like a forlorn baby, and it made Mouna want to punch him. "OK. You can go." "Mouna!" Mariam's voice was hoarse from the cough that still afflicted her. "Ali, 'afwan, you must excuse my niece. Sometimes she forgets her manners." But she had seen the look too, and she pulled her robe tight, holding it closed near her throat.

"Would you like some tea?" He didn't answer, and she reached for her purse. "Something for your trouble?" He shook his head. "My father said he hopes you feel better soon." And he ran down the stairs, not even bothering with the elevator. "Mouna, that was rude. What were you thinking?" Mouna couldn't answer—she didn't know why Ali's awkwardness made her feel cruel. Any more than she knew how to explain what she could see when his face was unguarded, the truth that he kept hidden most of the time. He hated them, all of them. The people who came into the bakery, rich and not so rich, but all richer than him; the men at the garage who teased him when he struggled with his heavy trays. Women, the ones who flirted with his father and condescended to his mother, working in the back, her head covered and her eyes low; it was the women he hated most of all. But why? She was too young then to understand.

Now Mouna followed Mariam upstairs, anticipating the smell of coffee, or food—a family had moved into the room across the hall from Deena's, where their grandmother was dying, and usually they would be making something to eat—but there was not enough water at the moment for cooking, or for anything else. The male surgeons were wearing scrub dresses. Dirty bath water was being used to flush the toilets. Keeping everything clean enough to avoid infections, Grace had told them, was an increasing challenge. Mouna's stomach churned. From the open door she could see Deena dressed and ready, sitting on the side of the bed, knees together like a little girl. "*Umma,*" Mouna said. "We're here." Deena stood up without saying anything, and Mariam took her little suitcase. She shuffled out ahead of them. *This is really no place for her now,* Nadim had said. *I don't know what we can do for her here.* What could anyone do for her mother, Mouna wondered? With the city—no, the whole country—gripped by mass craziness there wasn't much sanity on offer anywhere.

Across the hall, two little girls were sitting cross-legged on the floor, playing a clapping game. "*Shhhhhh!*" Someone shushed them. Mouna could, after all, smell food; they must have brought something in, for the last days of their vigil. Grace had said the woman wouldn't live much longer.

Deena was puffy-faced. She hardly ate these days, but the medication played havoc with her body, so she swelled up and lurched on puffy ankles. She moved like a zombie. It seemed cruel to Mouna that the pills that were supposed to make her less crazy should make her look more so. She was supposed to be improving, slightly, that's what Nadim had told them, that the new drugs were better, and she might soon start to come out of this cycle. When she held out her arms for a hug, her eyes leaking tears, it took all of Mouna's composure to let her mother touch her without showing her distaste.

They walked home, slowly. It was close enough even for Deena and driving was too dangerous now. Deena held each of them by the hand, as they picked their way over the tramlines that had crisscrossed the streets since before Mouna was born. Mariam and Deena had grown up with the trams, Mouna with their residual map of the city beneath her feet. The rails looked as if an earthquake had thrust them up, buckling and tearing them. Everywhere, bits of track had been ripped out to support the cobblestone barricades on so many street corners—impromptu protection for the *musallaheen* and their checkpoints. Every day when Mouna arrived at the camp the children made her run a mock gauntlet, mimicking the tense daily process that occurred across the city. They cocked their thumbs and pointed two fingers. *Religion? Parentage? Show us your identity card. Wrong one! Rat a tat tat. Pow pow.* Their guns were fingers or broken slats of wood. Last week Mouna and some friends snuck across to a nightclub in East Beirut—things were calmer there, at the moment—and they'd each carried two sets of ID ready for the drive back. They'd had to show both sets twice, praying each time not to make a mistake.

Deena was staying at Mariam's, their families now wholly grafted into one wonky unit. "When you come back from Europe," Mariam had said to Mouna last night, "we should talk." Mouna watched Deena shuffle up the stairs, clinging to Mariam's arm. Nasima opened the door, visibly upset to see her mother looking so frail and so much like the crazy people they saw more and more of now, wandering the streets or sitting in front of wrecked buildings, rocking themselves. Exhausted by the unfamiliar activity, Deena didn't seem to notice her younger daughter's dismay, and she soon disappeared to bed.

Mouna crossed her fingers that the night would stay quiet and they wouldn't have to go down to the basement garage, where all the apartment residents gathered when the shelling was bad. It stank down there now from the number of times they'd used it as a toilet. She made tea for Nasima and herself, dark and thick with sugar, while Mariam sipped from a small glass of what looked like arak. Mouna noticed suddenly how dry and fragile the skin on her aunt's hands had become, starting to look like crumpled tissue. *She's getting old.* They spent the evening playing cards; Nasima beat them both in a game of Memory, her eyes flitting over the cards, fingers floating above the table before she chose each pair. She almost never lost this game, and it calmed her to play it, the reason Mouna had suggested it tonight. She had seen the anxiety in Nasima's face every time she looked at their mother, the way her fingers started worrying each other. *Please don't let her have inherited Umma's curse.* Mouna knew what Mariam wanted to talk about once she got back from Geneva. What everyone was talking about these days. *When shall we leave?*

thirteen

Francine was singing in the shower. Her warble threaded the sound of water drumming on flimsy tin. "Somewhere over the rainbow, way up high, there's a land that I heard of…." In the bedroom, Lydia was sulking. Earlier that morning in the kitchen, she had been drinking coffee and reading a book. "What are you reading?" Farid looked over her shoulder. She could feel his breath on her neck, the warmth of his body behind hers. She turned the cover his way to show a muzzy landscape in English greens and browns.

"*Mill on the Floss*," he read aloud. "What's a floss?"

"It's a river."

"And George Eliot. Who is he?"

She saw his smile—hard to resist, full of sweet mischief that made him look like a naughty kid—and clicked her tongue. "Hah hah."

He leaned forward, still smiling.

"Tell me something. Why do you read this…" —he took the book from her, quoted the blurb—"… this 'classic of English literature' when you're in Greece? Why do you not read about Greece?"

Lydia could feel a lecture coming on, and as always when someone tried to instruct her, she began to harden and set inside herself, like a pudding with too much gelatin.

"I'm learning about Greece."

He snapped his fingers dismissively. "In the folkloric sense: 'Oh that woman who sold me the earrings was so *nice*. She was so *interesting*. Her life it is so *different* from mine.'"

Lydia pulled the book quickly from his fingers and its soft cover tore slightly, coming away from the spine. "How would you know what I think?"

"Why don't you read about the place you're in?" he asked her, and she shook her head. *You don't understand*, her impatient gesture said.

And it was true, he didn't understand it. "All you people with your books on the trains and ferries. Do you want to see what's in front of you, or not?"

Lydia sat on the bed in her underwear and picked at the sheets. What was the matter with her? She didn't give a flying fuck about Farid's opinion of her reading habits. Who did he think he was? She'd had it with his teasing, with the endless circular conversations about politics, with feeling apologetic or naïve. She didn't want to know about "the struggle," as he called it. Sooner or later that would lead to a discussion of the kind she most dreaded. *Fuck it all.* It had been a mistake to come and stay here with them. Though Francine and George seemed to be having a great time. Her inner monologue was as aggrieved as a cranky five year old's, which irritated her all the more.

"Lydia." Farid was tapping on the door.

"What?" She tried without much success not to sound like a child.

"Are you going to be angry with me all day? What about our trip to Lykavitos?" He made sad puppy sounds. First whimpers, then a howl. "*Aroooo*! Please come out and play, Lydia." Francine was behind him, wearing a towel. "After you," he bowed and as she opened the door he caught a glimpse of Lydia in her underwear, and saw that she'd started to laugh; she couldn't help herself. Neither could he: he had the beginnings of an erection, brought on by all these half-naked women. He stepped back into the kitchen, hoping they hadn't seen.

He and George hadn't been sure they'd hear from the girls again after Mykonos. But now they'd been here for almost two weeks, and things were fine. Things were good. It was nice to have women in the apartment, nice to go out at night as a foursome into streets that reminded him of what it used to be like at home: crowds of people, the young and the not so young, walking the streets, enjoying the summer night and their own preoccupation with nothing other than having a good time in this gorgeous, tolerant cosmopolis.

Yes, it was all fine; *eeazeem*, everything was great, except, so far, no sex. He could feel the tension between them that, unless he was crazy, meant Lydia was thinking about it as much as he was. But she was so prickly, so confusing in her moods. He couldn't tell what was going to make her laugh, what cause offence. Why, then, was he attracted to her? What was it that charmed him? Because he *was* charmed, there was no question about that. George said her body was too much like a boy's, and she looked too young—not his style at all—but Farid liked her slimness, was excited by her laugh, a helpless bark that always seemed to come as a surprise to her, and was somehow sexual in the way it involved her whole body, leaving her flushed and softened. At breakfast she wore her little blue and white kimono. A slice of white thigh flashing by as she stalked off to the bedroom after he'd offended her.

Lucky George. Last night, when the girls were both asleep, he had joked about Francine. "She's killing me, that one," he'd said, fanning his crotch as if it were burning. "And you? Any success?"

"Perhapsi yes, perhapsi no," Farid had said, in English, his hand tilting one way then the other, a wobbly bridge. George had smiled at the riff on Arafat's answer the last time he was in Athens to yet another question from an American journalist about "peace in the Middle East." (In Arabic, one word, *la'am*, did double duty, yes and no. *Perhaps.*)

The girls emerged, skin glazed with sunscreen. "OK, ladies. Let's go." Farid clapped his hands like a bossy tour guide. "Where's your umbrella?" Lydia scoffed. Tour guides at the Acropolis carried coloured umbrellas aloft so their charges would be able to identify and follow them. When they went up there together, Farid had made fun of the groups of disgruntled tourists, hot and tired, some very bored, but all docilely trailing after the umbrella. He picked up a dishtowel and waved it over his head, pretending to crack a whip, and they all laughed. Outside it was sweltering. Definitely the wrong time of day, hot enough to discourage most sightseers, but they drove to Lykavitos anyway. It would be crowded later, in the evening, but there was hardly anyone there besides them that afternoon. Farid parked by the road, behind a lone silver sedan, and they climbed the dusty path, looking up at the shrine and down at the city. They found shade under a scrubby tree and sat, closing their eyes against the heat. The occasional gust of wind gave a temporary illusion of freshness, but otherwise the air was still and heavy, with the thick scent of resin and dust. They chugged warm mineral water and, too lazy to talk, drifted inside their own thoughts. Farid lit a cigarette, his mind doing the usual involuntary shimmy. He was tired. Sleep was an unpredictable guest in his life, coming and going—four hours at night his usual, unless he'd managed the perfect narcotized balance of hash and alcohol. And even then. Here in Athens there were times in the day, whole days, when he was felled by a dreadful lassitude that sometimes followed the involuntary surge of adrenaline in response to a noise—a car backfiring, someone cracking open a cola—and reminded him how vulnerable he was to boredom. Anticipation of fear was hardwired into his expectations now, and in its absence he needed some other stimulus. "And if it's that way for me," he had lectured Lydia the other day, in one of their arguments on the subject, "please tell me what is to happen to those boys and girls in the camps who are born into it. How can they imagine peace? What can they hope for from one of your peaceful solutions? To be shepherds? To move to America and clean toilets or sell pizza?" He could tell that Lydia hadn't wanted to talk about it. She got that shut-down, turned-inward look that he saw whenever they talked about something that upset or bored her. He didn't think it had been boredom that time. Something else.

Half asleep, Lydia watched him smoke, his eyes squinting, his chest rising and falling under his blue T-shirt. His thin, boyish chest, with that bird-like hollow that for some reason made her imagine the way his mother might feel, looking at her skinny, undefended son. Would that feeling be any safer, less possessive than hers? She wanted to kiss him. Thinking about kissing him gave her a little electric shiver. What was he thinking about? She turned over and closed her eyes, the heat and the sound of crickets bringing back her first summer in Canada, when Toronto was swallowed in a tropical heat that they hadn't expected. Elise had arranged for Cathy, the 20-year-old daughter of one of her new colleagues, to come in daily, to "show them around" and keep an eye on them. A couple of half-hearted sightseeing trips and Cathy left them to it. She was engrossed in her plans for the next year at university and too old anyway to help with what they really needed: friends. She sent them off to the park in the afternoons, where they watched little kids at a day camp chase each other through the wading pool's shallow saucer and slide on their bellies along a wet plastic sheet. There was no pool for bigger kids. After a week of this, Elise agreed that Lydia, almost 13, was old enough to dispense with their half-hearted minder. They still went to the park and sat on the grass or wandered the ravine, where rabbits, snakes, and less visible animals scurried through the long grasses. They made careful circles round the teenagers smoking dope underneath the bridges or past the hillsides where ravine-dwellers marked their turf with plastic bags, old coats and tarps. Locked in the sludgy routine of these afternoons, Lydia felt stupefied by a combination of loneliness and the unfamiliar humidity that intensified the sun's heat to a slow scald. She and Matthew had an unspoken agreement to mimic happiness, even to each other; Elise was distant and precariously moody.

Near the end of the summer Rosalie came for a visit. At the end of two weeks, she cancelled her flight home and called her solicitor to ask him to arrange the sale of her small house. "There's not much for me in England anymore," she told Elise. The relief of having her there took the edge off Lydia's irritation, compounded by her first period, at being made to share a room with Matthew. School started in the fall and they gradually made their adjustments to a new set of social codes, if not painlessly then efficiently enough. Rosalie helped Elise with a down payment, and then there was another house, their own this time, compact but with three small bedrooms. Rosalie found her own apartment close by. Once Lydia had left home and Matthew had moved in with his girlfriend Ruth, Elise sold the house and bought a condo, a south-facing unit in a tall building off St. Clair, not far from the first place they'd lived. Her building overlooked the same ravine from further west; in summer, from her balcony, you could see a slash of green, follow it with your eyes as it cut through the city all the way down to the lake which, depending on the weather and pollution levels, was blue, grey, or a poisonous beige smudged yellow along the horizon. Grey was its variation on the afternoon that Lydia visited Elise just before Armitage's book came out. "There may be a bit of a fuss. Some of the details are controversial," is what Elise said then. "But nothing too sensational."

Lydia was startled awake when Farid ran a finger along her neck, tracing the downy arrow of hair along her nape. She shivered, and closed her eyes again to hide how aroused she was. If they'd been alone right then, she would have done whatever he wanted.

That night they went to the movies: a double bill at the open-air theatre. *Pink Panther* and *Beverly Hills Cop.* For some reason, the Athenians seemed to love Peter Sellers, howling with laughter at each of his gaffes. They sat on flimsy chairs and drank Fanta from plastic cups; Lydia and Farid, hyper-conscious of each other's bodies, could barely pay attention. Lydia's entire left side tingled, and every time Farid moved next to her the hairs on her arm prickled. Francine and George, already at ease together, seemed oblivious to the tension, laughing at Clouseau's antics, George's arm resting along the back of Francine's chair.

After the movies, they went out for dinner, long trestle tables under party lights, plates of shrimp and tall glasses full of beer. On their way home, Francine and George walked ahead of them, fast, eager to get upstairs. Farid put his hand on Lydia's arm. "Wait." He took her hand and they went round the side of the building, to the parking lot. It was past midnight, too smoggy for a clear view of the stars. The neighbourhood, the street, Palaio Zografou, its ledges and sills, doors and windows were all silted by construction dust that added itself to the heavy air. The perfect climate for a homesick Beirut boy. Or a Toronto girl. Farid slid his hand inside Lydia's white tank top and she leaned back, swaying as if she were drunk; she was intoxicated, but not by alcohol. When he pinched her nipple softly her whole body was seized by a quick convulsion. She sighed. Branches rustling. Grains of dust in the air. Dust weighing down the leaves on the trees, coating everything in a fine, grey haze. They stood there together, waiting to go in until the others were sure to be in bed.

When they finally went into the dark apartment, they didn't speak, neither of them wanting to break the spell that made each step inevitable. Farid took Lydia into his room, gave her a gentle push towards the bed. She sat down and he sat next to her, his breath on her neck. They hugged, pressing together, touching each other until they couldn't stand to be dressed any more. Her skin was hot. When they lay down he undid the button at the top of his jeans and wriggled, trying to get them lower. She slid her hands inside, then round his ass, one finger stroking just below his spine at the tender spot where his cheeks began to separate. He groaned, and slipped one finger into her, then ran the same finger over her clitoris. She was so wet, her fluids thick and copious. "You make so much…." He rubbed sticky fingers together and she tensed. *Shit! Have I insulted her again?* No. He felt her loosen, she leaned back and opened for him, and finally, there they both were. Home.

fourteen

Click, click. Click, click. Click.... Mariam took Nasima's hands off the dial to the stove. She held them and squeezed, not too tight. "*Habibti*, everything will be fine." She put her arms round her and rubbed her back, feeling each knob of bone in her spine. She didn't like this new tic with the stove, wasn't sure what it signified. Nasima had joined them about three years after Mouna, after Basman was killed, when a severe depression had led to Deena's first extended stay in hospital. May, her friend, had called Mariam: "I'm sorry, we all love her, but I can't take in another child," she said, she had five already, and so Mariam and Nadim agreed, it was the best thing anyway, they told each other, for the two sisters to be together. Unlike her older sister, Nasima's absorption into the family was almost instant; they fell for her right away. Her shyness, her fragile smile, her preternatural competence with household chores, acquired by necessity, no doubt. The naughty sense of humour that had surprised Mariam when she first experienced it. And for a family of card addicts, she was the perfect addition. "She cheats!" Farid had complained to his mother. True. But she was younger than them, and she wanted very badly to win, so they told him to be kind. And soon she didn't need to cheat. She was a more skilful gambler than any of them.

A month after Nasima moved in. Mariam folding laundry: *What is that terrible smell?* She couldn't see anything. Nasima's room was pristine but sulfurous. She bent down to pick up a dropped sock and the smell was stronger, coming from under the bed. She got her nose to the floor and squinted. Halfway under the bed, a small dish, two rotting eggs. What to make of it? She sat back on her heels, holding the dish. "It's an experiment," Nasima said, serenely, when asked. (What kind of experiment, she had refused to say.)

"Mouna won't be away long." Nasima's shoulders were so thin Mariam could see ugly protrusions of bone that looked like deformities. The pinched little face: an almost simian look about her mouth. All jaw, no flesh. The days of food experiments were over and now the list of foods she could tolerate was shrinking in inverse proportion to things she was afraid of. Not a little girl any more, but so slight she almost could have been. Her body was a stiff, brittle cage, but Mariam held on until she could sense her relax a little. "You and I will take good care of *umma* until Mouna comes back to us," she said, from over Nasima's head. Mouna had just walked into the kitchen and Mariam was speaking for her benefit as much as Nasima's.

Nasima made a restless movement in Mariam's arms. When Mouna took her hand she could feel the anxiety vibrating through her body.

"Don't go, I don't want you to go." Nasima pulled on her hand.

"It's not for long, monkey, *bou ee dik*, I promise. Auntie Mariam will take really good care of you."

"A month!"

"Three weeks. Monkey, you'll see, it's not long at all. I'll bring you back a fantastic present. What would you like?"

"I don't care." Sometimes Nasima was a little old lady, and sometimes she sounded so much younger than her age. She rarely had her period, and at almost 17 she looked prepubescent. The war had played havoc with her development—another topic, ironically, on Mouna's checklist for presentation to the committee in Geneva. Their first opportunity to report on the camps here, where already a generation of children had grown up, prematurely aged but emotionally and physically stunted. Like prisoners on day parole unable to navigate a supermarket checkout line, they wouldn't know how to function in a world at peace, if that world ever arrived.

Nasima went to bed early, like their mother, who was asleep in Farid's old room. At two in the morning, Mouna, lying on the couch, woke to the sound of shells, but nowhere close. She saw a shadow in the doorway. "Hello?" "It's me." "Can't sleep?" "The noise woke me up."

Mouna patted the couch. "Me too. *Yalla.*" Nasima's feet were icy. "*Aah!* Have you been sleeping in the freezer?" She rubbed her sister's skinny feet, trying not to shudder when Nasima wound them in between her legs. Then she held her like a toddler and sang to her, until she fell asleep again. Memory swooped in like an attack jet. She could see herself, very young, before Nasima, before Deena was ill, before Walid had left. They were driving home and had stopped by the road, maybe so she could pee, and Mouna hadn't wanted to get back in the car. She could see the wide road yawning, hear the tinny whine of other cars whizzing by. She could still smell the interior of that car though she hadn't seen it for years: tobacco, dust, and the remnants of Walid's sweets, which he ate while driving, spilling crumbs that lodged in the seams of the passenger seat, irritating Mouna's bare skin when she sat there, which wasn't often.

Her father's handsome face. The mole on his cheek. He was bored and absent, his usual defence against her tantrums. Had it been a long trip? She couldn't remember, though everything else was so vivid. He stood by the car, ignoring her. "You deal with her," he had said. Deena had crouched by her, holding her hands. "What's the matter?" The most gentle, tender voice. "I don't want to." "Why not, *habibti?* Do you feel sick?" "No." "Then what is upsetting you?" "I just don't want to!" Why? She couldn't remember. Perhaps she didn't even know then. Now she was swamped by the physical memory of her mother, her soft hands, the sweetness of her voice, the kindness in it, as if it didn't matter if they stayed there all day, figuring out the cause of Mouna's sadness. "Come on, we'll be home soon and I'll make you some tea with sugar and you'll feel better." *Forget this shit.* No point to it. Trapped beneath Nasima, surprisingly heavy, she could feel her legs going numb; pain where the couch springs knuckled her spine. While her sister and mother slept, Mouna was awake through the night.

Rah yiftah al matar—the airport is going to open—was a weekly rumour, but Beirut International was still closed indefinitely. The runway bombed by the Israelis when they left had not been fully repaired yet.

So by car to the airport in Damascus, Damascus to Paris, Paris to Geneva. Everything so fast that Mouna's eyes, her whole body, barely had time to register the shock of change, the astonishing sight of quiet, undamaged streets. At least there were mountains, and water, to mitigate the strangeness. The Damascus flight had been packed with people leaving Lebanon. Lots of tears, but also a semi-festive atmosphere. Getting away, going to safety. To join others in London or Amsterdam or Paris. Mouna knew one of the families—Leila and Tariq and their teenage twins, Sami and Khalil. Leila was glad to go, Tariq less so. Together they waited for the flight while watching a Lebanese soldier try and persuade his girlfriend to go with him. "What about your wife?" she pouted. Sami and Khalil nudged each other and snickered. When they arrived in Paris, they were met by a small crowd of Lebanese friends. Watching them, Mouna had a brief fantasy of missing her connection, slipping past the crowd, losing herself in Paris and not going on, never going home. She could hide, change her name, and never go back. No more ripped up streets, no more wounded children.

"Mademoiselle Ammari?" A man with her name on a sign at the Geneva airport. He drove her to the hotel, on Mont Blanc, right by Lac Leman. She was discombobulated: clean sidewalks, orderly people, and such pacific neatness. Everywhere parked bicycles, some not even locked. And each with a licence plate—*who but the Swiss*? She could imagine Mariam scoffing. She lit a cigarette in the taxi and could swear she saw the driver's nose twitch. What kind of taxi driver didn't smoke? He rolled down his window. Over his shoulder, he informed her that her hotel was near the Hilton, which was now the Noga Hilton, and that Saudis had started to crowd the promenades beside Lake Geneva with their veiled women. *Leurs femmes ensevelies*: he used the French word for shroud. She waited for him to say something about Arabs but he didn't. Instead, he asked if she planned to visit the casinos.

"*Ca ne m'intéresse pas.* Life's enough of a gamble without risking money."

"Where are you from?"

"Beirut."

He looked at her in the mirror.

"*Vraiment?* You live there? But it's so dangerous. *Trop dangereux, non? C'est barbare!*"

What was she supposed to say to that?

"Why don't you stay here?" He didn't mean Switzerland, surely, they didn't welcome foreigners, except on official visits or transient work visas. With his dark skin, she doubted he had permanent citizenship himself.

"I love my country."

Vous êtes folle. He shook his head. *How can anyone love such a crapheap?* He didn't say either of these, but he didn't have to.

Mouna had the luxury of some unplanned time, so she went to sit by the water, on the beach. She watched the fountains, and the people relaxing with their sunglasses on, shirts loosened, sleeves rolled up, others sunbathing in their bikinis. It was a beautiful early summer day but she couldn't get over the feeling that something would happen, any minute, to shatter this placid environment: a plane crashing into the lake; a bomb scattering the crowd of men and women enjoying the sunshine. Screams, mayhem, wreckage. Splintering the glassy blue like a burning sword.

But the hours passed uneventfully. She sat and drank a *citron pressé* at a small table; the lake remained calm, its promenaders undisturbed in their pursuit of sun. Next morning, she and a German colleague were to present their findings on the mental health of refugee children in the camps to a special committee at the UNHCR. Doctors and specialists of all kinds were meeting together for a week of talks. A week here and then she'd fly to Athens for two and a half weeks—*take a holiday, you need it,* her friend and boss Ramzi had said, *get some rest,* said Mariam, both leaving unspoken *you can't fall apart, we need you healthy*—to see her cousin. And then home again. She couldn't stay away too long, didn't want to; when you leave your home in a state of turmoil you never know what will have changed when you get back.

fifteen

Long ago, in that lifetime when Mouna was a little girl and Nasima not much more than a baby, it was Mouna begging someone—her uncle Basman—not to go out of town again, or, preferably, to take her with him as he babysat some foreign journalist through interviews and meetings.

"Why can't I come? I don't want to stay here."

"*Mish mneeha*." That was his answer, always—*it's not suitable*—and that may have been true, but it didn't make anything easier. Now she thought of how young he was then: just a kid still, and although she knew he'd had financial help from Mariam and Nadim, he had taken on most of the burden of responsibility for his absentee brother's wife and children. His job involved long hours talking, listening, charming strangers. Ferrying them from place to place, explaining, intervening when they caused offence inadvertently or, in some cases, deliberately. At home and at work, he was always taking care of other people's needs. Did he have a lover? Man or woman? Was there anyone who took care of him? Mouna didn't know, and she wouldn't find out now.

She had a clear memory of one of Basman's late visits after a long day at work. He sat on the sofa next to his sister-in-law, holding something out in his hand, a small package. His voice was hoarse with fatigue and hours of smoking and translating. *Take it*, he had said to Deena. A stranger was sitting across from them on a chair, smiling at Mouna. *J'ai une petite fille qui a presque le même age que toi.* The man's smile. Basman's clever face. His hand reaching for Deena's. *Take it.* Mouna hadn't wanted the stranger to see her mother like that, singing and too happy. She would have been angry with her uncle for bringing him into the house, if she hadn't been so tired. The man had sat with her while her mother and uncle went into the back room to talk; smiling, he tried to distract her from the sound of her mother's voice zigzagging up and down, each zag a danger signal. Her mood was turning, like it always did. The man showed Mouna photographs of his little girl: big eyes and a narrow, pointed chin. (What was that girl's mother like, Mouna had wondered? Did she spend days moving round her house like a sleepwalker, wearing the same clothes until they smelled?) He seemed kind, but she was very tired and she wanted him to go away so she could sleep. Deena had kept her up all night the night before in one of her too-happy moods that always filled Mouna with dread, anticipating their reverse. She had wanted Mouna to help her with the sewing, but she knew Mouna was no good with her hands. Sometimes Deena shouted at her for being so clumsy, so she had tried hard, hoping to keep her mother contented so that Nasima could rest, but Mouna was even worse than usual and ruined everything she worked on. It was all right. Deena wasn't upset, even though she had to do all of Mouna's sewing over. "Just sit up with me!" she sang. "Look at the sky, so beautiful!" She sang all night while she sewed; louder whenever she saw Mouna's head sag towards her chest. How could Nasima sleep through it?

One afternoon, the week after that visit with the French journalist, while Deena, on the downswing now, finally slept, Basman took Mouna away from her mother, to live at Mariam's. He took a few days off work, all he could afford, to stay with Deena until she was more stable, and May sent her oldest daughter to watch Nasima. Almost two years later, at Basman's funeral, Mouna looked for the journalist, but she didn't see him. There were other journalists there, one she recognized from a dinner at Mariam's, the night she'd insulted Carol Plakidas. He looked over at her and Deena once or twice during the funeral, but he stood in the back and left before it was over.

The plane began its descent to Athens airport. Mouna stretched her jaw and swallowed to clear her ears. She wondered how long it would take to clear customs. She had heard that security was tighter coming and going than it had been the last time she visited, but arriving from Geneva she should be OK. It would have been different if she'd flown direct from Beirut or even Damascus. Everyone was nervous about flights from the Middle East. When Rafa Ahmed hijacked the first El Al plane she was barely 20, younger than Mouna now. They thought they were going to change people's minds, Rafa and her comrades. Make them see. It seemed naïve, now, but for a minute maybe people did see the world, or their piece of it, differently. *Not for long.*

"Mouna!" A man ran towards her. Kissed her on both sides of her face, held her face between his hands. "Still so ugly!" She laughed. "*Merci.* You too." But she wasn't ugly at all, not any more. Farid could see that. She'd grown into her face, and her charisma made people in the airport pause to look at her, and look again, as if wondering who she was. She didn't seem to notice.

"How was Geneva?"

"Clean."

"Well, we're not so clean here. And there are four of us. We have two girls staying."

"One for each of you? *Eeafek!*" She linked her arm through his. It was so good to see him, his beaky face, his long hands, gesturing and pointing. "We have a car." It was old, but an elegant pistachio green. Trust Farid. He never made a mistake with colours. He had an eye.

To anyone who had watched them grow up, the closeness that existed now between Mouna and her cousin might seem miraculous. Mariam and Nadim in the kitchen, one night, about two months after Mouna came to them: "I don't know what to do with her. She's rude, hostile. And I think she bullies Farid when I'm not looking."

"Are you sure?"

"No, not positive. But something is going on."

"What does Farid say?"

"Nothing. But he might not tell."

"Well let's give it another month, and if it isn't better by then, I promise, *habibti*…" and he dropped his voice, as if he knew Mouna was listening, just down the hall. Though he couldn't have known she was there, she'd been as quiet as anyone could be, tiptoeing on her bare feet.

Mariam was half-right about the bullying: it wasn't physical, not like the day Mouna had pushed Farid. What she did was torment him with words, tease him about his shyness and insecurities, but most of all about his bike, which he was afraid to ride but desperately wanted to; his parents had promised him a boat trip if he mastered it. In private, Mouna called him a baby, a little girl. "Going to ride your bike today, *walad*?" she taunted him; he'd try and ignore her until he couldn't take it any more, then they'd start to fight. In return, he told her she was ugly, which she knew was true. Everything was too big on her face, and her teeth were crooked, but getting fixed now that she lived with her aunt and uncle. She hated the braces and the dentist visits, and she rarely smiled, not wanting to show her bad teeth, but at least Farid didn't tease her about that.

After overhearing the conversation between Mariam and Nadim, Mouna made a pact with herself: instead of teasing him, she'd help him learn to ride that damn bike. And then she'd get to stay. Because by then she had realized she didn't want to go home again, ever. Even though she missed Nasima terribly and found it hard not to cry after each visit, she no longer wanted to live with her mother. She would make her aunt and uncle want to keep her.

The hardest part was getting Farid to trust her. She'd tricked him too often and he was so used to her reversals that he didn't believe her when she said she'd called a truce and was going to help. "Why?" he said, staring at her, and when she held the back of the seat he wouldn't pedal. "You're going to push me off."

"No, I'm not."

"Yes, you are."

"Just try!"

"No." And so on, until an afternoon when she hissed: "*Na 'aaa*, crybaby, Faiza's right there." Faiza was sitting on a bench talking to another woman, not watching them, but she was a formidable protector, as they both knew, and Mouna had seen the back of her hand more than once. Farid stared at Mouna and nodded. *OK*. He let her give him a little push from behind and then he was coasting, trying to pedal, pedalling, round a corner too fast, wobbling... crash. He fell onto the grass, thankfully. He lay there for a minute looking up at the sky and she thought he was going to wail, like that day in the kitchen. Faiza still wasn't watching. But he dragged his bike upright and she went to help him again. By the end of the afternoon—after many arguments, one near fist-fight, and one fall that scraped his knee and did cause tears—he was riding free, pushing off by himself. They got home, triumphant. Faiza told Mariam: "Mouna helped him each time! And Farid *shujaa'*, so brave, weren't you, *habibi?*" Farid and Mouna looked at each other and started to laugh. The adults watched, nonplussed, while they giggled together.

Mariam put an arm round both of them. "I'm proud of you!" She wasn't just referring to the bicycle triumph, Mouna knew. After that day, things had begun to change, bit by bit.

And now... Mouna looked sideways at her cousin. Well now, after all this time, here they were. She was so happy to see him. A bit disappointed that he had guests other than her, though he was obviously thrilled about it. What kind of girls? She was about to find out.

sixteen

A rare occasion: Mariam alone in the apartment. Nadim, as usual, was at the hospital, Mouna in Europe. Nasima and Deena had gone to say goodbye to the Kasems, who were about to move to Cairo. And Faiza, taking a much-needed break from them all, was visiting her sister. *I should do something useful.* But what? Clean house? Prepare some notes for class, assuming that class would be taking place? Check the latest "traffic report" on the radio? Akhawi kept them all up to date on which routes were safe for whom, where the latest checkpoints were, who was manning each one. People tuned in to listen to him before they left work, went shopping, or, most important, let their children go anywhere. He'd become one of the few universally trusted men in Beirut.

No radio. She was too tired for *al-akhbar,* too worn out for news of any kind. Many mornings now she felt so wiped out it was difficult to get up, to put one foot, then another, on the floor. When the war had started, she was still young, still buoyed by the sense of her own life's drama and its possibilities, of time opening ahead, not closing behind her. Now she was afraid, indecisive, dithering. Like an old woman, she thought. Maybe it was her dwindling hormones, bearing her courage away with them as they fled. Maybe, if she were still young, her skin still smooth, her heart expectant, she could tolerate the future better. Not feel so exhausted. Nor have the sense that another life, her real life, had gone on in a parallel world without her, somewhere that didn't require identity cards and sandbags and taped glass and self-medication. How many cigarettes had she smoked since the beginning of the war? How many glasses of wine, cups of coffee swallowed? Too many to imagine counting. Arak and sleeping pills at night. Coffee in the morning, when she could get it. Coffee was her elixir. She had joked to Nadim that she could live without running water, without power, without fresh meat and vegetables, even without bread, but the day they ran out of coffee and the small reserve of water necessary for its preparation would be her last in Beirut. At least for now, water was restored, so coffee was no problem. She cleaned and filled the espresso pot, and put it on the stove. The pot was so old that almost the entire bottom half was stained brown, as if the coffee had seeped from the inside out. They had bought it in Venice, on a trip, years and years ago. Venice, where she was delighted by the excellence of the espresso all over the city and drank so much of it she was constantly high. In the morning at their hotel, the evening, at terraced restaurants, at two o'clock, in tiny bars with stand-up counters where Venetians stood to down their shot of espresso or little tumbler of red wine, eat a stale panino. Every morning now—even when they had to line up for water, she always hoarded some for this purpose—Mariam followed the long-practised routine: pour the water into the bottom, pack the aromatic grounds into its little circular tray. Screw on the perforated lid, then the top half of the pot. Set it over the flame and wait, watching until it hissed steam and a small trickle spurted down the side. Then the thick, chocolatey espresso was done. The routine itself would be almost Zen, if it weren't that Mariam's nerves were always crying out for that first rush of caffeine.

Did this poor pot ever think it would lead such a violent existence? Instead of sitting peacefully on a Venetian stove, it gets flung into the sink when a shell hits too close, coffee spurting everywhere. Its owners crawl towards it on their stomachs, below the line of fire, instead of strolling leisurely through their warm, placid kitchen. This other life, where did it go? They had photos, visible proof that once upon a time in a fairytale all they had to worry about was whether dinner that night would be as good as the one before. How crowded would the museums be? And would they make love before or after breakfast?

The before or after question was not one Mariam and Nadim asked each other at the moment. Sex had gone the way of peace. Mariam looked at her hands. She was starting to get age spots, and the rest of her body was an untended country, unplucked, unshaved, unsmoothed. What would her friend Leila, who lived in the language of women's magazines, say? *Just because you live in a war zone doesn't mean you have to look like one.* Leila had just left, for good—Paris—but she'd be glad to know her influence was still felt.

Louis, Mariam's favourite hairdresser, had been bombed out of business, but a woman up the street had rigged up a generator and did hair from home, and if she went there this afternoon maybe she could get it cut and the dye refreshed so she didn't look such a hag. But she was so tired. Before she had finished articulating that thought, Mariam found herself lying down on the kitchen floor, cheek on the stippled linoleum, ears ringing, her body absorbing the aftershocks of an explosion somewhere much too close. She lay there even when the pot started to bubble, then boil, then squeal, even when drops of scalding water spattered her cheek. She flinched then but still she didn't move. Not until the pot boiled over and a fountain of coffee doused the gas flame—Nasima's nightmare, the stove on, unlit and leaking gas. Not until then, and very slowly, did Mariam get up. She turned the stove off and listened to the spilt coffee bubble and hiss. The pot was fine, too sturdy to ruin. She burned her hand trying to pick it up, dropped it in the sink, cursing. What a waste of good coffee! Standing over the ruins she was surprised by an unfamiliar noise. Whose voice was that, so raw and rough? She listened and listened and it began to dawn on her that the voice was hers, the apartment filled with the sound of her weeping.

seventeen

Lydia and Farid lay in bed, listening to Mouna and George and two other friends, Sami and Michel, in the living room. Laughter, voices rising. George was hollering, one of his comic turns. Lydia needed to pee but she didn't want to go past the living room in her underwear and she couldn't be bothered to get dressed. And even if she did, there was Mouna to deal with: her bored scrutiny, its knife-edge of mockery. Who the fuck did she think she was? Her look, when they were first introduced: down her long nose, laughing. "*Ay*, I see." Did she really say that? What the hell did she think she knew about Lydia, just by looking? *Bitch*.

Best to forget about Mouna and concentrate on Farid's words; for once, he was talking about home. "My mother had the best parties in the neighbourhood. Everyone came. Even after the war started." This was one of the rare times he'd mentioned the war in a personal way. He told her about his cousins coming to live with them, first Mouna— "How we used to fight!"—then her little sister. "What about their parents?" Lydia asked. Mouna was hard to imagine other than as a fully-formed adult, so self-possessed and forceful. Stifling, in fact, Lydia thought, like some of the narcissistic actors and theatre people Elise used to bring home.

"Their father went to Jordan," Farid said, "and their mother...." He interrupted himself, maybe thinking of Mouna in the other room with her audience, two men who had shown up just after she arrived, seeming to hone in on her presence by radar. The apartment reeked of their cigarettes and dope, and the bedroom was starting to get stuffy.

"Shall we go to the movies tonight?" Farid nuzzled Lydia's shoulder and ran his finger along her neck, and she forgot entirely that she needed the toilet, the ache between her legs sublimated by another, more powerful, ache. Even his casual touch set her off, tingling, breathless, but she tried to hide it, wary of being completely transparent about his effect on her. He was looking at her, inquiring. *What was the question? Movies, right.*

"Is there something good on?"

"Oh, most likely no." He told her how he missed his favourite cinema in Beirut. "Everyone talks to the screen, all the men are smoking. Sometimes there's so much smoke you can't see the action." He mimed a karate chop.

"You like action movies?"

"My favourite. Chuck Norris. After the war started, some cinemas were bombed, others shut down, but not Saroulla."

"Weren't you afraid to go there?"

"My parents were afraid, but me, when I'm at the cinema I forget other things. So I went without telling them." He was caressing her still, slowly, and her concentration was impaired. She wanted him to keep talking like this, not one of their arguments but real conversation, so she could know him in his other life, have more of him.

"Where do your parents live?"

"*Ras Beirut.* Near the university where my mother teaches. They would like to leave, but my father is needed at the medical centre. And my mother can't leave Deena, my aunt. Mouna's mother."

"Is she ill?"

"Sometimes. Her husband left her alone with the children, a long time ago. Then our other uncle died. He was taking care of the family. And now her daughter Nasima, Mouna's little sister, is not doing so well. Too much stress—the war makes people sick." Lydia tried to put together his calm description and the trauma it contained. He gestured to the door. "Shall we get out of bed and join the others?" Then he saw her face. "I've made you sad." She turned red and her eyes filled unexpectedly, which embarrassed her.

"No, I mean yes, sad for your aunt, and your cousin. And Mouna, of course... and—" Her voice was trembling and she stopped, afraid that he'd think she was about to cry, which she knew would not be the right thing, not now. "And me?" He smiled at her, half-teasing, refusing seriousness. "And the whole of Beirut? That's a lot of people." He sat up and pulled her by the hand. "Let's join the party."

"So, young lovers," Mouna called out as they came out of the bed-room. "You're awake now?" Lydia ignored her, slipping behind Farid and into the bathroom, locking the door. Her face in the mirror was flushed, the look of a woman freshly fucked, on the verge of tears or tantrum, or all of the above. She splashed water on her cheeks and did a little deep breathing. It was exquisite relief to empty her bladder. The thought of joining the others smelling of sex prompted her to have a quick shower, and when she finally came out Mouna looked at her wet hair, raising an eyebrow (Did anyone actually *do* that, outside of nov-els? What was her problem?), but didn't say anything. The men were talking animatedly in what Lydia assumed was Arabic. Francine had joined them, patting the couch next to her for Lydia to sit down. Her tanned shoulders and long legs gleamed and she was smoking a joint, relaxed, her curly hair spread over the back of the sofa. Lydia shook her head at the offer of the joint. "You don't smoke?" Mouna made the question vaguely insulting, as if Lydia was branded a prude, or a petu-lant child. "OK princess, let's get you a drink. I bet you could use one." Well at least that's one thing they could agree on.

Princess. Lydia would have loved to tell Mouna to fuck off, and if they were alone maybe she would have. The woman drove her crazy. One minute she was feeling sorry for her, the next ready to strangle her. *Grow up, Lydia,* she told herself. *Jesus, think about what she's been through.* It was Mouna, after all, who had the sick mother and sister, lost father, long list of dead friends and relatives. But somehow none of that helped. Hop-ing her emotions weren't doing their customary ticker-tape display across her face, she gladly accepted a tumbler of wine from George. Soon everyone but Lydia was stoned. To compensate, she drank quickly, wanting to erase the feeling of being out of step and alienated by her own sobriety. Mouna and the men had naturally switched to their own language, so Francine and Lydia talked to each other, about a letter Francine had from her father, and about the possibility of taking a trip to Turkey. They kept their voices low, not wanting to intrude on the others, but Farid tuned in to the word *Istanbul.* "We should all go!"

"Oh yes, you can't go alone, girls. What about the white slave trade?" Mouna again, mocking. Lydia pretended she found it funny.

It was hard to believe Mouna had arrived only three days ago. When Lydia and Francine came back from the market, there she was, sitting on the floor with a glass of tea and a cigarette. Her bags were sprawled in the hallway and she looked completely at home, relaxed and amused, as if she'd been there for weeks and they were the ones just arrived. Lydia had wanted to like her, and for a minute she almost did, but then they said hello to each other and almost immediately something was off. Once in a while, she thought, you meet someone like that; you just know it won't work between you. No matter what you do—in fact, the more you try, the worse it is; better to leave it alone. The place felt crowded now: by Mouna's personality, and by all the people, mostly men, an occasional woman—who had suddenly materialized, with booze and drugs and messages from other friends. "Mouna, *habibti!*" "*Ciao*, Mouna," "Mouna, *dis-moi...*" all wanting to hear about home. Mouna had letters and news for some of them; others were hoping she'd take something back for them. The apartment had turned into a mini-hotel, a constant party, but it was not just recreation. There were political debates, with even more of the kinds of pronouncements that Lydia hated, the danger zone of discussions she didn't want to have, especially not in Mouna's company. And when her friends weren't there, Mouna filled the room with her outsize presence, taking up space, pushing the oxygen out so that Lydia could hardly breathe.

"I'm going out for a minute," she said suddenly. She needed air and it was still early. "Anyone want anything while I'm out?" Farid shook his head, lazily, and the others ignored her and kept talking. "Hey, I'll come with you." Francine pushed herself off the couch, at which Farid sat forward as if he was about to change his mind and say "me too," but Mouna put a hand on his arm, talking to him but looking up at Lydia. "You don't have to chase after her all the time. Play some cards with me, little cousin."

"Oh, old lady, I can beat you." He smiled at Lydia. "Don't be long. We'll go somewhere nice to eat tonight, for celebration."

Outside, Lydia could feel the drinks, too early in the day, making her logy and bad-tempered. She sighed.

"What's up?" Francine took her arm.

"Nothing."

"Liar."

"I feel a bit claustrophobic, that's all. Too many bodies."

"I know what you mean. It's only for a couple of weeks, though, right? While Mouna's here." Two weeks of Mouna seemed intolerable to Lydia at that moment; she didn't say it, but Francine was no fool. "You don't like her." It wasn't a question.

"Other way round."

"Oh, she's just being a tad possessive. Farid's crazy about you and she can see it." Spoken like a loyal friend, but of course, it didn't hurt Lydia to hear it.

Francine looked thoughtful. "What if we did go to Turkey for a bit, just me and you? A week, maybe ten days, would give us all some space. Mouna can have Farid to herself, so she'll be happy, and you and I can hang out. Just us. We haven't done that since we first met, you realize that?" She was right. They'd paired off quickly with Farid and George and since then they'd been a foursome or separate couples, only rarely alone together, and then just for an hour or two. Francine gave her a little punch in the arm.

"Remember that first morning at Steve's? I thought you were a 16-year-old runaway."

"Come off it."

"No, it's true! You looked about 12! And you were in such sad shape, all pale and sweaty, coughing your little heart out. I couldn't believe you were travelling alone."

The ridiculous description made Lydia smile. "From 24 to 16 to 12, in 30 seconds? If I could bottle that I'd sell it and be rich."

The streets were crowded with people surfacing from the afternoon siesta, riding by on scooters, waving at friends in the street. Around the newspaper kiosks, men chatted and smoked or walked by, calling to each other. Most were dressed casually in beach sandals with thick plastic straps, small leather purses swinging from their wrists. On the scooters, young women clutched their boyfriends around the waist. The women almost all had long hair and wore heels and summer dresses, skirts tucked sideways so they wouldn't fly up, or so short that exposure was moot. One anomalous woman rode solo—*Mouna!* Lydia thought, for a minute, but of course it wasn't her, just similar hair, cropped and boyish; dressed like her too, in a crumpled white shirt and Capri pants, a half-crushed cigarette pack sticking out of her back pocket. Like her fellow scooter-riders, pseudo-Mouna allocated pedestrians full responsibility for their own safety; Lydia and Francine sprinted out of her way just in time, stumbling into each other. They recovered at one of the stand-up bars where working men downed shots. Doses of transparent liquor—*down the hatch*—heightened the shimmer of heat and their already tipsy state. They realized how hungry they were and stopped at a little place for "toast:" buns stuffed with cheese, olives, tomatoes, fish, and chopped egg, in any combination, pressed flat on a grill. Their fingers were glossy and wet with oil and the paper sleeves holding their sandwiches soon transparent with grease. "Holy shit, that's good." They were leaning on a low wall as they ate, paying full attention to the food, when someone stopped in front of them: the big American woman from Steve's Hotel. "Good, aren't they?" She nodded to their sandwiches. "Mind if I join you?" Five minutes later, she had her own sandwich and was sitting on the wall beside them. "So where have you been? Island hopping?"

"Yeah," Francine said, curtly, not her usual friendly self. Lydia wondered why.

"What's on the agenda today?"

"Nothing special." Francine said at the same time that Lydia answered: "We're looking for a travel agency."

"Where do you want to go?"

"Turkey."

"I'll take you to the best place. They've got great deals on flights to

Istanbul." So they followed her to a travel agent off Syntagma. Inside, the usual posters showed islands in uniform: white houses with blue roofs, sugar-cube steps that led down to white sand and the sea. Santorini stood out, in volcanic black, and Lydia remembered it, the sand burning her feet as she ran to the water like a cartoon character, *ow, ow, ow, ow, ow, ow… aaaah*. She'd almost expected her feet to sizzle and smoke when she reached the sea.

The woman at the travel agency showed them a schedule for flights from Athens to Istanbul, for a very good price, as promised. "This offer ends today." "Should we wait?" Francine asked. Lydia thought about it. What Francine had said earlier made sense. "No, let's do it." Let Mouna have Farid all to herself. That was the adult thing to do. And on the childish side of the scales, he'd see how much he missed Lydia when she wasn't around—or so she hoped. They booked a flight for Sunday, three days away, and thanked the woman from Steve's— "Cyndra," she reminded them—for the tip.

"I can't like that woman," Francine said, as they watched her walk away, her broad back disappearing round the corner. "She creeps me out." But thanks to her, they were all set for Istanbul. On the way back to the apartment, Lydia started to worry. Would Farid be upset that she'd gone ahead without him?

When they got home, there was a rowdy poker game in full swing. Cigarettes, drinks, tea. Music on the stereo. As they stepped inside the apartment, Farid was getting up to put a record on, and soon a woman's voice filled the room: high, mournful, almost keening. The men started to sing along, heads thrown back and eyes shut. Mouna rolled her eyes at Lydia and Francine in a way that was complicit, almost friendly, and reminded Lydia, strangely enough, of her grandmother. "Who's that singing?" she asked.

"Umm Khalthoum. Farid must be homesick." Mouna got up and lifted the needle off the record. "No nostalgia, please, boys. I'm on holiday." She changed the record and another kind of female voice, almost as high, started. Blondie. *Rapture*. There was a knock on the door and Farid turned the music down a little before he answered it. "Our neighbour isn't happy." But it was another friend, bringing pizza. Farid followed him into the kitchen and waved Lydia in after him. The man set down the box and when he turned to be introduced he was wearing a white T-shirt with a familiar image stencilled on the front. Black-and-white: great contrast between the woman's kaffiyeh and her hair, her doe-eyed, almost flirtatious look and the heavy gun on her shoulder; her slim hand and the ring on her finger, refashioned from a grenade pin. The image had been standard bedroom decoration in the 70s for student radicals and anyone who sympathized with the PLO and the PFLP, and was still popular on posters, T-shirts, or cards in tourist shops around the world, next to Che or Mao. It never failed—this time was no exception—to give Lydia a jolt, like spotting the other half of a bad break-up just down the street. Cross the road, get out of the way. Put some space between yourself and the enemy. She turned away from the new arrival to see Mouna watching her.

eighteen

Tonight was just the five of them, killing time while they decided what to do with the evening. For once they were eating in—Mouna had said she wanted to cook something. Lydia could smell lamb.

"So, cousin, how much do we know about these girls? Have they told you their life stories yet?" Mouna's English was excellent, even better than Farid's.

A little bit stoned, Francine laughed, resting her head on the couch. "Not much to tell. I'm on holiday from my life. Like the song says, my man done me wrong, but instead of shooting him I left town."

"*Eeafekeh*. Bravo." George stroked her arm, and she smiled at him.

"And you, Lydia, why are you here?" Was it just Lydia, or did the question sound vaguely insulting? A fraction too much emphasis on "you."

"Just a holiday."

"You're both Canadian?"

Double chorus: "Yes."

"But you, Lydia, you weren't born in Canada, no? You sound more... English?"

"I was born in London."

"Ah, London. Nice city."

"Piccadilly!" George exclaimed, goofily, and they all laughed. Mouna suddenly lost interest in their background details and started chatting with the men instead.

Listening to the back and forth between Mouna, Farid, and George, Lydia could hear how long they had known each other. They spoke familial shorthand, even in English, "Remember...," "Yeah, that guy," "You know." Words left out. No need to explain themselves. She had to strain to follow anecdotes, about friends, about sisters and brothers. "Paris. Everyone's leaving," Mouna said, at one point, answering Farid's question about someone they knew. She was casually possessive of both men and in small, deliberate ways—"George doesn't like taramo," when Lydia talked about Greek food; "Farid, show her how I take my tea"—she made it clear that in her eyes Lydia and Francine were bystanders, without a serious claim on her boys. Her scrutiny, her mocking tone, put Lydia's back up. She was used to dealing with the occasional condescension that came from looking younger than her age, but this was different. Dismissal, deliberately impersonal, as if Mouna had slotted her into a category—lightweight—and that was it. If Lydia mattered at all, it was only in how she affected Farid, and she had a feeling that if Mouna could do anything to limit that she would.

When Mouna talked about her family, Lydia could sense a couple of points of connection they might have made, had they liked each other better. Like her, Mouna was protective of her younger sibling, and she obviously had an equally complicated relationship with her mother, the "Deena" who loved Umm Khaltoum and who, Farid had hinted, was unstable in addition to being traumatized by losing family members and friends. But the door was slammed as soon as she nudged it open: "Farid says your mother's been ill?" Lydia asked, cautiously.

"Permanently. She's a manic-depressive."

"Oh, I'm sorry."

Curtly: "It's not your problem." Mouna was busy rolling a joint and caught Lydia off guard when she said suddenly, looking up: "What about *your* parents?"

"My mother lives in Toronto. My father died in a car crash when I was nine." "Car crash" was a fudge that Lydia had adopted years ago. Farid looked up, surprised. "I didn't know that." She moved her shoulders, not quite a shrug. "It was a long time ago."

She got up and headed for the bathroom, where she leaned her head for a second against the cool mirror, fogging the glass with her breath. She stood back and wiped the glass to look at her face. She had a little bit of a tan, despite all the sunscreen she used; her eyes looked darker as a result. Phil's eyes, green with the same tawny ring round the centre. Why did people always say that? *She has her father's eyes,* as if he plucked them out and gave them to her?

She could hardly remember Phil now—was no longer sure when her memories were real or amalgams of things people had told her or she'd read in the papers. His death had been a sucker punch that had sent them all reeling. It had been impossible, at first, for Matthew and Lydia to believe in the irrefutable difference between that day without him and the many others that preceded it. Though, soon enough, it was obvious that there was indeed a rupture between their lives before— mostly predictable, occasionally tense, inflected by the complex forces that pushed Elise and Phil together and apart and divided them from their kids—and after, limbo-land, lopsided and out of whack. But in spite of the fact that Lydia had read his obituary in all the newspapers, including *The Times,* and that her mother was both grieving and, more mysteriously, angry, for months after his death, she hadn't been con- vinced that her father wouldn't pop up—*surprise!*—grinning like the Rasputin jack-in-a-box he had brought her once from Moscow. One day, she'd hear the high drawn-out squeal of taxi brakes, the motor of the big black cab chuffing like a Clydesdale while Phil paid his fare, and then he'd shoulder open the door: Holiday Dad, on his way back from another extended assignment, suitcase full of presents and a new batch of tall stories: jeeps and sandstorms and feasts watched over by vigilant gunmen.

For the first few years after his death, she could hear his voice al- most as clearly as if he were in the room. Could summon it, the same phrase even, a little recessed button in her auditory memory that she could press at will, banal but comforting: "How's my bunny?" Some- times it would wake her up at night as vividly as if he'd come into her room and called her. Gradually, it became more like someone on the telephone, first local, then long distance, attenuated and drifting away, and now… now the voice was gone and she rarely dreamt about him any more, though occasionally she did still wake from a dream whose details were already fleeing while she tried to grab on to them, and a sense that she'd just missed seeing him, one more time. She shook her head, splashed some water on her cheeks, dried off and went back to the party.

Mouna and George were going back and forth from the kitchen and the living room with dishes of food and plates for everyone. Olives, salads. Mouna brought out stuffed vine leaves and tabbouleh, as well as the usual Greek spreads. And she had prepared some lamb kebabs, which she wafted under George's nose. "Aaah. Thank you," he said, taking a stack of warmed pita bread from the oven. He handed the hot plate to Lydia and she took it gingerly by the fingertips into the living room.

Francine rubbed her stomach. "That smells so good. I'm starving. I can't believe you're cooking for us, Mouna, *we* should be feeding *you*." Farid cleared the ashtrays and a hash pipe off the table. There was a little spilled ash, which he rubbed off with a piece of newspaper.

"Housekeeping is lazy." No one cared. The food looked delicious: shiny black olives sweated oil and the lamb was flaky and aromatic.

Mouna handed Francine a plate. "Mmm."

"Help yourself."

They ate until the plates were clear, leaving a mound of olive pits, turning dry and grey, little shreds of olive meat clinging to the ridges.

"Lydia, I don't understand how you can eat so much and stay so small." Farid squeezed her leg, testing for plumpness.

She laughed, pleased, and because it tickled. "I have a hollow leg."

"What?"

"It's an expression. Something Phi—my father used to say."

"Your father." Mouna mimicked a bad, vaguely Southern American accent. "What did Daddy do for a living?"

"He was a journalist."

"What kind?"

"All kinds, really. Travel, politics. Arts." Lydia spoke quickly. "Anyone else want a glass of water?" She went into the kitchen and filled a glass with bottled water from the fridge.

"What's her family name?" Mouna asked, to no one in particular.

"You mean her last name? Marcus." Francine was rosy with wine and sunshine. "Why?"

Farid looked at his cousin questioningly and she shrugged. "No reason."

In the kitchen, Lydia stopped to look at a framed photo on the wall, by the kitchen table where they had their morning tea. A group of people sitting at a picnic. She had sat in front of it every day for the last few weeks, but now she looked properly. She could see that there were a handful of children in the picture, but none seemed to be Mouna: maybe it was taken before she moved in with them. She recognized Farid, and smiled. He was so skinny! There were horses in the background. At first she thought it was a farm, but some of the horses wore numbers, for racing. She felt a hand on her shoulder. Farid had come in behind her. "Why are you looking at that old picture?"

"Just seeing if I can tell who's who."

He pointed to the woman with a high forehead and beautiful, intelligent eyes. "My mother."

"She's lovely."

"I don't get my nose from her, you can see." An older woman with a headscarf and some people in the background were turned away from the camera, watching the horses. "That's the Hippodrome, the race track. My horse won!" He lifted his hands in mock victory. "I was excited." He put his arms around her and nuzzled her neck. "I'm a very excited boy." She was shy of the possibility that Mouna might walk in on them, but his breath on her neck made her dizzy, set off a little flutter at the back of her knees.

Once, when she was 16, Lydia had had her hair cut very short. Shorter than now, even, almost a brush cut. She had visited Rosalie right afterwards, and on the way to Rosalie's apartment had kept her vulnerable head covered babushka-style—it was a bitter winter day and the wind crept under the scarf, up her now exposed neck. When she took off her scarf and coat, Rosalie stood behind her in the close, cramped living room and, so unlike her, Our Lady of the Brisk Touch, she reached out a finger to stroke Lydia's neck, the cool, razored nape where the hairdresser had trimmed close and then used clippers. Startled by a caress so out of character, Lydia had stood still while Rosalie

fingered the faint dark arrow of down and lazily, delightedly, mur-
mured: "Beautiful. Like a young boy." All of a sudden, Rosalie had
dropped her hand, and together they'd looked out the apartment
window at the ravine. A grey, snow-heavy sky. Swollen clouds waiting
to drop their cargo. The subway exit was right beside Rosalie's building, its doors set in the centre of a half-moon shaped wedge of concrete
from which people emerged on their way home from work. Hunched
in their heavy coats and boots, trolls coming up from the Underworld.

After supper, everyone but Mouna went to the disco. Farid didn't react
when Lydia first mentioned that she and Francine had decided after all
to go to Turkey, but later, after a few drinks, he said into her ear, loudly,
so she could hear him clearly over the music. "Don't go." Music
thumped in her chest, and the lights spun.

"Whoops!" She leaned into him, tipsily, and he held on tight.

"After Mouna's gone we can travel anywhere you want together."
Lydia felt a ripple of pleasure at the way he said: "after Mouna's gone,"
casually, as if he didn't care one way or the other, as if by far the most
important thing was what happened between him and Lydia. *So there,
Mouna.* But she wanted him to know she could be magnanimous.
"Won't you have more fun together without us?"

He shook his head, grabbed her, and they started dancing again.
Francine and George were somewhere in the middle of the crowd of
happy partiers, arms flailing, bodies moving wildly to the music.
Mouna had said she didn't feel like dancing, and was going out somewhere with her friends.

Later, when Lydia was even tipsier and the huge room was steam-
ing from the heat of all those bodies confined, Farid took her outside.
They stood tilted against the wall, looking up at the smog-blurred
lights and a haze of stars, feeling the building throb behind them like
a huge, frantically pounding engine.

Farid put his arms around her and she laid her head on his shoulder. He kissed her cheek. The door opened behind them and someone
came out, a whole group of people, oblivious, talking and laughing.

"You know what?" he whispered into her ear, once the people had moved past. "What?" She was talking into his neck, half drugged by his hand stroking her back. He didn't answer right away. Then: "I think I'm a little in lo-o-o-ve with you." He drew the word out in a half-joking way, then held her away from him to see her reaction. Measured air between his thumb and finger. "Just a little." What he saw when he looked at her seemed to reassure him. He hugged her again and held her against him, the two of them rocking back and forth, gently. Which led to them hurrying home so they could fall into bed. The apartment was quiet, and soon the only noise in it was theirs. They didn't hear the others come back, first too engrossed in each other's bodies, and then asleep—one of them, at least. For once it was happiness, not anxiety that kept Lydia from drifting off, as she lay awake replaying what Farid had said outside the disco, the way that he had looked at her.

She was not the only one awake. Mouna had changed her mind about going out and had fallen asleep reading, on the couch. She woke when she heard them come in, but before she could sit up they moved at such a pace into the bedroom that she thought they must have stopped in quickly to pick up something—more money, maybe—and would go out again. Instead, soon she was listening to the sounds of unbridled, passionate lovemaking. *Shit.* It doesn't matter who it is, the sound of other people's sex is alienating to an involuntary eavesdropper. And in this case, more so. Mouna wanted to go in and pull Lydia off Farid mid-fuck, throw her out into the street. She grabbed her cigarettes and went out on to the balcony where she wouldn't have to hear them. Sleeping with the enemy, was that it? Did the little bitch get a vicarious thrill from fucking a Lebanese man? Her mother was Jewish, so it said in the journalist's book. And her father—Mouna would like to see the smile fall off her face when she mentioned, casually, that Rafa was a friend of the family. That would stop her in her tracks. *See how much you like your boyfriend then, Lydia. Because deep down, like all Jews, you don't trust any of us.*

nineteen

"Friend or Foe?" by Edward Armitage
from his book *In Love with Danger*

So who was Phil Devlin going to meet, his last day on Earth? His contact, a local interpreter and fixer, can't tell us, since he perished with Devlin. Yves Levy, the photographer he worked with on most of his foreign assignments, doesn't know. Levy and I were his most trusted colleagues, but Devlin was notoriously protective of his sources, and what he told us was that he was going to talk to a local chief who knew something about a PFLP base in the area. His widow, the inscrutable, elegant Elise Devlin (née Marcus) has never challenged the official version that he was off to interview people who were strangers to him, members of the PFLP at their camp on the southern border of Lebanon. But now Mrs. Devlin has decided to lift her veil of silence, to breach the implacable front she kept at the time. Now she is suggesting another theory, one that has been whispered for many years: that Devlin was on his way to a rendezvous with his lover, a terrorist, a woman in whom, in an extraordinary lapse of his journalistic acumen, he placed his trust. This lapse—inspired by lust, or by something more profound, perhaps a crisis of belief—may well have caused his death.

The British government has not seen fit to respond to this or similar theories, and some say this is because Devlin was one of theirs; like Graham Greene, an intelligence agent who used his standing as a journalist to gather information from diverse sources. It should be said that there's no material evidence to support this theory, but the rumours persist about a man who was an enigma to so many, including his family.

The government's silence and whatever that may imply doesn't faze Mrs. Devlin. "It's time," she said, in a stunningly forthright interview, "to set the record straight. Time to come clean and stop living a life of rumour and dissembling. That kind of life, the life that my husband lived, is no longer ours." She and her children now reside in Toronto, Canada, where they have done their best to shake off the past. Elise Devlin now feels that may have been a mistake. "We need to face facts," she said, in the same interview. "My children have each had their problems, their own struggle to come to terms with their father's death, and I think the lies have been part of it. For them to be fully realized human beings they need to hear the truth about their father, then they can make their own judgements and move on." In particular, her daughter, her oldest child—nine at the time Devlin died—has had trouble putting the past behind her. "I think she feels responsible, in some way, feels that if we'd been a closer family and she a better daughter, whatever that means, her father might have stayed with us, and thus stayed alive. I want my children, and the families of other people like Phil, to know that the choice to live such a reckless, duplicitous life has nothing to do with them. A man like Phil is addicted to risk, to intrigue, and to the idea that causes are what make one special. I no longer believe any of that, if I ever did."

Coming clean is her personal decision, and Mrs. Devlin wishes to protect her children from intense media scrutiny; she has authorized only childhood photos to be used here and has asked that the media respect their privacy, even though they are now both young adults.

So the questions remain, but are closer to being answered. A path can be traced from Devlin's prior knowledge of the release agreement in the case of Rafa Ahmed, to his trips to Lebanon and Jordan in the early 70s, to his presence in that rocky gorge in 1972. The link in each case is Ahmed, the woman who has now been confirmed to be his lover. The most famous face of 1970 and one of the most admired and most vilified women in the world.

Was it a surprise? That face, in the English journalist's book. So similar as a child, those big eyes: frank and open but wounded already, even before Daddy's death. Why hadn't she seen it before? *You think you've got problems? Try ours, princess. Try living where we do. You think Rafa is a murderer? Talk to her about murder. How many, by which killers. Never got over your father's death?* Na 'aaa. Desolée, princesse. *The same eyes as him, almost.* Though his weren't vulnerable, not at all. When she saw the name, recognized the face, she felt sick. If it hadn't been for him… now she remembered him sitting on Deena's couch, showing her the photograph: "*Voici ma fille.*" She had thought he was French. He had been kind, she remembered, he'd wanted to soothe her. *Fuck him. Fuck his sad-eyed daughter, too.* Getting into things they didn't understand, dragging other people with them, doing so much damage in their ignorance. Tending other people's fires and then blaming the world when they got burnt.

The balcony door slid open behind her.

"Princess asleep?" She tried not to sound as sarcastic as she felt, but Farid wouldn't have noticed anyway. He looked—she glanced over—yes, he looked happy. Happier than she'd seen anyone look in a long time. "*Ay.* I think…." All of a sudden he was shy. "Forget it."

"What's up?"

"Nothing. Ah… I think that girl is falling in love with me."

"Is that good?" But she knew, from looking at him, what the answer was. Her plan to tell him about the book, about Devlin, Lydia's identity, her inevitably fucked-up worldview, shrivelled and blew away. She couldn't say anything. "Wait a minute." He went inside and came back out with two little glasses of ouzo. Handing one to her, he made a toast. "*A l'amour.*" She clinked the glass, but didn't repeat the toast, as was their habit—let him think her words got lost in a swallow of booze. She tossed back her drink. It made her cough, and he knocked her on the back, between the shoulders, gently, like a father burping his baby. Like Phil Devlin with his babies, perhaps. His voice when he talked about his daughter, that fond, loving tone. No wonder Lydia mourned her daddy. She was his little darling. After Farid went in, Mouna stayed on the balcony, alone, smoking and watching the sky, waiting for the sun to come up.

twenty

The next afternoon, Francine and Lydia were at the open-air market, browsing for something to buy for dinner—Lydia determined to be the one to cook this time—and there was Cyndra, feeling a tomato. Francine elbowed Lydia—"Quick, let's go." Too late. They'd been seen. She was already walking towards them. "Hey! Hi!" She stood too close, as always, and peered at the stack of postcards in Francine's hand, unaware, it seemed, that this might be considered intrusive. "I haven't seen you around the hotel." Francine didn't respond and Lydia stepped in. "No, we're staying with friends." She wondered for the first time if Cyndra was all there. She'd have to be singularly unobservant not to have realized they weren't staying at Steve's. They only used the place as a mailing address and to cash traveller's cheques, like a lot of other tourists. Well, maybe Francine was right and she was always stoned.

Cyndra nodded. "Good score. Save on rent."

Francine still said nothing, arms folded.

"Hey listen. They serve an all-day breakfast at the Hilton. Wanna come?"

Lydia could feel Francine staring sideways at her fixedly, trying to get her to look over and receive the signal, but she couldn't find it in her to say no. Cyndra's over-tanned face seemed extra-vulnerable today, her eagerness for their company just a notch below desperate, and she had gone out of her way to help them get a deal on the tickets to Istanbul. "Sure." So they paid for their vegetables and followed her to the Hilton, where soon they were sitting in front of plates of thick pancakes and dry bacon, watching as Cyndra drenched her plate in syrup. "Ah, comfort food." It was a muggy day, the opposite of good pancake weather. Francine picked at hers, but Lydia found that Cyndra was right; there was something soothing about the familiarity of the food. She ate more than she had expected, and drank two cups of

"American coffee." The meal recalled brunches with Tree or with Colin, when she was still seeing him. Lazy Sundays with the paper spread out on the table and constant refills from a sleepy-eyed waitress. She had been one of those waitresses herself, cursing the late night recklessness that made the Sunday brunch shift a gritty-eyed, dry-mouthed chore.

Francine snapped her fingers in front of her face and she jumped. "Sorry."

"Cyndra was telling us about Turkey." *And you're the one who agreed to join her,* Francine's glare said, *so you'd better goddamn listen.*

But they were both spared when Cyndra remembered she was supposed to help Steve with afternoon arrivals. She drained her coffee cup and stood up. "Thanks guys. That hit the spot." She left the table without putting money down, and walked off. Francine looked at her retreating back and poked Lydia in the shoulder. "See!" "Oh relax. It's just a few bucks. Think of it as our good deed for the day."

"Up yours, Jiminy Cricket."

But she split the bill with Lydia and followed her outside, where they could see Cyndra, just ahead of them; she had turned around to call something when they heard the toot of a scooter's horn. "It's Mouna and George!" Francine perked up. Mouna indeed, on a red scooter she must have borrowed from a friend, George behind her, leaning back on the seat, casually, one hand holding on, the other spread loosely on his thigh, something only men seemed able to do. They pulled up to the curb, risking the lives of a woman and a small white dog. The woman swore at them.

"Where are you going, kids?" Mouna asked.

"We just had a late breakfast with Cyndra."

"Who's Cyndra?" Lydia looked around to point her out but she had disappeared.

"Must be shy." Mouna nudged George and he hopped off the scooter and slipped his arm through Francine's. "I'll walk with you."

"Come, Lydia, take a ride with me." Mouna laughed when Lydia hesitated. "I won't bite. It's a promise." Lydia accepted the challenge and climbed on.

"Scared? Hold on to me," she said. Lydia ignored her and put her hands behind her like George, holding the metal bar at the back casually, but at the first turn she felt herself slide sideways and as the bike picked up speed and she bounced awkwardly on the seat she quickly clutched Mouna's waist. She heard laughter. Mouna's white shirt was untucked and billowing in the wind and her skin was cool under Lydia's hands, stippled with tiny goosebumps in involuntary response to the breeze. Lydia tried to hold on without gripping too hard, shivering with a mixture of fear and exhilaration as cars and scooters whizzed by.

Mouna said something but her words were shredded by the wind. "What?"

She turned her head and for a second they were almost cheek-to-cheek. "I have to stop at...." This time the rest was lost in the sound of traffic.

They turned onto a winding, uphill street with much fewer cars and Lydia relaxed her grip, but suddenly the bike swerved right and she had to hold tight to avoid slipping off. They pulled up to the curb with a lurch. When Lydia stepped off she could still feel the vibration of the engine in her thighs, and her legs were unsteady. Mouna reached over and patted down her windblown hair as if she were a dog—yet another of her mockingly intimate gestures.

"Watch the bike for me." She disappeared into the dark interior of what looked like an amateur garage. It was a small place, but Lydia could see a car and a couple of scooters in different stages of disassembly. Mouna walked towards the back, a cluster of people working and talking, the smell of oil, the sound of metal on metal, and an engine being started and then stopped. The sunlight outside was bright, and all Lydia could make out was a dark outline of bodies and vehicles. She heard a shout—Mouna calling her name. "Lydia! Bring the bike in!" She fumbled with the kickstand, then flipped it up and wheeled the bike awkwardly inside, halting for a moment as her eyes adjusted. "Nico will take it." Mouna nodded to the man in a grease-streaked T-shirt and jeans. Lydia recognized him from the other night; he'd been wearing the Rafa shirt. His hair was a lighter brown than most of the Greeks she'd met so far, and he had a spray of milky freckles across his nose and cheeks. He said something to Mouna in Lebanese, then added in English for Lydia's benefit:

"One half hour." He smiled at her. "Maybe your friend will like the coffee at Aspa's."

"Well, friend," Mouna's intonation was ironic, "we've got time to kill. Let's relax and get to know each other better."

Round the corner there was a café with a yellow painted sign— *Aspa's*—and four tables under a ripped awning. After they'd ordered their drinks Mouna flipped her sunglasses up on top of her head and lit a cigarette, holding the package out. Lydia hadn't smoked since a six-month stint in her teens, but for some reason she accepted one now and let Mouna light it for her. The tobacco was strong, and although she managed to refrain from coughing, she was soon light-headed, almost stoned from the unfamiliar rush of nicotine. The taste, while bitter, was not unpleasant, like the smell of gasoline in Nico's shop.

"So, how do you like the bike?"

"It's fun."

"Not too scared?"

"Nope."

"So brave!" Mouna was already lighting another cigarette. Dizzy from the nicotine, Lydia let hers burn out in the ashtray.

"So, Lydia, I've been meaning to ask you…" Mouna inhaled to make sure her cigarette was properly lit, pausing to suck in smoke.

"… have you ever tried windsurfing?"

"Why?"

"I have a friend who's promised to teach Farid and me before I go home. Shall we all go?"

"It doesn't seem like Farid's thing." Lydia couldn't imagine him on a windsurfer.

"You know so much about what he likes, already?"

Sleepy and irritable in the heat, Lydia didn't respond.

"And does he know what you like? It's important, between lovers, no? To share your tastes. Exchange your histories."

Shit.

"Does he know all about your father?"

"What about him?"

"Phil Devlin. That's your father, no? I've seen your mother's book."

"Armitage's book." Lydia spat the words out.

"But this Armitage, he must know your mother *very* well, no? For her to tell him all about you, how sad you were after your father died."

"It's none of your fucking business."

"It's the public domain, no?" Again Mouna jumped tracks: "How do you feel about Arabs, Lydia? Palestinians?"

"How do you feel about Jews?"

Mouna seemed pleased by some part of this conversation, though which part Lydia couldn't imagine, and she was too angry to try and work it out.

What was the game? Was Mouna trying to protect Farid? Did she think things were getting serious between them? And were they? Suddenly Lydia wished she and Francine were alone again, free, like they had been before. She would have liked to leave the café right now and if she'd been more attentive to Mouna's route she would have: fuck her, she'd find her own way home. But instead they both finished their drinks in silence and pretended to focus on the street instead of each other. After some deafeningly quiet minutes, Mouna checked her watch. "Should be ready."

The gunpowder smell of sparks from a welding tool as they walked into the garage. Nico smiled at them and gave them the thumbs up. Mouna paid him cash and slipped him something else, "a little extra," she winked at Lydia. Dope, probably. Then she wheeled the bike out into the street. Lydia was just trying to work out how to avoid riding back with her when Mouna said: "Your turn."

"You mean the bike?"

"I'll show you what to do. It's easy." She laughed. "Don't worry, you can trust me. I won't let you crash." What was she up to? Lydia was determined not to be intimidated. Mouna pointed out the ignition and the brakes, showing her how to increase and decrease speed, then climbed on behind and held her round the waist. "OK." Following her instructions, Lydia started the bike and kicked off. "Go!"

It was easier than she'd thought, but still needed enough concentration that she couldn't stay tethered to her anger. Some of the tension left her body as she sped along the streets, anticipating the turns, watching out for other drivers and pedestrians, hyper-conscious of Mouna's hands around her waist, her breasts against Lydia's back. It was quite different up front, with the wind directly in her face and her own body in charge of the motion of the bike. They passed a fountain and a gust of wind pushed the spray in their direction, spritzing their faces as they passed. "This way!" Mouna shouted, tapping her shoulder and pointing up ahead, and Lydia turned left as indicated. "Slow down." They were going downhill and the bike had picked up speed. Lydia obeyed Mouna's instructions and turned left again. She was looking ahead at a stopped car with its hazard lights blinking when a brown dog ran out into the street just in front of the bike. She swerved to avoid it and the dog yelped and skittered away. The bike's wheels skidded, its frame shuddering as she fought to keep control. For a second it felt as if they might crash, but Mouna helped use her body weight to straighten up and Lydia felt the bike right itself; once they were past the car, she pulled over and stopped. Up the street, the dog, unscathed, licked its paw beside a parked car. They both climbed off the bike. Lydia's hands were shaking again, with good reason this time, and for once Mouna refrained from mocking her. She even squeezed her shoulder—"You did OK." Five minutes later, after switching places, they were turning uphill again on another street, towards Palaio Zografou. Mouna left her at the curb and waved casually behind her as she drove off, Lydia watching her go. She thought about the look on Mouna's face—proprietary, almost maternal, a quality she would never have associated with her—when she said Farid's name. How much of their conversation would get back to him? Lydia had better beat her to the punch.

But it wasn't that easy. There were always people around, Mouna among them, with a cat-got-the-cream smile, as if she thought she had Lydia wrapped up. And then whenever Lydia and Farid were alone, she found herself hesitant to break the spell of intimacy. After she got back from Turkey, maybe. Would it really matter? They didn't see eye to eye politically, but that hadn't bothered him yet. If anything, of the two of them she was the one who worried more about their differences. Mouna seemed to suspect her of some perverse motive, when it was just her bad luck that Armitage and Elise had decided to collaborate, just the luck of the draw that her lover was a Lebanese man who preferred Palestine to Israel. Was it, though? Or was that the draw? Mouna had a way of making her question everything, of mistrusting herself. If she told Farid about Phil then she would deprive Mouna of the ability to make trouble between them. Unless Mouna knew something about Farid that Lydia didn't? And on and on she rode the anxious lover's wheel of unanswerable questions.

As it was, their trouble came from another direction. Lydia had been too drunk in the disco to remember exactly how the conversation about Turkey went; misjudged Farid's understanding of the whole thing. He was furious, as she found out right before she left.

"We agreed to go together."

"But, I thought…."

"Wait, and I'll come with you."

"We're going tomorrow!"

Now she could see how angry he was. "You don't want to go with me."

"That's not it. I just thought…."

"So you can be free to meet men."

"No."

"More holiday boyfriends."

"No, I…."

"You're like all the tourist girls. You want to go home with as many lovers as you can."

"Fuck *you*."

"How can you fuck me if you're in Turkey and I'm here?" She'd never seen him like this.

His face looked thinner than ever, and cruel.

"I'm not going to…."

"Oh you're not going to fuck me? Only Turkish men? Well thank you *mademoiselle*, and don't bring me your second-hand pussy when you come back."

When she slapped him, it shocked them both. She thought he was going to hit her back but perversely he seemed to calm, suddenly, and to look at her as if he saw her again, as herself, not some enemy slut.

She was angry still. "You fucking idiot, I don't want to sleep with anyone else."

He held her hands. "You love me."

"I… what?"

"So why are you going?"

"I thought Mouna… I thought you…"

"Why do you talk about Mouna?"

She was almost crying in frustration at his stupidity, at her inability to explain.

"I love you too."

"What?"

"I love you too, Lydia. What should we do about that?"

Now she was crying for a different reason and he kissed her cheek. "Don't cry. Go to Turkey and have some fun. But when you come back, I want you to stay. Promise."

Later, she said, "Are you still angry?"

"No. I was glad when you hit me."

She sat up in bed so she could see his face properly.

"That's when I knew you were serious." He kissed her again. And with all they had to say to each other then, dredging up long-ago family history seemed unimportant.

twenty-one

In the morning, Francine and Lydia took a cab to the airport while the others were still asleep. They were hustled through baggage check with a cursory once-over, making way for a film crew. A news team from Britain was shooting a special about airport security, now that Athens was at Number Three on a *New York Times* list ranking the world's ten most dangerous international airports. Rome was Number Four, courtesy of Abu Nidal. (Both, of course, trumped by Beirut International Airport—when it was open—at Number One.) Francine and Lydia listened as some of the passengers played a parlour game, their scores depending on the answer to: *How Many of the Top Ten Have You Been Through?* The winner by a wide margin was Roy, an Australian teacher travelling with his two young boys. He'd been to eight of the ten hot spots, six with his sons in tow.

Roy sat across the aisle from Lydia and soon started a drawling monologue about his travels: how cheaply he'd been able to make his way round the world, what a good education it was for his sons, Joshua and River (no mention of their mother), how adaptive they were. Both boys were tanned and white-blond, brush cuts bleached by sun. Their names made Lydia think of a rabbinical/animist jazz combo. Joshua, the older, shy and serious, would be the bass player; River, the charmer, the front man—sax or trumpet. A Disney child with long-lashed blue eyes, pointy chin, and triangular smile, he'd already charmed the two stewardesses, who kept bringing him sweets, but they didn't seem to know what to make of his brother, who had the haunted look of a person who frets all the details; Joshua's long thin face watched Lydia while his father talked, skin stretched over his cheeks as if he didn't ever get quite enough to eat, and she could see where he'd get worry lines when he was older. *I'm not after your dad*, she wanted to tell him, *it's OK*. When she smiled at him he blinked as if she'd caught him out. "When

Aussies travel," Roy said, "we make it a real trek, 'cos it costs so much to get anywhere." He made "trek" sound like "trick." His hair was darker blond than the boys', his skin dry and toasted, years of sun exposure leaving his arms speckled with silvery blotches. When he took his sandals off and crossed his thin ankles in front of him the soles of his feet were cracked and black-seamed with dirt. Francine grimaced and turned aside, pretending to sleep, nudging Lydia in the ribs every now and then at some comment of Roy's; Lydia would have been tempted to laugh if it weren't for Joshua watching her, his intelligent eyes sensitive to insult. The flight was so short that soon they were making their descent.

The travel agent had booked them into a cheap hotel, clean and safe as promised, close to the Bosphorus. That evening they stood on the roof looking across at the old city, a fairy-tale image to match the allure of the old name: Constantinople. Lydia looked at the glistening ribbon of water, the careening lights and tilting horizon, the buildings dream-like, trembling inside a pinpricked gauze of light. She felt indistinct herself, as if she might melt into her surroundings or disappear on the spot.

They went looking for dinner, following directions from Erhan, the young hotel manager, to a street crowded with tiny restaurants and outdoor cafés. The street was so narrow that the roofs on either side made an awning over the space in between, which felt intimate and boisterous, loud with men's voices, talking and laughing. Of the handful of women, all foreigners, they were the only ones not accompanied by a man, and they had the feeling of being closely observed. Three men followed them back to the hotel, calling after them, asking to meet them the following day. "No thanks," Francine said, "our husbands are waiting for us." They linked arms and strode on but the men dogged them right to the door. Erhan waved them off and invited Lydia and Francine to join him for mint tea. "Mouna's favourite," Lydia said. "Farid calls it Bedouin tea."

"Who is Mouna?"

"A friend in Athens," Francine said. Not exactly how Lydia would have described her, but never mind. Erhan brought them their glasses of tea, heavily sweetened and heady with soaked mint leaves.

"Thank you, Erhan." Lydia said. "I'm glad we came here." He smiled indulgently. "You like our beautiful city?" he asked, unsurprised when they both nodded. Lydia showed him the list of things they'd marked off to see. He circled Topkapi Palace and then drew a little map for them. He pointed to another street and wrote something on it. "Here, one of the oldest hamams in the city. You must try it." He explained the baths to them, and promised an experience they wouldn't forget. "Take a taxi there and back." He offered them a nightcap, but they were too tired. When they went up to bed he returned to his books—he was studying chemistry.

"Do you think you'll ever go to Beirut?" Francine asked when they were lying in bed with the lights out.

"Not while there's a war on. Why?"

"Just asking. George and I are almost out of gas. But you and Farid, it seems like it's more serious. Am I right?"

"I don't know."

"But you want it to be?"

"I…"

"… don't know?" Francine laughed. "You're not exactly an all or nothing kind of girl, are you?" She was quiet for a moment, mulling something over. "Listen, I've been waiting to tell you."

Lydia felt a small surge of anxiety, a dinghy rocked by a sudden ripple in the tide.

"I might have a job with Carnival." When they first met Francine had said she wanted to look for work on a cruise ship, but it had sounded like a casual fantasy and Lydia had forgotten about it.

"I didn't want to say anything until I knew if I had a chance, but they called me and said to come in for another interview when we get back."

Lydia felt embarrassingly like a sad-eyed kid about to be left with strangers by her family. "I hope you get it," she said loyally.

"Liar," Francine laughed at her. "But thanks. I'm pretty pumped."

She sat up in bed, hugging her knees. "I'd love to just hang out indefinitely, but... the show must go on. Now that I've made it all the way here I want to be like all those Aussies, see a nice big slice of the world before I go home."

It was hard to imagine Francine as she described herself at home. Straitlaced, quiet, going to her job at the bank, wearing pantyhose every day, saving money, planning her engagement party with Joe—until Joe got her pregnant, drove her out of province for an abortion "because we don't want anyone to know our business," and then dumped her. "I'm not ready to go back to normal life yet, that's for sure," she said now. "And you're going to stay with Farid, right? No, wait, don't tell me... you're not sure."

"Oh, mock me all you want. I'm just a natural second-guesser," Lydia said. "And I don't believe you were ever a bank teller, by the way. You're a twentieth-century adventuress."

"Adventuress. I like that. I'll miss hearing you say things like that. But let's not get ahead of ourselves. They may not want me after all."

"They'll want you," Lydia said, and they both knew she was right.

It took her a while to fall asleep after that; she was back in the worrying game. Wondering what Farid was doing now, back in Athens. Playing cards? Lying in bed playing with himself and thinking about her? Or had Mouna dribbled her poisonous words into his ear, reminded him that the world was his oyster, he should be looking around, Lydia was too young, too English, too Jewish, too hostile to Palestinians, too fucked up by what had happened to Phil. For all she knew, he could be in bed with someone else right now—a thought that made her break out into a jealous sweat.

In the morning the sky was overcast, washed in grey light. They walked to Topkapi Palace early, to be there before it got too crowded. There was a small playground in the adjacent gardens and they watched the children, monitored carefully by their guardians. The girls kept their skirts tucked tightly between their legs on the slide. One man stopped his daughter at the top and rearranged the material before she began her descent, her knees rocking with impatience. It might have been Lydia's imagination, but he seemed to frown at them for looking. Ramadan was about to begin, and there were soldiers home on leave, wandering around the palace and its gardens. Lydia and Francine weren't allowed inside most of the mosques, even with headscarves, but what they could see offered filigreed eye-ports into another world. Lock and key, notch and groove, the designs of the mosaics, the wrought-iron work through which they looked at inaccessible court-yards were emblems of foreignness; more than that, reminders of everything they didn't know about this world—exotic, and sealed to them, but ordinary to the initiated. This cross-hatched view, hinting at what it hid, counterbalanced the lurid details that had dogged them, first at the airport and later at their hotel.

When they had checked in, Erhan told them that his hotel was where the girlfriend of Billy, from *Midnight Express*—the real Billy, not the actor who played him—had stayed while trying to get her boyfriend out of prison. (Images of the bitten ear, dank walls, night-mare scraps of story that travellers swapped in hostels.) Later, they overheard the proprietor of the place two doors down make the iden-tical claim. It must be what the hoteliers thought they all wanted to hear, a bit of second-hand danger to titillate anxious and impression-able people far from home. Francine laughed at Erhan—*I swear to you, it's true*—and they both laughed when they heard the story being told a second time by the other man.

Three days following Erhan's map of Istanbul, drinking mint tea, looking at carpet shops, visiting museums. They went to the hamam he'd recommended. The stone building was one of the oldest in Istan-bul, run-down, pocked walls made even more beautiful by decrepi-tude, its stains and discolourations. Wild birds flew over the roof. Inside, a bare-breasted woman with a cloth around her waist padded up to them in rubber sandals and showed them where to take off their clothes. She looked at least 60 and she treated them with benign in-difference, as if they were a neighbour's kids she was babysitting while she tried to get her chores done. They were the only ones there. She led them into the first chamber, the steam room, then next door where water poured from spouts into wide stone basins. Scrubbed and scoured, dead skin rubbing off in waxy grey pellets, they were appalled at the evidence of the dirt that accumulated on their bodies daily, unawares. After hot water came cold, poured over each of them in an icy rush. Francine and Lydia gasped like fish, scaled and cleaned, on the marble tiles. While they were drying themselves, the attendant flicked one of Francine's breasts, casually, with a long, water-puckered finger. "You, madame." To Lydia: "You, mademoiselle."

Tingling and a little stunned, they emerged into the open air, where the taxi was waiting. The driver must have known the routine. "You look very clean," Erhan teased them, pretending to sniff. "Your boyfriends will be grateful." They laughed. It was still grey, and colder; the weather had turned. Lydia wondered if it was cold in Athens, too. The end of the summer heat. Erhan had the night off and they all went to dinner at a cheap, noisy place full of other tourists; they were a little loopy still from the physical release of the hamam; Erhan, too, was relaxed, pleased to be away from his job and studies for the night. They ended up laughing a lot. Afterwards, they went to the roof of the hotel, taking a bottle of wine with them and sweaters to protect against the evening chill. They watched the illuminated buildings and the water curved below in its shimmering sleeve. Lydia remembered a night on the balcony, just before they left, when Farid had said something that confused her until he explained it. "We used to watch the hotel battles from the roof. They were beautiful, like cinema." Then he told her about creeping up at night to watch the shelling in the hotel district, where armed gunmen had staked out the Holiday Inn and the St. Georges, looting and shredding carpets, burning sheets, stealing chandeliers or just smashing them. At night the sky was a *son et lumière* that people went to their rooftops to observe; once he and Mouna had snuck after his parents, and his mother, Mariam, caught them and while hustling them towards the stairs conceded that yes, after all, though dangerous, it was beautiful. "Even though we know what it is we're seeing," she had said. "Destruction, murder—make no mistake about that—the ruin of our past and future." Just when she said that, there had been a particularly gorgeous eruption and Farid and Mouna had made the same "Aah!" as thousands of fireworks enthusiasts on patriotic holidays in more peaceful countries. Farid tried to describe the look on Mariam's face then. "Not afraid, but angry—not at us, you understand."

"What is she like, your mother?"

"Like that. Strong character. But very charming. And of course I'm her baby still." He pouted and made a silly face at her.

"And you, Lydia? You don't talk about your mother."

"We don't get along so well."

"Ah, like Mouna and Deena. It's more difficult between girls and their mothers, I think."

"You've got that right." She yawned.

"Are you tired?"

"A little. Maybe I'll go to bed." He had stood up with her and hugged her, holding her close against him and pressing his cheek to her hair. She'd been very tired, caught between wanting to lean in and to pull away, and then he'd kissed the tip of her ear and the decision was made for her.

All at once she wanted him so intensely she sighed. "You OK?" Francine asked, and Lydia was startled back to the rooftop. "Just sleepy. I'm going in." The others had moved their chairs together. "OK. I'll stay out for a bit." Asleep, she only half heard Francine come in, much later. At breakfast, Francine and Erhan exchanged private smiles as he pitched the Billy story to a new set of tourists.

On the flight home, a patch of heavy turbulence set the plane shuddering and rocking. Seeing her tense in her seat Francine patted Lydia's hand. "Athens is only Number Three, remember? Don't worry. You'll see your honey soon."

twenty-two

Is there anything duller than someone in love? Not in Mouna's opinion. Surprised by Lydia's sudden decision to make the trip to Istanbul with Francine, she was almost—but not quite—sympathetic to the fact that it had caused trouble between the lovebirds. But mainly she was glad that the two women were away for a while. She wouldn't have to spend the rest of her time in Athens watching Farid fawn over Lydia. He swore he'd never been in love before, not since he was ten years old with a puppy crush on Grace. And who wouldn't have a crush on Grace, with her gorgeous breasts and the streak of grey swooping through her hair—Mouna remembered her coming over to the apartment one day laughing because a woman at the salon had said: "*Dites moi,* what colour do you call that?" "Natural grey," Grace told her. The woman had nodded wisely and turned to the stylist and asked: "Can I get 'natural grey'?" Grace's warm, confident laugh. But Grace was one thing, Lydia quite another.

It turned out that Farid without Lydia was possibly more annoying than the two together. Wrapped up in his horny fantasies, he found ways to bring her into the conversation, Mouna could swear, just so he could say her name. He was like a teenager, or a stupid virgin in a romance novel. It might not be so irritating if Mouna liked or respected the object of his idiocy. On the other hand, it just might. Mouna hadn't realized that she'd been nursing a fantasy of her own about this trip: she and Farid and George would recreate a little of their childhood— not the fights and tantrums and tricks they played on each other, but the good stuff, games and jokes and sitting side by side on the sofa, watching TV. Not having to talk. She missed that. But there's never any point in trying to recapture the past—it doesn't exist, for one thing. Never did. The past is the present, as it was then. The future just the present arrived. Say you're walking up the street and you anticipate stepping inside your house, putting the kettle on, making tea, the taste of that tea, hot and sweet and comforting, but as soon as you take the first swallow, of course you forget the steps leading up to it. You're inside that moment; it's inside you. The minutes before were present, and now they're gone. The quality of the moment isn't what counts, either. Perhaps the house isn't cosy—the windows are taped up against bomb blasts, there's no fuel for the stove, no water to boil, the tea will have to wait. Or perhaps you're in a strange apartment, and instead of comforting you, the tea is hardly noticed because your cousin is going on about his damn girlfriend, a doe-eyed innocent whose outrage at "political violence" makes you want to shake her senseless. When all you wanted was a dose of home, that impossible past—a taste of something that home itself can't provide any more.

The irony was that Mouna knew Farid wanted nothing more than for her to share his happiness. He had love to burn, enough for both of them, enough for everyone in the goddamn city. He was like a puppy on speed, panting with eager joy, and while she didn't have the heart to wreck his ride, not yet, she was only human. One of these days she would have to pull out that book from her suitcase and show him. *Look, see who she is? How can you possibly love each other?* It had better be soon, before his living, breathing doll came back and suffocated all resistance with her sweet kiss.

twenty-three

"A Dish Served Cold" by Edward Armitage
from his book *In Love with Danger*

Revenge. Sooner or later—usually sooner—in this part of the world, you'll hear it talked about—and by more than one source. Who is going to seek retribution (or already has)? Was this murder of an Israeli settler Hamas or Fatah? That killing of a Maronite politician in Beirut arranged by Syria or by local political rivals? (Perhaps both.) Who bears more responsibility for Sabra and Shatila, the Phalangists who committed the murders or the Israeli army who stood by? What is self-defence? What's murder? Who's right? Who's wrong? To anyone not raised in this volatile climate, it can be overwhelming, the sense of centuries-old blood feuds gone wild.

Phil Devlin would call such bewilderment wishful thinking. *If the conflict is that old, that complicated, that intractable,* he said, *it can never be solved and we can wash our hands of it. Like Northern Ireland, only worse.* Such a scenario, he maintained, suits many of the participants, even more of the bystanders, but the people of Beirut, the Palestinians, the citizens of Israel all deserve better. We, his colleagues, heard this speech more than once over drinks, in some dusty bar or clapped-out hotel lounge. It's become a popular position now: other commentators make similar statements all the time. Back then it was less common to talk that way.

When Devlin became passionately attached to a woman who did believe in revenge, what happened to that speech of his? Did he change his beliefs, or conceal them? Or did he reassert them in the company of his lover and her friends? If so, was his death a rebuttal, meant to show that the instinct for revenge can't be whitewashed? Punishment, or—and this theory has been touted by some observers—was he, at least partially, a willing sacrifice?

This man Armitage couldn't seem to make up his mind, Mouna thought. Now he was trying to sell Phil Devlin as a hero. *How is it that the foreigners who die in Lebanon are all heroes, the rest of us just victims, collateral damage?* One journalist dies trying to hunt a story—or "become it," to steal Armitage's pompous rhetoric, and he's a flag-bearer for justice. What if he was just in the wrong place at the wrong time? And so his "driver," his "interpreter," *the one you don't give a shit about,* the man "raised in this volatile climate," gets wiped out because of an ignorant fool's mistake. *How does that sound, Monsieur Armitage? Or wouldn't that sell books? And who should get revenge for that kind of mistake?*

twenty-four

"*Umma*! Concentrate!" Nasima was trying to teach her mother poker. Deena laughed at her bossiness.

"*Habibti*, it's not my fault. The medicines have made my memory even worse."

Nasima sighed. "OK. But try. Two of a kind is better than nothing. But if you have a full house...."

"What's a full house again?" Nasima's head snapped up. "*Nikteh*! Joking, I'm joking! I wanted to see the look on your face." It was amazing, Mariam thought, listening from the kitchen. Deena was more lively than she'd been in years. With West Beirut in the middle of a surge of violence so extreme, even by its own standards, that they were almost entirely confined to the apartment (and at the worst moments to the garage below), she seemed to have been revitalized. Mariam didn't want to break up the false honeymoon, not yet. But soon someone was going to have to raise the subject of leaving. Who and how and where to. Things were starting to get desperate and she was worried about Nasima's emotional health under all this terrible stress.

She wondered about Mouna in Geneva, Europe's most tranquil capital. What could it possibly be like, in that most peaceful of cities, trying to explain all this? Mariam looked around for the beans. She had some, where did they go? She felt a surge of disproportionate rage that she was reduced to this: dried beans a precious commodity. She needed them for the soup, there wasn't much else in the apartment and it was too dangerous to go out. Here. Here they were. At least something was where it should be in this woefully depleted kitchen, the same kitchen that had been the hub of so many wonderful dinner parties.

Mouna as an eight-year-old, disrupting one of those parties. Carol Plakidas stomping out, Tom ineffectual in his efforts to calm her. Tom.

The thought of him made Mariam's stomach turn over. Her one affair, when she had thought it too late, when she was looking the other way. He taught American history and had come into her office one afternoon to talk about a student. While they were talking, he had picked up a photograph, a relic of vanity—ten years younger in the photo, she liked to think she looked a bit like Sophia Loren might if Loren were actually human. "You're much more beautiful now," Tom said, and she'd known then that he must want to sleep with her. It had shocked her awake, made her hot where she'd been cold, wet where she'd been dry, aware of herself as she hadn't been since the first few years with Nadim. She still loved Nadim, but—it happens. It's the most banal story of all. You get swallowed by life, distracted, lost to yourself—the truth is, she thought, it's yourself you fall out of love with, not your husband, and when someone offers you a new way of seeing yourself, something more like the old way....

She mocked herself now for having been so transparently susceptible. So easily flattered. She'd been oblivious to any man's attention for some time, almost afraid of being touched by Nadim, whom she did still love, still found attractive in the abstract, at least, just not up close. She used to sniff his armpits when they had sex, used to lick them like a salt-deprived animal—the deep, skunkish smell of his testosterone aroused her. But some time in the last year or two she had stopped being able to smell him. Was it a physical change in him? Hormonal fluctuation? His or hers? (*They say it happens to men, too.*) Or a symptom of marital trouble that wasn't mentioned in any of the manuals? It was as if he'd become bodiless to her. If it weren't for the heavy sound he made coming up the stairs when the elevator was out of service, which was almost always, she might not know he was there. She knew what he would have told her, in his scrupulously honest way, if she could have admitted it to him. *It has more to say about you than me.*

"Do you have any time tomorrow to go over Bashir's transcripts?" Tom seemed unnerved by her stillness.

"Tomorrow would be fine. Late in the day, though."

"*Eeazeem. Merci.* Do you want to meet here?" Inside, underneath the banality of conversations like these there must always be an inaudible dialogue that makes nerves buzz, the body's hidden parts pulse with awareness. Between her legs she felt warm, as if a lustful little animal was nosing there, opening her.

"If you like."

"Or… how about my house, if it's safe enough to get there? We can relax, have a drink."

"That sounds fine."

"Shall we meet in the parking lot at six?"

"At six. Yes. I think I know your car."

She had turned to her papers, a signal that he should go. Where had her usual charm gone? Even listening to his footsteps down the hall she had been stiff, self-conscious, as if he (or someone else, someone cold-eyed and unforgiving), were still watching.

She had never used to be this easy. Was it just because he was a foreigner, no matter how longstanding his family's involvement—two generations—with Beirut? (Why did people always use that word, "involvement," as if Beirut were a difficult woman, an unwed mother who had to be supported but kept at arm's length, a problem more than a source of life?) Or because she knew he was chronically unfaithful to Carol, who had left him and Beirut early on in the war to teach history at a small campus in Iowa? No, just more mid-life crisis, she scoffed at herself. The animal was still there, still sniffing intrusively. *If there's water tonight I'll shave my legs.*

When she went down to the parking lot the next day, he was leaning against his car, waiting. He opened the passenger side for her, and she could see the dark hairs, the vein on his forearm through the open window as he pushed the door shut. Tom still lived in the family house near the Swiss consulate. His parents now alternated between the United States and their home in Greece.

When they arrived at the house, he checked the security system and unlocked the door. It was warm inside and he threw open the window and the French doors at the back. He took Mariam's jacket and hung it up for her.

"Drink?"

"Scotch, please, with ice."

He began immediately to talk about Bashir, the student who was the subject of their meeting. She'd always liked him for this kind of diligence, for his sincerity. Bashir was an emotionally delicate and talented boy who had convinced himself that to leave Beirut voluntarily would be a kind of disloyalty. Tom wanted her to help him obtain a scholarship to study in the States, where he had some relatives.

"I think it would offer him an acceptable way to get out of the country and preserve his emotional health." Keep him safe. Boys especially, even apolitical ones like her son, were vulnerable to getting caught up in the conflict, and she and Nadim had determined early on to get their son away as soon as they could, though the two of them were committed to staying at AUB. The students deserved the loyalty of the faculty, the hospital its doctors. But when do the benefits of living somewhere saner, somewhere safer, outweigh principles?

She and Tom talked Bashir's situation over for some time, and as they talked the tension between them relaxed a little. "What do his parents say?" She sipped her Scotch, felt the alcohol travel, lighten her head.

"They want him to go. They're worried about him. They tried to send him at least for a holiday to some relatives in Jordan. He refused. But if he got a scholarship and felt that it was his duty to the university, to his family—I think he'd go. He loves school. His marks are good, but there are so many foreign students in the States, the odds of getting one of those scholarships... it's like playing the lottery. We need to find at least some of the money from one of the funds here."

"I think there's still some available. I'll set up a meeting with the scholarship committee."

"Great. Thank you. I knew you'd.... Thanks. Would you like something to eat?"

"*La, la*, I'm not hungry, thank you. Another drink would be nice." She was too nervous to eat, a sign she recognized from her earliest dates with Nadim. So long since that time, when she trembled at his slightest, most glancing touch.

"Of course, sure." Tom took her glass, a heavy tumbler, poured an inch of Scotch into it, with some ice. She noticed that his hand was trembling; he was nervous. He gave her the glass, leaning slightly forward, and she put it on the side table, keeping one hand lightly on his wrist. He was caught, slightly off-balance, looking down at her. His breathing was rough and he made a noise—a sigh or an exclamation—as she held his wrist and pushed until he was half-crouched in front of her. "I'll give you what you want," she said. She leaned forward and touched him. He flushed, with desire or perhaps embarrassment. She had a moment of uncertainty—what if she was mistaken, what if she were about to humiliate herself—then none.

"I…. Let me…."

"Ssh. Ssh. Fuck me. Isn't that what you want? To fuck me?" He flushed more deeply, aroused by her sudden, unexpected use of an obscenity in his own language, and almost tore her blouse in his haste to free her breasts. *More flesh than he's used to,* she was sure. His wife had small, high breasts, and the women she'd seen him with were all young, girlish, unaltered by childbirth. *He's probably seen no more than a handful of stretchmarks in his life.* But he seemed inflamed by the sight of her: dark, enlarged nipples, flesh low on the ribcage, lower than when she was younger, but still lush—ah, she wouldn't have thought that the week, or even the day before.

She hadn't told anyone, not even Grace. Talking about it would have made it real; making it real might have necessitated action, or at least reflection of some kind. Continue, or stop. Tell Nadim, or don't. Admit your weakness, or lose yourself, let yourself go, defer thought. She and Nadim had always had a good sex life, but this was different, some other kind of release. She felt it now in her flesh, remembering. She and Tom hadn't wanted anything from each other but this—no comfort, no war talk, no emotional intimacies, barely any conversation. Since that first time they hadn't discussed work when they were together. And what they did together was basic, wordless, not pretty in its urgency. *I've become a cliché.* She had been so scathing about men—including some of her friends—who hit middle age, panicked and cast about for a willing 20-year-old to help take the edge off. Now she understood. Tom was no 20-year-old innocent, he wasn't that much younger than her, but she'd used him just the same. Told herself the same lies everyone did: *well, it can't last, nothing's clearer than that. So is it really necessary to tell anyone, with all the hurt that would ensue?*

In the end, of course, it had had to stop. It had threatened the tiny portion of order and sanity that still existed in her life. Tom was too obvious, too naked in his responses to her. She could feel it starting to turn dangerous, and she couldn't risk that. She was lucky that Nadim never found out. She didn't want to lose him as well as everything else: their whole way of life, their future, such as it was. Couldn't add that loss to all the others. So many people, dead or gone.

Dinner, long before the affair. Tom and Carol (tense with each other). Carol telling him she wanted to go home and get pregnant, Grace told Mariam later, not play faculty wife in Lebanon. Grace was there, of course, she'd been at almost every significant event in Mariam's life since their friendship began; Leila and her husband Tariq, now in Paris; Grace's boyfriend at the time, Emile—years since Mariam had seen him. And Basman had shown up late with his journalist friend, the English man. A mixed crowd. The kids were up, excited by a party, stealing sweets from the kitchen. They'd "helped" Faiza and Mariam with the preparations, tasting everything and making a mess. Farid spilled some honey on Mariam's favourite blouse and she'd had to change. Suddenly Mariam wanted to see her son so badly it was a wire dragging through her chest, sharp and jagged. He'd said he was taking a year off from school two years ago, wicked boy, wasting his time with George, drinking and smoking too much. He was safer than anyone else in his family, but it never stopped, this worry, no matter how old the kids or where they were. Mouna and Nasima too, they were hers almost as much as Deena's, she who had hardly even wanted one, selfish cow that she was. It had taken hard work—sometimes it felt too hard—to reconcile herself to mother-love, so visceral, so uncontrolled, so free from what characterizes love between adults. Grace said—and Mariam's love for Grace was almost boundless—you love adults for their qualities. Your children you love in a different way, you can't help it; it's animal and painful. The clichés about being willing to die for them—those are true. Not because you become more noble, or because you think you should, but because you protect them by instinct, without being able to choose. Grace, childless, loving Mariam's children, Mariam loving Deena's, Deena, barely keeping her head up, they all knew this.

How had it started, that night? A conversation about Rafa Ahmed. Leila, wasn't it? Of all things, she had started talking about Rafa's jumpsuits, how good she looked in them. "The bitch, she dresses like a man, like a soldier, and still she manages to make the rest of us look like frumps!" She pouted, secure in the knowledge that she was anything but frumpy in her tight orange wraparound dress, her cleavage all creamy and plump (like a baby's behind strapped to her chest, Grace had whispered into Mariam's ear). Grace and Emile had brought pastries from the new French place in Hamra—a white box with a lilac ribbon—and Tom his guitar, of all things. "What is it with Americans and their guitars," she heard the journalist ask in his flat English accent. "Well, hey, we did invent rock and roll," Tom said. "My friend, that's where you're wrong. Your blacks invented the blues; rock and roll was the rubbish that fell out of their pockets and you white boys picked it up and thought it was gold. Anyway, England's got the best rock and roll musicians." That started some good-natured cultural chest-pounding that ended only when Nadim put on some of his own music to divert them. So the mood was already spiky—maybe it really started then, with the journalist.

The food was good—Mariam prided herself on that, everyone knew they would eat well at one of her parties—and there was a temporary lull while the first wave of hunger was satisfied. No main course, but plates and plates of mezze: kibbeh, hummus, all kinds of salads, stuffed peppers, okra, lentils with lemon and herbs, cheese, all manner of sweets for when the urge hit; Nadim had a terrible sweet tooth. And there would have been devilled eggs, no doubt, because he loved those too, though Mariam couldn't stand them—even the smell of them. Their swirled, creamy centres with the little waves of pepper-dusted yolk that always seem to her to have a slightly sulfurous odour, perhaps even more since the day of Nasima's experiment. *I must have loved him to make those.*

Everyone had eaten and drunk a fair bit by the time Leila mentioned Rafa's jumpsuit. Even Carol was drinking, unusual for her. She was flushed, over-animated, staying distant from Tom, further still when the music debate began. They must have had a fight on the way over, Mariam had thought then, and later that evening she found out from Grace that she was right.

Somehow Leila's fashion tips started a debate on America's Middle East policy, and the ethics of violent dissent. Leila lost interest almost at once—that kind of discussion bored her to tears. Mariam couldn't blame her. She'd heard one too many similar conversations between foreign academics—they seemed to feel that coming to Beirut made them more knowledgeable, more justified in their positions, whatever those were. But they were only too happy to leave when trouble hit.

Carol argued with the journalist. "There is no justification you could give me."

"None offered," he said, smiling at her. It wasn't an unkind smile, but it irked her, Mariam could see. Tom had his arm on the back of the couch and he tilted forward like he was about to play the voice of reason between participants in a bar fight. Farid was engrossed in backgammon with Emile and Grace, Nadim... maybe talking to Leila? And Mouna right in the middle of the debate, sitting on the floor, listening, in that way she had.

Both Carol and her opponent spoke French and half-decent Lebanese, even in the heat of their discussion, which is how Mouna was able to play her part.

"It's none of your business," she said, loudly. They both stopped, arrested by the sound of a child's voice.

"What isn't?" The man said, amused.

"Rafa Ahmed, *nize*'"—Mouna choked a little, swallowing saliva, nervous—"the… the struggle, it's our problem. You should worry about your own problems and leave us alone." She was looking at Carol when she said the next thing. "*Rja' 'al bayt.* Go home if you don't like it here." There was silence. Mouna was trembling, having shocked even herself. Farid stopped playing backgammon and gaped at her.

"You should learn some goddamn manners, little girl," Carol said, in English.

"Carol, for god's sake, she's just a…." Tom tried to put his arm on hers but she threw it off so violently it bounced against the couch. "Leave me alone."

Grace looked at Mariam and stood up. "*Desolée*, everyone, I'm a bit tired," she yawned. "Carol, walk me home? We could both use some rest, I think."

But first Grace knelt down beside Mouna and gave her a hug, whispered something in her ear. For a minute, Mouna stood as stiff as a cardboard mannequin and then she put her head down low and said to Carol, "I'm sorry." Carol was too angry to be gracious, but she nodded, an acknowledgment of the apology, if nothing more. "*Merci,* Mouna," Grace said, nudging her over to the journalist. "No need," he said. "I never apologize for my beliefs, and nor should you." For a minute, Mariam had thought it was all going to start again, but Grace steered Carol away—"I'll be back," she mouthed to Mariam. Nadim took the kids to bed. Mariam went in later to talk to Mouna, but she was asleep, or pretending to be. After Grace came back, they stayed up late, drinking more wine, playing cards. Tom stayed too. The journalist was a great player, and very funny. He and Nadim developed a drunken rapport; as for Tom, not a word was said by him or anyone else about going home to his wife.

In spite of herself, she was drifting back to that first time with Tom, the swamping desire, the thrill of it, when a shriek from the sitting room surprised her.

"See, *Umma*! You won!" Nasima and Deena were both laughing.

"So I did." Deena sounded as gleeful as a little girl.

twenty-five

Plucking her eyebrows on one of those mornings. The kind when all you can remember is the worst you've done: a feast of remorse on your own petty lies and small betrayals. Major ones too. The kinds of thoughts that used to come to Mariam in the middle of the night, or when she travelled alone, but now that the night was cacophonous, as unlikely as midday to yield quiet or privacy, her shameful sins swooped and attacked guerrilla-style, when and wherever they could.

Classes were cancelled, again, and she had taken the opportunity for some furtive grooming. Bent over her pocket mirror she accepted the sting of each depilation as penance; took satisfaction in the small, irritated patches that blossomed along her brow-line, minor self-fla-gellations. This one for her unkindness to Leila on that holiday ten years ago; that one for what she'd said to Nadim about his mother; this for Tom, that for Tom too, and that; this for her impatience with Deena this morning. Deena, so slow, so tentative. Sometimes, like today, her ponderousness and self-deprecation ground Mariam's patience too fine and she almost snapped. Other days it moved her. A woman shouldn't be that humble in front of her own children. Should not have to surrender their care and her authority to their aunt. Deena's swath of greying hair (badly in need of a cut), falling over her eyes, hiding any reflection of her private resentments. The heavy, slow fingers, trying to help in the kitchen, or folding clothes. No good for sewing, not any more. "I'll do it," Faiza said, when Deena tried to clear the table. "You drink your tea." Deena sucked her teeth, her only show of frustration.

There was a tap on the door and Grace came in without waiting for an answer. Mariam looked up, conscious of the pink tattoo across her forehead. She couldn't quite see Grace for the sunlight behind her, and she shaded her eyes, sun-blindness a mild disorientation that delayed her awareness of how unusual it was for Grace to leave the hospital during the day. Then it hit her.

"Nadim?" She stood up.

"He's busy in the O.R. I said I'd come."

Not him then, dear god. In a few seconds Mariam would know, but not yet. For a few seconds longer she could wait, as if she had all the time in the world, her brows stinging and her hands unnaturally still. She and Grace, standing awkwardly like strangers introduced and then abandoned by their host at a cocktail party.

"Deena. Nasima…." Grace covered her mouth to stop the words from falling.

They had been walking to the market. Deena had insisted, now that it was safe enough to go out. She was going to make dinner. They knew this because Faiza had been there when she announced it. *About time*, Faiza had thought, though not unkindly.

"I'm coming with you," Nasima had said. With an unconscious look of solicitousness that made Deena both ashamed and angry, though she hid this from her daughter. She couldn't bear it any more, this half-life, this feeling of not being a mother, or even a person. She would make a meal for her family tonight, no matter what anyone said.

It was so strange to be outside, her nerves sharp, not coated in the fuzzy sweater of drugs now so familiar that she felt naked without it. This strange clarity, the enhanced sense of perception. Colours looked sharper—the soft green of Nasima's shirt, her red tank-top underneath bright as blood, the green of the shirt almost the same shade as the seats in Farid's car, in the photo that he had proudly sent them. Her senses heightened, walking along Deena could isolate smells that would usually run together in her olfactory subconscious: cooking oil, incense, gasoline, brick dust. And something slightly bitter in the air that she couldn't identify. A spice? A chemical? There was a buzzing at the edge of her nerves, almost like being drunk—though Deena had only been drunk once in her life—just before you tip from that exaggerated sense of awareness into the mixed-up blur that follows. Even the edges of the clouds looked sharp, as if someone had outlined them with a pen.

"*Umma*? You OK?" Nasima looked worried. Deena smiled at her reassuringly, though now in fact she was starting to feel panic at the openness of the wrecked streets, at being unsafe and outside. All the people rushing past, the head and armbands, green and red, like Nasima's clothes only never the two at once. People kept their heads down, hurrying to do what was necessary and get off the street, get inside again, which was what Deena wanted to do, now, at once. But she was going to cook dinner. She had promised her daughter and, perhaps more important, herself. She turned and noticed for the umpteenth time that her younger daughter had almost the same profile as her dead uncle. Same jaw-line, same nose, same almost pout, caused by a slight overbite. Bittersweet.

Someone was waving at them from across the street. A woman. The street seemed huge. "Do you know that woman?" "Who?" Nasima turned to point. A pigeon cut through the air, someone called from an upstairs window " ... '*Ajjil*! Hurry. Don't forget..." and then a second or two of pain, a terrible heat, and what was not to be forgotten, her daughter's face—everything—was lost to Deena forever.

Run, Mariam's brain said, but her feet stayed put. She noticed with some interest how calm she was. How little she needed the hand Grace put out to steady her. "*Ma fi shi, ma fi shi,* it's OK," she said. She could hear herself say it. But just to humour Grace, she let her hold on. Just for a second. *No more.* Then she had to move.

On the way to the hospital Grace gave her what details she knew about Deena's death. Snipers, no one knew who or why. Probably random. Nasima, shielded by her mother's body and by a car door that suddenly opened, was... Grace looked for the word... *not lucky* Mariam thought. *Please don't say lucky.* "Alive," is what Grace said. A bullet in her arm and a broken rib, possibly a concussion when she fell, they were still trying to determine, but not the terrible mangling, the raw insults to flesh that were so often the gift to those who had "luck" enough to survive car bombs or shelling.

"Does Nasima…" she wanted to say "know," but instead Mariam observed herself double over mid-sentence, fists on her knees, retching in the hospital parking lot. Grace rubbed her back and tried to pull her along at the same time. "Come inside, it's not safe." Shells had been known to hit the parking lot. "She's in surgery, at the moment. Nadim is with her."

"And Deena's body?"

"Downstairs." That meant the morgue.

"I have to reach Mouna."

"I don't know if the phones are working."

"I'll use the one in the president's office if I have to."

Then everything moved very fast. The phone calls, the burial arrangements, the strings pulled, the flights fixed, connections made, connections missed, messages left, letters delivered. Doors locked.

twenty-six

"We're coming with you." There had been no question about it.

Farid sat next to Mouna on the couch while George began to make calls. She sat passively while he held one of her hands and rubbed it between his until George was off the phone. One of his contacts had been able to get them a flight the next day. Weirdly, the airport had opened again since Mouna left—*rah yiftah al matar* not just a rumour any more—and they could fly direct, surely the only people in the world who wanted to go to rather than away from Beirut. Farid had written a letter explaining to Lydia what had happened, asking her to take care of the apartment until he got back in three weeks. George added a note to Francine. Farid enclosed a cheque, made out to Cash, just to make it easy, in case there were any apartment-related expenses, but the rent was paid for several months. In the taxi the next day he felt the envelope in his pocket. Shit! There was no time to go back. It was George who had the idea: "We can leave it for them at Steve's!" The girls picked up mail and cashed their traveller's cheques there regularly; sooner or later they would get it.

Farid wasn't completely happy with the arrangement, but making it to the airport on time, catching their flight, was more important. Lydia would understand. George ran in while the taxi waited. The desk clerk knew Lydia and Francine, she said, and would make sure they got the letter. George gave her the phone number at the apartment, too. "Please call in a week if they don't come before then." She assured him she would. Then the three of them were on their way. Ramzi, from Mouna's work, met them at the airport. Less than an hour later they were at the apartment in *Ras Beirut*.

twenty-seven

"Hello? Anyone home?" Lydia unlocked the door and shouldered it open. The apartment was quiet and still, as if the air inside hadn't moved for a while. Francine came in behind her and they stood there, looking. Lydia had half-expected Farid and George to meet them at the airport, but was unperturbed when they didn't. In the taxi, as they got closer to the apartment she could feel her pulse speeding up, a lightness in her forehead. She was almost home—yes, she thought of it that way now. Not because of the place so much, this nondescript apartment, but because of Farid. They dropped their bags and went into the kitchen, where Francine put the kettle on. She opened the fridge, almost empty, sniffed a carton of milk and made a face. "Gross."

Where was everyone? There was no mess—no chaotic pile of clothes or uneaten food to indicate that they had left in a hurry. No note, either, no *gone to the islands, back soon* or *emergency, had to fly home, will call.* Nothing.

"Weird." Francine's voice sounded loud. "Do you think they're away for the weekend?"

Lydia felt dopey, thick-tongued, and full of an obscure, inexplicable dread.

Francine was staring at her. "Earth to Lydia."

"I don't know. Farid didn't say anything." She still hadn't told Francine about the admissions they'd made to each other, about *love, never leave you,* etc.

Francine plopped down on the couch. "There must be a note somewhere." She looked around the room, taking in the details, suddenly alert. "How long do you think they've been gone?"

It was stuffy in the apartment. The fact that there was no mail didn't tell them anything; like so many other temporary residents of the city, Farid and George used a box at the post office. The plants were dry, but not dead, so they couldn't have been gone that long, but more than an afternoon. More than a day.

They searched the kitchen, the living room, under the coffee table. Each of them checked the bedrooms, twice, even the bathroom, but there was no note anywhere.

Standing in the living room with her hands on her hips, Francine's face went pink. "Well fuck a duck. George. Where the hell are they?" For a minute she looked as if she might cry, but she stomped over to the balcony instead and unlocked the door and slid it open to let some air in. The breeze had a cold edge to it, and she shivered. "I'm going to take a shower. Do you want to water the plants?"

Although it was a small relief to do something practical, it didn't diminish Lydia's anxiety. She knew that she was a disaster scenarist by nature, but still, this didn't make sense. Where could they be? Had Farid left no note on purpose, to punish her for Turkey? That wasn't like him, but his outburst before she left, his anger, wasn't like him either. Or was it? Had he changed his mind about her? Did Mouna get to him after all? Did she turn him against Lydia, persuade him that the whole Phil and Rafa show was a sinister motivation for Lydia's attraction to him, instead of the old history that—increasingly—it was? Francine would say that was irrational. And so it was, as well as being an interpretation that allowed Mouna more power than Lydia was willing to cede her. *Fuck. I don't know.* She found the old yellow watering can on the balcony and filled it at the sink. The plants were thirsty and she had to refill it twice. She pinched the fat leaf of a jade plant as if it might give up some useful information; suddenly start talking. Outside was grey, and a gritty wind blew. Yes, the weather had changed here in Athens, too.

Francine came out of the shower and stood in front of her, dripping on the floor in her towel. "Do you think they left a note at Steve's?"

"Why would they?"

"They know we get mail there, maybe they weren't sure if we had our keys, or... I don't know, Lydia, it's a long shot, but I have to go there anyway to check on messages from Carnival. I have that fucking interview tomorrow." She got dressed faster than Lydia had ever seen her, and a couple of minutes later she was at the door, hair still wet. She looked over her shoulder as she opened the door. "Are you coming?"

At Steve's, Gary handed them a small pile of mail: a letter from Matthew, something from Francine's dad and the confirmation from Carnival; nothing from Farid or George.

"Oh crap…." Francine dashed out the back door beside the bar. Lydia understood when she heard a familiar voice.

"Hey, how was Istanbul?" Cyndra, with her perverse knack for showing up when she was least wanted. "Hi, Cyndra, sorry, just on my way…." Lydia tried to imitate Francine but Cyndra grabbed her arm. "Hey!" Her strong fingers dug in, and for a second her face was openly hostile, her jaw thrust forward and her eyes hard; just as quickly her arm retracted and she wore her customary shaggy dog look, the one that suggested she was slightly out of it, you could say anything, she wouldn't really hear you or care if she did. "Everything OK?"

Lydia's forearm felt bruised. She was tempted to tell Cyndra to fuck off, but she might know something useful. "Did anyone ask for us while we were away?"

Cyndra actually looked thoughtful and Lydia felt a spasm of optimism. "Two men, maybe with a woman?" She considered the questions so slowly that Lydia wanted to grab her and shake the answer out of her, in the process perhaps leave a few bruises herself.

"… Nope, sorry, can't say I saw anyone. If they show up what should I tell them?"

"Never mind." It was a non-starter anyway, she should have known.

"See you."

Francine was pacing up and down the street behind Steve's. "Find out anything?"

"Nothing."

"Shit." She pulled an unopened pack of Marlboros out of her bag.

"I didn't know you smoked."

"It's been a while. I just bought these from Gary." Francine lit one and offered the pack to Lydia. "No thanks."

"I'm getting a head rush." Francine puffed hungrily and they walked along in silence for a bit. "Something must have happened back home."

"But...." Lydia stopped. That did make some kind of sense, but if so, she couldn't understand why they hadn't left a message.

"Let's go back to the apartment and see if we can find a phone number for family in Beirut, and if not, maybe try one of their friends—that Nico, maybe? Or what's-her-name, Farid's old girl-friend?" *Giannoula.* They'd met her twice and she had been surprisingly friendly to Lydia, even telling her that she was a better match for Farid. It's rarely wise to trust an ex who says things like that, but Giannoula had seemed genuinely at ease with the situation. She had a new boyfriend and Farid said she was happy with him, they were talking about getting married, having a baby.

"I think I have her number somewhere."

Back in the empty apartment they didn't turn up much. They searched everywhere for phone numbers and addresses but couldn't find anything that would help. No list, no daytimer, and Lydia was wrong: she didn't have a number for Giannoula and didn't know her last name. She had no idea where Nico's nameless garage was, either—she had lost all sense of direction on the way there and back. But wait: she remembered something: Aspa's, the place where she and Mouna had had coffee just round the corner. They looked it up in the phone book and then found it on the map.

They had to take a bus to get there. An Orthodox priest sat near the front of the bus, bearded and straight-browed, his expression as he stared at his fellow passengers so severe that it put some steel in Lydia's spine. She sat up straighter. By the time they reached the garage, however, she was almost feverish with anxiety. What if Nico told them something terrible had happened? But he had not seen Mouna since before they left, hadn't heard of any emergency at home, and "so sorry, but I do not know any number there." He spread his arms wide to show that he couldn't help them. Something about his manner implied that they would have that number already if they were meant to. "Mouna didn't say anything at all to you?" "No." He shrugged and smiled again. "Sorry. I hope everything is OK." As they walked away Lydia looked back once to see him watching them. He waved without smiling and went back inside his shop.

"I need a drink," Francine said. "And something to eat, before we try again." There was nothing in the apartment, so they bought bread and cheese and some fruit at the grocer on the corner, and a couple of bottles of wine. They sat on the living room floor, drinking faster than they ate, so that soon they were more than a little drunk. "Why did we fall for these guys?" Francine wagged a finger at Lydia. "We should have known they'd be trouble. Should have kept our panties on." Then she sighed. "Oh Lydia…." She started singing. "*Lydia, oh Lydia oh have you seen Lydia, Lydia the tattooed lady….*" She trailed off. "I can't remember any more." So Lydia sang her the whole song, which Rosalie, of all people, had taught her when she was fourteen. "*La la la, la la la….*"

For some reason that made her think of something Phil had told her when she was much younger. "Hey did you ever hear George Bernard Shaw's fish joke? The one about how illogical the English language is?" Francine laughed loudly. "Lydia, I swear to god you're the only person I know who would bring that up in conversation." She waved a hand. "No, I love it. Go ahead." Lydia repeated the joke that had tickled her when her father told it. "How do you spell fish?" "Shoot." "GHOTI. GH as in laugh, O as in women, TI as in nation." GHOTI. Fish. Francine shook her head. "Who told you that?" "My father."

A minute later, after some more wine. "Miss him?"

"Yup. Do you miss George?" Although she'd said they were almost through, Francine seemed almost as anxious as Lydia.

"No, I mean your father."

"Oh. Not the way I did at first. But yeah." Rare flashes, once in a while, still surprised her. Not in the heart, always the stomach. Heartbroken had never seemed the right description for what she had felt in the early days, it was more like a fist to the guts, a violent clutch of longing. Whether for Phil, or for the illusion of safety and solidity that he'd managed in spite of everything to carry with him, she wasn't sure.

"Car accident, right?"

"Sort of."

"Sort of?" It was time, finally, so Lydia told her almost but not quite the whole truth. She described Rafa as a source of Phil's, implicated in his death, but didn't add that she was also his lover. "Anyway, Rafa Ahmed is a heroine to a lot of Palestinians. And to a lot of people in Lebanon. She's Lebanese—mother from Palestine. Like Mouna."

Francine whistled. "No wonder you and Mouna...."

"Yeah. Oil and water, that's us."

"But why should that matter to Farid?"

"I'm not sure that it does. But Mouna said... she thinks I'm bound to be prejudiced against Arabs, Palestinians anyway. I don't know. Maybe she's right."

"No way. Though jesus, who could blame you, after what happened to your dad? Oh screw Mouna, What does *she* know?" Good questions, both of them. Francine yawned. "What a fucked-up day. I'd better get some sleep, or I'll definitely flunk that interview." She struggled up off the floor. "Wanna have a pyjama party?" She pointed vaguely in the direction of the bedroom she usually shared with George. "Pretend it's Grade 8 and talk ourselves to sleep?"

Lydia was touched. "It's OK. I think I'll be up for a while and I don't want to disturb you. Better get your beauty sleep."

"I guess you're right. OK. See you in the morning. Try not to worry too much."

"Night."

Francine paused at the doorway. "Listen... I'll miss George and his kind heart, and I want to know he's OK. But we both knew from the beginning that it wasn't going to last. Maybe you should... oh what do I know? Night."

Maybe I should what? Forget about Farid? Would she feel better right now? Less sick and forlorn? The wine was making her dull and sleepy. Instead of lying awake, she went to bed too, and slept heavily. She was still asleep when Francine left for her interview. There was a note in the kitchen. *Hope you don't have a hangover like mine. It'll be a miracle if they hire me looking like this. See you this aft. xo F*

Lydia made herself some coffee and sat by the phone. Her hands were shaking a little. If she tracked down the number through directory assistance, what then? What if she got through? Who would answer? What language would they speak? What would Lydia say? At first it seemed moot. She called the international operator but every time the operator tried the line was either busy or inaccessible. In some ways, a relief. She was unprepared, a little spaced out when she did finally hear the voice of the Beirut operator, speaking first Lebanese, then French. "*Oui allo?*" "*Ah… allo? Je cherche un numéro pour…*" God, suddenly she couldn't remember Farid's father's first name, or his mother's. "*Monsieur Salibi.*" "*Addresse?*" *Damn.* She didn't know. The voice was impatient. "*Il y'a beaucoup de Salibi. Prenom?*" *Shit.* Wait. When Farid was showing her some photos he had said his father's name. "*Ah! Nagib, non, Nadim.*" There was more! "Oh, and… *il est medecin. Et il habite Beirut Ouest.*"

"*Bien sûr.*" The voice was dry. There was a wait. The operator gave her a number. "*Mais il faut avoir patience. Les lignes ne sont toujours….*" "*Merci, merci.* Thank you."

It felt like a huge achievement just to have a number, but after the first euphoria, a slump. She still didn't know what to say if and when she got through. She didn't even know if he was there, and if he was, what if he didn't want to talk to her? Maybe he was hoping she'd get the message and leave before he came back. But it was only ten days ago that they'd talked about living together. Could his feelings have changed so radically in that time? Maybe Francine was right, she'd taken the whole thing too seriously instead of accepting it was the usual temporary romance. And maybe Mouna was right and it would never work. No. *Screw Mouna.* That thought made her dial the number.

Unexpectedly, she got through on the first try. A woman answered. "Salibi." His mother. She sounded older than Lydia had imagined. "Um… *c'est Madame Salibi?*"

"*Salibi, oui.*"

"*S'il vous plait madame, je cherche Farid Salibi, ou sa cousine Mouna.*"

There was silence at the other end. She tried again. "*Farid Salibi?*"

"*Non.*" His mother said something in Lebanese. Farid had said she spoke both French and English fluently. Lydia tried again, in English, her face hot with embarrassment.

"*Is Mouna there?*"

Mrs. Salibi didn't answer at all this time. The quality of her silence made Lydia think that she might be crying.

"*Je suis une amie, Lydia.*" *Oh god, didn't amie mean lover in French?*

Mrs. Salibi sniffed and hung up.

Francine was home an hour later. She rushed in, obviously excited. "Hey..." Then she noticed that Lydia was sitting with the lights off. "What's up?"

"I got through."

"What? Hey, great! Did you talk to Farid? What did he say?"

"He's not there. His mother hung up on me."

"Why?"

"Who the hell knows?"

"Call back."

"What if she hangs up again?"

"Don't be a wimp. Call back." But this time, as the operator had warned Lydia, she couldn't get through at all.

"You must have been cut off."

"I don't think so... she sounded so strange."

"Strange how? Angry? Upset?"

"I'm not sure. She was speaking Arabic, so I couldn't understand."

"Something *must* have happened. Try later."

"Yeah... I will. But it doesn't sound like he's there."

"Well she must know where he is. She's his mother, for god's sake." Francine seemed distracted, hyped up. "I have news. Are you ready?"

Lydia already knew, from the energy that was flying off her like sparks of light.

"I got the job!"

"That's amazing! Congratulations!"

"Yeah, there's just one catch. They want me to start tomorrow."

They stared at each other. "You mean... training?"

"No, I sail tomorrow. They're short a hostess on their next cruise and they need someone right away. They'll train me on the job. That's what took so long—I had to get a physical."

"Wow...."

"It's such an opportunity."

"Wow." Lydia knew she sounded witless, but she couldn't think of anything else to say that wouldn't betray her.

"I know! Listen, I have to buy a few things. Come shopping with me? And then we'll try calling Beirut again."

"And Lydia..." she took Lydia's hand and squeezed it, obviously torn between her own excitement and sympathy for Lydia's distress "... if we don't get through and you don't hear from him in the next couple days, maybe you should go stay at Steve's. Trust me, it'll be easier to get your head straight." She didn't say "before you move on," but they both heard it.

twenty-eight

When the phone rang it had shocked Faiza, alone in the apartment. It sounded too loud. She picked it up to hear a girl's voice. A foreign woman speaking French, a language Faiza didn't understand more than "allo," "oui," "non." She could hardly grasp Farid's name, so mangled by this girl's strange accent. Mrs. Salibi the voice said. It must be someone from the university, one of the teachers or their wives. When the girl said Mouna's name, Faiza covered her mouth. Mouna was at the hospital, sitting with Nasima. Poor little girl! Faiza couldn't speak. She was about to hang up anyway when the telephone lines went dead.

twenty-nine

"Holy shit." Lydia and Francine were staring up at a behemoth: a massive floating resort hotel. The passengers wouldn't arrive for hours yet and there was no one on the top deck doing the ebullient goodbye wave so familiar from movies. Just an adamantine wall of white looming over them. On the taxi ride to the docks they were quiet, each too caught up in her own thoughts to speak. Near the end of the ride Francine took Lydia's hand. They had meant to stay up late on what had suddenly become their last night together, but in the end they were both tired, and Francine had said that maybe Lydia was right and they should, after all, get an early night. She was already transforming, sliding back into her professional persona, the one Lydia had never quite believed in. Now she was starting to be able to see Francine as the bank teller she'd been in Edmonton: sleek, organized, self-possessed, a different woman from the sun-kissed party girl with tangled hair and flip-flops. Lydia helped her with her bags and asked the taxi driver to wait. He nodded and turned to the soccer scores in his newspaper. "*Epharisto.*"

"So this is it." They hugged each other.

"What do you think you'll do?"

Travel is like trouble—it creates swift, close bonds between strangers, makes them comrades-in-arms, however briefly. There's a privileged insight that comes when you meet someone out of her element, off her guard, a moment when each of you might perhaps reveal your truest self. Francine's truest self, Lydia thought, was valiant. An adventuress, as she had told her. And Lydia's? She didn't want to know. *Coward*, her inner demons whispered. She shook her head, overcome by the reality of saying goodbye.

"Send me a card to the Carnival office." Francine pushed a scrap of paper into her hand. They hugged again. For a moment they both wavered; then Francine braced herself and Lydia watched her walk up the ramp, her long legs taking it in a few easy strides. She was met at the top by a man who shook her hand and motioned her ahead of him into a glassed-in corridor; straight to work, whatever that entailed. *Entertainment facilitator* was her job title. "I'm supposed to make everyone feel like they're having a good time," she'd said. "Like whatsherface on *Love Boat*." She didn't turn to wave one last time.

Back at the apartment without her, after another failed phone call and a couple of hours of pacing and fretting and wondering what to do, Lydia already felt slightly unhinged. Why wouldn't Mrs. Salibi talk to her? Why hadn't Farid left her a note? Was he OK? What if he was hurt, or ill? But then wouldn't George, at least, have left a message? Or could Mouna somehow have turned both men against her? But even so, why would they just abandon their home? *Why* didn't Farid...? etc., etc.

No matter how much useless tail-chasing she did there was the unavoidable, pressing question: *What now?* What if they never came back? With an open-ended ticket and no concrete plans, she had allowed herself to drift over the last few months, not really thinking about what would come next. Now, when she thought of explaining to anyone else what she had been doing, how she'd been living, it seemed aimless, seedy. Ugly, even. She and Francine living off two men they had met on holiday. She could feel it all dissolving, slipping away from her. Lydia stretched out on the couch and picked up a book from the coffee table, hoping to distract herself rather than simply wait for the phone to ring or the door to open. It was a report, one of Mouna's on post-traumatic stress in refugee children in Beirut, full of the kinds of facts that used to obsess her father and that, according to others, made his journalism so powerful: the name of a kid's dead teacher, the bald patch on a boy's head where he kept pulling out his hair, the ability of a three-year-old who'd stopped speaking to mimic the sound of shells exploding. This was the kind of story that had justified, in Phil's mind, though not Elise's, his long absences from home. He had a certain look after coming back from a war zone, as if they were strangers—for a couple of days he'd walk around the house like a man lost, smiling abstractedly when they tried to claim his attention. Sometimes not smiling at all. Lydia used to resent those children, the ones he talked and wrote about; to fear that he cared more about them than her and Matthew. And maybe in a way he did—how not to be more concerned about a child whose parents both died in front of him than your own safe, well-fed son and daughter? She'd heard Armitage describe Phil's habit of giving money to bereaved children and their families as an act of guilt—contrition, is what he had called it. Penance. Very Catholic, he'd said. No doubt Mouna would agree about the guilt angle. "You need shaking up, you Americans," she'd said once. "Canadians," Francine had corrected her. But they were all one to Mouna. "All of you." Shaking up was her intent in this report, obviously. And as for the kids whose lives she detailed, was there a solution other than to remove them from their traumatic environment? But where could they go? She left that question for her readers to wrestle with.

Lydia closed her eyes. If she slept now, she would wake in the middle of the night and be up until dawn. But she couldn't move. She fell into a fitful doze, a dream in which she could hear, but not see, a child crying. She woke with a start, sure there was someone in the room. "Hello?" She heard a rustle, a soft sound. Her pulse was trapped in her throat. She sat up with her hands on her knees, trying to calm herself. "Who's there?"

Something fell in the kitchen with a crash and she jumped up, trembling, and on her way to the kitchen almost fell over the intruder. "Oh!" A cat pressed itself against her ankles. She dropped back onto the couch. "How did you get in?" It must have slipped through the balcony door, though how it got up there.... Small and black, it rubbed against her insistently. It was skinny and very dirty. It must be hungry. "Come on, you, let's get you something to eat." She went into the kitchen. She'd bought milk on her way back from the docks and she poured some into a small bowl and put it on the floor. The cat lapped it up, its scrawny sides shuddering with each hoarse breath.

There was hardly anything else in the fridge, just a container of olives and some yoghurt frilled with blue mold. On top of the fridge was Farid's photo album. She hadn't noticed it up there; it was usually in the sitting room. The apartment was uncannily silent except for the cat's purr, the watery burble of the fridge and the sound of Lydia's breathing. She sat down at the table with the album and opened it, starting at the beginning, wanting to soothe herself with pictures of Farid in his childhood. Beirut had been a beautiful city. Wide avenues; a square with people walking; cars parked, a hand waving from a car window. Some kind of monument: a figure on a pillar. Handsome red-roofed buildings of a style she hadn't anticipated when she thought of Lebanon. Boats in the water just off the bay. Farid with his parents, in tennis shorts. It made her smile, his thin serious face, and the skinny knees. His tennis shoes looked huge—hard to believe he could walk in them, let alone run. He was no camera-hog; shying away from being seen in most of the photos, especially the ones of him and a solid, frowning girl. They stood at a good distance from each other, obediently looking at the picture taker, but Lydia had the sense that if they could they would have edged even further away from each other and out of the frame. Even then Mouna looked intimidating. No wonder Farid wanted to stand at arm's length. More pictures of them, one or two where they actually seemed relaxed, riding their bikes; picnics, Farid's mother, Mrs. Salibi: very attractive and with such a look of intelligence in her face she seemed to be pushing her way out of the photograph. Mrs. Salibi at the university with a group of what must be her students. Together with Mr. Salibi, leaning against each other with a sexual ease that was riveting and palpably adult. It caused a kind of pain under Lydia's ribs. *To have that with Farid*, to be with him long enough to develop that between them. She kept turning the stiff pages. Other people: family friends, an older woman, not quite old enough to be a grandmother, who was in a lot of pictures with the children; parties, a country place that Farid had talked about "in the hills." In many ways a similar kind of life to the one she and Matthew had had with their parents, would have had for longer if Phil hadn't died. There were several pictures of Mouna with a woman who looked enough like her that she must be her mother; she looked less at ease in those pictures, Lydia thought, than in the ones with Mrs. Salibi. One photo, out of chronological sequence, of a very young Mouna with a man who also looked like her—she was sitting on his lap and holding his arm as if she'd never let go. Her father, before he disappeared? To Jordan, Farid said. And here was one of Mouna with a little girl, arms around each other, Mouna protective but so relaxed and warm that to Lydia she was almost unrecognizable. That must be her little sister.

Another photo of the same man, with Mouna's mother. Something about his face made a ripple in her consciousness, something slipping, snagging then moving in and out of focus. She shifted, trying to place the source of it and the cat jumped off her lap. It was almost dark outside now, and suddenly she knew she was not going to stay. She washed her face, packed and tidied, picked the photo album up and put it on the kitchen table. She took one look at the last page, at a photo of her and Farid on Lykavitos, arms around each other. Francine must have taken that one. She closed the book. Should she leave a note? He hadn't left one for her and she couldn't think what to say.

"What about you, little one?" She knelt down and stroked the cat's fur, which was stiff and oily. She sniffed her hand and wiped it on her jeans. She couldn't leave him in here, so she picked him up, holding him awkwardly in one arm while she shouldered her knapsack and shut the door, dropping the key through the slot. He let her carry him downstairs, and she set him down on the street. "Bye little guy." He followed her for a bit, and then stopped, sitting on the sidewalk, licking his paw. As she walked down the hill, she thought she could hear the sound of a phone ringing in an empty apartment, on and on.

"Yeah, there's a couple of beds." Gary the bartender looked her up and down in his usual way. "Or you can always stay with me, darlin'." His usual routine. *Thanks but no thanks.* "Oi, Cyndra." Lydia turned to see her hovering near the door. "Get the key for seven, will you?"

"So you're back."

"Yeah."

Cyndra followed her so closely that when Lydia turned round she almost bumped into her. "Need towels?" "Thanks, Cyndra, I'm OK. I'll get them when I come down."

She stepped inside the room and locked it behind her. Alone.

Thank god. She could feel Cyndra standing outside the door, god only knew why, and waited until she heard her move away.

Four hours later, and Lydia was not herself. Who would have thought it was possible to get so drunk on Steve's watery beer? Shit. She didn't even like beer. She lay back on the bed and watched the ceiling spin, tried to sit up to steady herself—*uh-oh*—as she felt her stomach rise to shake hands with her throat. At least she made it to the bathroom, doubly blessed to find it empty, no one in there to hear her ugly retching or to smell vomited beer and chips. She sat on the floor, hugging the toilet for dear life.

Vomiting dissipated the spins a touch, there was that to be said for it. She took a shower to wash any lingering smell of puke off her. She leaned her forehead against the tiled wall, letting the shower pound the back of her neck and snake down her spine in ropes of water. Her legs were trembling. She had a sharp image of herself in blue light, curled up into a foetal ball, but she was still upright, still drunk, though less so, still ready to fly out of Athens as soon as she could. Back in bed, shivering, she tried to reconstruct the night. Cyndra, she remembered, at the bar. Talking on and on about her family: brother Dexter, political aide to a senator—"to-tally straight arrow"—and sister Susan who ran some kind of ecologically sound co-op in Minnesota. They didn't understand her, Cyndra said, the kind of people who thought they knew everything just because they'd got a mortgage and a permanent job. Gary gave Lydia a hand signal at one point; a kind of "do you want me to get her off your back" thing, but by then she was already too far gone to respond. And at least listening to Cyndra allowed her to take her mind off things. Farid disappeared, Francine gone, Rafa—no, Mouna, somehow they were merged inside her head—smug somewhere. How did she get to bed? Someone must have helped her.

Cyndra? Gary? She didn't sleep with Gary, did she? That would be the last straw. She felt cramping in her gut and groin. She must be getting her period, along with everything else. She fell back to sleep, too tired to check.

When the plane touched down in Toronto, it was a typically dreary early winter night, sleet trying to be snow and never making the full transition, a damp wind cutting through her jacket, letting her know she was underdressed. Gentler weather than her first winter in Canada, when the snowstorms had seemed ridiculously excessive, a caricature of what they'd expected, but in its own way more dispiriting. Lydia started shivering the moment she stepped off the plane and didn't stop until after she'd taken a hot shower and tucked herself into bed at a Traveller's Friend close to the airport. She couldn't sleep. She sat propped up against the pillows until dawn, listening to planes take off; through a gap in the curtains she watched white lights glisten on the highway and in the air, red blips punctuate a milky haze. At the last minute she had felt an urge to turn back, at least leave a letter, a way to reach her in Toronto. If there was some reasonable explanation— though that seemed less and less likely—for Farid's disappearance, what would he think when he came back and she was gone? *Oh for god's sake, Lydia*, she told herself, *Francine was right. You took it too seriously. It was a fling. Time to get on with your life.* Mouna was right too, in her awful way. It would have been too difficult in the long run. Forget them and their goddamn civil war and their murderous politics and their gun-toting heroines. Have done with them.

In the morning she called Matthew to tell him that his wayward sister was home. She had expected to leave a message on his machine, but he answered in person. "Hello."

"Hey, Moo."

"Lydia! Is it winter there yet?"

"Actually, I'm here."

"Here? Where?"

"In Toronto. I'm at the airport." She didn't say she had arrived the day before and checked into a motel overnight. "Would it be OK if I took a cab to your place?"

"Stay there, I'll come and get you."

Before she could protest he hung up. He didn't even ask which terminal. She had just time to shower and get some breakfast and rush over to Terminal 2 so she could wait with her suitcase like any other traveller just arrived. She waited outside the terminal doors, despite the cold, shivering like one of those puny hairless cats, feeling just about as unprotected and far less valuable. She kept scanning the curved drive in front of the terminal, looking for Matthew's car. There he was, in his used beige station wagon. She could hear the engine before she saw the car. Not one of those men who spent his income on automotive status symbols, her little brother. She loved that about him, his lack of interest in visible glamour, often a source of barbed teasing from Elise, who thought he should be more concerned with appearances. He honked the horn and Lydia dragged her unruly trolley over. He was half out of the car, about to hug her, but a security guard waved at them to move on, so Matthew popped the lock and Lydia hefted her bags into the trunk.

When she climbed into the passenger seat, Matthew was beaming at her. "Hey, you!" He waved off the security guard. *I'm going! I'm going!*

"Buckle up."

He waved again at the long-suffering guard—"OK, *OK*,"—and they rolled away, out of the driveway and into the collector lane for the highway. The engine was so noisy it sounded like a newlywed's car with tin cans trailing behind. They had to raise their voices to hear each other over the rattle, and the heater, cranked up high.

"I can't believe you're home. Ruth was sure you'd move to some idyllic island and never come back."

"Wishful thinking." She could feel Matthew's attention on her, his sensitive radar cranked up a notch or two.

"I did meet someone, but it didn't work out."

"His loss."

"Oh…" she remembered Farid's furious words when she'd told him she was going to Turkey without him. "It was just one of those holiday flings. I thought it might turn into more, but it's probably a good thing it didn't."

"And now you're home again."

Jiggety jig.

thirty

When you can't mend things any more, can't replace what's been lost, what *can* you do? What compels you? Guilt, for one. Revenge, another. At first Mouna was too busy with Nasima, nursing her, comforting her, planning for their future. But soon her thoughts turned in another direction.

The address she'd obtained was near Souk Tawile. When she knocked on the door she could hear children playing inside, and a radio. The door opened a crack, onto darkness and a smell that involved stewing food and too many bodies in a confined space. It opened wider and a woman looked her up and down. She sucked her teeth before she directed Mouna to a gutted luggage shop—"headquarters"—as if the makeshift sandbag and barrel setup could be called anything so official. The *musallaheen* hanging around were boys, barely out of their teens, strutting attitudes they'd picked up at the cinema. She walked up to the door and one of them stepped out with a gun in his hand. For a minute Mouna was whipped back to that afternoon with Sara, eight years ago. Like an animal in the wild that's just sniffed a hunter with blood on his knife, she froze, her skin prickling, but the kid's gun wasn't raised. Even so, something about him communicated violent misogyny—he'd threaten a woman, perhaps beat or rape her, just for the thrill of it. She recognized the type, met plenty of them at the checkpoints and on the streets, sometimes inside the camp, enjoying the crude power their guns bestowed on them. She'd negotiated with more than one of them on behalf of the camp's residents, or herself.

I have news about your mother's shooting. After she'd put the word out, eventually a message had come. And so here she was.

She held her hands wide, non-threatening, but it would be dangerous to show this kid any more deference than that. "Where's Sunny?"

"He's not here."

"Where can I find him?"

He shrugged, resting his gun on shoulder and hip. It galled her, his stupid macho show of indifference, but she knew better than to let him see it. "Is there someone in charge?" She asked the question dismissively, implying his junior status, hoping that this would goad him into giving her the information; instead, he signalled his irritation by shifting his gun so that it made a noise, metal and canvas rubbing together. A shiver ran down her back: had she made a mistake, insulting his pride? He didn't answer her, but his eyes had swivelled sideways, to where a group of men had rounded the corner of the street and were standing outside a gutted building. She called out the name.

"Sunny!"

One of them looked over at her flatly, but not with overt hostility, not like his idiot comrade. She thought of Mariam. "They like their Marxist rhetoric, these clowns," she'd said, just the other day. Mouna walked towards Sunny, suppressing the unstable mixture of fear and anger that all these guns in one place inspired in her.

"You sent me a message this morning?"

He nodded, seeming neither surprised nor particularly pleased that she'd responded so quickly. His friends stood behind him, watching. The way they were looking at her made her wish she'd brought a gun of her own. A week ago, a woman's body had been found, raped and shot, the woman last seen alive pulled screaming from a taxi at a checkpoint.

"Is there somewhere we can go?"

He jerked his chin towards the building. "In there. *Yalla*."

She followed him inside. Black scorch marks on the walls. The light fixtures were either broken or completely removed. Shelving had been ripped out, all the merchandise, looted. Shreds of plastic sheeting littered the ground, a broken strap from some piece of luggage, and near her foot something gleamed—a tiny lock and key, the kind that people use to protect their suitcases against nosy baggage handlers. She had an urge to pick it up, just for something to do, but she restrained herself.

163

He gestured to a broken chair. Not a chance. She wanted to be ready to run. "I'll stand." She waited for him to speak. He was the one who knew the script, but he didn't say anything, so she tried a prompt. "Obviously I got your message." No reaction, but there was some slight gradation of attentiveness in his face. She coughed, her throat irritated by all the dust in the building.

"White Mountain Bakery."

The non sequitur confused her. "What?"

"Your baker has a son who joined Amal. Ali."

Mouna felt the hairs on her arms lift, again like an animal smelling its doom. Her bladder fluttered, she thought she was going to lose control and wet her pants. Sunny looked knowing, even sly, and his previous blankness was preferable to this look. His clothes were dirty and even with the wind gusting through the holes where the glass had been blown out of the windows, she could smell him. By now she was used to many different kinds of stink, including her own, but it added to her fear. At least he looked more human than his friend outside; more human than many of the faces she saw every day on the street and in the camps. Perhaps more human than she did, lately.

"… this Ali…"

It had been a mistake to come here. Her pulse was soaring; she didn't want to hear, she began to move away from him, back towards the hole where a door should be, but he continued, raising his voice….

"… Amal has been targeting the refugee camps." Only the most recent of the militias to do that. Everyone, it seemed, had taken a turn. Echoing her thoughts, Sunny said. "Everyone turns on the Palestinians, you know that." He coughed. "They're going after staff as well. It's possible he was looking for you." Not a random sniper, then. The thought made Mouna break out in a sweat.

"And so?"

"So you want vengeance against such a coward." He said it calmly, as if it were a known truth about all humans, this desire. And he wasn't wrong, in Mouna's case. She could feel herself go limp with hatred, an awful kind of relief as that feeling replaced her fear.

"Ali's father, shouldn't he feel what you feel?"

A sudden image: a zigzag of flame, a spray of blood, an explosion that would leave the same shaped hole in Hamid's life as there was now in Nasima's, in hers.

"Isn't this why you came here today?" His smile was small and dirty with meaning.

She turned away from him blindly and stepped through the broken wall without answering him. *Nothing will come of it,* she told herself.

"Sister, *yalla.*" He yelled after her, trying to call her back. "We can do it."

She shook her head. "*La.* Thank you for the information."

Two streets away, she flagged a gypsy cab, leaning forward to assess the driver and the back seat for a long moment before getting in. If the inside handles had been gone she would have waved it on.

She stared out the smeared window. The driver had put a protective cover over the seats and her jeans caught on cracked plastic, raising a thin welt of pulled thread.

Ali. Of all possibilities, this one, obscure enough to be unimagined, now seemed half-plausible. She remembered the look she'd surprised in him with her rudeness, when they were both children. The anger and frustration that must have been there always, cooking. Getting stronger as he got older. Was it just toxic resentment of the social scheme that kept him and his family down near the bottom? Who knew? Not Mouna, for sure. And did it matter? What was a restless, alienated kid going to do in this nuthouse? In peacetime, he might turn delinquent, maybe, most often wind up hurting himself first and foremost: he'd be paralyzed in a car accident, jailed for a little dope-peddling or petty theft, hospitalized for an involuntary OD. Or maybe he'd hit someone else with his car; bash someone's head in on a drunken break and entry. Any of these could end in grievous bodily harm, but the harm would still be accidental, tangential (not that that was much consolation to anyone caught up in it). But without those simpler opportunities Ali had welcomed the chance to join the *musallaheen,* and, if Sunny was right, to take revenge on people he'd known since childhood—sudden flash of him as a ten-year-old, sneaking free pastries to his friends, then his beautiful eyes looking coldly up at her under thick lashes. She saw his face in the hospital, drawn with pain and barely recognizable. Who cared what had stoked him? *We should have let him die in that hallway.*

She tapped the driver's shoulder. "Stop here." She could hear sounds of shelling, not close enough to worry. A boy walking by bounced a soccer ball with his hand and it spun, black-and-white hexagons blurring into each other. Another boy snatched it away from him and they tussled. She recognized one of the boys, a neighbour's son. Then she saw Hamid in front of the bakery. She pretended to be fumbling for her cigarettes and didn't wave back. She couldn't look at him, not then.

Mariam and Farid were sitting in the kitchen when she got in, talking. "Where were you?"

"Visiting a friend."

"Ramzi was here. He has news for you."

"What news?"

"About the visas." Another step in the process of leaving. Ramzi had promised to help. Even now, Mouna didn't want to go, but the choice wasn't really hers any more.

"He'll come back tonight." Farid played with his coffee cup, turning it round and round.

"And you? What are you up to?"

"He wants to get back to his girlfriend." Mariam had the dissatisfied tone of a mother who wanted more information than her son was willing to provide. "Tell me, Mouna. What is she like, this mysterious girl?"

Why is it that when the opportunity arrives to say what you really think, it so rarely seems opportune?

thirty-one

"About ten weeks." Dr. Klement snapped off his gloves and tossed them in the bin. Talc from the lining left his skin chalky and his hands as pale and inhuman as plaster when he held them up to the light. He interlaced his fingers and stretched until his knuckles cracked. Then he pushed his glasses up his nose and said: "Do you need a referral to a clinic?"

"Not yet."

"Well, don't wait too long."

"I won't. Thanks."

"Cheer up. It's not the end of the world. Far from it."

He smiled at her and left the room just behind Sophie, his nurse, who crossed Lydia's name off the list.

Fuck a duck, as Francine would say. *Shit shit shit.* Lydia's mental dictionary swooped from expletives to the pragmatic language of clinics, procedures, termination cut-off dates and on to the Victorian terminology of mistakes, drafts of gin, hot baths, and swan dives off high tables that she'd grown up with: Rosalie and her friends gossiping in lowered voices after a quick look to see if little Lydia was listening. Obviously, she hadn't listened hard enough. How could she have been so stupid? So careless?

One of those moments that seem unreal when they happen to you. You've heard about them, seen them in soap operas and movies of the week, read them in magazines and novels, but there you are, there Lydia was, facing one of the female population's most ordinary dilemmas, and she felt as if it must be happening to someone else. She sat on the streetcar home leaning her head against the window and wondering what the bloody hell to do next. The sidewalks were slushy grey furrows through snow splattered with brown and yellow stains that made the whitish drifts nastily evocative of used toilet paper.

Should she talk to Rosalie about her "situation," as her grandmother would call it? She certainly wasn't going to tell Elise, and not Matthew either, not yet. He'd worry, and also, less nobly on Lydia's part, he'd be bound to tell Ruth, which she couldn't stomach just yet. *Stomach, ha ha.* She felt as if hers had grown since two hours ago, when Dr. Klement confirmed what she already knew. There was no question about what she should do: head without a second thought to the phone and make an appointment at Morgentaler's clinic or one of the others. But often there's a gap between knowing what's necessary and actually doing it, which is why that evening Lydia sat in her kitchen, summoning the gumption to call Rosalie. The kitchen, like the apartment, was old, with its dark green linoleum and huge double sink. It must have been a pantry once, before the house was divided into flats, or maybe a laundry room where a woman up to her elbows in soapy water pummelled dirty clothes. The kind of chore Rosalie had done when she was young while her father measured suits and her mother cleaned houses for middle-class gentile families in London. Ruth had always said it was strange how little either Lydia or Matthew identified with the Jewish side of the family, how little Rosalie talked about it. But Rosalie was a secular London Jew. When Lydia said that to Ruth, and that she didn't feel Jewish, or much of anything for that matter, Ruth had answered, in a way that seemed irritatingly smug, that feeling neither here nor there, "in other words chronically displaced," was a quintessential characteristic of Jewishness.

She was procrastinating. She lifted her feet off the cold floor and tucked them up on a rung of her chair and sipped some tea made the way she had had it as a child, strong and lukewarm with a splash of milk and so much sugar that when she was done her spoon would stand up in an inch of sweet undissolved sludge—also Rosalie's recommended formulation for shock, though Lydia couldn't claim to have been surprised by Dr. Klement's diagnosis. Before she made the appointment she had twice in a row (just to make sure) sat in her bathroom on the side of the tub watching the little porous strip of paper turn Mediterranean blue.

The tea, her grandmother's medicine, finally prompted her to make the call. She listened to Rosalie's voice on the new answering machine. Her grandmother loved gadgets and was always accumulating more, an anomaly in her general thriftiness. She'd had a VCR before anyone else in the family, and more multi-purpose mixers and electric toothbrushes and ionizers and digital radios than one person could reasonably use. The answering machine was her latest purchase. Lydia left a message asking if it was OK for her to come by for a visit tomorrow night after work. She was temping again, at a consulting firm this time, and freelance editing as usual, on the side.

Five minutes later, her grandmother phoned back. "I didn't hear the telephone. I have a meeting that ends at six, why don't you come for dinner at seven." Rosalie had so many projects and meetings that Lydia couldn't keep track. *Meals On Wheels,* home library delivery, reading to the blind: she'd become a professional do-gooder, like the wealthy Victorian widows. If she wasn't quite wealthy, Simon had left her what she called "a tidy nest egg," and she'd been careful with her money. She was more than comfortable, she said. "I'll have something to leave you all." She still collected her pension from the British government, watched over some carefully tended investments, and her only extravagance was the gadgets, which she bought mostly from a used appliance store.

The following night, Lydia made her way in the wintry dark to her grandmother's building. She came up out of the ravine-side subway exit, under a purple sky. After snowing all day the temperature had dropped again and the air glittered with crystalline particles so fine that it was hard to tell if snow was still falling or being whisked from its powdery drifts and blown around by the wind.

Lydia stamped her boots on the mat and let Rosalie take her coat. She sat with a glass of sherry in one hand and tried to think of how to start. In the end she just blurted it out. Rosalie looked at her unreadably. "Who's the father?"

"Someone I met while I was travelling."

"You're going to tell him?"

"I... no."

Rosalie shook her head. "It's a mystery to me how you girls today conduct your private lives." When it was clear that Lydia had nothing to say in response, she asked: "What *are* you going to do?"

"I guess it's obvious."

"Is it? Then why bother coming to me?" Could Lydia get away with murdering her grandmother if she claimed hormonally induced insanity? But it was a damn good question.

"I don't know." The glass of sherry tilted in her hand as she slumped forward.

"Give me that." Rosalie took it from her and put it on the side table. She sat back and sipped from her own glass. "Well, you don't have any money, there's that to consider. And you haven't much of a career. Other than that you're perfectly competent."

Lydia snorted. "Thanks." She put her head back on the couch and looked at the ceiling. "God, can you imagine mum's face if I told her she was going to be a grandmother? She's barely recovered from the trauma of taking care of us."

"Your mother did what she could manage. And you couldn't ask for a better brother."

"I know." Before Lydia could say "or grandmother," Rosalie reached over and gave her hand a squeeze. "That's more than most have. You're not the first to be in this situation, Lydie, and you won't be the last. You'll get through it." Later, as she cleared the table, she said: "You owe it to this fellow to contact him. If you go ahead."

She went down the hallway to the bathroom and while she was gone Lydia looked around, trying to identify what was different. For the first time that she could remember Rosalie had a menorah on the mantelpiece.

She fell asleep soon after she got home but woke in the middle of the night sweaty and dry-mouthed. Rosalie was right: if there was any question about what she was going to do, she should try and contact Farid. But *why* was there any question? She wasn't the kind of person who "went ahead" with an unplanned pregnancy. She was too irresponsible.

Two days later: two more people consulted. Tree was her usual unfazable self and said she could get Lydia a referral easily when she was ready. Matthew promised not to say anything to Ruth until she'd made up her mind, but Lydia didn't hold out too much hope that he'd be able to stick to it. Of the three people who knew—five if she included Dr. Klement and Sophie—Rosalie was the only one who'd seriously considered the possibility that she might not have an abortion. It made perfect sense, so why was she dragging her heels?

Having resigned herself to the idea she wouldn't see or hear from Farid again it was hard to imagine calling him. Her wounded pride was the biggest obstacle. He had Matthew's number and he'd never tried to reach her. Obviously, he didn't feel the way he'd said, or he'd thought better of it. But still she'd begun to write to him seven or eight times now: *I'm wondering how... I hope you're... are you... I'm sorry that... why didn't....* Her writing table was an old school desk left by the previous tenant; names and insults cut into the soft wood evoked other tests, other tortured compositions. *Miss Treharne is a dike*[sic]. *Math sucks. Adam Little is a perv. Helen loves Tony Tse.* Nothing to help her there.

She kept each draft until the sight of it embarrassed and disheartened her enough to throw it away. Then she started another one. But thoughts of Farid always turned into a curdled mixture of sadness and resentment, so she went out with Tree or Stella or Gavin, an old boyfriend with whom a failed romance had turned into comfortable friendship; she went to the movies, read, had tea with Rosalie, caught up on her work. As well as temping, she was busy with two editing contracts. Each one had a life that began when the first pages arrived and ended when she signed off on the final copy, hoping that it wouldn't turn undead and haunt her with posthumous questions and changes. Time-consuming but intellectually undemanding work that left plenty of room for recreation and a little too much for thought. She had joined the community centre and went there almost every day in late afternoon to jog the sloping track that circled above the gym for a birds-eye view of the exercise classes, or to swim in the pool. (Rosalie tsked about the jogging. "Until you decide, it's best to be careful," she said.) From above, the participants in the aerobics class looked like beached synchronized swimmers themselves, performing their ungainly earthbound choreography. This vaguely routinized existence was more ordered but not much more purposeful than Lydia's life in Athens. She was in a holding pattern, she knew. Something was going to change and maybe this was it.

It had to be faced. Wherever he'd gone, why ever he'd left, he must be home by now. The next morning she called the Athens apartment. "*Ne*?" A woman's voice, one that Lydia didn't recognize. She was hit by an acid wave of jealousy. Was this a new girlfriend? "*Ne*?" The voice was curt, impatient, which made Lydia think of Mouna, but it wasn't her.

"*Parakallo*... do you speak any English?"

"A little."

"Could... could I speak to Farid Salibi?"

"Who?"

"Farid."

"There's no Farid here. Wait." She heard the woman turn to talk to someone else, there was a pause, the clothy sound of a palm covering the receiver, the far away reverberation of a voice speaking indistinctly to someone. Waiting, Lydia dropped into a muffled sea-cave of quiet and struggled to stay alert. "Hello?" The voice was back, and she resurfaced from the grotto and shook water out of her ears. "No, we don't know him. He lived here before, maybe. We just moved."

"Oh... do you have the landlord's name and number?"

"We go to an office. It's a..." the woman said a word in Greek then found it in English "... a dentist. Megas. On Syntagma. Wait." Again, the null space. The woman came back with a phone number.

"OK, thanks for your help."

"*Parakallo*." The voice was a bit warmer now.

Lydia phoned the dentist: his receptionist, who was also his wife, said they didn't know any Farid Salibi, never had. Lydia put the phone down heavily. It was her fault. She'd waited too long, given up too easily on calling Beirut last time. She was on her own with this. Her last card from Francine, still working for Carnival, said she had never heard from George. He had disappeared too.

"You always have me," Rosalie had said last night, when they were sitting on the sofa. Then she had announced, suddenly: "I had a miscarriage, once." Lydia wondered if she was using a euphemism. "It was after your mother, and the doctor said it was dangerous to be pregnant again."

"Was it a planned miscarriage?"

Rosalie flushed. "An abortion? No." She seemed to be remembering. "Your grandfather was so angry. He said I was jeopardizing our family, playing with my health. But I lost the baby early and I was fine." She looked into a corner of the room, away from Lydia. "Funny, I still feel it, sometimes."

"I'm sorry, Grandma."

"Nonsense. It's your situation you should be thinking about."

She wondered what Rosalie would say if she told her this baby's father was Lebanese, that its aunt (god, Mouna would keel over! Lydia almost smiled thinking about it) was a Palestinian activist. *Baby.* She'd said it, if only to herself.

thirty-two

She had gone, just like that. Gone and taken the money too. "Yeah, she was here. Sorry, nothing here for you. No letter," the woman at Steve's said. Nothing for him, not even a note. The woman looked uncomfortable at his obvious disappointment. More humiliation. He'd been right, he was just a holiday fuck, she hadn't meant any of it. *Bitch. Whore.* He hated her. He had wanted, needed, to tell her about Deena, about Mouna and poor little Nasima. To be comforted by her. Now she wasn't here, and who could he tell? Giannoula, whose eyes welled up in sympathy. "I'm so sorry," she said, kissing two fingers and touching his forehead. She was pregnant already, they'd just found out, and she pressed one hand to her stomach as if to protect the foetus from such tragic news.

Giannoula said she was surprised about Lydia. She poured him another glass of wine and watched as he drank it too fast. "She was in love, I saw it." She shook her head as if the mysteries of life could never be explained. She and Christos had decided to go ahead and get married, quickly, so his mother wouldn't be upset. Farid wondered if there was something about him that stopped women from being able to love him. He was weak, like Mouna had said when they were children. *Walad.* Weak and pathetic. He didn't ask Giannoula, didn't want to hear her try to reassure him.

It was just a game for Lydia, then. And in the end she stole from him too. She didn't even have the decency to leave the money. He should have listened to Mouna. *Bitch, whore, Jewish cunt.* "You know she's a Jew," Mouna had said, though she didn't explain how she knew. He'd been pissed off. "*Ay*, and so?" Mouna was the one who cared about that, not him. You couldn't blame all Jews everywhere for what was happening in Beirut. That's what he'd said to her. "What do we have to do with all that? We're just trying to live." But was she right?

Had it been impossible for Lydia to really love him?

He had a tantrum in the apartment, throwing things around, and then had to clean up, sweep up a broken plate and glass. He didn't want any trouble to come back and haunt the man who held the lease, a friend of George's cousin. George was in Jordan now, working for another cousin, and wasn't coming back to Greece. And Farid was off to Paris. Time to grow up, time to move on. He left the keys at the dentist's office, after hours, and then went to the airport. He cheered up on the flight, a little, thinking of all the French women. How jealous Lydia would be if she saw him sitting at a café with a beautiful Parisian girl. *Tu ne me manques pas.* Lydia, her long neck, her big eyes, that look of wounded fury when he had accused her of wanting to fuck other men. She had looked at him with love. *She had.* Maybe, for a little while, she had even fooled herself.

thirty-three

An American woman has been found dead at Piraeus. Nico had sent her the article from *The Herald Tribune.* Mouna looked at the photograph. It wasn't a face to be noticed. Memorable only for its blandness. One of the army of foreigners in Athens, most as unremarked when they leave as when they arrive at the docks, the ferries, the airports, constantly replaced by the next wave. But Mouna thought she recognized this woman. She had seen her, with Lydia and Francine, had heard them talk about her. Cindy something. There was the name, under the photo. Cyndra Hansen. *Following us around,* one of them had said. Was that it? Or was she following someone else? Not everyone in Athens went unobserved: most of Mouna's friends there were PLO members or supporters, used to being watched. The photograph looked like it came from a mug shot or an identity card. *Do you know her?* Nico's note asked. These were her last days at work, getting ready to hand everything over to her replacement. There was too much information, too many case files, too many vulnerable kids, she didn't have time to spend on much else. She looked at the face again. *Who are you, stranger?* She had no idea.

thirty-four

Now that Lydia was visibly pregnant, she had become public property. It was almost like being a sexpot, only a different set of admirers. Strangers leaned in to touch her belly or accosted her at Loblaw's or Shopper's with cloying demands to know whether "it" was a boy or a girl. They smiled at her knowingly, frowned if she was buying a bottle of wine at the liquor store, gave up their seats for her—or looked doggedly the other way—on the bus. To some people she was now invisible, to others, surrounded by neon arrows. It was almost as exhausting as pregnancy itself.

"What are you going to say when people ask?" Elise wanted to know.

"Why?"

"Well, isn't it... awkward?" They were only just on speaking terms again after a mutual freeze-out following Elise's response to the news that Lydia was: a) pregnant and b) not having an abortion. Elise was, she had said, "appalled" that Lydia was "throwing her life away. Ted agrees with me," she'd said. Armitage was now living with her, when he was in town, and Lydia had finally had to modify her practice of referring to him in conversation as "slimebucket." But the idea of Armitage being consulted, let alone appalled, was too much for Lydia. "Fuck him," she'd said, and Elise had hung up on her. Then called back a day later to say she was sure that Lydia would have come to her senses, but Lydia hadn't answered. She'd lain on her bed listening to Elise's voice on the machine, feeling that shudder of resentful disgust that women have felt since the cooling of the earth when their mothers— *Finally! Thanks for nothing!*—offer censure masked as advice. Lydia had fallen down another of life's rabbit holes into a world she had not expected, ever, to be a member of: the strange alternate universe of the single mother. Whether out of her own perverseness, or fate, or love, it didn't matter. Once she'd crossed the Rubicon she couldn't go back.

"Awkward for who?"

"Whom," Elise said, automatically. She was driving Lydia to buy a crib and a car-seat, for which Lydia knew she should be grateful. Damn it, she *was* grateful. She almost felt sorry for her mother—it was Elise who was finding it "awkward" to explain that she didn't know who the father of her daughter's unborn baby was. Among the university-educated children of her friends this was an anomalous situation, and she had settled on "he is no longer in Lydia's life," as if Lydia were, like her, a widow, or had been abandoned by the feckless son of the laird. Lydia supposed she was doing her best. They both were.

"Have you seen your grandmother?" From Elise's grim tone, they too must have had one of their fallings out. "She's been so odd and un-communicative lately. Dot says she hasn't been doing Meals on Wheels for weeks."

"Maybe she's got a boyfriend!" Lydia grinned at the thought.

"Don't be ridiculous."

They drove in huffy silence. Lydia wondered whether Elise knew about Rosalie's newfound attendance at synagogue, but her mother seemed so frazzled that she didn't ask. She did, however, drop by her grandmother's the following afternoon, a Sunday.

Rosalie didn't look exactly thrilled to see her. "I'm in the middle of something."

"Sorry, Grandma, I'll go...."

"You're here now. Make us some tea." Lydia heard her muttering to herself as she went down the hall to her bedroom. "... some people.... no consideration...."

Lydia could never dissimulate with her grandmother. Once Rosalie had joined her she said, "Mum wants to know if you're all right."

"She can't ask me herself?"

"Dot says you haven't been doing Meals on Wheels."

"Why is it that when you get old people assume you have no private life?" Rosalie stared hard at Lydia. "They think they can just barge in when they feel like it."

Lydia was too interested in her grandmother's response to feel chided. "It *is* a man! I told her!"

Rosalie snorted. "Don't be ridiculous, Lydia." Sounding quite like Elise, though not as affronted. She turned the cup of tea in her hands, sitting quietly, looking at the pattern round its rim. Lydia waited, but that was it.

"OK. What shall I tell Mum, if she asks?"

"That she can pick up the phone and ask me herself, missy. Now tell me, how are you feeling?"

Lydia described her latest encounter with an elderly man who had followed her into the elevator at the obstetrician's, insisting that he could tell it was going to be a boy, she was carrying high. Rosalie laughed. "Men! Typical."

By August, Lydia was thoroughly sick of being pregnant. She moved like a water buffalo, wading and rippling through the humid streets. *Be prepared,* Rosalie had said, *the first is often early. Keep a night bag by the door.* Lydia had a couple of false alarms, the cramps that would come and go. "Braxton-Hicks," Ruth told her, knowledgeably, with a touch of the smugness that sometimes made Lydia want to smack her. Everyone, it seemed, was eager to impart the language and lore of maternity, as if Lydia were an idiot child who couldn't be counted on to find out for herself. She got used to the cramps and wondered: would she know when it was the real thing?

She needn't have worried. The last weekend in August she was at the corner store buying some juice when she gave a shout of surprise. "Holy crap!" She lowered her head and gripped the counter. "Eeee!" The woman at the cash looked up from her magazine, said "uh oh," and handed her the phone. In the middle of calling Matthew, who had insisted on being her designated driver to the hospital, she had another contraction so intense she dropped the phone. She picked it up to hear Matthew shouting:

"Lydia? Answer me! Lydia?"

"I'm... hooo!... fine. This might be it. I'm up the street, at Sun Convenience."

He was there in five minutes, the advantage of living so close to her. Ruth was going to meet them at the hospital with pyjamas, pillow, etc. Rosalie wasn't home but Ruth said she'd track her down and let her know. Lydia gripped Matthew's hand. "Don't call mum, not yet." He patted hers, keeping his eyes on the road. "Let go, Lydie. I need to drive." She grabbed the edges of the seat, bracing herself as if the car were driving through a hurricane. She made sounds like a goaded moose, Matthew told her later. The ride was agonizingly slow. There were roadworks everywhere, the curse of Toronto in summer, and each lurch, each dip into a pothole added depth and dimension to a pain so different from any other pain she'd ever felt that it was mind-blowing. Spectacular pain.

There was a brief lull when they got to the hospital and she was able, with relative equanimity, to let Matthew leave her to be admitted while he parked. After that, everything was raw and loud and then quiet and then loud again, waves and jags and spurts of pain and fluid and straining flesh. "Her pelvis is very narrow," the nurse said. "We might end up having to do a C-section."

"Give it time." That was Rosalie. *When did she get there? Why was it so bright?*

Rosalie handed her an ice chip to suck on. "Push, Lydia, push. Squeeze my hand." Lydia gripped Rosalie's arm as if it were made of iron; later Rosalie showed her the bruises. She was feral with pain, furious with it, more inside her body than she had ever been. It was all there was. Hours of cycling, pulsing waves and circles of pain, blunted by an epidural but still—*OH!*—so strong. Then, when she was about to give up, to say *I can't do it, I changed my mind, make it stop*, the doctor said "Hey! Don't you want to look? Your baby is being born." She lurched up on her elbows, put her hand down and felt wet, matted fur like a cat's. At first she thought it was her own pubic hair, but then she saw the head, covered in black hair. The little pouch-eyed, smeared, wrinkled creature that finally slipped out in one wet, sloppy gush, like a baby calf, was hoisted up by the doctor and put on her breast. "Good girl," Rosalie said, and kissed her sweaty forehead. The baby was a boy.

thirty-five

Mouna had entered her own alternate universe. Six months after Deena's death, with the help of IVOW—Innocent Victims Of War— and her friend Sara Halil, as kind as ever, now a medical resident at the Children's Hospital, she and Nasima were heading to Montreal. "You'll love Montreal," Mouna had heard her say before they left Beirut, via a pirated telephone line rigged by Mariam's ever-resourceful neighbours. Sara had sounded excited and nervous, her voice full of restrained anticipation, remembering their stolen kisses and the handful of passionate letters they'd exchanged. But also, perhaps, aware of the reluctance to leave that made Mouna twitchy and moody, and that she'd been trying to keep hidden, from Nasima most of all. Mouna's own sense of guilt—for so many things—and Nasima's dependence had bound her into a web of need and expectation, different, and for her, so much more difficult than the demands of a job that she knew many people would find harrowing, but that was easier for her to confront than this. This intricate set of responsibilities was too personal. Sticky. She had to get it right, for Deena, for Nasima. Her sister was too vulnerable for her to fuck up.

After the chaos of getting out of the city—driving past collapsed apartment buildings, the carcasses of cars, a scattering of shoes left in the road when their owners ran, men with guns who turned to stare at the car as it passed—the plane's quiet had been as surreal as Geneva's waters, a limpid oasis of calm. She stretched out in her narrow seat, trying to relieve a cramp in her foot.

"*Café?*" The stewardess leaning over her was very pretty, though her creamy foundation was too pale for her olive skin and ended at her neck, mask-like. In the closeness of the cabin her makeup had turned filmy, glinting on the hairs above her upper lip. Her tight blouse was unbuttoned to show cleavage; as she tilted the carafe to reach the man by the window her breast pressed against Mouna's arm, an action, like the smile, seductive in a neutral, automatic way. Mouna leaned back slightly, pretending to adjust the ventilation nozzle above Nasima's sleeping head. Curled under the coat that Sara had warned her to bring, Nasima looked tiny and much younger than her age. "Your daughter?" "My sister." The stewardess smiled again. "*Elle est mignonne.* Coffee for you?" "Tea, please." "I'll be back in a minute." Mouna lit a cigarette, holding it away from Nasima to avoid waking her.

She could never sleep on airplanes and she didn't feel like reading. When the tea arrived it was terrible, stale and bitter. She left the cup on the tray and was glad when another stewardess took it away. Instead of sleeping, she drifted, hovering but not allowing herself to land in any one emotion. It was still hard to believe that she and Deena would have no more opportunities to frustrate and disappoint each other. At the moment, these and other facts floated above the pain and guilt that usually came with them and she slid into a half-memory, half-dream of another flight, the one home from Athens with Farid and George. Farid had been looking out the window, watching the city fall away below them, then the dotted islands. Beside him, Mouna had tried to lean forward to look, but her body was pushed back into the seat and held there by gravity as the plane climbed its ladder of air. Surreal powder-puff clouds blew by the window. The plane bumped giddily, then settled. Farid had talked about tennis, about the indoor courts in the old gym on the AUB campus. He had asked Mouna whether they were still in use, their metal walls dented and pocked by bullets. Then he began to talk about what he would eat, his first meal home. She'd had to resist snapping that his choices would be limited. Like everyone who left, he seemed to have half-forgotten what it was like there now. He had been in an anticipatory mood, despite the inevitable dangers and stresses of their arrival and the reason for their journey, and his concern over Lydia, who would come back to find them gone. Not that he had talked about her, for which Mouna had been grateful. Grateful also that he hadn't asked her to pretend about her complicated feelings for Deena. He never had. There were not many people she could be so unguarded with about her strained relationship with her mother. Even close friends had the capacity to make her feel—as Deena in her unhappiest moments had maintained that she was—unnatural. As if he knew what she was thinking, Farid had stroked her arm, though he was still turned towards the window, exclaiming like a child at the beauty of the sky. The airport, when they landed, had been chaotic, re-opened for who knew how long, guarded by jeeps, patrolled by soldiers, and full of people saying goodbye, leaving indefinitely or forever. Ramzi, waving them over to the car he had waiting. There was a crater beside the road on the way home, the massive scar from some prior attack.

Suddenly, without wanting to, Mouna saw that luggage shop, Sunny's dirty smile, heard his siren song: "We can do it. Isn't that why you came here today?" She pressed her hands against her eyes so hard that it hurt. "Are you all right, miss?" The stewardess again. "Fine, thank you. Just a headache."

When they landed at Mirabel, she and Nasima were both hovering in the surreal zone of traveller's exhaustion. *Can those sniffer dogs smell last week's marijuana?* Mouna wondered. Their luggage took forever and they stood watching the black slats of the conveyor belt fan and contract as the luggage retrieval room echoed with the irregular swish and thump of heavy bags falling down the chute. Not much conversation; people concentrated wearily on the bags circulating hypnotically, lurching into action when theirs showed up. Finally: Mouna's suitcase. Another five minutes passed before Nasima's appeared. At least they'd travelled light. There hadn't been much to bring.

Once they were through customs, Mouna pushed the trolley out into the Arrivals area, which, in contrast to Baggage Claim, was throbbing with movement. Women with flowers, cab drivers with hand-lettered cardboard signs, weeping relatives, boyfriends, small children hoisted on shoulders, waving, all turned expectantly towards the sliding doors, caught in an agony of anticipation, and there was Sara: tall and slim, wearing a tailored overcoat. She looked far more sophisticated than Mouna remembered. In the past few years she had become a poised, gorgeous woman, with long wavy hair and a face as dreamy and romantic as the tone of her letters. Nasima pointed. "Sara!" She tugged Mouna's sleeve. "*Shoof!* There she is! Sara!" She ran ahead, leaving Mouna to push the cart up the long ramp.

Sara lifted Nasima up, trying not to show dismay at her skinniness. "Little monkey. Can I still call you that?" Nasima snuggled into her like a child, her eyes closing as if she might fall asleep instantly. Sara held her tight and bent over with a chaste cheek-kiss for Mouna. They were both at a bit of a loss.

"I could see you through the glass. What took so long? Did they search you?"

"They stopped a family in front of us. And of course our bags were some of the last off the plane." Mouna tried to smile too, to break through the black mood that had been descending on her throughout the flight. Sara turned her attention back to Nasima. "*Incroyable!* You're a young lady now." Nasima giggled drowsily, a sound so sweet and unrestrained that Mouna was struck by how rarely she'd heard it in the past six months. Longer.

Sara beckoned them outside. "Come. My car's over here." She had a little blue Toyota, with a blanket thrown over the back seat. "I hope it doesn't smell too much. Lucie was in here earlier." "Who's Lucie?" "My friend's dog." She popped the lid to the trunk and they put their luggage in. One bag went in the back with Nasima. Then they were on the road, the long drive to downtown Montréal. *Avenue du Parc* was the name of the street they were heading for, but Mouna didn't notice anything that looked like a park on the way, and said so. "You'll see it tomorrow. I'll show you the mountain."

Dazed and preoccupied, Mouna was immune to curiosity. She watched mindlessly as the highway unscrolled ahead, while in the back seat Nasima sat wide-eyed, head propped on her thin wrist. A truck with a cylindrical load—*Gaz flammable. Avertissement,* a skull and crossbones leering from the rear of the cylinder—signalled late and turned onto an exit just in front of them and Sara had to brake so fast that Nasima's head snapped back. "*Merde. Pardon.*" The truck's gears gasped, the cylinder swung wide, and then the road ahead was clear again. By the time they reached Sara's apartment, jetlag had pounced. While they waited for Sara to park the car, Mouna looked in the window of a street-level shop that said it was a drycleaner but had a hand-lettered sign advertising other services: *Assurance Passeport Visa Lam-inat.* She could see her reflection, small and hunched from the cold.

Determined to keep them up late enough that they'd have a chance of sleeping properly, Sara suggested a shower and then supper at a place close to the apartment. Nasima said she was too tired to eat but, astoundingly, she drank most of a vanilla milkshake. Mouna had soup and tea, and five cigarettes. Sara shook her head. "You've come to the right city." The air in the restaurant was blue; everyone but Sara and Nasima, from the waitress on break to a customer fumbling for change, had a cigarette going.

When Nasima started to droop over the dregs of her milkshake, Sara asked for the bill. They walked slowly back to the apartment and she guided them up the metal staircase to her door, almost indistin-guishable from its neighbours. "You must take my bed, monkey. *Et toi, Mouna....*" Mouna was not ready for this. "Why don't you share with Nasima? I'll have the couch." How could she have forgotten Sara's tact? Sara never made assumptions about others, almost never imposed her own desires. Sometimes her discretion used to frustrate Mouna, but tonight she appreciated it.

Before she fell into unconsciousness, she had a moment of dread so intense, so acute, it threatened to rip up sleep for the night. But her fatigue was too powerful. She woke in the very early hours, judging from the density of the blackness around her. Nasima had flipped onto her back and was snoring. Mouna didn't want to disturb her, or to wake Sara, but eventually the urge to pee was so strong that she had to get up; she slid carefully out of the bed, pulling the top blanket with her, and tiptoed to the bathroom, her feet shrinking from the cold floor. She wrapped the blanket tightly round her shoulders and found her cigarettes in her bag, which she had left in the hallway. Then she pulled on a pair of Sara's boots and slipped out onto the fire escape at the back of the apartment. It was bitterly cold, but still better outside in the night air, where she could see the lights of other insomniacs and early risers pricking holes in the darkness. A cat startled her, landing with a thump on the step in front of her, on its way to some other home. She flicked her cigarette off the balcony, a spray of orange sparks before it was extinguished; she went back to bed and lay for an hour or two, sleepless, thinking of what was ahead and trying not to count her losses. What would she do now? Faces punctuated her waking dreams: Deena, Ali, Farid, even Lydia Marcus/Devlin was among them, her narrow face accusing.

Part Three

thirty-six

Off and on, Lydia wondered where Francine was now and what she was doing. Her last letter had been returned with no indication of a forwarding address, and Lydia had assumed that was it: the connection had been broken. It happens, sooner or later, when odd-matched travellers go their separate ways. But one day from London: stamped with a little rosy-tinted queen's head, a letter. *Hi Chiquita, Bet you thought you'd gotten rid of me, but no such luck. How the hell are you?* Lydia laughed out loud. Francine was one of those rare people who sounded the same on paper as they do in life.

She hadn't been at Carnival for almost two years now, she wrote: *those bastards.* They'd stiffed her on her severance pay. The job soon got stale, and after her contract was up she decided it was time to return to real life. *I went back to Athens, stayed at Steve's for a few days. No sign of the human leech, by the way. Imagine what a disappointment that was.* She had looked up George in Athens but there was no sign of him either. She didn't say if that was a disappointment or not.

An Australian girl she'd met on the ship invited her to go to London, where they found a two-storey flat to share with three other people... *you wouldn't believe how expensive rent is here. No one can afford to live alone.... One of the guys in my apartment is in finance....* He got Francine an interview for an entry-level position at Credit Suisse— *and guess what, they offered me the job!* Next week she was moving to Basel, *to live like an adult again.* No time for dating, she said—*got to get my skills up for this job*—nothing but a few one-night stands since her fling with a fitness instructor on the boat, *kind of a space cadet, but hey, he looked like Robert Redford.*

Any news from Farid? Remember driving around in his old car on Mykonos? Do you think they ever finished the construction in Zografou? It seemed like such a long time ago. And so far away: Palaio Zografou, the white-hot afternoons, the balcony and sliding door with its broken latch, the little shop whose toasted sandwiches in greasy paper sleeves were so often their staple meal of the day. The outdoor seafood restaurants that Farid said reminded him of a resort town back home called Jounieh. Farid in bed. Laughing at the movies. Leaning on the balcony while he reminisced about explosions in the night sky. Miles and miles away.

I've missed you, girl. Write me. xoxo Francine

She held the letter in her hands and read it through again. *I've missed you, too.* Did she mean Francine or Farid? Both. Francine already had an address in Basel, where, she said, Lydia could reach her for at least the next six months. Tonight, Lydia would write her back. What would she say? *So good to hear from you... glad you're doing so well. No, I haven't heard from Farid, but I've tried to reach him, because...* that was a bombshell, wasn't it? Felix.

Speaking of Felix: if she didn't leave now she'd be late picking him up from daycare. He'd been going full days for a year now. In an ideal world, she would have waited a bit longer, but the spot came up, and they were like Wonka's golden tickets, those subsidized spots. Elusive, floating, then suddenly in your hand and you had to grab them or someone else would snatch them from you. But it had been hard. On Felix's first day, he had yelled and sobbed and held out his arms to her as Irene, his new teacher, carried him inside. Lydia had cried too as she left the daycare, unable to let go of that awful moment, the sight of his frightened, bawling face, his pleading arms. It felt like such a betrayal. Do children ever get over being abandoned, she wondered, even in supposedly small ways? Would he remember this later? "Don't worry, he'll soon get used to it," Yolanda, the daycare administrator had said, handing her a Kleenex. "I know it's hard, but it's better if you leave quickly, helps him adjust." She had sniffled all the way home, all the while guiltily aware that she also felt a vast, horizon-stretching relief. She had longed for time to herself, some respite from the dullness, the yawning afternoons that, as much as anything else, were parenthood. Well, she had earned her solitude, more time to work and find new editing clients, and to think. And Yolanda had been right, Felix was fine.

A question loomed as she hustled down the damp street under a sky that was dense and lowering: a storm on the way. *Any news of Farid?* How long could she pretend, to herself, and everyone else—to Felix, most of all—that Farid didn't exist?

thirty-seven

Mouna was waiting for the salt. She had asked someone to hand it to her ages ago, she could see it in the distance, silver and glinting, passed from hand to hand while the table got longer and longer and the salt further and further away. She was so hungry. Suddenly there it was, floating through the air, sailing towards her. She reached out to grab the glass container but it turned soft in her hand and burst. Lit powder everywhere.

She woke to voices down the hall, in her kitchen. She struggled to remember whose they were, which kitchen, which apartment, which city… before impressions settled into present reality. Sara and Nasima. And the newly painted kitchen was salmon-walled (Nasima's choice), cold-floored like the rest of the apartment. The city? Not Beirut any more, nor Athens, but Montreal. What had actually woken Mouna was the sound of Nasima's laughter, her distinctive snort-hoot in response to a joke. "What's going on out there?" Mouna called.

"*Yalla!* Come and find out, *ma belle.*" Sara's voice teased. As always, Mouna set her feet on the bare wooden floor before she remembered how cold it was. "Ahh!" Where were her damn slippers? Her groping feet were no help. She got down on her knees and saw them under the bed, where she'd kicked them last time. The floor was furred with dust and she could see uncapped pens, an empty Tylenol bottle and a book, all too far back for her arm to reach. Grabbing for her slippers, she inhaled a noseful of dust and sneezed, twice, sitting back on her heels. She might as well get dressed. She did it quickly, shuddering. This was only her second full winter, sun-deprived days, streets scoured with wind, and the simultaneously domestic and desolate sight of people jumping snowdrifts and hunching their shoulders against the coldest draughts; blue winter light, steps tongued with snow in the corners or thick with snow right after it had fallen. Sara had described it all too well. Mouna was still shivering as she walked into the kitchen, feeling in the back pocket of her jeans for cigarettes.

"What's so funny?" Sara was laughing now, Nasima singing, mimicking a Lebanese singer they saw a few nights ago. A well-meaning friend had invited them out for dinner at a Lebanese restaurant, hoping to do them a favour and transport them home, temporarily. Expecting traditional music, instead they got warmed-over Madonna and a variety of other cover songs delivered with torchy theatricality. "Like a Ver-her-her-her-djinn." Nasima vamped and sashayed, all scrawny arms and non-existent hips. She fell heavily onto a chair, fanning herself, mock-exhausted from her exertions, and Sara applauded.

"Did it snow again?" Mouna peered out the window.

"Not yet. What's your hurry?"

"I thought it snowed in the night." She shivered.

"Poor baby." Sara put her hands on Mouna's shoulders and rubbed vigorously up and down. The friction made her tip on her heels like a toddler being towelled dry. Her shoulders stiffened and Sara stopped and turned to put the kettle on.

"Hey, Sara, maybe you should hire that singer... what's her name? Fa-tee-ma." Nasima fluttered her eyelashes. "For the club."

"Oh yeah, the girls would love her. Over-the-hill torch singers are a big draw here. Especially virgins." Sara went back to the *Week in Review*; she was a newspaper junkie, and it was Sunday, so an eviscerated *New York Times* was spread over the table, sections on top of each other, overlapping, sheets of paper drifting to the floor.

"Who's playing tonight?" It was club night—the lesbian supper club that Sara and a group of friends ran every third Sunday, popular with artists. Strictly Sara's private life—none of her work colleagues knew this side of her. The club hosted performances by local actors and singers and raised money for various causes. The music was good and it was always packed with women and a handful of gay men. The food was good too, thanks to her friend Myles, a chef, who donated his Sundays off. Guests could drink hard liquor or beer at the bar or pay a small surtax to bring their own wine. It was a drunken affair by the time the doors closed, early Monday morning.

"It's retro night. Lisa and Vania are DJing."

This new life had taken some getting used to. It was surprisingly freeing to escape the claustrophobic gossip factory of Beirut, but Mouna missed her work, the people whose lives had absorbed her (especially the children), friends and colleagues who shared her sense of urgency about what was happening. Now she had a job at the *Centre Pour Des Femmes Réfugiées* that many would call equally important, and a readymade household. Family, condensed: sister to protect and nurture, would-be steady lover waiting patiently for her to make a full-blown commitment. When she wasn't working, Mouna drove Nasima back and forth to school and to her therapist, watched over her meals and doled out the vitamins that were so important after the deprivation to which she'd subjected her body. She spoke to Mariam as often as she could, to update her on Nasima's welfare and, until three months ago, to ask once again when she and Nadim were going to leave. *I'm taking a sabbatical,* Mariam had told her then. *In the States.* She had said *I,* not *we.* She phoned Mouna after she got to New York, to give her the number where she would be living for at least the next year.

There were mornings when Mouna woke up in a blind funk, suffocating under all this routine. After the initial effort involved in getting health coverage, finding work, settling herself and Nasima in, she'd come smack up against it. Trapped. Cut off from the deep political engagement that she craved and the travel that she loved, both of which had protected her from the emotional claims of others.

But how could she resent this new life? Just look at her sister. Nasima wasn't unmarked, of course; she had more than the usual ration of psychological tics and a new diagnosis of Obsessive Compulsive Disorder, but nonetheless, she was eating (the occasional relapse to be expected, the therapist said in a family session), slowly gaining weight, and back at school. Her social life could stand improvement and she still looked both younger and older than she should, but at least her body was no longer so visibly undernourished. Mouna looked at her now, sprawled on the chair, almost happy.

No, she couldn't allow herself to resent or regret having come here. So why did she have that too-tight-in-her-skin feeling, little pulses of electricity zapping and threatening to spit flame?

"Are you staying tonight?" she asked, suddenly, following an internal line of thought without having paused to assess its effect. Now she watched Sara try not to seem upset at the abruptness of the question. "I don't think so. I've got a pile of abstracts to read before I drop in at the club." She'd been planning to read them early Monday and go in late, draft an excuse to tell her supervisor, carve out a little extra time with Mouna before the club and another grinding week of call at the hospital, but she was a deft liar.

Nasima was not so politic. "You can't go! You *have* to stay tonight—we said we'd all go to the club together. Tell her, Mouna...." Neither woman answered her.

"Well, I've got a couple of errands to run. If I'm not back before you leave...." Mouna gave Sara a quick kiss, squeezed her arm, and was moving away before, she hoped, Sara had time to register how perfunctory her touch was. "See you later."

"Stay out of trouble."

"Always." Mouna's tone was slightly mocking but still affectionate. "You need anything at the dépanneur?" she asked Nasima, who shook her head. Bystanders to a sudden eruption of activity, the two of them watched while Mouna located scarf, coat, hat, boots—all things she had trouble keeping track of in this new life. She was constantly losing one glove, finding her scarf mashed at the back of the closet, on the floor. She stepped outside into the crisp air that smelled, she would swear to it, of impending snow. She suddenly realized she'd been holding her breath. She was so relieved to be outside and alone. She looked back at the apartment. The houses all seemed perched, poised for something adventurous. Flight, like her. She passed the dépanneur without going in, strode past the wine store, the bakery, the dollar store. All that mattered was her overriding need to escape the domestic closeness of the apartment. Her feet were carrying her without any other purpose. No errands, no meetings to get to. She walked on and on, very fast.

Once she could breathe again Mouna began to think about coffee (she'd started to develop a taste for her aunt's beloved espresso) and an uncensored smoke. Nasima had been infected by the North American health bug; she had started to worry out loud about second-hand toxins, and Mouna had capitulated, grudgingly, to the point of stepping onto the cramped balcony when it wasn't too cold for her to bear. The sight of Nasima's anxious face took most of the pleasure out of smoking indoors, anyway.

"Why do we all feel guilty for leaving?" Sara had asked last night in bed, head propped on her wrist, her long body curving towards Mouna.

"I don't." But it wasn't true. She shook her head as if insects were buzzing around her on a hot summer day, instead of a stinging wind on what should be spring but instead was one of winter's finest, and made an abrupt decision to stop at Luna. She had just stepped through the door when someone called her name: Safia, one of the student volunteers at the refugee centre who was also on the committee for the *Peace and Reconciliation* conference that Mouna had been asked by the Palestinian Students' Association to co-organize. Safia and her boyfriend—what was his name?—Luca, were beckoning her over, both grinning at her. It took some getting used to, the way people smiled here, so easily and indiscriminately, a toothy salute often bearing little relation to what they were saying or feeling. By all appearances these two were sincere, though Safia's attraction to Mouna was coloured by intimidation and Luca's by some alloy of curiosity and sex. Maybe he was one of those men who were titillated by lesbians; she'd caught him eyeing her when Safia wasn't looking.

She was about to put them off, then changed her mind. They'd distract her from her mood and maybe she could catch up on a little shop-talk about the conference. They were sitting near the back, close to the cinema, where it was darkest and the smoke thickest, and they each had a pack of smokes in front of them.

"So, kids. What are you up to this weekend?"

"I was at the office this morning." Safia paused. She seemed excited, more vibrant than usual. She started to play with the sugar packets on the table, twisting one between her fingers until it broke and the sugar spilled in a small gold heap. The look of sudden dismay on her face was comical. She was a sweet young woman—too sweet, it woke the devil in Mouna, and in Luca, too, sometimes, she'd noticed—less militant than some of the others at the Palestinian Students Association, but haunted by her family's stories about lost land. Her father was the Scheherazade who kept her imagination fuelled with a mixture of longing and outrage. Luca's motivations were less clear. He came to rallies and stuffed envelopes, but Mouna was not sure why he was involved and for that reason she didn't entirely trust him. He seemed committed enough, but in an impersonal way that had made her wonder, on occasion, if he was spying. She was too cynical. Maybe it was love, and he was doing it for Safia.

"A fax came in from Jordan." Safia paused again.

Mouna caught the buzz of her agitation, but didn't say anything; already she felt light-headed. The news they'd been waiting for.

"Rafa Ahmed will be at the conference."

Black sparks danced in front of Mouna's eyes. Safia couldn't have known all the implications this news would have for her. As soon as they'd heard Rafa's travel ban had been lifted, Mouna and her colleagues on the committee had gone to work. Equally passionate about her attendance, still none of them could have had such a personal connection, such a gut-deep, physical longing to see her, hear her voice, be in the same room with her. Rafa was Mouna's childhood *coup de foudre*. Everyone has at least one, the one you long to shine for, the one who blinds you, and she had been snared as soon as she saw her first image of Rafa, electrified by her presence, her bravery, her dedication. Her beauty, her face in the newspaper photographs, graven images no less mesmerizing than the woman herself, all of it even more potent now that Mouna was far away from home. She was back in that stuffy hallway on a hot summer day listening to Rafa's low voice floating out from Mariam's office, her laughter; burning with the desire to be the one who could make her laugh. Or speak to her as an equal.

Safia was still talking. "She wants to be part of the panel with the

Israeli foreign minister." She was watching Mouna, waiting for a reaction that hadn't materialized to her satisfaction. She asked, tentatively, "Maybe we could see if we can get her to do a Q & A, or an interview for *The Link*?"

"That's one possibility." Safia looked deflated by the non-committal answer. Luca ripped open one of the glossy, chocolate-coloured tubes of sugar; its tiny sleeve deflating as well as he poured the stream of pale gold granules into his espresso. Safia reached for her bag. "Oh, I forgot. There's something here for you. I was going to drop it by your place." While she scrabbled among a mess of papers and books, Mouna was aware that Luca's scrutiny was less covert than usual; when she tried to stare him down he didn't look away.

"This is good news, right?" Luca stirred his coffee, still watching her.

"Rafa?" Mouna nodded.

But there'd be practical consequences. Security, which was already intense, would have to be heightened, that was if the Israeli foreign minister would still consent to participate. There would be extra attention on the Centre, and on all pro-Palestinian groups in the city— in the country, come to think of it. PLO representatives would need to spin hard and fast if they wanted the press to talk about anything outside of Rafa's titillating history and her status as former pinup for radical liberals. It could be they'd want to stress the fact that she hadn't been one of theirs, strictly speaking, when the hijackings occurred. RCMP and CSIS would be all over her and the conference; unmonitored interviews weren't likely.

Safia had found what she'd been looking for. She pulled an envelope out of her overstuffed bag—"I call that bag her *bosse de veuve*," Luca said. "She's going to turn into a little hunch-backed witch if she keeps packing everything but the kitchen sink in there." He was not the first man to do this in Mouna's presence: serve up his girlfriend as somehow smaller, cuter, less consequential. It was a minor form of sexual betrayal that she frequently evoked, not without satisfaction. She didn't have time for it now. Safia's cheeks were slightly flushed, from embarrassment or annoyance, or both. They'd argue about Luca's behaviour later, Mouna thought.

She recognized Farid's handwriting. *Fragile, Photos, Ne Pliez Pas.* "Thanks, Safia." She finished her espresso and put three bucks on the table. "I'll let you kids enjoy your coffee. I'd better get home." Safia looked disappointed, Luca mildly curious, but they just smiled and nodded at her. "We'll talk more on Thursday. Ciao." Something about Safia's slightly wounded look pricked the bitch in her. "Watch that hump, *Cendrillon.* Luca's right, you need to lighten your load."

She had walked another block before she decided to step into a second café for a leisurely read of her mail. She wasn't ready to go home, and she wanted to enjoy Farid's letter in solitude. She picked a spot in the corner with empty tables all around. The waiter came up to her, tip-tapping his fingers on his blue menu, waiting. If she drank more coffee she'd pop a fuse, and nobody here made tea the way she liked it: Bedouin-style, strong, pungent with fresh mint and thick with sugar. She asked for *eau minerale.* The bored waiter barely acknowledged her order, but he was fast and efficient. It wasn't until he'd set glass and bottle on the table and left her alone that she began to open the envelope.

She looked at the photos first. Farid in Paris, with some familiar faces. Leila and Tariq, inside the restaurant they'd started—*Leila's mezze are* mash-hoor, *all the rage,* Farid had scrawled on the back of the photo. In front of Pei's glass pyramid, with some other friends. And two photos he'd included *for old time's sake,* left over from Athens. He wasn't a prolific photographer, obviously. There was one of her and George, together, and one of the five of them: Farid, George, Mouna and the two Canadians, taken by someone else. It seemed like so long ago, now, that summer's end. She looked at Lydia's image. Did she know how much she revealed in photographs, that one? She didn't seem to be able to put on a face, to pose. Instead, her body, the way it was angled, and her face, naked even in its guarded intensity, managed to communicate every one of her mixed emotions. Happiness and unease, love and anxiety. Mouna smiled to herself. The unease was probably because Mouna was sitting next to her. She set the photos aside and began to read the letter. Farid gave her his news: that he was working for Tariq and taking some classes, to finally finish school. He was seeing a girl, but "it's not serious," he said. His parents had separated temporarily; when his mother had arranged her sabbatical in the States, Nadim had insisted on staying in Beirut. *They say it doesn't mean a divorce, but who knows?* Mouna thought about it. It didn't surprise her, exactly, but after everything her aunt and uncle had faced together, it was sad. She had been intimidated by them when she first moved into their home, and had converted that into mistrust and anger, but she loved them now and wanted them to be happy. Perhaps childishly, she was unable to conceive of their happiness apart from each other. *Forgive me, some war news,* Farid's letter said. *Remember Ali, Hamid's son?* The thin paper felt brittle in Mouna's hands, suddenly, it rasped between her fingers. *Umma tells me he was killed. Hamid may close the bakery. She says his heart is very bad and he wants to leave the city and go to live with his brother. The girls left when Asma died.* Asma, sour and unfriendly, hidden away in the back near the ovens, tormented by the sight of her husband flirting with all the Sunni and Christian female customers; she coached her son, so Mariam once said, to inherit her terrible bitterness. The girls, Ali's sisters, had always been invisible, not allowed to work in the front of the bakery, but not to attend school either. Did they miss their brother? Mouna lit a cigarette, then another one. *What have I done?*

The waiter had read her radar correctly—*I'll tip generously, just don't bug me*—and he left her in peace after he brought the bottle of water. When she looked up again from her fourth reading of the letter, her ashtray was full and it was almost dark outside, and she felt slightly calmer. She was momentarily disoriented, having missed the shift of light as it passed through the shuttered time of day when streets narrow and warm rooms begin to expand. Like her, the place was in limbo, caught between its afternoon role as café (a handful of people sitting alone, writing in journals) and its evening identity as bistro and bar, with diminished tolerance by the waiters for solitary brooders; soon it would start to fill up. One of the tables near her was occupied now by a chic young woman—definitely no earnest scribbler—who looked at her watch, checking the time. She was cute, and from the way she sat, theatrically poised, fingering a silver hoop in one ear, she knew it. Mouna admired her for a minute before she signalled to the waiter, paid her bill, tipped double the cost of her water and headed out to the street where it had finally begun to snow.

On the way home, she stopped at the dépanneur for bread and more cigarettes, keeping the envelope inside her coat, held tight under her arm. The house was dark when she got in. Nasima was out, at the library, no doubt—so much more studious than her older sister had ever been. Mouna stamped her feet automatically to free her boots of snow. The old stuff was packed hard and what was falling was soft and light, fluff sitting on the tops of her boots and floating to the ground when she moved. Standing in the hallway, one hand braced against the wall as she pulled her boots off, she felt suddenly dizzy. Too much coffee and nicotine, not enough food. Too much news. She bent down, head near her knees. The envelope dropped to the wet floor and she snatched it up. *Breathe.* She waited for the feeling to pass and stood up slowly, envelope in hand. Nasima was no snoop but Mouna hid the letter anyway. She walked past the kitchen and through the living room to the bedroom, which was still infused by Sara's perfume. Not here. Back in the living room she knelt in front of a stack of old LPs. They didn't have a record player anymore but she couldn't let go of her vinyl. She pulled one from its sleeve, doubled it up with another, replacing it with the envelope and adding two others that had been hiding behind the records, then slid the album back. Marvin Gaye, *I Heard it Through the Grapevine.* Hearing Nasima's key in the lock she stood quickly—too quickly, dizziness again—and tripped on her way to the sofa, where she fell in such an awkward position that she was still laughing at herself when Nasima opened the door.

"What are you laughing at?"

"Nothing. I tripped." Automatically, Mouna lit a cigarette, and they were both diverted by Nasima's instant look of disgust. She fanned the air, frowning.

"You have to wait until the exact minute I come home?" Her voice rose at the end of the sentence, a warning signal. Mouna stubbed it out. "Such a pain, my bossy little sister."

"I'm not bossy."

"No? Soon you'll be telling me I have a curfew." She raised her hands, adopting a voice their mother had sometimes used when she was exasperated. "Please god, tell me, what did I do to deserve this terrible woman, this pervert, for an older sister...."

She was suddenly afraid she'd gone too far, ripped their fragile peace at the seams with a stupid joke. Nasima's cheek trembled. Her hair was beaded with drops of melting snow, sparkling in the dim hallway light. She stepped close to Mouna, leaned down and shook her head like a wet terrier, drops spraying over her sister, who recoiled, laughing. Thank god. Nasima was laughing too. Seeing her mischievous face, Mouna felt a rush of confirmation. This was the right thing, coming here. The next minute she remembered Ali and felt sick. Like a short-cycling manic-depressive, up down, up down. She ground the cigarette again, snuffing out its last embers. She should eat something; settle her stomach. "There, mademoiselle. Just for you." She pushed herself off from the sofa. "I'm gonna make some toast. You want some?"

"I'm not hungry."

"Were you at the library?"

"For a bit. Then I met Salma and she invited me for tea." Probably that meant she'd dropped by Salma's shop to join one of her card games. Nasima was happiest in the company of women who reminded her a little of her mother or Mariam. She had been adopted by a little circle of older Lebanese women, including Salma, who babied her and didn't seem to mind that she whipped them regularly at whist and euchre.

"How much did you make?"

"Thirty bucks."

"*Eeafekeh!* Wow! Enough to buy my drinks tonight."

"*Je crois que non.* I've got better things to do with my money than pay for your immoral habits." She said the word "immoral" like an old

201

schoolteacher and wagged her finger, eyes glinting with mischief.

"I'm going to have a shower." Still teasing, she pranced towards the back of the apartment, to the little chip-tiled bathroom, her favourite retreat—complete with what Mouna called her "Barbie shelf," stuffed with pink- and mint-coloured lotions; loofah, pumice, bubble bath, nail polish. After the years of living with an erratic water supply, Nasima revelled in all ways and means of keeping clean, smelling sweet. Today this allowed Mouna another short spell of solitude to collect herself so she could prepare for a night at the club. What had she done? Who could she ask, who would know exactly what had happened to Ali? She needed to think it through, but now was not the time.

The last time Mouna saw Hamid, she had thought he looked ill. He had called out to her in the street and, seeing him struggle to walk towards her on his swollen feet, she had slowed down. His colour was bad and his breath sounded stifled and wild, as if there was a small animal trapped in his chest labouring to get out—congestive heart disease, he told her. This was after Mouna's meeting with Sunny and she had found it hard to look at him. It was mutual. Now she wondered if he'd heard the same rumour she had. He had offered her some bread "for your family," a sacrifice in today's market, avoiding her eyes. He seemed ashamed of how his illness had weakened him, shy of her grief, or perhaps his own. Asma had died not long before. He looked up once, as he gave her the bread, searching her face for something, she didn't know what. He'd had the haunted eyes of a man with not much time left, but now he'd outlasted his son.

thirty-eight

Felix had dozed off in the chair next to her. Sensory-deprived by her head-phones, Lydia flicked her eyes his way periodically and kept her heavy coat on, ready for a fast getaway. Even now, he was occasionally known to wake up from a nap with an ululation of surprise that shocked strangers.

She was here several times a week for clients, and she knew her way around, so she had ordered her videos and found a free monitor quickly. Other people were hunched over their tiny screens, and in the booth next to hers a couple was watching *Psycho*, sharing a pair of headphones, gasping and gripping each other's arms at the scary parts. Lydia's video was an amateur production and some of the images were hard to decipher. The camera was shaky and people walked towards it as if they were going to confront the filmmaker but then stepped away, their faces dodging in and out of the frame. There were sounds of gun-fire and shouting, pop music in the background. Then an open-air market where men weighed beans and rice and a baby cried where it sat in the middle of a barrel of chicks. The chicks climbed over and around him, peeping. A boy wheeled bricks; another delivered tea to a scrapyard where men in overalls squatted beside broken cars. Then a woman running from a bomb blast, covering her face with her skirt. The camera lurched all over the place, its operator either unsettled or inexperienced. Lydia didn't know much about the process of making films or videos. But sound was added later, wasn't it? So were the noises authentic? The camera lingered on some small boys playing with wooden guns. *Rat-a-tat-tat.* They mimicked the noise of machine-guns, and pretended to stop passersby to check their identity cards. Zoom onto a still shot: a postcard view of the main square, orderly and picturesque. A new frame, live footage of the same place with trees amputated, statues shattered and fallen.

She wasn't surprised by the destruction she saw—no one could be that naïve, not after what George and Farid had told her, not to mention the average daily news story or those dizzying reels of World War Two footage in Grade 12 history class—but she couldn't fathom how or whether Beirut's inhabitants and exiles could have become used to the damage. How long before their initial feelings of disbelief and unreality wore off? Did each new defacement of their city have an equal effect? Did it, cumulatively, eventually, come to seem normal? Or did it persist as a waking hallucination, a nightmare?

The couple next to her jumped in shock: Felix, not *Psycho*. He'd opened his eyes and started straight into a full-throttle roar. Lydia muttered an apology, scooped him up, and carried him over to the elevators. Felix squirmed and pushed. "I want to get down." "Look, Felix! Look how high up we are!" He stopped struggling and stared up at the bright atrium and the plants trailing over the balconies and snaking their tendrils into elaborate, clinging friezes. The doors to the glass elevator opened and they made room for a couple of students to step out, then went in. She pointed up again. "Let's ride to the top!" Hearing her sugary, slightly crazed tone, she wondered if any mother in the world could avoid sounding like that at least once in a while. Felix was fascinated by the view and wanted to ride up and down a couple of times, looking out at the light and the wide staircase and the different levels with carrels and numbered stacks and open areas, whose straw-coloured tables were full of people, stooped over their books and magazines. Lydia peered down as they passed Level 3. A woman whose back view reminded her of Rosalie was browsing the stacks in History. She looked again coming down, but the woman had moved. "OK bubba, that's enough of the elevator." Felix opened his mouth again and she thought he was going to argue, but he said, "Look mumma," and pointed at a mobile on Level 2, a seagull turning slowly in the air, its wings shimmering. She looked down at her son's amazed face and was drenched by a rush of love almost liquid, so sudden and complete.

When he was six months old, Felix had developed a bad cold, followed by a wheezy little cough. One morning Lydia had taken him with her into the shower, door closed, hoping to fill the room with steam that would soothe his lungs, when she noticed a shallow depression just under his ribs, the skin there sucking in and out like an extra fontanelle. The room was fogging up and at first she mistrusted her eyes. But no, when she carried him out to the bedroom it was still there. In, out, in, out. It looked terrible, like a wound underneath the skin.

She wrapped him in a big towel and sat on the bed rocking him, beside herself— more like above herself, hovering, watching, disbelieving—while she phoned Tree, whose instructions were no-nonsense: "Take him to Sick Kids Emergency right away. They need to see him. Page me and let me know what they say." After Lydia hung up the phone she was momentarily paralyzed. Moaning, talking out loud to herself, she stood up, looking down at Felix on the bed, then suddenly snapped to it like a runner at the starter's gun: *Right! Dress him! Get his blanket! Diapers! Sleeper! Bottle! Just in case!* (He'd refused a bottle until then and never did take one, from her breast straight to a cuplet improvised from a bottle lid. At six months he was still too small for a proper cup and feeding him had been a slow and painful process, but any attempt to ease a rubber nipple between his lips was met with his turned-up stare: baleful, stubborn, and then by a howl. *Don't you dare try and trick me!* The real thing, or another thing entirely, for her stubborn child, no false substitutes.)

Coat on, Lydia had phoned Ruth, who listened to her incoherent blathering at the end of the line without comment, then said: "I'll meet you at the hospital." Too upset to drive safely and not wanting to let go of Felix, Lydia took a taxi. Ruth was already there when she arrived, waiting at Admitting and making a list of questions for the doctor. The sight of her was a relief (of the lifeline-to-a-swimmer-in-shark-infested-seas variety). Even Felix seemed to relax, to breathe more easily. On the alert for an aggressive respiratory virus that was sweeping the city, the doctor saw him quickly, scheduled a test and had him admitted. Ruth went to phone Matthew to tell him what was going on. Lydia had dreaded going home by herself, but now she was a basket case, sitting beside his bed trying unsuccessfully not to cry, listening to him wheeze and cough while a busy nurse explained what had to be done, in order to keep him alive. The nurses were sympathetic to her anxiety, all except one, who came in on the second night. After watching Lydia for a while, she said: "Pull yourself together. It's not about you now. Your baby needs you calm."

It would be overstating the case to say that there was one moment when Lydia felt suddenly capable of her enormous responsibility. After the first sickening certainty that she would never be able to take care of this tiny, vulnerable animal, there was no one moment when a light bulb went *poof!* But that night was one of the turning points. Felix didn't have the dreaded virus, or whooping cough, as they'd feared, or anything very serious in the long haul, but she'd had to stay alert, monitor his breathing, make sure he got enough fluids. The hospital kept them there for four days. Ruth was with them a good chunk of that time, and Rosalie too.

Elise came to visit once. Tilting her head in alarm at the dim lights and glowing machines, she whispered theatrically: "Oh, how is my darling Lydia? And how's the little one?" (She almost never used Felix's given name, even now.) She hovered near the door and watched while Lydia fed him Pedialyte. Rosalie stepped out to get some coffee and by the time she came back Elise was gone, a spray of yellow roses in a vase on the bedside table. Rosalie looked at the flowers and said neutrally: "Those are pretty," and handed Lydia a tepid, waxy hot chocolate.

Lydia found the washroom on the library's ground floor, and took Felix in for a pee. He was smiling at her now and talking about how high they had gone in the elevator. When he was younger, she often thought how frustrating it must be for him to not have words at his disposal yet. Sometimes he had looked as though he was bursting to speak, other times she had been sure he was hoarding language, deliberately waiting. When he was almost two, she had consulted the doctor, who had said that it wasn't unusual for boys to be a little slower than girls, and it wouldn't be long. Back then, Felix said a few words, but the rest was fervent hand signals and "oo oo oo" when he wanted something he couldn't name.

No such problem now. "I want some apple juice." There was a small cafeteria on the main floor, and she took him in there for some juice and crackers. She sat him at a table near the counter, and ordered a coffee for herself; while she waited for milk, she scanned the posters and ads on the wall, apartments for rent, used textbooks, lost wallets. Readings and events at the library or local venues close by. Except one: *Peace and Reconciliation: The Future for Palestine and Israel. April 12– 14. Guest speaker, Rafa Ahmed.* Babump. The sound of her heart thumping. She tore off a flyer and took it with her to the table, where Felix was wearing a sticky beard of juice and crumbs. She wiped his chin and gave him another juice box.

There was more. "For information, please contact Professor Riva Hirsch or Mouna Ammari, Peace and Reconciliation Conference, Room 214, Concordia University, Montreal." *Holy shit.* Lydia's mouth was open and she pressed one hand to her chest as if to hold her heart still, or as if she were about to take an oath. A sensation of falling. "Mumma. Pffffft." Felix make a fart sound and waited for her to laugh, but all she could do was stare at him, then back at the piece of paper, to make sure she wasn't hallucinating.

That night she paced the apartment, checking on Felix once in a while just to make sure he was breathing, a ridiculous habit she hoped to grow out of soon. Tomorrow, she knew, she'd be so tired that she'd fall asleep sitting up, over client work stained from the things she spilled on it when she lurched awake. And she would need to work full tilt to get the most pressing contracts out of the way. The conference was only three-and-a-half weeks away.

thirty-nine

For all Lydia knew, Ammari might be the Lebanese equivalent to Smith or Jones and not her at all. But, granddaughter of a fatalist *par excellence*, she didn't believe in that kind of coincidence. It was too ironic, too unexpected, too fitting. Mouna and Rafa in the same place at the same time, each with crucial information about people she'd loved. She had to go.

She also knew that she had to face up to the need to find Farid and tell him about Felix. It was her job, as that unsympathetic, plain-talking nurse had once told her, to jettison her own small injuries (in this case pride, mainly) and think first of her son. At the time she'd been told this, Lydia had spilled a few tears of humiliated rage—chided, labelled self-pitying at the exact moment that she needed reassurance!—but the nurse, damn her flat, Sister-knows-best eyes (Lydia could even now feel the sting of that look) had been right.

She'd have to ask Ruth and Matthew if they could take care of Felix while she was gone. It was only two days, but she had never been away from him overnight before. She knew that Moo would say yes, no questions asked; Ruth was the one she needed on side. She didn't want to let on her reason for going in case nothing came of it. When Felix was a baby she would have asked Rosalie for help, but he was a handful now and her grandmother was getting too frail for strenuous babysitting. So she steeled herself and called Ruth at work. "Montreal? Why?" Ruth asked bluntly. "It's for one of my clients. He can't get to this meeting and he wants me to go instead, so I can help draft the report." "He can't send anyone else?" "Well, he really wants it to be me." It sounded lame, even to Lydia. "What are we supposed to say to Elise?" *Bloody hell.* She'd totally forgotten her mother's birthday. "You know how much she'll bitch if you're not there." "I know, but this client…." Lydia's voice sounded high and implausible in her own ears, and she stopped.

Just as the silence began to defeat her and she was about to come clean, Ruth caved. "OK. Don't sweat it. We always love having Felix. And I think it's great that you're working so hard." Lydia's hands felt sticky with her own duplicity. Ruth sighed involuntarily at the prospect of Elise's birthday. "You can make it up to us when we have our own kids."

"Sure thing." She'd be walking a tightrope until she was safely on the train. There was going to be a lot of news coverage—she'd be lucky to get away before Ruth heard about the conference. Surprising, now that she thought of it, that Armitage wasn't going, that he hadn't at least mentioned it. In one of life's ironies, Felix adored Armitage. He climbed all over him whenever they visited, which Armitage seemed to like, so much that he pretended to be oblivious to the danger signals Elise sent whenever he focused for long on someone other than her.

Lydia had thrown out her signed copy of *In Love with Danger* in a fit of drunken pique the night of Armitage's launch. But she had read most of it later, in small painful doses, when she sneaked the book from Matthew's shelves in spite of herself. It had been hard to forgive him the chapter about Phil's death. The bits she hadn't been able to bring herself to read she could guess from the news coverage and reviews. Get over it, Lydia, that's what Rosalie would say. Had said, in fact. And she was right. Now that her mother's attachment to Armitage had taken on the ordinary solidity of fact, there was no longer much point to extreme umbrage over old history. Besides, she had more important things to confront.

forty

"Dinner for Two" by Edward Armitage
from his book *In Love with Danger*

The Lebanese have two obsessions: politics and food. Famously generous hosts, the people of this tragically embattled country think nothing of inviting a stranger home for a sumptuous meal, where the conversation is always lively—fuelled by arak, and, with any luck, one of the superb wines from the Bekaa Valley—and always political. At one such feast I found myself being tutored in the history of Palestinian radicalism by a child.

Any journalist visiting Beirut before the war, and even since, could relate similar experiences, though Phil Devlin spent his time more clandestinely than his colleagues, and his diet was heavier in political rhetoric than mezze. Devlin was caught up in events that, even now, are hard to unravel. Perhaps especially now, after so many years of war, of revenge and retribution, people are reluctant to name names, and I've had to go slightly beyond eyewitness accounts and my own personal knowledge to extrapolate what happened. The result is, of course, at least partly speculative—dramatic reconstruction as well as history—but I've been careful not to veer into outright fantasy. I've allowed myself to imagine emotions or sensations, but not crucial facts. The stakes are too high.

One May evening in 1971 Devlin returned to his borrowed apartment, ready to shower and relax after too long playing nice with people who saw him as a human telephone, useful mainly in his potential to convey messages. He had spent the day in the company of PR boys for the PLO, hoping for an interview with Arafat. The promised interview had ended up being postponed; part of the way Abou Ammar builds up his mystique. Devlin's reputation as a widely respected journalist was what got him in the door. That and the fact that he knew Rafa Ahmed personally; this made his handlers both amenable and cautious. The PFLP and the PLO had the same goal, ostensibly, but not the same leader, nor the same slice of the pie. At that point in history they were uneasy comrades and it seemed clear that Arafat intended to claim a broader power base.

With his eye on the prize, Devlin had been on his best behaviour, though he knew enough to display a little cynicism. The day had consisted of interminable rounds of car rides from one place to another, cigarettes exchanged and shared, enough glasses of tea to strain the most resilient bladder, an infinity of smiling pauses. Net result: some rumours, some useful information, and a sense that after failing in Jordan, Arafat was hoping to use Lebanon as a kind of sub-Palestine. There were whispers about a plan for coordinated guerrilla units in the south.

Two-thirds of what he'd been told could be discounted as propaganda, but there were a few little nuggets for a serious story, some analysis of what the PLO's new presence in Lebanon might mean in the future.

The phone rang. "Phil?" It was his interpreter.

"Yeah?"

"Abou Ammar will meet us now."

"Who called?"

"Mohammed, the one we were with today." Mohammed was a familiar figure to visiting journalists; he often played middleman. They had spent part of the afternoon with him, a long, stagnant period of sitting, smoking and drinking tea and watching a well-dressed young woman play with the fingers of his free hand while he talked, nuzzling his ear and whispering to him whenever he stopped. The girl had a small caramel-coloured dog with paws that looked as if they'd been dipped in ink. When anyone approached it jumped off her lap and spun in yapping circles, flamencoing the tiles with its hard claws. More than once, Phil told friends later, he'd had an urge to kick it.

No one knows quite what happened at that well-earned meeting. It was not a long one, which is a fact in itself tempting to over-interpret. Arafat is known to be an expansive, even garrulous subject, once he grants an interview, so why was this one so brief? Simple logistics: another commitment, for example? Or did Devlin cause offence, perhaps even alarm, by something he said? He himself simply described the meeting as "unproductive." No one else has been willing to comment.

Once the interview was over Phil was driven to a street near the restaurant where it's now known he met Rafa Ahmed. He asked to be let out somewhere short of his destination—he had not disclosed this assignation to his colleagues, though it was more than likely his interpreter, whom he trusted more than anyone, knew. Beirut is not an easy place to keep secrets.

He went home soon after that. Home, to his family and then on to the next assignment, whose location, as always, depended on the violent impulses of strangers. What did he talk about at that dinner with Rafa? Was it a simple lovers' rendezvous, or something more dangerous? Of the two people who could say for sure, one isn't talking and the other is dead. Next time Phil Devlin came to Lebanon he didn't see Rafa, only chased her shadow. Where that took him, there was no coming back.

forty-one

Mouna watched her neighbour hump a case of beer up the steep, slippery iron staircase. Sylvie, slight and trim, blond hair hiked into a high ponytail, rested the case on her knee and waved with her free hand. "Starting early?" Mouna called. "Hockey game tonight." They both laughed—why, Mouna was not exactly sure—and Sylvie lifted the case again and made it to the front door, where she rang the bell with her nose. Mouna laughed again, at the silly trick, and turned aside as one of the guys in the house opened the door. She and Sylvie quite often chatted on the steps, or when they ran into each other at the dép or one of the local cafés, but in the presence of anyone else they were both a little cagey, like married flirts afraid they'd get busted before they'd had a chance to actually misbehave. In summer, Mouna had admired Sylvie's slim shape as she went out for a jog or came in from classes. Something about her body, the way she moved, reminded Mouna of Lydia Devlin, someone she'd thought of just lately because of Rafa coming to Canada. She wondered what Lydia would think about the news, if she heard about it.

Quick mental picture of Lydia sitting in the Athens apartment: her body a mixed message as always, poised for getaway despite the easy way she stretched her legs out in front of her and tilted back in the chair. In warm weather, the resemblance between Lydia and Sylvie-next-door was accentuated by tank tops, summer uniform for both. Sylvie wore them with black jeans and seemed to keep waitress hours—how she earned her tuition, no doubt.

Mouna's neighbour to the left was a tiny storefront synagogue. She had missed the homely little sign until after they'd moved in—unexpected, slipped in between all the student apartments. The Hebrew lettering was gold on red, a colour scheme that Mouna thought of as Chinese rather than Jewish. She had spotted the rabbi on the street and in the small back garden in summer. He rolled up his pant legs and sunned his ankles, feet extended as if the light that lapped them was warm water at the beach, the way, aeons ago, she and her friends used to dip their feet into the ocean at AUB when they didn't feel like going for a full swim. He lived upstairs from the synagogue, Sylvie had told her, and took care of the garden himself. He'd built trellises and trained vines onto them with coarse green wire. There were herb pots too, like the ones Nasima filled with sage and basil. Mouna seldom saw anyone but the rabbi going in or out. At first it made her uncomfortable, being next door—it had felt like the windows were watching her when she walked by—but it was backdrop now. She flicked her cigarette into a flowerpot, where it made a tiny, hissing dent, and headed back into the house, kicking off her unzipped boots inside the draughty hallway. She shivered, rubbing her hands together. It was supposed to be spring.

It was too cold, she thought irritably, to smoke outside, even to appease Nasima's anxieties, which were piling on top of one another like hoarded newspapers. It took Nasima an hour now to get out of the house for school, checking everything first: the windows and back door, if not carefully locked, would let in thieves; the oven would be left on, leak gas and blow up the house; an improperly closed tap in the bathroom would flood the apartment. One morning Mouna overslept and woke to find Nasima pacing the kitchen, clammy with sweat, her coat already on. She couldn't remember if she'd fed the cat and couldn't bear to risk feeding him twice. A cross of Anxiety Disorder and OCD, the psychiatrist said. His treatment plan entailed helping her "manage" her anxieties like so many office projects, while he tried to attack their complicating factor: Post-Traumatic Stress, an occupational hazard for those who've fled war zones.

Mouna heard footsteps down the hall. "Have you seen my keys?" Nasima called. "I can't remember where I put them." The note of tension in her voice was within normal range, the average person's frustration over elusive property.

"On the table." Mouna went into the kitchen.

"*Merci.*" Nasima came in. "It's cold in here."

"Newsflash, *habibti.* It's cold everywhere in this city."

Mouna grabbed her bag from the back of a kitchen chair, and propelled her sister out without letting her start the loop. "Come on, I'll take you."

They were almost at the door when Nasima turned back to check the kitchen window. Mouna steered her outside, shutting the door firmly behind them. She jiggled the key so Nasima could see that the lock had engaged and the apartment was secure. When Nasima started for the bus stop, Mouna pointed to the car.

"The pollution…."

"You may want to freeze your butt off, but I prefer to take advantage of modern technology." She unlocked the car and gestured inside. "Your limo, mademoiselle."

She incurred more criticism by running the engine, waiting for the car to warm up. "Madame Gariépy says it's a myth that you need to let the engine run."

"Madame Gariépy doesn't have a shitbox for a car, *ana akid.*"

She took pity and pulled out into the street. "OK, mademoiselle, here we go, ready or not." Nasima was quiet, staring out the window and listening to the announcer give a deeply pessimistic weekend weather forecast in exhaustive detail. "Want me to pick you up today?"

"Salma's invited me for tea." She was silent the rest of the ride, even when Mouna reminded her that Mariam was coming in two days. Mouna watched her walk up the steps to the university, made sure she was inside and then drove off.

On the way home, she stopped at the Italian bakery on Parc to pick up a coffee. She left the car running—*desolée, Nasima.* Took a sip of her coffee before leaving the bakery. Instant infusion of warmth and comfort.

"Mouna." Luca, Safia's boyfriend. "Nice outfit." She had forgotten she was wearing pajama pants under her coat. "What are you doing up?" It was almost 10, but anyone who knew Mouna was aware how much she hated to get up before noon on her days off.

"What makes you think I've been to bed?"

He patted her cheek with a warm hand. "Pillow-crease." Held the door for her. It had started snowing again. "*Merde.*"

"Ready for the debate?"

"Is anyone?" The main feature of the conference would be a face-off between the Israeli foreign minister and Rafa A., reformed terrorist. The question period following would mostly be taken up by pre-assigned delegates, including Mouna. Questions had been submitted in advance and scanned by the committee to ensure "positive intent." Mouna's was a fairly innocuous one about refugee education statistics, but she planned to use it as a lever if she could. They'd been warned that the mikes would be turned off if there was trouble, but it wasn't that hard to project your voice if you had enough incentive. The thing would be to do it fast, before the debate was shut down. She could hardly be the only one making that calculation.

forty-two

Knowing her aunt was arriving today, Nasima hadn't wanted to go to class, but Mouna followed the doctor's recommendation that she stick to a routine, only gradually introducing minor changes and disruptions. The wisdom of his advice was confirmed earlier this morning as Nasima stood yet again in front of the stove, clicking the oven dial on and off in a helpless loop. Mouna gently took her hand off the dial. "Let's go. Auntie will be here when you get home."

Standing in front of the flickering information boards at the airport, she had a sudden, sharp longing to book a ticket immediately to somewhere far away. Skip the conference, leave Nasima's welfare to the gods, abandon a puzzled Mariam who would assume they'd missed each other and find her own way to the apartment, collect the key from its hiding place, let herself in, and wait in vain for her oldest niece to come home. Mouna's imagination skipped over any painful consequences—this was fiction, after all. Free again, she would be in the air, on her way to nowhere. The fantasy was so vivid that she could almost smell the dry, stale air in the long corridor from the departure gate, feel the wind press against the accordioned sleeve connecting the ramp to the plane, finger the nubbly apron covering the back of the seat in front of her. The only thing she couldn't do was picture her destination. Athens? Tahiti? Paris, to visit Farid? Beirut, back among the ruins?

Here came someone, the first drop in the flood arriving from New York. A pink-sari'd woman shoved Mouna aside, yelling. "Sheila! Sheila! Here!" A group of dazed travellers with nametags came next after Sheila, then a tired-looking pregnant woman with a toddler sitting in the top basket of her luggage cart, and then, just ahead of the rest of the crowd, Mariam. Mouna had that momentary sense of voyeurism that comes from scrutinizing a well-loved face before its owner has located you. She watched Mariam scanning the throng of people waiting, turning her head this way and that. She was thinner than when Mouna last saw her in Beirut, smaller somehow in her big grey coat and a red scarf brighter than anything else in the room, brighter even than the pink sari. Too bright for her face, which was drawn and pale. There was something fragile and tentative about her movements and suddenly Mouna didn't want to watch any more.

"Auntie!"

Mariam saw her and smiled, moving out of the way of other travellers, an overnight bag in one hand, purse in the other. For a moment Mouna had forgotten: this was a long weekend only, not emigration. They hugged each other.

"So tell me, *Umma*, do you feel like a New Yorker yet?"

Mariam laughed. "Take me home and I'll tell you all about it."

forty-three

When Mariam's old friend Ed Rahimi had called to say he could arrange a teaching exchange—he called it that though they both knew that there would be no one on the other side of the "exchange"—she had asked Nadim what he thought.

"I think you should do it." She hadn't been sure until then whether she wanted him to say yes or no.

Those first few weeks in New York she had been two-dimensional, dwarfed by canyons and plains, overwhelmed by all the food in plain sight: pretzel and hot dog stands, muffin carts, juice huts, pasta bars, sandwich delivery boys, a carnival of industry on the go: bicycle couriers leapt the curb, ardently sucking whistles like huge toddlers their pacifiers, Haitian men flogged racks of fake Guccis and Chanels, sidewalk artists sketched their quick, facile cartoons. The streets were paintings, angles and planes: from a corner thrust into permanent gloom by skyscrapers Mariam walked into an unexpected blast of white sunlight and a huge avenue zinging with cars. But to her ears the sound was muted: no guns and missiles, no rocket launchers, no shelling. No rupture of a sudden, massive explosion. In comparison, this hubbub was pastoral, except for an occasional *bang! crash!* that would start her heart racing with vestigial fear.

Kind Ed had arranged a sublet for her but she couldn't move in for ten days; until then she had stayed at the 47th Street Y, where she lay awake at night while students—overflow from NYU residences—escaped their tiny airless rooms to eat pizza in the hallway and complain about their assignments. Some of them might be hers, but she never saw them, they kept such different hours. Her room was near one of the men's bathrooms, and twice she'd heard, late at night, the sound of someone throwing up what they'd had to drink. She'd thought of her son and wondered how many times he had done the same thing. Not often, she guessed, since he seemed to have inherited her tolerance; his father's delicate system was another matter. She roamed the museums and Central Park, carefully, sticking to the busy areas like any other tourist, saw sunglassed women her age and older power-walking, elbows out, tiny arms and legs pumping along, spandexed twigs in clunky running shoes. Dogs everywhere, tiny ones scuttling along rat-like behind their owners or huge, loping show dogs, their processional hierarchy made her think of Edith Wharton. Not the dogs *per se*, but their elegance, or lack of it, the way they indicated the social class of their owners. More than once she saw a dressed-to-the-nines woman—real Gucci, real Chanel—on her way into one of the huge apartments near Central Park thrust a lap-dog into a doorman's arms, the doorman feigning gratitude. How Leila would love all this! How Grace would laugh!

Round the corner from the Y, there was a grocer with buckets of flowers and plastic umbrellas, rows of fruit outside; inside all kinds of food, a huge island of salads and take-out meats and pastas for those New Yorkers—most, it seemed—whose kitchens were too tiny to cook in. Mariam found herself joining them. The grocer had all the other necessary supplies: aspirin, cigarettes, wine, beer, milk. Beads of rain clung to the pyramids of waxed fruit outside under the false glow of the yellow awning, where it was impossible to choose between one photogenic apple and its siblings. Aware of the grocer's constant scrutiny and his cardboard sign—a hand-drawn picture of a wincing apple over the caption "Please Don't Squeeze Me"—she had usually grabbed one at random when she stepped inside for cigarettes and dinner on her way home. Walking to the Y, she'd rub it on her coat and pick off threads and lint before taking a bite: almost always disappointing, spongy or less flavourful than she had imagined. Still, its skin was luminous green or Snow White red and the rediscovered luxury of having fruit available all the time would compel her to eat it to its core before she tossed into a garbage can spewing coffee cups and pizza crusts. The people who passed her on the street saw: what? Another self-sufficient New Yorker grabbing a snack on her way home to her studio apartment and cat, or rushing to an improving night class.

She looked like what she was, probably, an academic with no personal life. Her colleagues, who so far seemed nice enough, conversed with each other mostly in a code that had to do with shopping. Ask someone how their weekend was and she'd tell you where she bought the chicken for Saturday dinner, or what kind of shoes she had picked up on sale. It meant something, all this information, but Mariam couldn't figure out what. She didn't really mind; there was freedom in being out of step. And to combat her self-imposed isolation she had started talking to herself, another common New York habit. She held one-way conversations with Grace or Nadim or Farid, with her nieces and sometimes even with Deena, found herself muttering and sighing often as she walked along. She must look like a crazy person. Sometimes the sigh was a sob, suppressed and pushed down so that it became a silent ache. Loneliness, she supposed.

Loss of her city, her home, was unlike any other: both more attenuated and more enveloping. Walid had been so distant even as a young man that she hardly thought of him. She didn't know how to contact him to let him know about Deena, didn't even know if he was alive. His death, if she ever heard about it, would be a continuum, not a fresh loss. When Basman died (and later, their parents), she had been surprised at the extreme and unpredictable swoops and plateaux in the course of her mourning, but after six months or so it had settled into a lesser vein. After a year, however, she had still found herself expecting to see Basman, caught herself thinking "I must tell him that," and even now, occasionally, the pain returned with an unpredictably savage sharpness that was almost welcome because, for a moment, she felt his presence. But this was a different species of grief. She was uprooted, strange to herself, full of guilt about Deena, whom she couldn't pretend to mourn in the same way, and another kind of guilt about Mouna and Nasima, fending for themselves, and still another kind about abandoning Nadim. Was this the end of her marriage too? Sometimes she felt so outside herself, so unreal that she was afraid she might not just seem to be losing her mind.

Her students had swiftly learned to read her signals. If she closed her book and got up to leave immediately after class, no one followed. No one showed up at her office later, asking zealous, teacher's-pet questions about their work. But if the book stayed open, they knew she was willing to linger and they could approach, walk beside her as she left the classroom and perhaps even accompany her to the coffee shop for further discussion, where her rich laugh was the reward for a particularly witty insight. She still had that most valuable teacher's gift—the ability to inspire her students to knock themselves out trying to impress her, though they couldn't know that sometimes it was their best qualities, their charm and intelligence, the sense of promise in their smooth young faces that infuriated her, made her impossibly angry at the thought of what so many young people at home, including Farid, Mouna and Nasima, had been deprived. On those days her door was shut.

The Brooklyn neighbourhood where she lived now was mostly brownstones, hived into apartments inhabited by the barely middle class or the upwardly mobile, hoping that thrift now would jumpstart a lifetime of income security. If she wanted to cook at home in her tiny kitchen she bought groceries near school. The local shops closed at night. By six o'clock or earlier, metal grilles were rolled down and locked, alarm systems turned on. Only the liquor store stayed open late, and its owner had a permit to keep a gun behind the counter. Mariam's only weapon was a green water pistol whose purpose was to deter Sylvia, a grey half-Siamese, and Ted, a mongrel tom, from jumping on the tables or scratching the sofa-legs. One of the conditions of the sublet was that she took care of the cats and protected food and furniture from their assaults. She found the pistol handy when she was eating her solitary meals at the kitchen table.

Max, her landlord, gave her custody of both cats and weapon the day after she moved in: "The professor left this for you. It doesn't hurt them, he says, but it sure does freak them out." He grinned, showing a gap in his back molars where his insurance had fallen short. "Between you and me, I think Ted and Sylvia like a good brawl." She smiled, caught him looking sideways, curiosity showing briefly in the tilt of his head. "Well, enjoy." And he was off to fix an outside light so that she and the other tenants didn't have to fumble with their keys in the dark. As a landlord, Max was near-perfect: quick to answer questions or complaints and showing no tendency to ask probing questions himself.

When she first arrived, Mariam had been relieved by the fact that no one around her knew her history, nor she theirs. She had no idea who was bereaved, divorced, homesick, or ill. Whether Max was the son of Holocaust survivors or a Baptist draft dodger from Illinois. If the man who sold her this unexceptional apple had made his way to America from Vietnam clinging to a raft or the more mundane way, economy class; whether he worshipped Buddha or Christ. She liked the fact that no one knew these things about each other, nor seemed to care. But other days, this freedom left her perilously unhinged, the physical boundaries of apartment, subway, and classroom invaded by random memories from the past that she neither invited nor could bear to turn away from, knowing that when she most longed for them they'd elude her or show up only in nightmares.

At night she took the subway, the Number 6 to Brooklyn Bridge, capital letters pasted on pillars and signs, a child's alphabet. The cinder smell of the subway platform made her cough. Once inside the train the smells were fleshy, warm, and rank. Wet wool, sweat, stale tobacco, piss, and other, more subliminal odours. To the exiled or bereaved, smell is the cruellest sense. Its synaesthetic properties tease with false promises, tag-ends of memories that shred as soon as you begin to examine them, scraps of a dream. For almost two weeks after she came home from hospital, Nasima had slept with Deena's sweater, the one that she'd left at the apartment when they went out that day. On the nights she'd been able to fall asleep she woke in the dark and held the sweater up to her face, inhaling the last traces of her mother— weaker every day as they mixed with her own smell, the smell of the bed, the household air. One day she couldn't find it when she woke up. She had run sobbing into Mariam's room for help, white-faced from the physical pain triggered by a frenzied tossing of the bed. Mariam found the sweater where it had fallen, underneath. Nasima snatched it from her and held it to her face, and then all of a sudden gave it back to her, still hiccupping swallowed tears. "Can you throw it out, auntie?"

"Really?"

"*Ay*. Please. Or give it to someone."

The smell that haunted Mariam here was some kind of plant that her neighbours grew, a bitter, piney smell that reminded her of the hills. It was very faint, of course, but on damp mornings it made her catch her breath.

Some of this, the less revealing details—nothing, of course, about that memory of Nasima's suffering—she described for Mouna on the way back from the airport. They parked the car and made their way up the steep staircase. A clangour of locks and the front door swung open. Nasima was waiting for them. "*Habibti*! You look so beautiful!" And it was true, she was a lovely girl again, a bit too thin, yes, but not a famine victim any more. They put their arms round each other and Mariam hugged her tight. "It's so good to be here, all of us together again!" she said. Each thinking of at least one person not included in that "all."

forty-four

"I'll call tonight and see how you are, OK, honeybun?" Instinctively with Felix, Lydia fell back on endearments from her own childhood, which meant quoting Phil; Elise, except for the actor's impersonal, multi-purpose "darling," not having been much for sweet talk. Rosalie only ever called Lydia and Matthew by their names.

"OK."

"And you'll be a good boy for Uncle Matt and Auntie Ruth?"

"Will you bring me a present?"

"You bet."

"OK, bye." He sounded so breezy. She'd been right about him hoarding speech: once he started, his vocabulary was surprisingly large and most of his syntax note perfect. *He's been spying,* she'd thought, *listening until he was sure he wanted to join us.* She remembered one night, before he was talking coherently, when she had brought him to a dinner party at Matthew's. They'd put him to bed upstairs but he'd woken up and come down in the middle of dinner; he had stood by Matthew's chair in his pajamas and delivered a monologue, unintelligible except for its tonal shifts and inflections. They could hear hesitations, the end of sentences, moments of surprise and alarm, without any understanding of what his story was actually about. He'd stopped talking abruptly, put his arms up for Lydia to carry him back up to bed, where she tried to suss out whether he'd had a nightmare or a pee accident. He was fine. He'd just wanted to say his piece, the content of which remained a mystery.

Ruth opened the door to them, looked at Lydia coolly and took the bag with Felix's things. Then she rubbed Felix's head and put her arm round him. "Hi, sweetheart. Did you say goodbye to your mom? OK, come and see the amazing new train-track Uncle Matt's built for you."

She waved goodbye quickly and shut the door a little faster than Lydia had expected, catching her unprepared. She stood alone on the porch for a minute, picturing Felix's face, his big, always slightly questioning eyes, dark hair standing up at the crown, intent, serious expression as he'd asked her about presents, his look of contentment as Ruth led him into the house. She felt the precipitous swoop of dread that his happiness sometimes invoked. Its source was indistinct, but something to do with the usual clichés about children's innocence and vulnerability; sentimental truisms that she shied away from in news stories because the child she knew best was so much more complex in his passions and rages, so much earthier and more vivid than those angelic victims of tabloid narrative. His pungent small-boy smell. His amoral impulses, slowly being reshaped by adult discipline. There was something that she saw in him, and in other children, a kind of unconscious integrity, not to mention the fortitude it took to negotiate the ordinary, unreasonable adult world, that, when she was feeling so inclined, caused her to make fierce and useless promises to herself to protect her son from harm forever.

She started for her apartment to pick up her bags. She zipped her jacket up to the chin and watched her breath puff ahead of her in the still-cool spring air, small clouds of engine smoke. Things at Ruth's had gone much faster than she'd expected, and on a whim she walked past her place without stopping and climbed the steps up to Casa Loma, to burn off some nerves. The steps had been part of her training route when she ran cross-country in high school, a memory that gave her psychosomatic shin splints. Ahead of her a woman had paused on the second landing to catch her breath. Bent over, palms on her thighs, she smiled ruefully at Lydia, still able to jog up the whole thing in one go, though unquestionably not as fast as she once could. At the top of the steps she turned to look, to locate her street and the house with her apartment on the main floor, four musicians upstairs; further east, she could see the top of Matthew and Ruth's street, but a curve in the road obscured their house. If she kept walking north she could go into the park, past the water treatment plant and down into the ravine that had wound through her first days in Toronto. Then, if she continued along the ravine she'd pass underneath Elise's and come up beside Rosalie's building. From up here the trees were spindly clumps. Spring was still tentative. She was catching the 2:30 train and she should hurry. She ran quickly back down the steps.

Before she left she phoned Rosalie. It took a long time for her grandmother to get to the phone, longer than it used to, and Lydia had recently helped her set the ringer on her answering machine so that she didn't have to rush or miss a call.

"Felcia?"

"Who?"

"Where have you been?" Rosalie sounded unlike herself, confused and querulous. "Lydia. Oh." She sounded disappointed now, but more alert.

"I'm off to Montreal, just wanted to call and see how you are."

"Fine, I'm fine. Busy." As if she wanted to get off the phone. Lydia could feel Rosalie's attention drifting away and circling back. "You won't be at the party?" Ruth had told her already.

"Mum knows. I'll bring her a lovely present."

The silence at Rosalie's end was blank, as if she was staring into space, waiting for the line to go dead.

"OK then… well, drink a glass of champagne for me."

"What?"

"Never mind. Have a good time at the party. I'll call you on Monday." Lydia hung up thinking that maybe Elise was right, that Rosalie was declining. She'd had one or two Transient Ischemic Attacks—*We call them TIAs*, the doctor had said, *nothing to worry about, we can't see any permanent damage on the scans*, but they may have altered her brain in some small but vital way. It was not uncommon for that to happen, he'd said, though it didn't always, and often not permanently. Just then Rosalie had interjected: *TIA. Sounds like an airline*, sounding completely herself. They had all laughed, she and Lydia and the doctor. *You may find you lose the odd word, or that your emotions fluctuate in unusual ways: you might be temporarily more volatile than usual, or less so.* Rosalie had nodded, seeming unconcerned, though to Lydia, for whom she had always been the most consistently level and sane person around, the thought of her being "less so," however fractionally, was disturbing. And now sometimes she did seem off balance, even a little depressed. Lydia would take her out for lunch when she got back, to the Coffee Mill, one of Rosalie's favourites.

The night before, Lydia had woken in the dark to find herself crouched on her heels in the middle of the bed as if something slimy had touched her feet. She couldn't recall what her dream was about, but the panic that came with it took its own sweet time to fade. Her room had looked foreign, shapes ominous, like sweater-monsters to a small child with the night-time heebie-jeebies. She had crept into Felix's room to make sure he was OK. He was sleeping on his back, arms wide, his duvet shucked down below his hips. She had pulled it up to his chin and gone back to bed. Inside ten minutes she was up again, putting the kettle on for tea.

There's no lonelier time than pre-dawn to assess your own wisdom; self-confidence bottoms out, your own small sins and bad planning make themselves known. Lydia had paced the kitchen waiting for the kettle to boil. What was she thinking, going to Montreal? Lying to Ruth, and, by omission, everyone else, all for this double fool's errand? How could talking to Mouna, of all people, affect the future in any positive way, any more than seeing Rafa Ahmed would ease the past? It wasn't as if Rafa would suddenly confess to Phil's murder, after all this time. Lydia should follow Rosalie's advice. Let the past take care of itself, worry about the future. But the past and the future refused to be neatly separated. Rafa Ahmed, Phil, Athens, Beirut, Farid, Mouna, and Felix were all mixed up together.

Dreams that included classrooms, microphones, metal detectors, and failed speeches had increased exponentially over the past two weeks. Some nights Lydia was delivering a keynote address but had left all her notes at home. The last coherent dream that she could remember featured Phil giving the Annual Safety Speech (the ASS) at her primary school in what would have been the year after his own death. Apart from that wrinkle and one or two others, the dream was remarkable for its verisimilitude in detail and atmosphere. In her dream she was un-fazed by Officer Phil's identity, as she was by the fact that the police-woman, at first a stranger—one of those faces plucked mysteriously from her visual memory vault—became Jenny Richardson, and, fol-lowing dream logic, took off her clothes. Phil ran through his topics and when he got to Suspicious Packages, Lydia was suddenly at St. Clair West subway stop, with Felix. An abandoned Adidas bag sat next to a rubbish bin. Which was the dangerous object? Bag or bin, bin or bag? She grabbed Felix's hand, yelled at him to run. Too late. *Boom!*

She had made her tea and taken it to bed, where she sipped it slowly. It was comforting to look around and take stock of her room's familiar contents: her chair and desk, the movie poster of a man and a rhinoceros in a boat, the man humpbacked with the strain of row-ing. On her dresser, domestic photographs: a childhood photo of her and Matthew, one of Felix (on her bookshelf there was a photo album crammed with pictures of him, most taken by his doting uncle) Ros-alie, and other family and friends. There was a snapshot of Athens from Lykavitos. One of Lydia and Francine that Farid must have taken. None of Farid himself.

She had told herself then that she would call Matthew and Ruth and come clean about this trip. But if she came back empty-handed— no news of Farid, no clearer sense of Rafa Ahmed's actions so long ago—what good would it have done to tell them? *Why isn't Armitage going?* It nagged her. Was it old news for him now that his book was done, and he was screwing, not to mention living with, his former col-league's widow? And what about the widow? What would she make of the news that Rafa was in Canada? Or, for that matter, that her grand-son was half-Lebanese? By the time morning had arrived and she'd dropped Felix off, the urge to confess had worn off.

Arriving in Montreal, Lydia had a strange, overlit feeling, like the pre-cursor to flu, electric and slightly queasy. She took a taxi from the station to the hostel where she was booked for the next two nights. Concordia had arranged special rates for the conference, and there was a small crowd at the front desk when Lydia checked in. The woman at the desk—Julie, said her nametag—was answering questions about door keys and directions to the university. A formal dinner for the more high-powered delegates was taking place that night. Maximum security, of course.

To get a pass to the conference had required some finessing. Outright fraud, really. Conference attendance was tightly controlled for reasons of demand and security, and most spots were reserved for students. Lydia had enlisted the help of her friend Dilip, who worked in the audiovisual library at U of T and had access to the office where student cards were validated each year. He took Lydia's old card and managed to sticker it with a graduate student tag, date and laminate it, and then together they forged a letter from her "supervisor" in Middle Eastern studies. Since her card was under the name Marcus, there were apparently no red flags raised about homicidal Devlins coming after Rafa, but Dilip forged an *i* at the end ("Instantly Italian!" he teased her), just to be safe, and two weeks later her authorization arrived. Dilip's only fee, he said, was a beer, at her expense, once the conference was over and done.

Lydia's first night in Montreal was dreamless, but not peaceful. Mouna's face, summoned from memory, hovered like a mocking gremlin, taunting her with the knowledge that she should call. There were no phones in the rooms, just one in each hallway and three in the lobby, but she had got the number from directory assistance and put it on the night-table beside the alarm clock so she'd have to face it first thing in the morning. Before she went to bed, she had called Ruth's from the hall phone, hoping to talk with Felix, just to hear his voice, but Matthew said he was asleep. Ruth came on the line briefly. "We saw Rosalie today."

"How is she?"

"A bit tired but OK. How's it going there?"

"Well, the first meeting...."

"Cut the crap. I read about the conference."

"I should have told you."

"Too late now. We'll all be at Elise's tomorrow night if you want to call. I hope it goes well for you." Ruth hung up.

Lydia imagined herself getting on a train, or better yet an airplane, zooming back to Toronto and scooping Felix up in her arms and taking him back home, to his own bed, where he belonged. Forget about Farid, Mouna, Rafa, all of them. She would stop fretting about the past; sink into her life as a mother, as properly dutiful daughter—which would mean that she'd spend tomorrow night celebrating her mother's birthday instead of here in Montreal. If she were another kind of person, that is, and if she hadn't come here to face both Mouna and Rafa. In spite of her embarrassment, it occurred to her that Ruth hadn't sounded really angry. Perhaps, after all, she approved. Next she tried phoning Rosalie, but there was no answer. She must be asleep early. Lydia's own sheep-counting was fruitless and she spent the night in a state of waking hallucination, not dream, not full consciousness, but certainly not sweet, blameless sleep.

forty-five

Conference day: cold but sunny, and the voice on her clock radio said it would warm up throughout the day. Lydia lay in bed listening to the local news. Closures on the highway due to an accident; a chunk of concrete had fallen from an overpass and hit a car. No one seriously hurt, which seemed incredible. The city had been promising for months to do minor repairs on that stretch of road and now there would be an inquiry. A big turnout, including protestors, expected at the historic *Peace and Reconciliation Conference* at Concordia's downtown campus. The university had considered making it a long weekend and cancelling classes for the day but decided against it, cordoning off an area surrounding the hall where the conference was happening and asking that students attending class avoid that route for ease of movement and their own safety. It was expected that the influx of people would balance out: some students would stay away voluntarily, while others were skipping their Friday classes to attend the conference.

A white scrap of paper beside the bed reminded her of what she had to do. She took a shower and went downstairs, where there was a table set up with coffee and pastries in the lobby. She grabbed a coffee and went to make her calls from a payphone. There were three cubicles with retractable wooden doors, like the ones in old train stations. She pulled the door to and then opened it again, overwhelmed by the funky smell of old sweat and humid breath so thick it was a palpable mist, sticking to the walls. She compromised and shuttered the door halfway. First Ruth and Matthew; early as it was, this was the time to catch them, before work, when she would be able to talk to Felix. "Oh hi, Lydia," Matthew answered. "Felix, there's someone here who wants to talk to you...." "Who is it?" Felix's voice. He sounded like a harassed CEO preparing to ask his secretary to take a message. "It's your mum!" Felix said what sounded like "no" and Matthew's voice was heard, wheedling. Lydia waited. She knew he hated talking to her on the phone, but she hadn't been able to resist, and this was her punishment, magnified no doubt because she had gone away. When she came home he would ignore her outstretched arms and stick himself to Ruth or Matthew, make her woo him back. She knew this because of what happened even when she left him with someone for an afternoon or was late picking him up from kindergarten. It might not take very long, but it was always painful in a small but exquisitely precise way. Now she heard the phone being passed and the sound of his breathing. "Hi bunny!" "Hi hi hi hi hi hi," he said, manically, and dropped the phone heavily. She waited. Matthew again. "That was it, I'm afraid. He's having a great time, but dying for you to get back, of course." He didn't mention what she was doing in Montreal, though Ruth must have told him by now about the conference, confirmed by his next question. "You OK?"

"Thanks, Matt... for everything...." She didn't know how to finish.

"Don't worry about it. Gotta go. I'm late for work and Felix has to get to daycare." She put the phone down feeling less like a mother than an unpopular, desiccated maiden aunt. She would have liked to phone Rosalie, but didn't want to disturb her so early. *OK, nothing for it.* She dialled one more number, culled from directory assistance.

"*Oui allo?*"

"*Je cherche Mouna Ammari.*" *Déjà vu.*

"*Elle est déjà sortie. Vouz voulez laisser un message?*"

"*Non... pardon, oui. S'il vous plait. Je m'appelle Lydia, et je veux... je vais essayer plus tard.*"

"Lydia...." The voice repeating her name sounded very young, polite but incurious.

"*Oui. Je voudrais laisser mon numéro à Toronto, si c'est possible?*"

"*Vous êtes à Toronto?*"

"*Non, non, mais j'habite là. Je rentre chez moi demain après-midi.*"

"OK." The voice was preoccupied now, eager to end the call. Lydia quickly left both numbers, the one at the hostel and the one at home, and hung up, glad to get off the phone herself.

The tray of pastries had been picked clean except for some sad-looking halflings and scraps, but she was too nervous to eat anyway, so she refueled her coffee cup and got ready to go. She felt so unready, separated from herself. She needed a jolt, a slap to wake her from this vagueness, this swimmingly dopey inertia that was so stupefying she could hardly get herself together to grab the basics, directions, coat and knapsack, money. For a minute she lay back on the bed, her body leaden with passivity. She closed her eyes and in spite of the caffeine fell instantly asleep. She came to, the sound of her own slow, heavy breathing, the clock ticking, and sat up, panicked—she had missed it all, slept through it!—but it was only a few minutes later. It was as if she'd gone into a tiny swoon. She yawned desperately and stretched her jaw as if she were clearing her ears on a transatlantic flight. *Wake up!* She jumped up and got her things and went downstairs.

The conference was very close to where she had arrived by train, which in turn was not far from the hostel. She walked fast, trying to guess which of her fellow pedestrians were also headed for the conference. Most of them, it seemed. Like the children of Hamelin they followed the tune, a trickle of people becoming a heavy stream the closer she got to the campus. When she arrived and saw the crowd, the news vans and police, she tucked her elbows in and straightened up, flipped her pass so her photo was visible and began the climb up the crowded steps.

forty-six

The phone rang twice and stopped. Mariam heard Nasima's voice from the bedroom, and soon after, she heard the shower start. "She'll check the water a few times before she's dressed, and maybe after too," Mouna had said, trying to prepare her aunt for the expansive range of Nasima's obsessions. She had gone in early to help brief delegates and find out if there were any changes to the schedule; Mariam was to help Nasima get to class and then make her own way to the conference with the special pass Mouna had arranged for her. "You take her every day?" she asked.

Mouna's answer was a shrug. Who else was there? Nasima would improve, the doctor said, over time; it was all part of the adjustment, part of grieving and recovery. Not at all unusual. *Eeazeem*, thought Mouna. *Great: thousands of crazies who spend their lives turning dials and checking thermostats.* Sometimes she had to leave the room so she wouldn't scream at her little sister to stop, please, for fuck's sake, stop flicking a switch for the millionth time. She didn't say this to Mariam.

"Try and reassure her, but don't get too involved or you'll never get her to class," is what she said. But perhaps Nasima was soothed by her aunt's presence; after she had done her usual rounds, she watched attentively as Mariam checked off the items on her fingers, and followed her out without checking the door more than twice. They had walked half a block when she put her hand in Mariam's, holding it tight like the little girl she still was in many ways. It gave Mariam a strange, precipitous feeling, memories of walking a child to school in the early morning. She had to remind herself that her niece was a young woman, not a child at all. Nasima's hand in hers called up reserves of tenderness that had sunk lower than she'd realized.

Mariam ruffled her hair. "You should be wearing a hat." She pulled Nasima's scarf up and covered her head, wrapping it round her until she looked as if she were in *hijab*. Nasima giggled. "It's too tight."

"Here." Mariam loosened it and was almost tipped off-balance when Nasima threw her arms around her. "I'm glad you're here, Auntie." She looked even frailer inside her scarf. She had a drawn look, still, around her mouth, as if that part of her face were aging much too fast, faster than the rest. Looking at her made Mariam angry, but she didn't know where to direct her anger, or at whom.

Her niece was telling her about political science, her elective course. "It's my worst day of the week."

"You don't like the class?"

Nasima grimaced. "I'm no good at it. It makes my stomach hurt. But Mouna says it's important. And I can drop it if I'm still doing badly after the exam."

"But you won't do badly, you'll study," Mariam nudged her. "*Ay?*"

"Here's the bus stop." The sun had risen properly now and the air was clear and bracing. Their timing was good: they stood there only for a minute or so before the bus came.

"*Merci, madame,*" from the bus driver, wearing vinyl gloves and a scarf that covered his chin, his dark blue down jacket thrown over the back of his seat. Slushy rivulets of melted snow flowed up and down the bus, in the grooves of the floor. Everyone's boots and hems were speckled with brownish-grey splotches.

Last night Salma came over and they played cards, Nasima winning until she went to bed. Then they opened some wine and talked about the conference, about friends back home, about Leila and Tariq in Paris, Farid, other friends in London. "And Nadim stays? Grace too?" Salma shook her head. Later, after Salma had gone home and Mariam was in bed she heard someone else come in, someone who went straight to Mouna's room. There was no sign of a guest the next day, but the unmistakeable sounds of a woman's stifled orgasm, very early in the morning. It was difficult now to remember what that felt like. The woman who'd loved early-morning sex with Nadim, who'd been consumed, however briefly, by lust for Tom, where was she now? Prolonged stress and sadness had made a celibate of her. The thought of letting someone touch her had become less rather than more plausible as the months, now turning into years, had passed since Deena's death, and the war went on, even now that she was far from it. It was scarcely self-denial, since she didn't even feel the lack. That part of her had closed up shop, gone dormant, and she hardly cared. *Maybe it's just age.*

"Here we are, Auntie." Nasima was pulling her hand. The bus had stopped in front of a concrete building that was unmistakably institutional; there were signs for the conference, but it was in a different part of the university, Mariam knew. "Watch her to the door and see that she gets inside," Mouna had said. "And if you could wait a minute to make sure…." The steps were crammed with students smoking, lounging as if they didn't feel the cold, were too cool for it in their leather jackets, bare-headed. There was a blur of frenzied activity at her side: Nasima, wrestling with the scarf to pull it off her head. "Shall I come in with you?" "No, thanks." Nasima switched her weight from hip to hip, jiggling, as if counting. "Did we close *all* the windows?" "Yes, monkey. Remember? Stove, fridge, back windows, back door, taps, front windows, front door." Nasima mouthed the items silently. Then she nodded, firmly, as if she had done the count herself. "OK." She leaned forward to have her cheek kissed. "*Ciao, p'tit coeur.*" Mariam watched her walk to the doors, giving a little wave to a couple of girls huddled against the wall; Mariam was pleased to see them wave back. "She has one or two friends," Mouna said. "But she spends a lot of time alone, or with Salma. And she likes to hang out with me. It feels safer, I guess." "She'll get there," Mariam had said, touched by the solicitousness in Mouna's voice. She felt guilty for having thought twice about coming this week.

Nasima turned and gave Mariam a minimal wave, then she was inside. Mariam hadn't heard a bell, but the crowd of students on the steps tossed cigarettes, bunched into a mass and started swarming through the centre doors. For some reason, she waited until the last one was inside. There was a vacuum then, still vibrating with the displaced presence of all the bodies that were whirling through it just seconds ago. It took the air a while to settle, get used to their absence. Mariam too. All those barely adult children, whose parents must trust they'd get through the day, the weeks, the months without trauma. All those parents, who could never have completely anticipated the weight of this particular love. She checked her watch. Time to get to the conference hall.

forty-seven

Around the building, on the steps, a military atmosphere: rows of uniforms, riot gear, police on horses; and everywhere, microphones and TV cameras. A throng of demonstrators, for and against. One or two of the protestors were wearing skull-masks of the kind once associated with anti-nuclear protests, but here they meant something else. Others were dressed Gaza-style, scarves pulled up to cover their faces. The placards had the usual terse, obdurate messages, in French and English. "Honour the Right of Return" was still predominant, spanning the years since Rafa's stay in her British prison, when Mariam's family, like Beirut itself, had been more or less intact.

Mariam pushed her way past the protestors, up the steps, clutching her pass in one hand and a coffee in the other. The police were inscrutable behind their riot masks as they held back the crowd, which seethed with unpredictable energy. Metal detectors had been installed in the foyer. Cresting the wave of people, Mariam shouldered her way down a long corridor to an improvised checkpoint where she was scanned and screened, warned not to use a flash camera or otherwise disrupt the proceedings. She was watched by a policeman as she dumped her coffee into the plastic-lined bin already half-full with cardboard and Styrofoam cups. Steam drifted up from the splashed black plastic, an ugly slop of liquids pooling at the bottom. There was a delay while a policeman questioned a student whose backpack contained a needle and kit for insulin. Every time the main door opened, there was a swell of noise, protestors yelling slogans, taunting the cops and jostling each other and anyone within elbow-distance. Anyone important, anyone who needed protection, had been ushered in safely via private entrance a half-hour or more earlier.

At first, the din inside the lecture hall was almost as loud, though less heated, than outside. On stage there was a long table, miked, with name cards at each seat. There was a podium to one side for individual speakers and next to it a small square table with a wide-mouthed jug of water and several glasses. On the wall behind where the panelists would sit was a long blue banner, with the words *Peace and Reconciliation/La Paix et La Réconciliation* in white.

Mariam had found a seat in the middle of a row and she kept her coat over her shoulders, where its bulk made the already tight space more cramped. She couldn't focus her attention on any one face or detail for long; her eyes skittered across the room like stones over a pond. Was that Mouna, in the second row from the front? She stretched to get a better look but couldn't tell.

She could smell sweet cinnamon. The man next to her was chewing gum manically, and he was so tall that his knees hit the seat in front as he leaned forward, unconsciously drumming on the back with his long fingers until its occupant, an older man, professorial, turned to glare at him. The drummer raised his hands in apology. "*Pardon, je m'excuse.*" There was a sociable, almost festive aspect to all the noise. Some people were laughing, others turned around to talk to their neighbours, making plans for later. Students were sitting in blocs of the like-minded, a tight community on either side. The whole thing was starting to have the feeling of a sports rally, Mariam thought. Any minute now, people would wave flags with their team colours, or start singing soccer anthems.

Suddenly the mood changed and the noise dimmed as someone walked onstage. False alarm. It was a technician, coming to check the mikes. He tapped the one at the podium. "Testing, testing." The sound of his fingers hitting the surface of the mike was a series of thuds, a bouncing ball. *Thunk, thunk, thunk.* He walked off and before the room had time to settle again panelists filed onto the stage and the moderator, a tall, middle-aged woman with high cheekbones and a brown bob of hair stepped up to the mike. There was one empty seat behind her. The room was silent now except for a few coughs. Everyone was waiting.

The moderator appeared nervous; she tucked her hair behind her ears in a girlish gesture that didn't seem quite right for her. "Welcome to Peace and Reconciliation. *Bienvenue à La Paix et La Réconciliation.*" She scanned the room. "I'm very happy to see so many of you here to participate in this landmark event." But the moderator certainly didn't *sound* happy. And the seat behind her was still empty; one very important person had yet to appear. Where was Rafa? Other people were wondering this too, obviously, starting to fidget. The coughs and sniffles got denser and more numerous. They must be bringing her on last, for security's sake.

"Before we start, I must tell you that there has been a change in the program." Now the room was almost entirely quiet, a silence attentive and ominous as the audience began to anticipate what was coming next. With fatalistic certainty, Mariam knew. "I'm afraid that one of the participants has had to withdraw due to…" the moderator stumbled "… due to a conflict." There was a low hum from the crowd. "Rafa Ahmed…" the hum rose, becoming a kind of exhalation of disappointment or disgust, almost a groan, "… is not able to join us." Silence from the audience, breath held in. Then the first drips of noise, followed by a downpour. "Coward!" a young man in a yarmulke shouted. "Censorship! She's been censored!" shrieked a woman on the other side of the room. A group of Palestinian students started banging their feet on the floor. "We want Rafa!" Now the chanting began. "Rafa! Rafa! We want Rafa. *Où est Rafa?*" As if the crowd was a single organism it stood and began to surge into the aisles, where it separated, as some people pushed for the stage, where the panelists were still standing awkwardly, like strangers at a dance, others, Mariam included, for the doors. There was a moment of stasis, then chaos.

forty-eight

The crowd was an animal with too many flailing limbs. For an unnerving few minutes, Lydia thought she might suffocate in the crush of people pushing blindly towards the open doors. All the exits were open and organizers were trying fruitlessly to impose some kind of order on the struggling mass. Once outside the doors, people spread out and streamed down the hallway and out onto the steps, and then the immediate danger was of being pushed from behind and falling, to be crushed underneath all those feet. The police were standing united at the bottom of the steps, their shields up in a row, a long, reticulated weapon to block even the most aggressive of the protestors. Lydia clung to a pillar and cowered—there was no other word for it, and she was beyond shame or self-consciousness. Just below her, two men were wrestling a sign away from a woman whose headscarf had slipped down to her shoulders. She hit one of them in the head with her placard and two policemen rushed the steps, yanking her off as she kicked uselessly at their shins. Another cop tried to arrest the boys; he got one in a headlock, but the other slipped free and disappeared into the mass of people fleeing the steps from the side. Another boy had his arm raised, opening his fist to show a rock in his hand, and at his signal, several of the pro-Palestinian protestors hoisted rocks as well, not throwing them but holding them high to make sure they were seen. Later, it would become known that these "rocks" were symbolic, made of papier mâché or Styrofoam, but at the time, who was to know? Not the police, evidently: that's when the first tear-gas canisters were thrown. Now Lydia went to try and push her way back into the building, but it was impossible to move safely forwards or back, so she crouched down behind her pillar, clinging with one arm and pressing a sleeve to her eyes in a vain attempt to protect them from the agonizing sting and burn of the gas. Tears ran down her face.

The noise was overwhelming: feet crunching on glass, panicked voices yelling at full throttle, stentorian orders from the police ranks. Lydia held on like a shipwrecked sailor until eventually the crowd thinned as protestors were arrested or moved out of the way. As soon as she relaxed her grip and stood up, she was hit from behind and she slipped, falling down the slick steps and landing heavily on her side, the wind knocked out of her. Mouna tripped over her a minute later.

Sprawled on the steps, gaping at each other, the two of them could have been survivors of a mining disaster. Some unknown substance blackened their faces and their tears had turned the smut into paste, drawing clown-like tracks on their cheeks. Their eyes were inflamed and reddened from the teargas. Lydia's hair was sticking up in spikes. Her pant-knee was torn, there were muddy stains on her shirt and she could feel a deep bruise starting to form on her hip. Somehow, she had managed to hang on to her backpack. Mouna reached over and tried to swipe some of the dirt off her, her hand brushing another bruise so that Lydia yelped with the sudden pain. "Sorry." She stood back and held her hands up to show it was an innocent mistake, then laughed, shaking her head. "I can't believe this." She laughed again. "You look pathetic."

"So do you."

Mouna's laugh turned into a cough and she bent over, hands on her knees, hacking away, big shuddering lung-bursts.

"Are you OK?"

"Never…." She coughed again and spat out some phlegm. "… better." She stood up and together they observed the damage. Placards and posters had been dropped and trampled, someone's TV camera smashed. A policewoman, whose hair had sprung loose in wild strands from her tight ponytail, stepped over and picked it up, turning it over in her hands to look for a media logo. Some of her colleagues, better protected in their shields and helmets but equally dishevelled, were also surveying the mess. Most of the protestors had run and a small group had been arrested, while another small group was still jostling, more tamely now, for the benefit of TV cameras. At the bottom of the steps, a man was crouched beside a sobbing woman. He rubbed her back in continuous circles, but she kept crying and eventually he stood up and horked his own wad of phlegm in the direction of the police-woman, who ignored him.

Mouna wondered where Mariam was. More experienced than most people here at anticipating violence, she was probably on her way back to the apartment. That had been their arrangement if they didn't find each other at the conference—or if anything like this happened. She felt broken glass crunch under her feet and looked up to see that the windows above the main doors were smashed. Her other foot snagged on someone's dropped kaffiyeh. She kicked it free and pulled Lydia by the arm. "Let's go." One of the news cameramen was still film-ing and he turned his camera on them, but Mouna moved quickly past, her arm up to block his view of their faces, dragging Lydia with her.

"Where are we going?"

"My car."

Lydia was shivering from cold—her coat was marooned in the conference hall, and all the doors were locked, with no way to get back inside—and delayed shock, and being inside the cocooned safety of a car seemed like a good idea. Except once they got there the car wouldn't start. Sitting in the frosty interior, hands clamped under her thighs and teeth chattering so that it was hard to get the words out, Lydia said giddily: "Well, we're shit out of luck today, aren't we?"

"It's the alternator. It'll start in a minute." Lydia nodded, still trem-bling violently. She looked out the front window trying to see what was happening. People were heading for their cars or towards the métro, some slowly as if dazed, others rushing to escape. Mouna leaned over into the back seat and grabbed a blanket, tossing it to Lydia. "Use this." Gratefully, Lydia wrapped it round her shoulders, and while she couldn't yet stop shivering entirely she could feel her body beginning to calm and settle. "Give me your hands." Mouna rubbed them be-tween hers, which were warm. She did it briskly, not tenderly, but the gesture was so kind that Lydia could feel tears—real ones, not chemi-cally induced—begin to well. She fought to suppress them. She was

not, fuck it all to hell, going to cry in front of Mouna. She tried tough-
ness instead: "So, I have to ask," she said. "What the hell are you doing
here?"

"Shouldn't I be asking you that?"

Their breath was visible inside the car and Mouna's words were
punctuated by small white gusts that seemed to emphasize what she
said. In spite of the words, her tone was not emphatic. She spoke softly,
in soothing cadences unfamiliar to Lydia, though they wouldn't have
been if she'd seen Mouna with Nasima, or in the camps, or here with
some of the women at the Refugee Centre. "Were you hoping Rafa
would confess to your father's killing? Was that the plan?"

Lydia sighed and answered semi-honestly. "I don't know. I just
wanted to see her."

"Me too." Mouna stopped rubbing Lydia's hands, but she continued to hold them, and she was so close that Lydia could feel the
warmth of her breath and smell the coffee she'd had with breakfast,
the acrid musk of cigarettes. "Anyway, it's too late to find out the truth
about your father now. Too long ago, too many versions."

"What do you mean?"

"*Rafa did it. The Israelis did it. Hezbollah.* You think anyone really
knows? Even the person who did it may not know why, or who for."

"There has to be a reason."

"Sometimes the reasons come after." Mouna coughed again and
covered her mouth for a second. "Why do you think there was a riot
today?"

"Because Rafa didn't...."

"Because we were all afraid. And fear made us angry." This didn't
sound like Mouna—not the Mouna Lydia remembered, anyway—any
more than the measured softness of her tone. "You know how my
mother died?"

"Your mother's dead? When?" Lydia began to sense, ghost-like, the
tentacular ramifications of this news. Mouna waved her hand impa-
tiently, as if to say *of course* or *what does it matter when?* "That's why
we're here. My sister was hurt. You want to know how it happened?"

"I… if you want to tell me."

"Are you sure?" She took Lydia's silence as assent. "They were shot. *Umma* died and Nasima was hurt because of me. A stupid old grudge, personal, not even worth remembering. But combined with the new politics of Beirut…."

"I don't understand."

Mouna laughed, and Lydia didn't know why. Then she switched dizzyingly to another track. "The big blond woman in Athens, the one who followed you around?"

Lydia's teeth had started to chatter again, and she felt sick. "Cyndra?"

"That's her." Mouna shrugged. "American. Or she may have been an Israeli. She may not be anyone, we'll never know. Maybe she was another mistake." She was squeezing Lydia's hands now, and it hurt, but Lydia barely felt it. She was hunched forward, remembering Cyndra's eyes moving restlessly, lighting on faces, on her and Francine, in what had seemed to be a random expression of loneliness. Mouna loosened her grip, patted Lydia on the hand, with a trace, but not much, of the old condescension, and let go. "Don't try and understand." And she said something Lydia thought she remembered hearing her say before, or something like. "We're not evil, you know. We're just people who never run out of bad news."

"Let's see if my old lady has warmed up." Mouna turned the key again and after a couple of grinding splutters the car gave a sick cough and started. "Now I have to pollute the environment for a few minutes, or we'll stall on the road."

The engine was noisy, and Lydia was very tired. The easiest thing was to lean her head back against the seat and close her eyes while Mouna let the car run.

"Where are we going?" Mouna asked, after a while. Lydia lurched awake from a hallucinatory doze. "What?"

"Where are you staying?" Lydia gave her directions to the hostel.

"Still traveling cheap. That's good." Less than ten minutes later, they pulled up to the door. "A hot shower and a Scotch, that's my recommendation."

Lydia took the blanket off her shoulders and put her backpack on her knees. She felt drained of all urgency, couldn't say what she needed to about anything: Rafa, Mouna's mother, Farid, Felix. Part of her wanted to stay in this kind of gentle limbo of twenty questions, inching closer to mutual understanding. Part of her knew Mouna was right—she might never understand. They might never understand each other. Or they already did, as much as they could. "Thank you for getting me out of there." She had one hand on the door, poised to open it. "I'm sorry, for…" for what? Mouna's losses? For her own? For her blindness, her slow awakening to Mouna's basic decency?

"You want to know why I wanted to see Rafa?" Mouna sat slightly forward. "I was going to ask her when sending kids to school will be more important than training them to destroy their future." She took her hand and rested it, just for a second, on Lydia's. "We all change, Lydia. Even me. Even you. *Tant mieux.*" And she drove off.

forty-nine

Mouna drove fast. Mariam must be home by now. Thank god Nasima hadn't been at the hall. She shook her head. Lydia—though she had almost expected to see her—had thrown her off, and now she was dizzy from tear gas and delayed shock. She pulled the car in back, into the little parking space behind the building, and slammed her door hard, something she was always telling Nasima not to do to the poor old shitbox. "One day that door'll fall off and then who'll pollute the atmosphere on your behalf?" When she went to lock the passenger door, she saw a brown leather wallet, half-hidden under the seat. Lydia must have dropped it. *Fuck.* Typical. She'd have to go back to the damn hostel. Not now, she needed to check on her family first. This time Lydia would have to wait for rescue.

She took the metal staircase two steps at a time, almost killing herself when she slipped on the icy top step, pinwheeling backwards for a heart-stopping moment and then lurching forwards, half falling through the doorway as the back door opened, Mariam on the other side. "Mouna!" Mariam grabbed her by the shoulders. "Thank god. We saw you on the news!" Mouna could hear the television from the living room, near the front of the apartment. "Auntie, some people were arrested!" Nasima called out. "It's OK, Mouna's home." To Mouna: "You're not hurt? We've been worried."

"I'm fine." Mouna splashed water on her face from the sink, poured herself a long glass of cold water and drank it down, gulping. She wiped her face with a kitchen towel, leaving black smudges. She turned to Mariam. "How did you get home?"

"I took a taxi."

Mouna turned around and bumped into her sister, coming her way at high speed. "I'm OK, monkey." Nasima was a little pale, but not in the state Mouna had feared, thanks to Mariam, no doubt.

"What did they say about the conference? Why did Rafa cancel?" No one had said anything at the briefing beforehand, and Mouna had tried to look for fellow committee members afterwards, but no luck. The dean and the other big shots had melted away, been spirited with the guests into safe limos and entourages, away from the anarchy on the front steps. No tear gas for them.

"She said something in an interview this morning."

"She hasn't given any interviews!"

"Well, that's what the announcer said." Nasima looked put out.

Mariam put her hand on Mouna's arm. "Rafa gave a taped interview. It was to air tonight, after the conference, but someone leaked it and apparently what she said made the administration decide to cancel her appearance. They say she violated the intent of the conference. We heard there was a riot... I'm so relieved you're okay." Her hands were at her sides, clenching and unclenching. She looked more like Nasima than Nasima did.

Mouna gave her a quick hug. "*Ma te'tal hammeh.* I'm fine. Everything's fine." Mariam motioned to the sitting room and Nasima followed them sulkily. "OK. Let's watch." Sure enough, when they switched on the CBC, they were playing the interview over and over. Mouna was breathless. *There she is. Rafa.*

Following the first half of Mouna's advice, Lydia had a hot shower and a change of clothes. She'd have to find herself another coat, if she could, to go home in. There was no television in her spartan room so she went downstairs to the common room, where people were crowded round the communal TV, chattering. "Ssh!" someone hissed. "Listen!" A low, speculative murmur continued, all the same. Barbara Frum was doing an intro, detailing the conference and the sensational background of her guest. The set was bland and bright, one of those nondescript backdrops where journalists and their subjects regularly confront each other. As Barbara Frum's monologue wound down and the camera began to pan, the voices around the TV set started to fall silent. A figure walked into the frame and there was a collective sigh from the people in the room. *Here she is, in the flesh.* Or on the screen, anyway, right in front of their eyes. *Rafa.* Frum shook Rafa's hand and she settled into a chair across from her host. Lydia imagined that she could smell the tainted alloy of nicotine and perfume on her skin. That face, deeply charismatic, still sphinx-like, even more so with some added flesh. Still beautiful, too, her head uncovered now, a crisp matron's haircut, a cigarette in her hand. She was a chain smoker, worse than Mouna. Worse than Phil.

Mouna and Mariam were leaning towards the set as avidly as winter campers before a fire. They scrutinized the familiar face, taking in the new hollows and grooves in her skin, her features both more sharply defined and softer at the edges, where she'd lost her youthful tautness. Each woman was assessing her for evidence of what her life had been like in the intervening years. Her voice was deep and slightly harsh, deeper even than Mariam remembered it, perhaps from all those cigarettes; smoking, she told Barbara, was her only hobby. Her charm had deepened too, but she was no longer flirtatious; there was nothing girlish about her any more.

What had she been doing since 1970? Barbara Frum asked her.

"A housewife." She smiled.

"That's not entirely true, is it?" Turning to the camera, Frum laid out the basic details of Rafa's career. She had been living in Jordan and Gaza. She had two children now. She was a security advisor to Arafat and had risen to a prominent position in his cabinet (some said a possible successor, if they could ever stomach a woman. Mouna had heard this rumour). Frum turned back to her subject and her voice dropped as if to match Rafa's.

"Some people call you a murderer. How would you answer that charge?"

"What is she talking about?" one of the students asked.

"I've never killed anyone." Rafa was still smiling.

"What about the British journalist Philip Devlin? It's been suggested that you were involved." Lydia had not realized that she'd been holding her breath but she let it out now in a little gasp that the woman standing next to her noticed.

Rafa shrugged. When she spoke she was no longer smiling and her voice was forceful, but relaxed. "You know, Philip was a friend of mine and a good man. I don't think he would have approved of this fixation on one foreign journalist when so many of our children are dying."

"Your children?"

"Palestinian children. Lebanese children."

"What about Israeli children?"

"The Israeli government is responsible for the suffering of its people."

"We'll come back to that. But Phil Devlin? Are you telling me you had nothing to do with his death?"

"I can tell you this. The Israelis thought that I would be with him on the day he was killed."

"Are you saying…?"

"I have nothing more to say about that." Now she leaned towards the camera herself. "What I want to talk about… what *I* want to talk about is the future."

"Can you separate the future from the past?"

"Can *you*?"

Theme music swelled and a commercial break was announced. Lydia was shivering again, as if she'd only just come in out of the cold. Someone passed around paper cups and a mickey of Southern Comfort; she took a cup gratefully, slugging it back.

I have to call home. But she had to see the end of the interview first. Lydia nodded at the woman who had passed her the drink. "Thanks." People were arguing about what had happened at the conference, and about the interview, but holding back, as if they didn't want to get into it until they'd heard how it ended. "It's censorship!" one student said, and others nodded. A girl with dreadlocks was starting to argue with him when the show came back on. "Sssh!" Leaving Phil Devlin aside, Barbara Frum went after Rafa now on the question of who was responsible for what. They were both so good at it—serious but not heavy, able to make their points and stay cool. Experts, though Rafa had the edge when it came to sheer charisma. Then came the two questions whose answers were rumoured to have caused the conference organizers to realize their mistake.

"Would you still die for the Palestinian cause?" In the paper the following day, a journalist would describe the look Rafa gave Frum at that point: *Dismissive, flat. Brutal.*

"Of course."

"Would you kill?"

"I think you have my answer."

"We all change," Mouna had said. But she was wrong, Lydia thought. Not everyone does.

fifty

"That's it?" Mouna flopped back on the couch and closed her eyes.

Mariam watched her, worried. "Surely she'll have more to say. Now that she's not in the conference."

"But not to us." *Not to me.* Mouna's eyes were hot and she wondered, dreamily, as if she were her own audience, *I'm not going to start crying, am I?*

Mariam had been fascinated by the performance they'd just watched: a woman the same and not the same, her authority fully charged now, still dangerous, still erotic, but with a matriarchal heft. Rafa had stopped just shy of showing contempt for her interviewer, but only just. "Do you know which hotel she's staying at?"

"Yes, but there's no… *merde.*" Mouna felt Lydia's wallet in her pocket and sat up. "I have to go out again."

"Why?" Nasima had a nervous tilt to her head. This was a lot of up and down for her in one day.

"Someone left a wallet in my car."

"Does it have to be tonight?"

"She lives in Toronto."

"Oh!" Nasima sat up. "She called this morning!"

"No that wouldn't have been her. I just left her now."

"Linda? Leda? Something. She said she was visiting from Toronto. She left a number."

Now why the hell would she have called here? Mouna wasn't in the mood for games. The tear gas had given her a sickening pseudo-hangover: her head ached and her eyes hurt and her stomach felt weak and jellied, trembling inside itself.

"Are you sure you're OK to drive?" Mariam's voice was full of concern.

"It won't take long. Half an hour, maybe." Mouna got her coat on again. She didn't mind going outside again, really, back into the bracing, cold air that might ease her headache and appease her awful restlessness. She took the steps more carefully on her way down. She could see where a small animal had walked across her car, a ghostly map of its prints on the roof, already frost-glazed. The wind was blowing and the light-bulb above her neighbour's door swayed on its cord and swung light into her face, shadows lurching. She let the engine run a minute and flipped open Lydia's wallet while she waited. Money, cards, a folded train ticket. Slip of paper with her telephone number on it and her name in Lydia's handwriting. She slid out Lydia's citizenship card—the kind that she and Nasima would have soon; in the black and white photo, Lydia was a girl still, unsmiling and solemn, her signature childishly rounded but recognizably the same handwriting as on the piece of paper. Lydia Rosalie Devlin. Her legal name. Height-Taille 160 cm. Eyes-Yeux Green. The wallet had a little window for a driver's licence, but she must carry that separately, if she had one. Instead, there were a couple of snapshots trimmed to fit next to each other: an old woman, and one of a little boy. Mouna switched on the roof light. The boy was about three or four, she guessed, dark, not like Lydia with her dark hair and light eyes and blue-veined translucent skin, but dark everything, eyes, brows, hair, olive skin, like a Spanish child. Or Lebanese. She frowned. He looked... she held him up to the light... no, she wasn't imagining it. He looked like Farid.

By now the shit would have hit the fan. They would almost certainly have seen the news —not when Felix was around, Lydia hoped. He was too young to understand, but he would know that the others were upset. If they'd seen the riots, then even Elise would know what Lydia was really up to, and she wasn't so callous as to allow her mother to fret about her welfare. She should have called earlier to wish her a happy birthday, anyway. She checked the time—10:30. Almost not too late, if she did it right now. Students surrounded the payphones in the hallway; all waiting to pour out their own excited account of the day's events. She went to the desk to ask about making a long distance call from there. "I have a calling card." She felt in her bag for her wallet; *jesus fuck, can I never keep my things in some kind of order?* Constantly thinking her keys were lost, her wallet gone, tearing things apart only to find them nestling where she'd first looked, the cruel mischief of inanimate objects. She patted her jeans pockets. Not there. The desk clerk watched as her fumblings became more frantic. "My coat. Oh." The wallet must be in her coat pocket, locked inside that hall.

"Why don't you call collect?"

She thought. "Can I make a local call first?" He handed her the phone and asked if she needed a phone book. She nodded; Mouna's number was in the wallet, along with everything else she would need to get home tomorrow. She found the number again and dialed—a different voice this time, an older woman. "*Allo? S'il vous plaît, je sais que c'est un peu tard, mais est ce que c'est possible parler à Mouna?*" The voice sounded amused at her tortured French.

"*Desolée, mais elle n'est pas ici. Elle vient de sortir.*"

"Shit!" The woman laughed, and responded in English with an elegant accent. "It's important, then?"

"Oh, I'm trying to find—I lost my wallet. I think it may be locked inside the university."

"Are you Linda?"

"Lydia."

"Lydia, yes." The woman repeated it slowly, and it was strange hearing a voice that she didn't know say her name that way, each syllable distinct. "She is bringing it to you now."

"Oh thank you! I mean, thanks for letting me know. That's so nice of her."

"Well you can't do much without your identity, can you?"

"No. Thank you, um, Mme., Mrs...?"

"Salibi. Mariam Salibi. It's nothing." Lydia's face flamed red.

"Ciao." Click.

"Everything OK?" the clerk asked.

"Fine, thanks." Anything but, but never mind. Following his advice, she dialed the operator and placed a collect call. Armitage picked up and she listened to him speak to the operator and accept before she said, redundantly, "It's me, Lydia."

"Lydia! We're so glad to hear from you!"

"How's Felix?"

"Fine, he's fine. How are *you*? We just saw the news."

"I'm OK."

"You'd better talk to your mother." A pause while he handed off the phone.

"Darling! It's so good to hear your voice!" Elise sounded tired, but not angry. "Listen, darling…."

"Mum, I'm sorry…."

"Darling, don't worry. Just get home tomorrow and you can drink a toast to me."

"Your birthday…."

"We burnt the lamb chops, thanks to you! We just drank lots of wine with our oysters, so we're all quite happy now."

"Tell Felix I send him a huge kiss."

She hung up and gave the phone back to the clerk. "Thank you. How much do I owe?"

"Local calls are free." He smiled at her. "Looks like you could use some rest."

"Yeah. Thanks again." She went to sit in the lounge, to wait for Mouna. It was almost empty now, people on the phone or going up to their rooms or out to party and rehash the drama.

"There you are." It was Mouna.

"Oh Mouna, thank you. This is so kind of you."

Mouna gave her the wallet. "My sister says you called this morning."

She was so tired and confused it was tempting to let it go, but even if she wanted to, the expression on Mouna's face said that she couldn't. "Yes. I called to ask… I wasn't sure if I'd see you at the conference, and I need to get in touch with Farid."

"A bit late, no?" The old tone was back.

"I tried before, in Athens. When we came back from Turkey. We didn't know where you were. Nico said he hadn't heard from you."

He didn't trust them, Mouna thought, and who was to say he had been wrong?

"Then I got through to Beirut and they said he wasn't with you. I didn't know what to do."

"We heard about my mother and sister and went home. You knew he was coming back. You had his note, and the money."

"What note?" Lydia's face was burning.

"At the hotel."

"No, I never got it." She tried to suppress the quaver in her voice. "What do you mean, money?"

Mouna shook her head. "Your friend said she'd pass it on to you."

"Francine? But she was with me." The suspicions she'd had when Mouna first mentioned her mother's death, in the car, began to spill and spread.

"No, another friend." Mouna tried to remember what George had said then. But it was just one small detail that had been less than important to her at the time.

"The only woman I knew there was Cyndra." Lydia's voice sounded thin and Mouna thought she might start to cry, but she didn't. Instead she knuckled her forehead, trying to understand. They looked at each other.

"So. A mystery. Why would she take your letter?" Mouna wondered out loud. She shook her head again, this time to clear it. She and Lydia spoke at the same time.

"Farid thought I just took off?"

"Why do you want him now?" Neither of them said anything for a minute.

"Shit." Mouna ran her hands through her hair. "His mother is at my place. Can you come tomorrow?"

"I have to get home. My…"—she almost said *son*—"mother is expecting me. It's her birthday." It sounded lame enough.

"Well, come back with me now. You can sleep on our couch."

When she didn't answer, Mouna said: "Afraid?" The same old mocking smile. "Come on." And held out her hand.

fifty-one

"Tired, *habibti*?" Nasima was perched on the end of the couch, legs crossed and one foot bouncing rhythmically. There were dark circles under her eyes.

"No." She put her fingers in her mouth and then, as if a voice audible only to her had said "stop!" took them out and folded her arms. The foot kept its rhythm, her slipper slapping against her heel.

"Let's play some cards, then." While Nasima went to find a deck, Mariam poured herself a glass of red wine in the kitchen and made a phone call. *The Ritz Carlton*, Mouna had told her. What did Gaza think of that? Rafa had never cared about luxury that Mariam could remember; she'd enjoyed good food and wine but she could do without and not seem to mind. *We all need more comfort as we get older.* That was something she had said to Grace, an apology of sorts for leaving, though it wasn't true of Grace, and she wouldn't have expected it of Rafa either. *You never know.* She reached the front desk and was told by a concierge that all messages would be given to Ms. Ahmed via a security person. Ms. Ahmed was not accepting any direct calls, he said, politely.

"What should we play?"

"Something I'll have a chance of winning against you. Which means not poker!"

They settled on blackjack, and Mariam was glad to see as they played that Nasima let go some of her tenseness, though they were both hyper-aware of any sound that might announce Mouna's return. Halfway through the third game, they heard the car pull up: feet on the staircase, more than one person, it sounded like. Mariam was suddenly nervous. Could Mouna possibly have brought Rafa with her? The door opened and Mouna came in, followed by a stranger, a young woman with big eyes and short hair, not a brush cut like Mouna's but more gamine, a swoop of hair falling across her high forehead. Her body was tilted slightly forward as if she were still in motion, not yet at rest. As if she might turn at any moment and run back down the stairs.

"*Umma*, this is Lydia. She's going to stay here tonight."

Mariam held out her hand to shake. "The one with the wallet?"

Lydia smiled. "That's me. Sorry about the expletives. I was in a state." Mouna noticed that her English accent, usually an echo inside her Canadian one, was suddenly stronger—nerves? Was it a mistake to bring her here? Too late now. Mouna opened another bottle of wine and brought it into the sitting room with a couple more glasses.

"Lydia is a friend of Farid's, *Umma*. We met in Athens." She wondered if Mariam remembered the name.

Lydia took a big gulp of wine. Her eyes were glossy, suddenly, but if Mariam or Nasima noticed, they were too polite to show it. "How is Farid?" she asked, her voice only slightly unsteady.

"Oh, the way most sons are. He doesn't tell me about his life—I'm his mother, after all."

"He's living in Paris," Mouna said.

"You haven't been in touch for a while?" Mariam sipped from her glass and looked at Lydia.

"No, not since Athens. We didn't... I phoned your house in Beirut, once, and spoke to a woman. I thought it was you, but she didn't speak English or French."

"Ah, Faiza."

"She said he wasn't in Beirut."

"No, he was there. You must have misunderstood. It was a bad time for us."

Mariam glanced at Nasima, who was staring at Lydia with her mouth open like a child at the zoo.

"I know, I'm sorry...." The awkwardness in the room was suddenly stifling.

Mouna took pity on Lydia. "*Umma*, Lydia has something to tell us, something important."

Lydia looked frozen with embarrassment and apprehension.

"The picture in your wallet?" Mouna widened her eyes, daring her. *Yes, I looked.*

"Uh…. Yeah. Mrs. Salibi…."

"Mariam. Please."

"I feel—I don't know how to—I thought Farid didn't want… so…."

Mariam set down her glass carefully. Now it came to her. *This is the girl he was in love with.* "You were a lot more than friends."

"Yes."

"Tell me."

"After I left Athens I found out that I was pregnant." Everyone in the room but Lydia, playing nervously with her fingers, was suddenly very still. "I couldn't find Farid, and I couldn't… I decided not to have an abortion." The stillness teemed now, like the conference hall after the moderator's announcement, about to erupt with noise or movement. Slowly Lydia brought out Felix's photo and held it out, watching Mariam's eyes move over his face. "This is my… Farid's son. Your grandson."

Mariam looked at the picture for a long time, holding it in her hand. Nasima put her head on her aunt's shoulder, leaning in to look.

Lydia's hands were clenched in her lap. "I'm so sorry."

"You thought he'd abandoned you."

"Yes."

"You must have been angry." Mariam sighed and looked up at Lydia. "And don't you think we should be angry? What about Farid?"

Lydia didn't say anything.

"What is his name?"

"Felix."

"Felix." Mariam said the name slowly, wonderingly, the syllables crisp and distinct, the way she'd said Lydia's name on the phone. "What does it mean?"

"I thought it meant lucky, but it's more like happy. Happy and fortunate."

"Is he a happy boy?"

"Sometimes. Mostly. He can be a bit anxious."

Nasima gave Lydia a tentative smile. "He's beautiful." She looked nervously back at Mariam, who patted her hand.

"I think so." Lydia smiled back at her, then took an audible breath. "There's more."

"More than this?" Mariam said, almost amused. "How many other ghosts do you have in your closet?"

"One big one. My father was Phil Devlin." No one said anything and she rushed ahead with the last part. "And I don't know if it matters, but my mother is Jewish. Which means that strictly speaking, so am I."

Mouna had been silent throughout, but now she said, "Farid never cared about that."

"You told me...."

Mouna shrugged. Mariam stood up abruptly, bumping the table with her knee and knocking over a glass of wine. They watched as it spilled over the edge, a thin purplish stream pouring onto the carpet. "*Pardon*, Mouna. I'll clean it up."

"No, Auntie, I'll do it." Nasima jumped up and got a cloth from the sink. Mariam went to the stove, where she lit a cigarette, then she stood by the back door and opened it a sliver to blow smoke outside. A draft of cold, damp air slipped into the room. She shivered, standing sideways with one hand braced against the frame as if she were a guest just about to leave.

"This is... quite a lot."

"I know."

"I don't think you do." She shut the door. "Your father was a kind man, Lydia, but not very wise. Maybe you take after him." She settled herself on the couch again, tucking her feet under her to avoid the wet spot on the floor.

"Did you know that your father worked with my brother, Basman? Mouna's uncle, who was supporting her mother?" Lydia's dumbfounded expression answered for her. "I thought not. Basman was killed with your father. He was his translator."

His interpreter and fixer, Armitage had written. The man in the photograph, whose face had been a mystery. Now a hazy memory

261

started to solidify. Phil's old photos, faces of people he'd met on assignment, friends, colleagues. She had seen that face before, in the jumble of others whose pictures she always found so fascinating—was jealous of, almost, for knowing her father in a way she never could.

"When I say your father was kind… he was very fond of my brother. He trusted him, relied on him. Too much—most of Basman's journalist friends did. But your father used to send money for the family because he knew Basman tried to help Deena, our older brother's wife." Mouna went to the kitchen table and took one of Mariam's cigarettes, just for something to do. She rolled it between her fingers, catching a whiff of sharp American tobacco. (*Take it.* Basman handing Phil's money to Deena.)

Nasima said: "I don't understand." Her voice quaked as if she were about to cry. Lydia, being closest on the couch, moved as if to comfort her, but she shifted away.

"After he died, your father's friend kept sending the money. He said Phil would have wanted him to. It was done quietly, so no one would know. There were a lot of questions about what happened."

"Which friend?" Yves? Lydia wondered.

"The one who wrote the book." Mariam looked at Mouna. "You met him, Mouna, though you may not remember; he came to one of our dinner parties. And Basman's funeral."

"*Armitage?*" Lydia felt as if someone was lifting the top of her head. She put a hand up to clamp it back down. She was standing in a cold, high place where the air was thin. She felt dizzy.

"That's the man. He didn't use Basman's name or photograph in the book, to protect us, just in case."

"In case what?" Mouna was waiting for the answer.

"We didn't know who was responsible. Maybe the Israelis, maybe someone close to Rafa. Your father, Lydia, was involved with things he didn't understand."

Now Mouna and Lydia were equally stunned.

Mariam looked very tired, suddenly, and frail. "I must go to bed. I might not see you in the morning, Lydia, but you won't hide from us again, I think." Her voice was scratchy with fatigue, but Lydia didn't miss the warning note.

"I promise."

Nasima got up too. For a minute they all hovered there, in limbo, before Nasima followed Mariam down the hallway. Mouna blew her a kiss. "Good night, monkey. If I'm not here in the morning I'll be dropping Lydia at the station."

Then it was just Mouna and Lydia, alone together, trying to compute this newly aligned set of facts. What if she hadn't left her wallet in Mouna's car? Lydia might have gone home without saying anything about Farid, might just have swallowed that nice little aphorism about how we all change, bye bye, *sayonara*, no hard feelings. A fuck-load easier than what sat between them now. Now she couldn't think of anything to say that wouldn't sound grovelling or craven, or just wrong. When in doubt... she swung the wine bottle towards her glass. *I'll have a hangover in the morning.* But it was morning already, getting on to 1:30.

"I'll have some too," Mouna said.

"Is this why you hated me?" It came out like that, naked.

"Why do you Jews think that anyone against Israel must hate you?"

"I've never really thought of myself as Jewish."

"Maybe that's your problem."

"I bet you didn't mind when Farid thought I'd run off with his money." *The money, the note. What a fucked-up mess.*

"I wasn't thinking of you, or Farid."

"Mouna, I'm sorry. I'm an asshole."

"This is the problem. You think all death is personal."

"But isn't it?"

"Not when it's hundreds, thousands. Then it's political." She sounded like Rafa.

"But each of those hundreds is only one. They're all personal to someone. Aren't they?"

She waited for Mouna to answer.

fifty-two

The couch smelled of cats and spilled wine and cigarette ash. Lying there in the dark, scraps of the day's conversation became nonsense in Lydia's head.

"*No cameras... drink coffee not war... we want Rafa! Rafa... no he was Faiza... you Jews are all smokers... happy boys are lucky... mother has flown home....*" The next thing she heard was her own name. "Lydia!" Mouna, shaking her.

"Come on. Your train." *Jesus, it must be close to noon.* She sat up, amazed to find that she had actually slept and that she had no hangover, but her bladder was so full that her eyes watered and her jaw ached; she ran to the bathroom for a pee and a quick shower. Even at top speed, she registered that the bathroom was not what she would have expected of Mouna: sparkling clean and girlish, all pink loofahs and bubble bath and jars of pastel salts. Her toothbrush was packed away so she squeezed some paste onto her finger, rubbed her teeth and rinsed. She wrestled her still-damp legs into her jeans and dressed again quickly, everything rumpled and reeking of smoke. When she came out, Mouna had her coat on and was shaking the car keys at her, lighting up a cigarette as they opened the back door. "Got everything? Your wallet?" Mouna's hair stood up in spikes and she had sleep crusts in the corners of her eyes. She drove with her cigarette clenched between her teeth, eyes squinting against the smoke. The perfect deterrent to conversation, not that Lydia had anything useful to say. They got to the station just as the train was boarding. Lydia handed Mouna the photo. "Would you give this to Mariam?" She surprised herself by kissing her. "And thank you." And she ran to the train, leaving Mouna standing there, cheek warm where Lydia had kissed it. Mouna sleepwalked back to the car. Once the train started, Lydia slept almost all the way home.

How does she do it? Somehow she always turned things upside down. The conference displaced by a small child, Rafa by Lydia *fucking* Devlin. She could call herself Marcus if she wanted, but Devlin is what she was, professional interloper and fuck-up. Chaos dressed up as innocence. Mouna's cheek could still feel the kiss. She slapped it away with the back of her hand, and with the tiny, stinging burst of pain, something dislodged. With a shock she realized that it was not Lydia who had made her so angry. *Not her at all, no.* Rafa, who must have known what would happen when she gave that interview. Mariam, and her lies. *How could you have known all this and never said?* She had wanted to ask her last night, but not in front of Lydia. And the money from Phil Devlin, from Armitage, what was that? Pay-offs? Compensation?

Mariam had decided to tell the whole warped story when what Mouna craved was the old beliefs, the old standbys, no matter what she'd spouted to Lydia about the mutability of truth. Outside the car someone yelled; she had made a right turn without looking, almost ramming a cyclist into a post. Anglophone, apparently, since he was yelling "stupid cunt!" his face stretched purple and oblong with fury. She almost gave him the finger but settled for a mocking wave and sped up, just in case. She didn't want a bicycle lock hurled through her window, thanks. When fear makes people angry, as she'd told Lydia, they do stupid things, damage multiplied. She cranked open her window to let in some air, warming up, snow melting, the damp breeze told her. Spring. Even the grey streets had a fertile, earthy smell. Mariam was flying back to New York in the morning, and the question was, how were they to get through the rest of today with all this new information between them? *Stick to the surface.* She didn't want to hash it all over with Mariam. She had her own plans.

Nasima was up, fully dressed.

"Where were you?"

"Taking Lydia to the station, I told you last night." She didn't mean to sound so irritable.

"I'll be late! I have a test!"

"Monkey, it's Saturday." Nasima gasped and then burst into tears. Mouna wanted to kick something. She should be calling committee members, trying to set up a meeting to talk about what had happened yesterday, to see if any of the other panels were still on today. "Come here." She hugged her sister and rubbed her back until the crying slowed down. "Why don't you make some of your special pancakes for us?" Shiver, shiver, sob. "O... O... OK." The front door opened and it was Mariam, advancing down the hallway fully made up and coiffed. What the hell was going on? They'd been up most of the night and already the apartment was a factory of activity. Mouna, the only one who had a pressing reason to be up, was wearing pajamas under her coat. "I went to get cigarettes," Mariam said, though no one had asked. "Is everything OK?" "Perfect." Mouna gave Nasima a little push. "Pancakes! I'm starving." Nasima sniffed and blew her nose on a paper towel. She began collecting her ingredients. It would be a slow, painful process, but she'd lose herself in it and the day might just recover from its shaky beginnings. Mouna went to wash and dress, hoping for a minute of privacy, but Mariam followed her. "I called the Ritz from the corner." She spoke quietly, looking back at the kitchen.

"And?"

"Gone already." Mariam shrugged. "I thought I might catch her, and then...." She made a *who knows* gesture with her hands. "Stupid. I was going to ask her for the truth."

"Which truth?" Mouna stared her down.

"*Habibti....*"

"Forget it. It's old news." Brushing past her aunt, she was ten years old again, confused, hostile, wanting to be anywhere but there. Her head was buzzing. She had a good long shower, drumming the thoughts out of her skull with hot water, stood naked in the tub when she'd finished, watching the steam rise off her skin. By the time she was dressed again she had figured out what to do with the afternoon. "How about a movie?" Too brightly, the others agreed, and after lumpy pancakes and coffee that's what they did. A movie, more coffee, an early dinner, then an early night, *we're all tired*, they said: all excellent protection against more conversation of any kind. When they took Mariam to the airport the next day, Mouna made sure not to look at anything beyond the road. The only time she spoke was to promise Mariam she'd call and let her know when Lydia had talked to Farid. Mariam nodded. "Thank you." Then she hugged Mouna, told her to stay in the car, waved, and was gone, back to New York, her students, her borrowed apartment. Mouna and Nasima went home. For Nasima, it was homework, studying for her test. For Mouna, the phone calls began: first to her colleagues in Montréal, then a friend of a friend in Toronto who might know how to find unlisted numbers.

Getting in touch with Armitage was something she'd rather do without Lydia's help.

fifty-three

The picture on the front page of *The Toronto Star* had been taken from the bottom of the steps, looking up: a clotted mess of panicked students caught in the middle of the turmoil. Lydia could see her own shoulder and the back of her ducked head behind the pillar. Not her face, thank god. The image came from another time zone; there had been such a rupture between the beginning of the day and its end, such a distance between what her expectations had been in the morning and what she knew now. More, and less, complicated. Rafa Ahmed a ghost, the witch of the west, nothing left but her empty, glittering shoes, while Mouna, Farid, Phil, Armitage, the Ammaris and Salibis, were inside her head, swarming. Farid's phone number and address were in her bag and every nerve in Lydia's body was tuned towards home: Felix. The need to hold his warm little body in her arms was an ache that had been growing in intensity since she left. Her cab drove along Front and the dog-leg across York to University, past the fountains, not yet turned on for spring, the war memorial where a young man was posing for a photograph underneath the bronze soldiers, then north to Ruth and Matthew's place.

Ruth opened the door. She looked terrible. "Oh Lydia."

"What is it?" Lydia went hot and then cold. "Felix!"

"He's fine. He's with Matthew and Elise, at her place. We tried to call you at the hotel, but they said you'd left."

"No, I'm sorry, I...." She saw that Ruth had tears in her eyes. "What *is* it?"

"Rosalie had a massive stroke last night."

"Oh my god. Where is she?"

Ruth touched her arm in a tentative way, not one of her usual repertoire of gestures, and Lydia knew before she said it: "She died, Lydia. Early this morning."

Everyone rehearses these moments. Practice for loss. What will it be like? How will it feel? What will I do? Lydia had seen her grandmother's increasing frailty, of course. Had realized in abstract that Rosalie would die, but she'd thought it and then pushed the thought aside. She'd concentrated instead on getting used to the slightly diminished version of Rosalie, dealing with the immediate present rather than the future.

In any case, none of Lydia's practice would have helped. Phil's death was too distant, her knowledge of him even at the time too limited, too vague—and it was surprising to realize this—to be of any use to her now. Her anticipation of Rosalie dying had been fiction. This was the real thing. She was emptied, scooped hollow. Then the pain swooped in, with claws, scraping. "I should have been here." Voicing that thought almost made her bawl. Ruth half-fell towards her and they held each other while Ruth cried. Lydia couldn't, not yet.

When Ruth had stopped crying, Lydia asked, "Can I see her?"

"She's at the funeral home. Lydia, there's something else."

"What?"

"Her will…." Ruth stopped. The words, her hesitation after them, felt to Lydia like bad melodrama and she wanted to laugh, even though she recognized that as displaced panic.

"She wants us to sit Shiva."

The laugh belted out from Lydia's throat before she could stop it, raucous and crude. Ruth was watching her like a compassionate nurse a mental patient. "Do you want me to drive you to the funeral home?"

They didn't talk on the way, thinking their separate thoughts. About Rosalie, no doubt. About yesterday and today—the huge gap between. Time was doing funny things this weekend, asserting its pull, making itself felt.

The woman at the funeral home reception was writing something when they came in but she immediately put it aside. *Jennifer Day* her nametag said. She had a nice, square-jawed face, with tightly pulled back blonde hair, and her manner was, Lydia thought, perfect: efficient but not impersonal, with none of the rheumy-eyed faux-melancholy that for some reason Lydia had expected (too many movies, probably, and too much Dickens).

"Your grandmother's body is in here." Jennifer Day took them to a room in the back. "I wanted to ask you," she said. "Her teeth. Do you want to take them?" When they were kids and Rosalie stayed with them she had taken out her teeth at night and put them in a glass to soak in denture cleaner; they had looked strangely appealing, pink-gummed and preternaturally white. On the handful of occasions Rosalie had come into the bedroom after lights out she had looked different without them, her face softer and, weirdly, childlike. "Yes, I'll take them," Lydia said.

She was nervous as she approached the coffin where Rosalie was laid out. What did she fear? Some of it was animal, visceral fear of death but it was also fear of herself, her own emotions. When she looked down at Rosalie's face, though, she felt instantly calmer. There she was, Rosalie and not-Rosalie. She would never have willingly let herself be so closely observed. It was one of the few things she and Elise had in common: a keen sense of privacy. (Secrecy, Ruth had always called it.)

Perhaps it was a well-founded instinct. Dead and helpless, Rosalie revealed things about herself that she might have preferred to keep hidden. Her face was beaky and gaunt, the flesh fallen away as if she had not eaten for days. Her right arm, where the emergency technicians had inserted a line, was bruised brownish-yellow. Without teeth her mouth folded in like an empty purse. She looked shockingly small. Lydia looked at Ruth. "Is it all right to touch her?"

"Of course."

She took Rosalie's hand and chafed it very gently, as if to warm her. Then she didn't want to be touching her at all.

Ruth and she stayed like that, waiting, for what felt like hours, but must have been only a few minutes. They heard Jennifer Day's footsteps coming towards them. She had a paper bag in her hand that she handed to Lydia. "Here you are."

They followed her to the front to talk about the other arrangements: the service; sitting Shiva; the notice in the paper that was waiting for Lydia to look at it before it was confirmed. Elise, surprisingly, had insisted on that. Then that was it. They went outside, where a light rain had started, misty and almost warm.

When they got back to Matthew and Ruth's, Felix was there. "Mumma! Nana Rosie died!" He said it buoyantly, as if he were pleased to be giving her this vital piece of information. Then he put his arms round her as she crouched beside him in the hallway, and spoke into her neck: "Are you sad?" "Yes." He'd asked the question kindly but dispassionately. It reminded her of a day when she'd been nagging Rosalie about some health-related issue, and Rosalie had said: "I'm not afraid of dying, you know." "Why not?" Felix's question had surprised them from the other room, a scientific inquiry made by someone who couldn't yet properly conceive of death. "I'm old, and I'm tired," she'd said, "and I wouldn't at all mind going to sleep and not waking up."

"Where is Nana Rosie now?" he asked. Good question. Where does a—even inside her own head Lydia was awkward with the terms— soul, spirit sit, between death and a funeral and whatever passage follows after that? What about when its owner was unclear about her faith, or lack of it? But Rosalie wasn't unclear, was she, if her stipulation about Shiva was any indication? Something had decided her, in the end.

Home, once Felix was asleep, Lydia took a very hot bath. She sat in the tub, sweating, her skin turning pink. Something about the heat, the water itself, released her so that she could cry. She let it out, loud and guttural, hoping that Felix would sleep through it, but not being able to stop anyway. She hadn't cried with Ruth or even when she saw Matthew, who had the jump on her, grief-wise, his eyes red from already-shed tears so that she hadn't wanted to force him to break down again by doing so herself. She wondered if he felt the same thing she did: that Rosalie was, to all intents and purposes, not their grandmother but their mother, and that now they were orphans.

fifty-four

Lydia's mouth had filled with saliva. She swallowed too hard and made a strangled throat-noise just as the phone was picked up. *"Oui allo?"* A stranger's wary voice, puzzled: perhaps debating whether to hang up on yet another heavy-breathing pervert. She was glad it was this unknown woman, and not Farid, who answered. Her next thought was: *He's got a girlfriend.* Of course. Why wouldn't he have someone by now? If not for Felix and her own untrusting nature, so would she. As it was, she'd had two months of late night visits from Roman, met at the library, sexually enthralling but hardly stepdad or even permanent lover material. He raced over on his bike after Felix was asleep for an hour or so of dirty, basic sex; she never let him stay over, not that he asked. It was almost porn, sex without context. Thrilling, but not built to last. Nothing more substantial than that over the last few years, she had avoided anyone who showed serious interest; the thing with Roman was less complicated, less likely to end in tears, though she hadn't learned how to master the loneliness that always swiped her after sex, when he'd gone.

"Allo?" A brusque, sexy voice, carelessly self-possessed, uninterested in who Lydia was or why she was calling. Lydia saw an elegant, stylishly dressed pouter with long hair and perfect breasts pillowing up and over a frothy French bra. No doubt she smoked Gauloises after sex. (*Question pour Catherine Deneuve: C'est vrai que vous fumez après l'amour? Reponse: Je ne m'ai jamais regardée.*) A cliché, but why not? Blame her poor imagination for having been stuffed with clichés from years of fairytales and novels, *Vogue* spreads and French films. And anyway, sexual fantasy, especially the jealous kind, is notoriously unoriginal. The young Deneuve gave her another number, the restaurant where, she said, Farid worked—hard to imagine him a waiter—and Lydia forced herself to call immediately, so she wouldn't lose her nerve.

But he wasn't there either. *Damn.*

The Coward's Dilemma. Now she was ready, now she could handle it. But what about later in the day, or tomorrow? When you've steeled yourself to a confrontation, especially long distance—the smoothest talker stutters and balks over a transatlantic line—it's doubly hard to be forced to postpone. Few gaps yawn wider than the one between the last digit dialed and the click of a phone being answered. How deflating, then, to find that the target—ex-lover, mother, Revenue Canada—who's got your stomach in knots isn't there, you'll have to go through it all at least once more. *Argh.*

"Mumma!" A shout from the next room, Felix awake, sitting up in bed, waving his "stuffie," a monkey that Armitage, of all people, had given him. "Hey, bunny. Are you all awake now?" He held his arms up like the baby he used to be. "Need to pee." She indulged him, carrying him to the toilet, and stood there listening to the stream of urine as it plunged into the bowl, a night's worth stored up. He closed his eyes for a second to enjoy the satisfaction of it and opened them to accept her praise. "You're getting to be such a big boy!" "I know." She lifted him into her arms, his bare legs wrapping around her waist, dampness where a drib of his pee seeped onto her T-shirt. She cradled him, swaying under his weight, while he tucked his head into her neck, snuffling like a piglet for truffles. "OK, let's get you dressed." He hopped down and followed her back to the bedroom, where she helped him choose his clothes. The automatic coffeemaker burbled from the kitchen, Matthew's present from last Christmas, her chemical catapult into each day.

Now reaching Farid had become urgent in the way that anything put off does, once faced. (Mariam's expression, half grieving, half angry, but also kind, when she had told her about Felix; Nasima's gentle voice: "he's beautiful.") She had cheated all of them of his first years. Cheated him, too, and why? A childish sense of hurt pride? Her paranoid conflation of Mouna and Rafa? Self-pity? *It's not about you any more.* That bloody nurse, back inside her head. Only the nurse had taken on Rosalie's vocal inflections now. This was the kind of music Rosalie would have wanted her to face.

273

Felix pulled himself up onto his special chair, low enough for him to sit comfortably with his feet on the rung. He had a little school desk in his room now too, and liked to sit there drawing pictures and playing with cars, which he lined up around its edge and rearranged constantly to reflect his current favourite. Today he was dreamy, telling himself a story over his cereal, a sub-conversational murmur; they had a quietly companionable breakfast together while she read the paper and by then, of course, they were running late, she had to rush to get dressed and brush both their teeth, hustling out the door.

The magnolias had bloomed overnight, were already dropping a handful of splayed petals, each tree an eerie burst of semi-fluorescence. Her favourite was a star magnolia, smaller than the others, two doors down. She didn't have time to stop and appreciate it, just kept walking, Felix's hand in hers, his legs whirring along, adding an extra half-step each stride to keep up. Most of his kindergarten peers were happy to be trundled to school in their strollers still but he refused. They had to stop to look at the garden gnome that he confused with Santa Claus, swerve to avoid a double stroller, empty of cargo—*shit, are we that late?*—barrelling in the opposite direction, its navigator speedwalking, headphones and sunglasses blocking out the world. "My shoe!" Felix yanked her arm and she stopped to help him take a stone out. He stood there unhappily.

"What is it, bun?"

"I forgot my toy." It was toy day, and they'd both forgotten in the rush.

"I'm sorry, love. Maybe you could do two toys next time?"

His lip jutted out. "I want my monster truck."

Shit on a stick. "OK, how about if I drop it off for you." He looked at her snake-eyed. "Promise?"

"I promise."

"Can I have a piggy-back?" She bent down and he threw himself onto her back, his arms round her neck in a strangulating grip that she loosened gently as she stood up.

On the walk back Lydia allowed herself a moment to pause in

front of the magnolia, incongruously graceful on the grass of a frat house, a delicate sister lending her refinement to the ugly old house, its goofy fraternity insignia emblazoned over the front door. The air was spiked and brightened by a cool edge, salad hues of grass and trees enhanced, the magnolia's vivid light sharpened. She was procrastinating still. She should finish a draft for the direct mail package she was editing before she tried Farid again. It would calm her down to do some work first; she wasn't likely to be calm afterwards.

fifty-five

Lydia's most recent memory of Paris was a tiny apartment she'd lucked into for two nights her last time there, thanks to a sudden cancellation, so when she thought about Farid, she imagined him in a similar setting. As far as size went she wasn't off the mark, but his home was more elegantly situated, thanks to a young Parisian whose wealthy family was content to allow her to slum it in the name of art, but not to live in a slum. Farid paid cash for a room in her expensive but cramped apartment in the *8ème arrondissement*. Nathalie worked part-time as a waitress at *Les Cèdres*, Leila's restaurant, which was how they had met; her boyfriend had left and she needed someone to help with expenses, "quelqu'un qui ne m'enerve pas," she told Farid, scrutinizing him as if she could tell by looking whether he would bug her or not. Now there he was, her room- and occasional bed-mate. She reminded him a little of Mouna, confident, unapologetic, except that she had none of Mouna's casual vices and almost no sense of humour. She never drank or ate too much, didn't smoke, rarely stayed up late except to work. She was determined to be a successful painter, and if talent didn't get her there, persistence might. Farid was always tripping over her sketches and paintings in the hallway. When Nathalie wasn't at home, school, or work she was at a friend's studio (Farid suspected she slept with him too) where she stored her larger canvases; she had told Farid that her ambition was to have her own solo show by the time she was 25.

His roommate was the kind of person Farid had never properly understood—he wasn't driven in that way, or maybe the drive had drained out of him somehow, diffused. He thought he must be too easily distracted to be seriously ambitious. Eventually, yes, he would have to do more with his life but for now he was happy at the restaurant. Leila let him keep all the tips from deliveries. He liked Paris and the offhand approach most young Parisians, other than Nathalie, had towards work—not too much of it, and never let it interfere with the real business of life. Time off was sacred. The kids who came into *Les Cèdres* flirted, enjoyed the food, and drank plenty of red wine. In spite of their apparent friendliness there were borders he knew he couldn't breach. A set of codes they'd imbibed with their milk when they were toddlers at the same nursery schools, trundled through the same parks by their au pairs, then had drilled into them by their teachers at the lycée together. They had money, these kids, which was great for Leila, since they'd decided that her place was the latest thing. (Their parents had started to discover it too, and there was talk of a second restaurant with a partner.) The girls sat and drank with Farid, let him take them out for coffee or Vietnamese, maybe even back to his room, but not one of them, he knew, would invite him home. Even Nathalie hadn't dared tell her parents that her new roommate was a Lebanese.

Some days, before the restaurant opened and if the weather wasn't good, he took himself to the Louvre. Once a month it was free on Sundays, but even so, he didn't mind the fee. He avoided ahead-of-season tourists all zooming in on homely little Mona Lisa, trapped in her glass case (*she has to smile, no way out for her*) and stayed in the less-populated areas, or found a seat and planted himself for a while. He knew Nathalie sometimes came here to sketch, which was unfashionable among her friends, who were all doing installations and video projects, but he admired her for it. More evidence of her determination—no matter what kind of art anyone made, she said, they needed to know how to draw. She wasn't there today, he knew; she'd gone to visit her parents. Across from the museum was a little shop he liked where they sold delicate, hand-stitched cotton dresses and skirts fashionable with bohemian girls. There was a peach-coloured skirt and a white sleeveless blouse with a round collar that made him think of Nasima. Tourist-priced, but the shop-women, who were Vietnamese (they had turned him on to a couple of good cheap restaurants), were nice, and they let him pay in instalments. Today he was going to pay the balance and then mail the clothes to Montreal, a surprise for Nasima's birthday. She'd like to have something from Paris.

He wandered the museum, backing out of the way of tours and their guides. Students like Nathalie and old people came here to sketch or nod off in front of the paintings. Regulars had their favourites, just as he did. (The man with a cane sitting in front of one of the Rembrandts, he'd seen him more than once in the very same spot.) Farid's favourite was a sixteenth-century carpet in *Islamic Art*. He could stand in front of it for a long time, losing himself in the intricate designs, his mind soothed by their never-endingness. It wasn't that he was depressed—if anything, he considered himself contented—but the old restlessness never seemed to leave him. Whatever he was doing he imagined doing or being somewhere else, with someone else. Kissing Nathalie's downy ear, smelling her personal scent, a little beige, a little biscuity, certainly alluring, he imagined kissing someone else. He was always watching the horizon. When he spoke to Mouna or to Mariam, or occasionally George—and even more occasionally, his father—on the phone, he gave them all the same report. *Ma te'tal hamm. Fine. Yes, I'm fine.* And he was. It was just that at the most unexpected moments, a choking sense of claustrophobia, a kind of panic came down, an allergy of the emotions that clogged his sinuses and made his throat close up. It swooped at random, in a movie, at dinner with Nathalie, flirting with a stranger, closing up the restaurant, waiting at the métro. It was more unsettling than fear or sadness because he couldn't say what it was, exactly. But the Mona Lisa knew. *Loneliness, pure and simple.*

He was thirsty, he realized. He left the museum and walked across the street to the dress shop, where the woman recognized him and went into the back. She came out with the package, wrapped in tissue, and put it into a little pink bag. He gave her the last 200 francs and thanked her for keeping it for him, then he went to get something to drink. He might as well go to the restaurant, it was almost time to start setting up for lunch, anyway. He stepped out of the way of a bicyclist and walked along, the bag tucked under his arm. "Someone called for you," Leila said, when he got to *Les Cèdres*. "Nathalie gave her the number." That Italian girl he'd met at the cinema last week, maybe. He'd given her his number but had not really expected her to call. "An old friend, she said. She'll try again, maybe at home." "Lebanese?" "No, I don't think so. Long distance. She spoke pretty good French but had a bit of an accent."

fifty-six

Cowardice, or common sense? She didn't know—probably a bit of both—but after that one phone message Lydia changed her mind. She would try and tell Farid about Felix in the gentlest, least hurtful way possible. Long distance, under stress, knowing she was about to shatter his peace with 30 seconds of talk, she couldn't say what she wanted. On paper she might be able to revive all those words that she had crumpled up and tossed into the garbage, unfold them, refine them, find the perfect way to explain how easily mistrust and doubt can flourish between two people with so much baggage. She unplugged the phone, turned up the radio, and in two painful hours was able to set down on paper some of what she had thought about saying for three years. It was as honest as she could be. Before she could change her mind she walked to the post office and mailed it off express to the Paris address Mariam had given her. The temperature had suddenly zoomed up ten degrees, a premature spurt of summer weather, and the people on Bloor Street were festive, coatless, smiling, sweating happily in the unexpected heat. She could smell garlic and onions frying. She stopped for a falafel, ate it at the counter, watched a spindle swollen with shawarma meat rotate, dripping fat under the heat. She went outside again and felt the sun on her neck, warming her throat. She bought a newspaper and some yellow tulips, browsed the cut-price books laid out in front of the bookstore. Then she walked home to finish her work before it was time to pick up Felix. All she could do was wait until her news reached its destination and life changed, again. It was out of her hands now; someone else would take the next step.

fifty-seven

Will you come home? Mariam couldn't answer, not even to herself. And now she had a grandson, a fact that she was waiting to tell Nadim only when she knew that Farid had heard from the boy's mother, Lydia. Lydia Devlin. What a strange, strange world: that Phil Devlin's daughter should be the mother of Mariam's first, perhaps her only grandchild. What would Rafa make of it, if she knew? Or Basman, if he were alive?

Nadim had written that despite the latest eruption of violence—a huge car explosion, 67 casualties to the AUB medical centre alone— there was talk of an end to the war. Letters came fast to New York, because the university had set up a courier service, so Mariam was lucky enough to hear regularly from both Nadim and Grace. *People are exhausted,* he said. *They won't tolerate this carnage much longer, no matter what their beliefs. I think it may really be over soon.* Then what? Nadim would stay, she knew, he had told her that, but could she go back? Did she want to? Loneliness in a new life is entirely different from loneliness in an old life that has transformed around you, every- thing you knew turned to dust. "Will you come home?" he asked. *I don't know.* There was something luxurious, fluid, about her solitude, to be self-contained again and not worry about his needs, or whether he'd survive the night at work, or the pain each day might bring. Bad news, the collapse of some other familiar place or institution, the death or maiming of another friend or acquaintance. Grace wrote as often as she could, though she didn't ask directly: *are you coming back?* She said that the hospital was hoping that if things stabilized they could lure back some staff and repair some of the services that had been out of commission for so long.

Mariam was out of coffee. She looked out her kitchen window at the sky and pulled on a raincoat over her weekend clothes, an old shirt of Nadim's and some trousers. It was warm, but with the rain the sky had paled and softened and the greyness reminded her of the early days of winter in Beirut, when snow on the mountains would still be a month or so away. Grey-brown weather in the hills, the same hills where they used to go in the summer to escape the humidity. They always stopped by the road to buy fat oranges or melons from one particular stall. The vendor had a wooden leg that fascinated Farid. When he was very young he had asked if he could tap it, to see if it was hollow. The man grinned and said *ay*, go ahead, waving off Mariam's embarrassed apology. He was Shi'a and usually had his wife and children with him, the woman holding her scarf across her face, sitting slightly back from the stall. The children played quietly and helped their father bag the fruit. Sun-shot plastic, shimmering yellow and orange, dripping slices of fruit. Mariam wondered if Farid or Mouna ever felt self-conscious, as she did, that they were so visibly on holiday, responsibility-free, while the vendor's children worked all through the summer selling fruit to spoiled Beirut brats and their families. She imagined that's how they saw the other kids, anyway, cranky and whiny from the car ride, squabbling with each other, and snatching at fruit, but the orange seller's children smiled, and showed no sign of resentment. She doubted if they went to school when summer was over. Like Ali, Hamid's son, they were too useful to their family to spend hours a day being educated for no particular purpose.

Farid had been awkward with Ali, once they were too old to play together. Mariam had experienced the slight burn of the boy's gaze when she paid him for his father's bread. But she had felt sorry for him, whereas Farid had seemed intimidated, Mouna to have a definite antipathy. Passing them on Hamra, on their way to the movies or when she was taking the kids to school, he was always working. Once the war started she sometimes saw him with a barrow of old car parts, wheeling them to the mechanic's. The last few times they had passed each other, before she recognized him in hospital that day, Ali had pretended not to see her. And now he was dead. An absurd accident, so Grace had said the last time they spoke. Killed by a bullet from a gun fired into the air at his cousin's wedding.

The bell over the door to the bodega jangled when she opened it and the owner looked up. He knew her by now, and was already reaching for her usual cigarettes, the unfiltered Camels that she loved. She shook her head. "Not today, thanks." She found her coffee—fancied she could smell it even through the vacuum packed foil—and went to pay for it, then changed her mind. "After all, I'll take one pack of Camels."

"I'm a bad influence." He smiled at her. "I should be telling you to quit, like me." He pulled a package of Nicorette from under the counter and waved it at her. "Oh, life's too short." She stepped outside to find that the rain had cleared, and not a trace of Beirut remained in the air. All Brooklyn, all New World. *Life's too short.*

fifty-eight

Closing routine at *Les Cèdres*: once the last customers had left (the most stubborn lingerers encouraged on their way, at a signal from Leila, by the stacking of upturned chairs on empty tables), the staff ate a meal together and finished off the open bottles. If necessary, Leila opened one or two of their cheapest to supplement the leavings. Next, they sorted the till and divided up tips, and then the cleaning began: the kitchen and main restaurant were swept, mopped, and wiped, garbage collected and put out, dishes washed and stacked. Leila and Tariq left well before the routine was over, trusting Farid to close up. It made for a long night and by the time he got home it was often two, or later. The métro closed at 1:30 and he usually missed it. It was a good thing Nathalie's parents had money and the apartment wasn't in the suburbs. Unless the weather was really foul he could walk home, a not-unpleasant way to end the night. He would fall into bed exhausted and half-drunk and sleep better than he ever had in his life. Bottom-less, these sleeps, a slow plunge that ended only when he woke up. But gorgeous as they were, they weren't his most treasured hours in bed. When he allowed himself to think about it, he could admit that his dreamiest, most honeyed nights had been with Lydia—*faithless bitch*—the feel of her small, cool body a soothing drug; only her belly had been hot, a little furnace of digestion and fertility that he sometimes imagined might glow in the dark, pressed against his spine. Sometimes the heat there made him sweat and he had to angle his body slightly away from hers.

In the small hours he had often woken up and marvelled at how silky her skin felt against his. She liked to spoon, never slept facing him—"morning breath," she said; she hated how in films the lovers always woke up face to face and began to kiss right away. "Who would do that?" she scoffed. "They never eat, or go to the bathroom either.

Have you noticed that? And not that I'd want to see anyone take a crap onscreen, but I might believe they were human if I saw them at least open the bathroom door." He had liked this prosaic aspect to her. And her tenderness. Sometimes when he was too wired to sleep, she had stroked his back, rhythmically and delicately, with the tips of her fingers, until he surrendered all the tension in his body, his limbs turning heavy and waxy-soft, his neck prickling with sensuous delight. It didn't always calm him, this stroking; sometimes he'd turn and interrupt her with his hard-on, and they'd fuck until neither of them needed soothing in order to sleep. On the rare occasions when she'd wanted to prevent this possibility her touch had been firm and more purposeful, signalling a therapeutic goal, not an erotic one. He didn't mind that, either. Hadn't minded anything about her, then, not her stubbornness, or her easily hurt pride.

He and Nathalie didn't sleep together; the times they had sex, usually in her bed, they generally separated for the night afterwards. She liked the boundaries strict and contractual, was up early and didn't enjoy the languor of morning lie-ins that might lead to more sex and interfere with her productivity. Lately she'd been away overnight, whether at the studio or one of her other lovers he didn't know. It was not part of the contract for him to ask—and since he was more grateful for the place to live than anything else he would have kept his mouth shut anyway. He had no illusions there.

She was out now, and it looked as if she had been gone most of the day, since he'd had to pick up the mail on the way in. The usual bills, something from a gallery for Nathalie, and then another letter that fell out from where it had been tucked in between the heavier envelopes: blue onion-skin, air mail, from Canada. A Toronto postmark. He used a butter knife to open the envelope, its dull edge tore the flimsy paper, right through the address on the back, but when he held the pieces together there it was: L. Devlin. She'd gone back to her father's name. In spite of being lighter than the others, the envelope had some weight to it, something in the bottom right-hand corner. When he tipped it open a small square fell out, face down, obviously a photograph. A spurt of adrenaline. Why would Lydia be sending him mementoes now? He didn't turn it over, didn't want to see her face just yet. Instead he marvelled at how he still felt such intense betrayal. Why? It was just a fling in the end, right? Just an unbelievably good fuck, just a dream gone sour. All she'd done was move on without warning. That and take his money, which had surprised and offended him more than he could have imagined.

When he opened the letter he felt the heat rush to his face at the sight of his own name, in her handwriting. When her fingers held the pen, when she wrote, or smoothed the paper with her hand to write some more, some of the oil from her skin would have transferred. Some of her was on this paper. Traces of the body that he'd fetishized even after she'd left him—he still masturbated to thoughts of her, in spite of himself. She'd left him, beached, high and dry. "She did love you," Giannoula had said. "I saw it." The thought just made him angrier.

Dear Farid,

I don't know how to write this, so I'll just go ahead. I've thought of you many times and wanted so badly to see or hear from you... surely she was joking... *but I gave up hope. When I saw Mouna in Montreal....* Until that point he hadn't even thought to ask himself how she got the address. Lydia and Mouna? How? *I called your home in Beirut, and tried to reach you in Athens once I got back to Toronto. I was confused and upset when I didn't hear from you, and no one seemed to know where you were. Mouna has told me about her mother and I think I understand what happened, or some of it anyway. I'm so sorry for her loss, and yours.*

Mouna also says that you left me a letter at Steve's, and some money. Please believe me that I never saw either. I thought you'd changed your mind about us and couldn't say so to my face. I know now I was wrong, and I guess I should have known it then. I'm sorry I... can't fix that now... want to explain... hoping you'll understand why... he couldn't follow it, the words were throbbing, his forehead felt tight. He stopped and turned the letter over to read the end. *I hope you can forgive me.*

Even if you can't, I'm hoping we can find a way to communicate, for his sake. Your mother seemed to think we might—she was so kind when we met—his mother! What the *fuck* was going on? *—but I'll understand if you don't want to.* How had she met his mother? For whose sake? He went back to where he'd left off and read until the end, from her halting explanation of misunderstood love to the astonishing hard facts. *I hope you can forgive me.* He went from hating to forgiving her back to hating her again. Now he knew what the photograph would show him. He turned it over to the child's face, huge-eyed, almost but not quite serious, biting his lip, as if he were about to laugh or run away from the photographer. His son. Whether what he felt was rage, love, panic, or all three, he couldn't have said. He put his head down between his arms, old breakfast crumbs crunching under his cheek, welcoming the small discomfort. For perhaps the third time since his own childhood, he cried. Then he got drunk on Nathalie's good brandy.

fifty-nine

At first Lydia woke each day anticipating a response from Farid, expecting to hear from Mouna, but then she and Felix both came down with the flu, and soon after that he needed some unexpected dental care. Human nature: life takes over and dramatic events are supplanted by more mundane concerns, and what seemed urgent is merely important, and then less so, something to get to when you have time. Then two things happened that brought it all back. The first she learned from the newspaper. She was indulging her habit of reading the obituaries first, laughing over one for a man who had been taken *into the arms of Our Heavingly Father*, where, she could only imagine, his soul was seasick, when she saw on the international news page the following Reuters squib: *A Palestinian official was slightly hurt and her bodyguard killed yesterday by a car bomb in Gaza. Both victims were rushed to hospital, but the bodyguard died on the way. Local sources say the attack may have been retribution for the killing abroad of an Israeli agent last year, though the Israeli government has made no official comment, or even acknowledged that such an agent existed. Unusually, both the alleged agent, an American national, Cyndra Hansen, whose body was found in the water at Piraeus, Greece, last year, and yesterday's target, the notorious ex-hijacker Rafa Ahmed, are female. Some have speculated that Ahmed might eventually succeed Arafat, though it is generally felt that neither the PLO, nor the wider Arab world, is ready to accept a female leader. A spokesperson for the PLO denounced what he called a cowardly and unfounded attack and said that Ahmed will soon resume all her activities.*

Lydia could hear Mouna in the freezing car, after the conference: *Maybe she was Israeli.* She hadn't understood at the time. Had Mouna known then or only suspected it? Cyndra taking the letter and the money, was that just greed or something else? Another question, more unnerving: how had Mouna known Cyndra was dead? Did she have something to do with it? And why would Cyndra have been watching any of them? Lydia tried to recall exactly what Mouna had said, but it was all mixed up, the aftermath of the riot, Mariam and Nasima, finding out about Farid. Then Rosalie's death eclipsed everything else for a while. *Think back.* She remembered Nico's shut face when she and Francine asked if he knew how to get in touch with Mouna. Had he thought *they* were connected to Cyndra? Fuck. Could any of them trust each other? Ever? As for the attack on Rafa, she didn't know what to feel about that. She should feel something. Another person had died, after all. There was always at least one other person, more or less innocent, who died with or without the "intended target."

The second thing that happened was a postcard from Farid, at last. *Thank you for your letter. I will be coming to Canada in July and I would like to meet Felix then. Let Mouna know what is convenient, she will make the arrangements.* No *love*, no *regards*, or alternatively, *why the hell didn't you tell me, you bitch?* And no *please call me.* Just this curt, formal, un-Farid: *I would like to meet Felix.* She should have been glad, or at least relieved, but what she felt, primarily, was dread. She couldn't sleep that night.

She had always suffered from a fear of the moment when she tilted over the ledge of consciousness and into sleep—had always fought it, did still—and the result was night terrors. Not so bad any more, though occasionally, like tonight, they arrived without warning. She crept into Felix's room and lay down on the bed next to him, hoping that his presence would soothe her, though it was supposed to be the other way round, wasn't it?

When Phil was at home he would sometimes come up at night and sit with her, on the end of her bed or propped against it on the floor, his clothes smelling of Scotch and smoke and aftershave. He'd said that her nighttime demons stemmed from a precocious fear of death, and his remedy was to talk to her about what he imagined the end of life to be like. "A long sleep. Think of how tired you are at the end of a day in your summer holidays, how lovely it is to put your head on the pillow and drift off with the sound of the sea. I think death will be like that." He couldn't have any idea though, could he? Even then, she had known that, known he was improvising in order to comfort her. And in the end, it would have been something else entirely for him. Noise, panic, fire. The wrenching apart of body and—what? Always that question, unanswered, for her. Soul? Spirit? The end of Phil's life would have been ugly and insanely chaotic. People screaming. Yves, the photographer, deafened by the explosion, running into the gorge after him, falling, slicing his cheek—black stitches like barbed wire when he visited them in London to pay his condolences, the bouquet of lilies he'd brought lying sideways on the coffee table, their cone of violet paper turning grey and soggy, stems dripping water that stained the blond wood, where they lay, unattended.

The frames of Phil's glasses, toffee-melted by the heat, found 30 feet from the car. Yves, Armitage had written, on his knees yelling *fuck fuck fuck*, unable to stop. Other melted substances she couldn't think about. What did her father think as he was killed? Did he have time to think anything? What about Mouna's uncle, ripped apart by the same explosion? Or Mouna's mother? Were their deaths immediate? Did they know terrible pain, the searing of their flesh? Please not. Please let it have been that sudden, total sleep that Phil had wanted her to imagine. That she hoped Rosalie had slipped into. Though the thought of not being conscious—of not thinking, not being—was as unbearable to Lydia as always. Her mind turned into a panicked rodent chasing its own tail and when she started on that track she knew from experience that she had to shut it down, to sit up, turn on the light, switch on the TV for the illusion, at least, of human contact.

In Athens, she hadn't needed the light, or the television. She'd had Farid, lying next to her. After that moment of intense, dark fear, as if someone had tightened a string around her and pulled, hard, she'd move close to him, curl into his back and hold him, feeling the movement of his breath as it filled and hollowed his chest, her heartbeat slowing in time to the rhythm. They both slept better together than when either was alone, or so he'd said, though more than once she'd woken in the middle of the night to an empty bed, gone looking to find him in the kitchen or on the balcony, smoking, thinking. About what? He wouldn't say. About the past, the future, both at once, probably, just like her.

No Farid with her now, and from the tone of his note, not likely to be again, not in her bed, at least. Now that she was responsible for the safety of Felix's sleep, her nights were all about protecting him. She put her cheek to his back and listened, to the sounds of life, his breath, his pulse, the workings of his body. He was so alive. He held her hand and his fingers twitched and tightened, as if he were trying to communicate his dreams. She was nodding off, finally, when he startled her with a particularly forceful tug from his hand. She eased her hand out of his but lay curved around him still, listening to his sleep-murmurs; like this, she fell asleep too, finally, until morning.

sixty

Mouna had seen the news too; she wasn't exactly surprised by the attack on Rafa, though the rumour that it may have been Hamas was unusual. But she was surprised by the other thing. It seemed, as she'd said offhandedly to Lydia, that the woman might really have been Israeli. She'd known about her death before now only because of Nico, hadn't heard any more since, but now her curiosity was tweaked again, briefly. Was Cyndra Hansen really a spy or just an aimless, unlucky loser who stuck her nose in and stole other people's mail? What could she have thought she would find out from any of them, from Lydia Devlin, of all people? Or was it because Lydia had been with Farid, and because Mouna had come visiting? It was no secret that anyone thought to be associated with the PLO in Athens was monitored. In other countries, too, but the Greek government's support for the PLO, its popularity in Athens especially, Arafat's visits there, meant close scrutiny from all sides. But really, was it worth anyone's time to watch some aimless Lebanese expatriates and their clueless girlfriends? Well, no point considering it further, in Mouna's opinion. It was just gossip and speculation of the kind that never stopped when it came to the subject of Palestinians and Israelis.

And now Farid's letter. He was coming, and would she please take him to see Lydia and the kid. From his letter it was hard to tell what his feelings were; such inscrutability was unlike him, but maybe he didn't know how he felt or what he wanted out of it. He'd be there in a few weeks. That decided it. Mouna would come to Toronto early and meet Armitage, ask him her questions. The broader question, that she wouldn't ask and that no one ever seemed able to answer to her satisfaction, was this: How was it that men like Armitage and Phil Devlin got tangled up in the lives of people like her? First they went to get their stories, then held out their hands, everywhere except where they belonged, at home. She didn't get these selective do-gooders, never would.

She wanted badly to see Sara. They'd not gotten back on track since the conference. Mouna had been preoccupied, and later, Sara made herself unavailable. She didn't answer her phone, or left evasive messages when she knew Mouna was sure not to be home. It was only when she couldn't have her love and attention that Mouna realized how much she counted on it. She felt disturbingly like a naughty child, willing to apologize for anything, including sins she didn't know she'd committed, just to have the warmth of Sara's unconditional love restored. Was she really that weak, that needy? She was disgusted with herself, and as a result, irritable with everyone, including Nasima, with Mariam, too, when she asked when Farid was coming and how long he planned to stay.

"I don't know, *Umma*, why don't you call him yourself?"

"Thank you for the advice, Mouna. What's wrong?"

"Nothing. I'm just tired."

"Well, get some sleep then." Mariam sounded almost as cranky as her.

"I can't. Too much to do. I have a damn wedding to go to this weekend." Safia and Luca were tying the knot, as they said here. To Mouna a knot meant a noose. So she should be glad, really, if Sara was cutting her loose. Why didn't she feel glad, then?

"Well, make sure you cheer up by then."

Then Mouna surprised herself. "Auntie? Can I ask you something?"

"What?"

"You've heard about Ali?"

There was a sigh, and then Mariam gave a strange little laugh. "Speaking of weddings. I wasn't sure you knew. Poor Hamid. First Asma, then Ali. What a ridiculous thing, a bullet falling from the sky."

"What bullet?"

"He was killed at his cousin's wedding when they fired their guns in the air. Isn't that what you meant?"

Mouna was so relieved that she started to laugh too, then caught herself.

"I know, it's terrible to joke about it, but it's just so absurd." Mariam's voice turned serious and she said it again. "Poor Hamid." They both had a moment of silence, thinking of him, each with a different but equally uncomfortable mix of sympathy and shame.

"Put a nice face on for your friend's wedding, enjoy yourself and then get some rest. Much as I miss the good old days I don't want my sulky little niece back. I prefer the grown-up one."

"OK, *Umma*, I get the point." She hung up, sat back. She felt a huge weight off her chest. *Thank god.* She was not responsible. Not her fault, this particular damage, whatever else was. It was just stupid fate, bad luck. Those, at least, she was familiar with.

sixty-one

Lydia made tea for herself and Ruth. They would never come back here, once they'd taken out the last of Rosalie's things. It had taken them longer than they had anticipated, but the apartment had been paid up for two months, and somehow it was easier to do it a little at a time. Now the bookcases were empty, and would soon be gone. The prints were off the walls. Ruth came out of the bedroom, pushing a box ahead of her with her foot. "This was in the closet." It had Lydia's name on the side in an outsize, black marker version of Rosalie's handwriting. There were other boxes, all labelled by Rosalie, two for Matthew and Ruth, including some of Simon's old law books, and a small jewellery case for Elise. Rosalie must have known her time was running down, and she had started to put her things in order. Only Lydia's box was taped shut.

Lydia stared at the box. "What's in it?"

"Papers, photos. I didn't open it." Knowing Ruth, that was true. Her high-mindedness was sometimes almost scary. Lydia would not have been able to resist the temptation. She was the kind of person, her friend Tree had once observed, accurately enough, who would snoop through your underwear drawer when she house-sat. Not Ruth. This seemed like as good a time as any to tell her: "Listen, Ruth…." Then Lydia gave the spiel she'd rehearsed, that "Felix's father" would be coming soon for a visit. Ruth coughed sharply. "Does Elise know?" She held up her hand with a *stop, don't tell me* motion. "Why am I asking you that? This family is the fucking Bermuda Triangle of secrets."

Lydia admitted that she hadn't told her mother. "Actually, it's a bit complicated."

"So who is he?" Ruth sounded determinedly casual.

"Someone I met in Athens. He's Lebanese. The tricky part is that Farid—that's his name—his uncle knew Dad. He was his translator in Lebanon."

"The one who was killed with him?"

"Yeah."

"No wonder you haven't told Elise. This is kind of unbelievable."

"No shit."

"What are you going to say to Felix?"

"It depends. I'm waiting until I know how much Farid plans to be involved." Which would depend on whether they could mend some of the damage to their short-lived, fragile affections.

When Lydia got home after picking up Felix from his friend Liam's, she left Rosalie's box in the hallway, thinking she was too tired to do anything with it tonight. But after Felix was tucked in and asleep she changed her mind. She hauled the box into the kitchen and poured herself a glass of wine. Once she sliced through the tape with a knife, the flaps of the box were soft, easy to open. She had no idea what Rosalie would have thought was important, and she began to flip through, hoping for photos. She'd always liked other people's photographs. It was never landscape that interested her in paintings or photos, but faces, clothes, expressions. (Farid, she remembered, had accused her of shallowness once when she'd confessed that.) She used to read her own family photographs as if they were runes, looking at the miniatures of Phil, Elise, herself and Matthew, asking herself: *What were we thinking then? Was that the day we went to visit so and so…? Which assignment was Dad home from?* She hadn't thought about her father in that way for some time. He'd slipped deeper into the past without her being aware.

The box seemed to be full of things Rosalie had picked at random. A couple of books: her grandfather's old atlas with the dark blue cover and a silver-etched globe on the front bisected by latitude and longitude lines, an old law book—wrong box, it must be meant for Matthew. There were envelopes, used wrapping paper flattened and folded. The way Rosalie hoarded and reused things had always driven Elise crazy. She said it had embarrassed her when she was little, that Rosalie was unnecessarily and ostentatiously cheap. "It's not as if we couldn't afford new things—my father was a successful lawyer." Simon Marcus had married Rosalie Blum when she was 18 and he was almost twice her age. Lydia and Matthew had never known him—he'd died of a heart attack when Elise was in her teens.

Lydia smoothed a piece of wrapping paper, so old the pattern was faded and the tape marks had turned brown. Birthdays in London: Rosalie taking presents away from her and Matthew, her firm hands prying them from their sweaty ones—they, of course, would have ripped and shredded the paper in a frenzy of desire for its contents—to carefully peel off tape and unfold corners, then give the presents back, all revealed, surprise ruined, wrapping preserved for another occasion.

An envelope stuffed with papers, business documents. A prospectus for a company called *Reclaim*. The name immediately made her think of a pharmaceutical product. *Recover lost hair follicles! Boost your diminished sex drive! Reclaim!* There was a handful of donation receipts made out to Rosalie; it must be some kind of charity. The first page was a Mission Statement. She read it through once, and then again. *Wow.* She'd been way off. *Reclaim* was a foundation for tracing Holocaust survivors and victims, *the murdered and those who may have survived, but were lost to their loved ones.* All Rosalie had ever said to Lydia about the Holocaust was that she was very lucky to have left Poland so young, "long before all that," to have suffered no more wartime hardship than the average Briton. To have lost—in either sense—no one. Lydia had taken her at her word on all counts, which in itself was strange, as Ruth had said, more than once. "Aren't you curious?" Lydia had been irritated by the implied criticism. "What about? Why should Rosalie talk about the Holocaust if she doesn't want to? Because she's Jewish?" The handful of times they'd chased this one round the room, Ruth had assumed her know-it-all, I-feel-sorry-for-you-but-I-understand-you-poor-little-ostrich look, the one that always made Lydia question how much she liked her irritating but really very likeable sister-in-law. *What's it to you, anyway?*

Well, what was *Reclaim* to Rosalie? Belated curiosity? Going back to her roots? Or just one of her causes, something less physically strenuous than Meals on Wheels? Here were more papers: photocopied pages from historian Lewis Winton's *Holocaust* and *The War in Poland* that were eyewitness accounts of what had happened to Jews living in towns and villages near Warsaw before and during the war. Names and dates, highlighted by Rosalie, notes in the margin in her small, girlish hand-writing. Not all the notes were legible. Lydia had a sudden and distinct memory of catching sight of her grandmother in the reference library, in the history stacks. At the time she had dismissed it as an illusion, a woman of similar age and appearance, but she was sure now it had been Rosalie, in that burgundy coat she wore in all weathers except high summer swelter. Was this what she'd been researching?

In high school, along with the rest of her classmates in Grade 10 History, Lydia had seen the standard reels; she had been horrified and grossly embarrassed by her own half-sexual fascination with the im-ages; the obscene intimacy of the still photos, all those helpless naked people, women with their raw, fleshy hips and thighs, others visibly starving, stretched racks for skin and tendon, all of them waiting to die. And then footage of the Allies going in to clear the camps, corpses rolling over each other in the bulldozer's mouth, like sticks in the jaws of giant dogs. She had been easily moved then, crying over wrenching stories she read in the paper or tragedies on television; but on that oc-casion what she felt was uglier, tainted with shame. Each day of the two weeks of "Holocaust studies" she went home relieved to forget about it, only to find she dreamed about those images, woke in the night with them playing behind her eyes, an unstoppable reel.

Something else: a letter to Mrs. Marcus informing her that *Reclaim* researchers had been able to confirm the murder of Felcia Blum at Auschwitz, *please see attached*. There was no fee, of course, the letter said; this was essential to *Reclaim*'s mandate, but all donations were greatly appreciated. And here was a large donation, again in Rosalie's tilting script, painstakingly legible this time: *In Memory of My Beloved Felcia*. Lights seemed to shimmer on and off and back on again, though there was no light on except the lamp on the kitchen table. Lydia could hear her own breathing, constricted. She thumbed tears away from the corners of her eyes. Then she repacked the box and put it in the store-room in the back, camouflaged by the junk there, old winter coats, a suitcase, a pair of broken skis. She washed her face and went to bed, but lay awake for another hour. When she did fall asleep it was to an image of Rosalie on a train platform, tiny and far away, waving.

sixty-two

When she called the number she'd obtained, Mouna heard his very English voice answer the phone, the long vowels, the crisply articulated "r," not their sway-backed North American cousins.

"Armitage."

"Mr. Armitage, my name is Mouna Ammari."

A long pause in which he waited for her to say more, but she didn't. "Yes?"

"I'm a friend of Lydia's."

Now he was the silent one. She wondered what he made of that strange piece of information.

"I've read your book and I'd like to ask you some questions."

"Now is not the best time."

"Later. In person."

Another long pause. "About the book?"

"When I visit Lydia in three weeks, could we make a plan to meet?"

"If you'd like." He was too experienced to sound surprised, or to suggest a time or place until she did. "Why don't you call when you're here, and we'll set something up?"

"OK."

"You're Basman's niece." Armitage's face was as flat and calm as a Swiss lake on a windless day. (Mouna would be less fanciful in her description to Lydia, later, when she arrived at her house that evening.)

"That's right." So this was the man. He seemed so ordinary. She wondered: *does Lydia still hate him?*

"You know, we've met before."

"Yes?" Mouna noticed how intelligent his eyes were. *Old fox.*

"Twice. The first time, you put me in my place. Most impressive at the age of—what, nine?" He was using what Lydia would have recognized as his best camouflage, manufactured to cause others to underestimate him: his posh accent, wasted on Mouna to whom it merely sounded English. "It was at your aunt's apartment."

"Really. I must have impressed you, to remember this after so long." She saw that he was unoffended by her tone and not going to offer anything until she asked.

"Oh I'm well-trained. You can't be much of a journalist without a good memory." She looked at his chubby face, the bright hazel eyes, long-fingered hands resting on his big stomach. His legs were unexpectedly slim and elegant in proportion to that stomach, but still it was hard to imagine him in the field, hard to think of him ever having moved fast, urgently, running, running, to where his friends had just been hit. He'd been lean and dark, wavy-haired then. In some people a younger self, a child, even, is visible, looking out from the adult face; in others, you have to search, wait for a movement, an expression, that will unlock that past self. *There!* Running through the woods or peering out from behind a tree! The visibility of this phantom self has little or nothing to do with the aging of the body, more to do with camouflage of personality, the layers of protection a person has assumed. Armitage was the hidden kind. No sign of the child, or even the young man he had been. He was fat and what hair he had, grey going white, was combed and oiled so it lay close to his scalp, back from his high forehead. His nose was sunburned and peeling, but even that—a boyishly vulnerable detail—didn't reveal him to her.

"I was sorry to hear about your mother. A friend in Beirut gave me the news." She liked the way he said it, naturally, not too sad. It was strange, but she almost liked *him.*

"Thank you."

"What can I do for you, Ms. Ammari?"

Enough politeness. "Mouna. I want you to tell me about my uncle, his connection to Lydia's father, and Rafa Ahmed."

"I'm not sure I can give you anything you don't already know. If you've read the book, or talked to your family, you've pretty much got it."

"And I should believe that?"

He looked at her. "You haven't changed, have you?"

She shrugged.

"Why now?"

"Something my aunt said. And please, if you haven't noticed, I can't seem to get away from this family."

"They might say the same about yours."

"So let's hear all of it."

Half-way through retelling this encounter, somewhat edited, Mouna suddenly stopped. Lydia waited for a second, for the story to go on, then followed Mouna's eyes to the doorway, where Felix stood in his pyjamas. "Mumma?"

"What is it, bunny?"

"I can't sleep."

"Are you thirsty? Do you need to have a pee?"

"I can't sleep because my eyes don't fit." He rubbed them with his knuckles, for emphasis. "They don't fit and I can't fix them."

Mouna laughed. "I know exactly the problem." She held out her hand. "It's OK?" She looked over at Lydia.

"Of course." Felix climbed onto her lap as if she were an old and trusted friend. The way he did it set off a little quiver in Mouna's stomach, echoed low in her spine. "OK, close your eyes." He did so obediently. "Now put two fingers over each eye and just hold them there, don't press. Keep your eyes closed, but move them left to right, under your eyelids. Can you feel it?" He nodded, half-squinting them open. "Don't open them!" He squeezed his lids shut, so deadly serious that Lydia bit the inside of her cheek to keep from laughing.

"OK, that should do it. Open your eyes."

He put his hands down and looked at Mouna, staring wide, without blinking, as if to test the results.

"What do you think? Did it work?"

"How did you know what to do?"

"Happens to me all the time. Bad-fitting eyes. Big problem." A choked, snorting sound from Lydia, her face pink with held-in laughter.

"Thank you." He put his head on Mouna's shoulder and his arms round her neck, confidently waiting for her to return cuddle for cuddle. Again that shiver in her gut. Hard to imagine there were still kids like this in the world, so trusting and relaxed. Farid had been a little like this when she first met him—one reason she'd resented him, wanted to hurt him, trip him, push him off his bike, watch him lose some of that sweet innocence that other children, she and Nasima, for example, had never had even before the war. These kids, so loveable and loving, they were dangerous. They could make you think it wasn't as shitty out there as you knew it to be.

Lydia eased Felix off Mouna's lap and carried him to bed. She came back still smiling. "I think he's just over-excited, you know, having guests, meeting Farid tomorrow."

"Does he know?"

"Not yet. I don't want to confuse him before they meet."

"Who does he think his father is?"

"I've told him that it's someone I knew for a short time, that he had to go away before either of us knew I was going to have a baby, but that I'm going to try and find him."

"True, more or less." Mouna knew she sounded sarcastic.

"Pretty pathetic, as explanations go, but I was looking for damage control."

"He seems very… he seems to like people. He expects them to be nice to him."

"Yeah, we'd better fix that too."

Lydia seemed different, here, with her son. More adult, both alert and relaxed at the same time. Not always waiting for someone to challenge her. Certainly not the injured innocent, not any more.

"So, tell me more about Armitage. What did he say?"

"The same as his book."

"He's slippery, though, isn't he?"

"He's not a stupid man." They sipped their tea.

What Armitage had told Mouna was that he had given up, in most situations, on knowing the whole truth. "Strange thing for a journalist to say, isn't it?" He reached across and lit her cigarette for her, then his own. "Depending on the source, I've been told that Rafa killed your uncle and Phil Devlin. That your uncle was a spy. That Phil was a spy. That the Israelis were responsible. Or the Syrians. Or the PLO. Or the PFLP."

Mouna could hear an echo of herself, talking to Lydia, but now she was unwilling, as Lydia had been, to accept a wide-open possibility, *perhaps*, *la'am*, as her answer.

"And what do you think, yourself?"

"I think that Phil forgot what his job was, and your uncle died as a result. And I think that Rafa Ahmed set them up because she didn't trust Phil."

"Why didn't you write all of that?"

"I wrote what I thought I could verify. That's my job. The rest is up to other people."

"*Was* my uncle a spy? Why did Phil Devlin give us money?"

"He gave Basman money because he loved him, and he knew there wasn't enough. I continued because they were both my friends, and I felt responsible."

"You?"

"By extension. We're all there for the news. But then where are we, later?"

Mouna had thought that same thing many times. After she left, she realized that he hadn't given her a definite answer to her other question. But either way, he had told her what she'd refused to believe for years. Whether she did the deed herself or not, Rafa killed them. Why, now, did Mouna trust Armitage? Perhaps because he wouldn't say any more than he knew for certain, and because he was not the self-important, careless fool she had expected. He protected others, he held himself accountable. So there it was, one way or another: *Rafa killed them.*

She yawned now, at Lydia's table. "I agree with Felix. My eyes don't fit."

"More tea?"

"No thanks, I'll try and sleep."

sixty-three

They were getting ready to leave when the phone rang. It was Ruth, sounding harassed.

"Lydia? My custody case has turned into an abduction—I have to go in."

"Shit." (Felix, to Mouna: "Mumma said the s-word.") "Don't worry about it. Good luck."

"OK. Gotta go." And off she went.

Felix again, lobbing previous moral instruction back at her: "You said the s-word."

"I'm sorry, bun. That was Auntie Ruth. She has to go to work so you can't visit her this afternoon." She smiled at him, stalling for a second while she thought what to do, aware of Mouna behind her, waiting. School and daycare were closed this Friday. Elise was bad with last-minute changes, especially ones that involved requests to babysit, and Tree was at work. She couldn't think of anyone else on such short notice. Nothing for it: "Would you like to come with us to the airport?"

"Yes! The airport!" He circled the kitchen making airplane noises.

Mouna looked amused at his excitement. "I know Farid will be happy to meet you Felix. He's a nice man. You'll like him." Lydia had rented a car for the weekend, and she grabbed Felix's car seat from the back room, where she had stashed Rosalie's boxes the night before. "OK, let's go then. We don't want to be late." He ran ahead and Mouna took the opportunity to say, quietly. "It'll be fine."

"I know." She knew anything but; still she was grateful for the kind thought. Had Mouna always been like this, Lydia unable to see it? Or had they both mellowed? People change, that's what she'd said in Montréal. *Tant mieux.* It seemed less and less viable to be suspicious of each other.

It was a hot afternoon, the height of it, but they were starting early, trying to beat rush hour. Felix's nap-time, usually, but he'd caught the sense of occasion, if not anxiety, and was full of vim, singing, bouncing, asking questions. "Mumma, know what?"

"What?"

"Tosh has a new bike."

"Wow, lucky Tosh."

"It's red. Can I get a new one?"

"Let's put it on your birthday list."

He looked out the window. "Red. Black. White. Orange, no... yellow. Red!" He had invented a mind-numbing car-spotting game where you got points for each red car—his favourite colour—seen and called out before your opponent. "You go." "I'm going to concentrate on driving, bun." "Can I play?" said Mouna. "What do I do?"

While they called out cars, Lydia made her way to the Allen and then the 401. Eglinton was busy, as usual, and she drove slowly. She checked her rearview and saw Felix picking his nose. Almost as soon as they were on the highway, he got quiet. "He's asleep," Mouna said, looking over her shoulder.

"Good."

"You're worried?"

She repeated herself from the previous night. "I don't want Felix to be confused." But it was Lydia who was confused. She didn't know Farid now, and the more time passed she felt as if she'd hardly known him then. They'd gone from innate mistrust to attraction to love—yes, she'd call it love even now—then anger, sadness, the healing over, the required hardening. Back to mistrust again, and so easily—it had taken so little for them to go back to that. She was as guilty as he was there. Perhaps guiltier, all things considered. Maybe Mouna was right and history did matter. Could their worlds—Lydia, Farid, and Mouna—their versions of the world, ever come together? She didn't want Felix to be their disputed territory.

Mouna looked sideways: Lydia, eyes on the road, rigid-wristed as a little old lady driving her husband's car on Sunday. She wasn't used to being a passenger, it drove her nuts to go at someone else's pace. And especially this, so tame and slow. They'd be driving forever. *Calme toi.* (Out of nowhere, Sara's voice.) They were both nervous, she thought. She wondered what Farid was feeling, now that he was almost here. Would he be looking out at the clouds, trying to imagine the moment he would arrive, how it would be when he saw their faces? He wouldn't be expecting Felix at the airport, Mouna had told him the little boy would be at home, but *c'est la vie.* They'd all adjust, more or less. She opened the window wider, saw Lydia glance her way. Whump whump of cars passing them, Mouna's fingers tapping the edge of the window. *Come on!* Feeder lanes rivering on and off the highway, gaunt hotels with their rates posted on banners high above, a little white plane showing them the way to the airport. Lydia swerved to get into the right lane fast enough. "Sorry." Felix grumbled but didn't wake up. Soon they were following a wide curve to the left, and into the parking lot.

"It'll be easier if I wake him now." Lydia climbed into the back seat next to him. She stroked his leg. "Bunny, time to wake up." Mouna could see his chest rising and falling with the deep breaths of sleep. Kids are lucky, she thought, and well designed. They look so beautiful, so vulnerable when they're asleep it makes you want to take care of them. Except for some, the feral ones in the camps or beside the roads, throwing rocks at cars.

"Felix... it's time to wake up." Lydia squeezed his knee gently. He opened his eyes, blinking in an oddly adult way, like a professor trying to clear his head before a lecture. "Where are we?" "In the parking lot at the airport." He shuddered and his face screwed up to whimper. "Carry me." "OK, but just for a bit. You're getting awfully big and heavy." She lifted him out of the car seat and he clung to her, his sweaty head lolling over her shoulder, his feet dangling past her hips. She staggered along the walkway, Mouna behind, feeling just a little surreal and wondering if strangers would think she was the nanny, though she didn't look much like one in her cut-off jeans and T-shirt. Ahead of her, Felix and Lydia were a waddling four-legged animal. Lydia carried him over to a bench and sat down, talking to him, patting his face. He sat up, restored at the mention of some treat or other.

It was cold inside the terminal, over-air-conditioned, and they all had goosebumps. Felix said he needed to pee, so she sat and had a smoke while Lydia took him off to the washroom. When they came back, Lydia bought him a hot dog; she and Mouna sipped coffee, unable to make conversation. The last stretch of waiting, particularly to leave or for someone to arrive, is a null zone. You can't settle to anything, can't read or relax. There's not enough time to start any activity that might properly distract you, too much to allow you to forget your anxieties, whatever they may be. Felix chewed his food in a desultory, vacant way. Mouna and Lydia were silent. Neither of them had slept well last night, and now each was caught in her own worries: Lydia, of course, Farid's imminent arrival and what it would mean for Felix. Mouna was wondering how Nasima was managing with her away. She was staying with Sara, who would take good care of her no matter what was going on between her and Mouna.

"I'll be back in a minute." Mouna stood up and pushed her chair back abruptly.

Lydia looked at her watch. Five minutes. "If we're not here we'll be at the Arrivals gate." Felix put down his hot dog. "I'm full."

"That's OK, sweetheart."

"Nana Rosie says it's a waste." The present tense tugged at her. Would he remember Rosalie at all when he grew up? Probably not.

"It's OK to stop when you're full."

"OK."

"Do you want to play X's and O's?"

He shook his head, distracted by all the movement around him and by the proximity of airplanes; she took him over to one of the glass walls where they could see the edge of a plane's wing. "Where is it going?"

"I don't know. Where would you like to go if we were taking an airplane somewhere?"

"Africa."

"Why?"

He looked at her and shrugged, a *stupid question* gesture. "Lions eat zebras, you know."

"Yuck. I know."

There was a hum around the arrivals gate, as if everyone had received a subliminal signal at the same time, and Lydia put an arm round Felix and steered him up to the barrier. She felt a little sick. She wished Mouna would come back so that Farid might see her, not them, first. Too late. The doors had started to open and people were coming out. Faces, more faces, someone's luggage cart stuck. And there he was, searching the crowd. He saw her and stopped, the woman behind him bumping into him, pushing past him, irritated. Other people pushed by him and still he stood. "Is that your friend, Mumma?" He'd started towards them, frowning at first, then he began to smile, and she felt a little of the pressure in her chest ease up. But the smile was for Mouna, just behind them. "Farid!"

The walk to the car was disjointed, Felix hopping up and down, Mouna and Farid talking, Farid looking at Felix, trying not to stare, then at Lydia, his eyes flickering over her, Lydia like a pinball, her attention socking back and forth, smiling, though her cheeks felt bruised from the effort. She could hardly look at Farid. How was she going to drive in this state? When they got to the car and Mouna offered to drive, she was relieved. "Sure." She had her hand on the back door but Farid said, "Will you mind if I sit in the back?" "Sure." She tried to sound casual, and moved aside, their hands brushing each other. "It's so good to see you," he said. (To Mouna, not her.) He seemed bigger— she wasn't sure why. Still thin, but there was more sinew to him, more muscle.

In the car, Lydia's ears were stretched with the effort of listening without seeming to.

"Have you ever been to Africa?" Felix asked him.

"No. Have you?" They both laughed, as if it were a big joke. The back of her neck felt scalded; she turned sideways so she could see them without having to focus on one face. "How was your flight?"

"Fine, thank you." Polite and dispassionate. She remembered that. The way he could suddenly and totally withdraw, mouthing ordinary words that were slivers of glass, absent of any warmth. There you were, face to face with a wall, and he was somewhere else entirely, barely conscious of you, bruising your fists and heart on stone. She'd been too proud, their relationship too new, for her to challenge those fits of withdrawal or let him know how much they hurt, but she knew she wanted to protect Felix from the same experience.

"Felix, has your mother told you anything about me?"

"You used to live in Greece. Is it hot there?"

"Sometimes."

"She said you're a good swimmer."

"Yes?" He glanced her way.

"Do you go to school, Felix?"

"Soon I will be. I'll be in JK."

"What is JK?"

"Junior kindergarten," Lydia said.

"I *know* that," Felix said. "Junior kindergarten," he repeated to Farid, as if he might not have heard Lydia. "Do you have kids?" he asked.

There was a pause. Lydia turned frontward, quickly, to avoid the sight of Farid's face. She could feel Mouna waiting, like her, for the answer. "Yes." Farid's voice was hushed. Felix was in question mode and she dreaded an excruciating catalogue: *How many do you have? Boy or girl? What is he like? How old is he? Really? My age exactly? Where's his mum?* To forestall him, she blurted, "Felix, did you know Mouna and Farid grew up together? They're like brother and sister, like me and Uncle Matt."

"Mouna's your sister?"

"Almost." Farid began to explain, and then Mouna made a joke and the danger zone receded, temporarily. Lydia felt like an outsider, watching Felix mirror their attention, laughing and chatting. He was comfortable—she could tell because he was being goofy and playful. She had wanted that, wanted him to be relaxed and oblivious to the adult tensions, for this first meeting to go smoothly, but now she felt

shut out and sick with shameful, ridiculous jealousy at his impervi-
ousness. Even so, by the time they got to the house, she was calmer
than she'd been when the day began. It would get easier, she told herself, bit by bit. But it didn't matter how much she had prepared herself
or told herself to expect it; she was bitterly disappointed to realize how
very angry Farid was with her.

sixty-four

The boy was so beautiful. Look at him, his thick black hair, his eyes. He was talking but Farid couldn't focus, too busy taking him in.

What is he saying? "Have you ever been to Africa?"

"No, have you?" Laughing hysterically, he heard his own laughter, stupid and too loud. "Are you a dad?" *She* smiled a little, he thought, and he had to fight his rage down, down, shove it down, out of sight. *Fuck you.* He was even angry with his son, for not knowing, for being the unwitting object of such an egregious theft. Angry with Mouna for not seeming outraged on his behalf, though of course she'd hardly show it now, here. The little boy was trying to be funny, his feet kicking back and forth in his car seat, hands wiggling, head bobbing as he used a kooky voice to make them laugh. He wanted Farid's attention, his approval. Did he sense something, some connection between them, after all?

Lydia looked the same as he remembered. No, there was a difference. The woman he remembered—no, she'd been a girl then, another difference—would have been visibly nervous. She was so calm, waiting for him to be the one to make a scene, to lose his cool. Her face was blank and serene, which made him want to hit her, provoke her. Didn't she feel anything? He talked to Felix, listened to him, at the same time fizzing with awareness of her.

He'd never catch up. He was so angry with her for that. "She couldn't find you," Mouna had told him. "She thought you'd left her." Which is what Lydia had said in her letter, but he didn't believe it. She should have tried harder; she would have if she'd wanted to. *OK. OK. Here you are now. So much you have to do.* Get to know Felix, woo him, gain his trust, tell him about his family, his history, his language. His grandmother and grandfather. Farid had talked to Mariam on the phone before he came and he knew she'd be waiting to hear what had happened, how it had gone. "He looks just like you." It had pissed him off beyond belief that she'd known about Felix before him, but that was the least of it. Look at the boy! Mariam was wrong: he looked like Lydia, Farid thought, not him. Her eyes, the way they almost talked to you without words. Felix had spilled ketchup on his T-shirt at the airport and the red smear was turning crusty brown, the shirt already blotchy with faded stains from other meals, other days. He was clean—the shirt had been washed many times—but not too neat, Farid was glad to see. Not shy, the way he had been as a child. He smiled at the boy and Felix's face lit up. It hurt.

Lydia was panicked: she'd made a terrible mistake. Farid was going to stay with them in the apartment, share a room with Mouna—there was her bed and the couch, plus a sleeping bag if one of them preferred the floor—while Lydia shared with Felix. But this felt awful, almost unbearable.

Mouna had to drive slowly—they'd hit rush hour—and for Lydia the trip became a prolonged quiet agony. She couldn't tell what Farid was feeling, apart from that instant leaching of all warmth when he looked at her. It was miraculous really that Felix didn't notice, but she was glad he hadn't. She was trying so hard to behave normally, to seem calm, to hide the fact that it was difficult to breathe in this atmosphere of hostility. There they all were, faking it for his sake. Lydia fake-calm, Mouna fake-oblivious, Farid fake-happy, Felix the only one who seemed to be having a completely marvelous time, mugging for the adults, enjoying the attention that, as an only child, he was quite used to from Rosalie, Matthew, and Ruth; even from Armitage, if not Elise. The car might as well have been a sealed box transported from one place to another by laser beam for all the awareness Lydia had of anything outside. She dimly felt the heat of the sun and the density of the traffic, but the car, the emotions trapped inside, was her prison for the 40 minutes or more that it took them to get home.

Finally, here they were. "Felix, please wait until the car's stopped," Lydia said without looking around. He had his seatbelt undone already and Farid was reminded of Mariam, who had seemed to have eyes not just in the back of her head but all over the apartment, zooming in on wherever he was, whatever he was doing. It was particularly unnerving in his adolescence when his sins became more private, more complex, and much more embarrassing: bags of dope at the back of his dresser, a condom hidden inside a sock, crusty sheets pushed down in the hamper to conceal the stains. Even when he was away from her she had seemed to be able to see him, to know, for example, when he'd taken a forbidden, dangerous route home alone from visiting George. She'd been waiting for him, pale and angry. "*Yalla*. Listen to me, this is not a joke," she'd said. The war, she meant; the possibility that the worst might happen: the wrong person stop him, a bomb or a bullet rip through him. "None of us goes out alone." After that, for quite some time, when he or Mouna left the house someone had to be with them, if only the two of them with each other. When they were older, the war had gone on so long that it wasn't possible to maintain such rigid standards. Every time they stepped outside, they were at risk. To be lucky under such conditions meant being grazed by a bullet, like George, rather than hit. Or like Farid, standing next to a man who got shot in the neck, then running inside a shop, from where he'd watched the man fall to the ground outside.

He helped Felix get his arms free of the straps on the car seat and followed him out of the car. The street was wide with lots of trees on both sides, shadows on the pavement quivered with shifting, rippling patterns. The house that Lydia's apartment was in had a covered porch at the front and two bicycles pushed to one side; there was a folding chair and a little saucer filled with cigarette butts—Mouna's, he was sure, confirmed when she stopped and tapped out a cigarette. "Want one?" He shook his head. "I'll be in soon, then." Lydia unlocked the door and waited for Farid and Felix to go ahead of her, then she followed them past Felix's room, through the big kitchen that functioned as dining room and playroom as well and into the second bedroom, where Felix showed Farid the couch and the sleeping bag. "This is where you and Mouna sleep," he said. "Mumma sleeps here, but not now." Farid dropped his bag on the ground and when he stood up saw that Felix had unconsciously leaned into Lydia for a cuddle. The sight set off a series of small, contradictory explosions inside him. He hated her for the fact that Felix didn't know him well enough to do the same with him, loved the sight of the little boy, so relaxed in her embrace, remembered with shock her body, the feel of it, the nights they curled up in bed after making love; carnality appeased, melting into comfort, Lydia's cool fingers stroking his back, soothing, calming. He was yearning. Thirsty. "Can I have some water?" He sounded like a little boy to himself. "Of course. Here." She went to the fridge and took out a green bottle of mineral water, poured him a tumbler. He drank it quickly, glugging and sneezing as the bubbles went up his nose. "Bless you. Felix, why don't you show Farid the bathroom and the back garden and I'll make some supper for us."

Farid followed Felix out back, heard running water, the clink of a pot being set on the stove, other dishes knocking against each other, then outside sounds, dogs and voices, a mower somewhere close by, he could smell cut grass and gasoline as they went to the back of the garden—narrow but long, with a hedge on one side and a fence on the other. Felix showed him a little bench, a loveseat, that he said had been there when they moved in. Someone had planted flowers and herbs in the garden—Lydia? Farid had trouble imagining that—and there was a wading pool, a big frog's head with eyes on the side, upturned and face down on the grass. The frog's eyes stared as he sat down on the bench, heavy and passive, watching and listening to Felix, who had a whole slew of things he wanted to tell him. He slid next to Farid, keeping a couple of inches between them; gradually, while they talked, he got closer. When he asked Farid a question about airplanes, he unconsciously put a hand on his knee; the softness and warmth of it made something release inside Farid's chest and for a horrible second or two he thought he might cry. He sat very still, as if Felix were a bird who might be frightened by a sudden movement, so badly did he want to prolong his son's touch. The two of them were sitting like that when Lydia came out to call them in for supper. Felix jumped up and took Farid's hand in the proprietary way of small children with adults they've decided they like. "Come on."

Lydia had opened some wine and made pasta with a fresh tomato and basil sauce. There was a bowl of finely grated cheese and a green salad and some olives in a dish. Farid had thought he wasn't hungry— flying always disturbed his stomach—but the food was so light and delicious that he ate a bowl of the pasta and a handful of olives and drank two glasses of wine. Sitting round a table together, it was impossible for him and Lydia not to speak to each other—*pass this, do you want some more of that*—and it began to feel both more and less normal. More like an ordinary interaction with someone you know slightly, and less like being with someone you've known intimately, someone you've been close enough to that they can still make you crazy with anger. "I'm trying to keep you up so you get a decent night's sleep," she said as she made coffee, and he smiled at her before either of them remembered he shouldn't. Her face opened and shut in response to his—like a sea creature, stretching and fluttering in warm water, snapping shut when it was poked with something sharp.

Felix was half-asleep, his head in Lydia's lap. She stroked his hair and Farid heard her voice shake a little as she said, "Would you like to read Felix a bedtime story?"

Felix sat up and answered for him. "Yes!"

Lydia looked at Farid questioningly and he nodded. "Of course."

"Just one story, bun, it's past your bedtime." She helped Felix off her lap. "Let's do your teeth first, and then you can be all comfy."

"No teeth." He was showing off for them all.

"Teeth, or no story." He stuck his chin out at Lydia and she tickled him, teasing; he squirmed away from her, but went obediently with her to the bathroom. Farid noticed that Mouna was watching them with a very mellow expression, as if she approved. *Hey!* he wanted to call out. *You're on my side, remember?* She saw him looking, and shrugged, then stood up with her cigarettes out. He got up to follow her, but she said: "If you smoke now, Felix will tell you that you smell bad." *So she's already done this routine with him?* He felt jealousy of Mouna now, added to everything else. Felix was right behind him. "I'm ready." *I'm not,* he thought, but he followed Felix to the bedroom and watched him slyly pick one of the thickest books from his shelves. Farid remembered this from his own childhood, trying to stay up as late as he could wangle, even when he was dead tired. Especially on nights there were guests, bargaining with Mariam for an extra hour or two.

He began to read what was obviously a very familiar story, as Felix mouthed some of the words. "I can read already, you know," he said, watching to see if Farid believed him.

"Can you, *habibi*?" It slipped out.

"What's that?"

"What?"

"Habbi... Ha... baby?"

"*Habibi?*"

"Yes."

"It means darling in our—in my language."

Felix looked affronted. "I'm not darling!"

"Doesn't your mother say that you are her darling?"

"No. She calls me honeybun."

"Someone must. Your grandmother?"

"No men do. Uncle Matt calls me bud."

"Well, where I am from it's OK. But never mind. No darlings."

"Read more." He went a few words on and Felix interrupted him again.

"What language do you speak?"

"Lebanese—it's close to Arabic. French, and Arabic. And of course English."

"Mouna can speak French you know."

"I know, she's half-Lebanese."

"So can Mumma. Nana Rosie spoke Polish when she was a little girl."

"What about you?"

"I speak English. And Rachmanian."

"Ukrainian?"

"No, Rachmanian." Felix looked up at the ceiling. "*Zeedle blobba doo.*"

"What does that mean?"

"It means *I like you.* Can you read another book? I'm bored of this one."

"Didn't your mother say one only?"

"You can do one more, she won't mind." He batted his eyelashes like a silent movie star. *Zeedle blobba doo.*

Farid laughed. "OK, but let's pick not such a long one." He found a rhyming book about dinosaurs and read it quickly. Felix seemed ridiculously happy to have snuck in another book and achieved such a tiny disobedience.

After finishing the dinosaur book, Farid went back into the kitchen. "I think he's almost asleep."

"I wouldn't be surprised. It's late for him." She didn't thank him for reading the story and it wasn't until later, lying on the floor in his sleeping bag, that he realized how graceful that omission had been. Thanking him would have made him even more of a stranger, a guest. She was trying to make space for him, trying—he remembered this of her—to apologize without having to say the words. She had confessed to him once that she found apologizing one of the most difficult things in the world. "It's like peeling off strips of my skin," she'd said, "even when I feel truly sorry, I can't say it."

"I think I will go to bed too," he said. "What about you, Mouna?"

"Me? No, I'll stay up for a while. You take the bed."

"Good night." He kissed her on each cheek. Then said from the doorway, "Good night, Lydia."

"Night." Even tired, she looked beautiful to him. He shut the door.

Mouna rolled her eyes, to no one, and Lydia didn't ask. "You want to play cards?"

"Backgammon? I'm better at that."

"Now I remember. You're not a good card player."

"Let's sit out back, then you can smoke." *How did this happen?* Lydia thought. *Suddenly Mouna and I are best buddies?* Something to do with Felix, and with Farid's arrival. She was too tired to think about it now, a little drunk, besides.

The back porchlight was on and it was still too early to be seriously worried about bugs, so they sat on the back steps and drank some more wine, playing backgammon and swatting away the odd fly or mosquito. No heart to heart, just the game. Then Mouna went in, and Lydia moved inside, to the storage room, where she sat in the old armchair, in the dark, unable to sleep in spite of being so tired.

sixty-five

Lydia woke abruptly into the choking certainty that Felix had been taken. She bolted up, dry-mouthed and aching from her hunched position in the chair and stumbled on stiff, awkward legs to his room, where he was sleeping, perfectly safe, mouth open, arms and legs flung starfish-wide. She stood there watching him, her hand over her heart like the high-strung heroine in a melodrama. *He's fine, he's fine.* She pulled his sheets up where he'd kicked them off and went into the kitchen, poured herself a glass of water and leaned against the sink while she drank. 3 a.m., the absolute worst time of night for rational contemplation, best for fear-mongering. (Ruth: "My custody case has turned into an abduction.") She didn't seriously believe that Farid and Mouna were planning to snatch him, but what about a custody suit? What if all this newfound camaraderie with Mouna was sub-terfuge? Tomorrow, if she could steal a moment in private, she'd call Ruth about seeing a lawyer. She couldn't believe she hadn't thought of it earlier.

Having made that decision, Lydia felt calmer, but wide-awake. She turned on the little standing lamp, looking for something to read. *Shit.* All her books were in the bedroom. Nothing in the back room but Felix's old stroller, a pile of winter coats and boots, boxes of things they had no room for or planned to give to Goodwill. Except for the box Rosalie had left for her. Its contents felt dangerous now, and confusing, she didn't want to read them again and try to decipher what they meant. Maybe she'd look at the atlas. But as she pulled it out, some-thing was stuck to the back cover—a photograph. A very old one, almost sepia. She pried it off very gently, afraid she might damage it. A very young Rosalie with another girl. *Felcia and me,* Rosalie had writ-ten on the back. They looked so alike. Who was Felcia Blum? A cousin? Why had Rosalie never mentioned her? Lydia stroked the photograph with her thumb, staring at the soft young faces, their puffed hair and dark clothes.

She pushed the door to the hallway wider to let some air circulate. The back room was an add-on, uninsulated, cold in winter and hot in summer, warm now that the temperature outside had shifted. Whatever had happened or would happen, she'd never be able to unhook her memory of Farid from summer weather. Early or late in the season. Here or Athens. The last whiff of lilacs as they crumpled into compost, or the dry, pungent air of the hills in Greece. Broken stones. Dust. Farid's thin face, his shirt billowing behind him in a smoky breeze that scattered grit and offered no relief from the heat. His smile. Then, not now—now it was tight and unfamiliar. It was on Felix's face that she sometimes saw a version of his father's old smile, that beautiful spasm of mischief and amusement.

The room had turned stuffy. She got up and unlatched the back door quietly, inhaled the silky air, the water-fresh breeze that would have entirely disappeared by August, when humidity would sit like a blanket of sweat over the city, pressing it down into its sweltering bowl. Then she went back to her chair, and the photograph. She hadn't noticed a light turn on in the bathroom behind her. She heard the toilet flush and the door open, the click of the light being switched off. Someone was standing there, watching her from just outside the room. "Mouna?" "It's me." *Farid.* She shoved the box under a broken chair with her foot and closed her hand over the photo.

"Is everything OK?"

"Thank you, yes. It's fine. But I can't sleep anymore now. You know, jet-lag."

He stood in the doorway, his face in shadow, and she peered up at him, trying to see if he was looking back at her.

"Are you crying?" His voice was neutral.

"No."

"You still have trouble sleeping?"

"Yeah."

"Me too, still." He pulled out his cigarettes and opened the door.

She got up to leave but he touched her bare shoulder with two fingers. "Will you sit with me outside?"

The first touch since he'd arrived, it could have been imagined, so quick and light.

"I'll get cold." Full summer heat hadn't settled in.

"Here." He pulled off his sweatshirt and gave it to her.

"Then you'll be cold."

"So stubborn, always."

She took it and thanked him, and sat, leaving as much room between them on the step as she could.

Neither of them said anything while he lit his cigarette and took the first few drags. She felt something rustle in her pocket and realized she'd slipped the photograph inside. She pulled it out gently, afraid she might have creased it.

"Who is that?" He leaned over to look.

"My grandmother."

"And the other one?" Lydia looked at it again. "I'm not sure." "May I?" He held the photo carefully, far away from him and she wondered if he needed reading glasses already. "She looks like you." His thumb was beside Felcia's face. Lydia took the photograph back and stood up, and he put an arm up as if to stop her from leaving. "I'll be right back." She stepped inside and tugged the box out, then put the photo in, carefully, with the other papers. When she came back outside he was already lighting another cigarette. Tired, and in the grey early morning light he looked younger, softer. This time when she sat down she shifted on the step, a little closer to her. He seemed to be waiting to say something. For some reason, the smell of smoke made her think about making coffee. "He's a good boy."

"He is. I—we're very lucky."

He didn't answer for such a long time she thought what she'd said had made him angry again, but then he said: "I did not come here to take him away from you."

She held herself still. They both did, as if the subject between them was alive, a wild, skittish creature, and they had to edge up to it, make their approach softly, without sound. Slowly, so slowly, creeping through the undergrowth, he put his hand on top of hers. "Shall we try to be friends again first? And then parents?"

sixty-six

In her sleep, Mouna was running, running, running through an abandoned building. A goddess burst through the ceiling, her body punching light into the centre of the black room. People Mouna couldn't see were also moving through the ruined space; she could hear glass crunch under their feet, laughter. The room changed, suddenly turned bright: now an office suite empty of furniture, green carpet lozenged with darker green where filing cabinets and desks had blocked the light. No, not carpet, but leaves and trees; roots caught at her ankles and poked through broken windows. She was at the old racetrack, the Hippodrome, having a picnic with friends. She waved to Sara, who looked past her and turned away. Horses were riderless, there were no spoons for the picnic. She was back inside the building again. Pigeons sat on the wires outside, their watery coos thickened the air, getting louder and louder. Where was she? There! Rafa Ahmed, pulling her arm. "Come, let's go. Follow me." And with a flash of joy Mouna took her hand—warm and strong, throbbing with vitality. She was running with her—trying to run, but her legs were so heavy, she was falling, she couldn't keep up. It was dark again. And Nasima was standing in the dark corner, watching her. Someone called her name, loudly: "Mouna!" She woke in a froth of anxiety, sure that she had heard a live voice. The lost promise of Rafa's warm hand brought tears to her eyes. The birds outside her window were making an incredible ruckus. She remembered where she was. Lifted her head and saw, yes, she was alone in the room.

What time was it? Low voices outside. Farid and Lydia were talking. Mouna listened drowsily, barely able to hear them over the singing birds, they were speaking so quietly, but she thought they sounded peaceful, or at least not angry. Trying to reach some kind of understanding. This was strange territory they were all moving into here, somewhere between friends and enemies, lovers and family, coasting together into the unknown, the way she and Lydia had raced downhill on that scooter almost five years ago, tilting round corners, surfing the currents of air in the hot streets, leaning into the curves. Testing their luck and their ability to trust one another. She had said to Lydia then: "I won't let you crash. Trust me."

But could any of them trust each other? If not, what was there to hope for? She listened again to the tentative murmur of their voices and wondered how long the day—and each one that followed—was going to be.

Acknowledgements

While I have made reference to some actual events and people in *No Place Strange*, its story and characters, even where based in fact, are from my imagination.

Thank you to Zoher Hakim, Caroline Hariz, and Jaye Jenkins for their kindness and patience in answering my questions, and to Farah Haider for being so unstinting with her time and knowledge of spoken Lebanese.

Of several first-person accounts of life in Beirut I am particularly indebted to Jean Said Makdisi and her marvelous book *Beirut Fragments*, whose glossary of war-time expressions I've plundered, and to Gladys Mouro, author of *An American Nurse Amidst Chaos 1975–1998*.

While writing this novel I received financial support from the Ontario Arts Council and financial and editorial support from the Writing Studio at the Banff Centre for the Arts. My thanks to both, and to the editors at *Alphabet City* and *The New Quarterly* for publishing excerpts and earlier versions.

Two people have given me hours of their time, encouragement and editorial advice: Martha Magor, and particularly Jane Warren, my editor, whose dedication and attention to this book have been almost as long as mine. I am extremely lucky to have such a fine editor.

I owe a huge debt to my family and friends (many of whom have read and commented on the manuscript as it developed) for their support.

For his example as an artist and his generosity in pretty much everything, my gratitude, respect and love belong, always, to Jerry Berg.